Peter Beale started as a film industry office boy, and worked his way up to be company executive, producer and director. The films he contributed to include: *Lawrence of Arabia*, *Dr. Zhivago*, *Touch of Class*, *Star Wars*, *Alien*, *The Empire Strikes Back*, *The Omen*, *Julia*, *Rocky Horror Picture Show*, *Elephant Man*, *Five Days One Summer*, *When 8 Bells*, *Toll Tam-Lin*, *The Arian Couple*.

Peter worked with some of the greatest Directors including David Lean, George Lucas, Irvin Kirshner, Dick Donner, Ridley Scot, Fred Zinnemann, George Cuckor, Charles Creighton, Ronnie Neam, Roman Polanski. Later he headed Showscan with special effects legend Douglas Trumbul, and Illusion, both high tech companies and pioneers in interactive and virtual reality entertainment. His interests include the environment, transpersonal psychology; alternative healing, sailing and family. He, and his wife Francesca, have two children and two grandchildren and now live in Spain where has just finished an environmental short film, lectures and writes. *Lucky Lancaster* is his first novel.

LUCKY LANCASTER

Peter Beale

LUCKY LANCASTER

Pegasus

PEGASUS PAPERBACK

© Copyright 2023
Peter Beale

The right of Peter Beale to be identified as author of
this work has been asserted by him in accordance with the
Copyright, Designs and Patents Act 1988.

A CIP catalogue record for this title is
available from the British Library.

ISBN 978 1 80468 046 9

*Pegasus is an imprint of
Pegasus Elliot Mackenzie Publishers Ltd.*
www.pegasuspublishers.com

This is a work of fiction. Names, characters, businesses, places, events and incidents are
either the product of the author's imagination or used in a fictitious manner. Any
resemblance to actual persons, living or dead, or actual events is purely coincidental.

First Published in 2023

**Pegasus
Sheraton House Castle Park
Cambridge England**

Printed & Bound in Great Britain

Dedicated to my wife,
Francesca
and
Yasmine, Sean, Joaquin, Katie, Shane, and Olaya

In fond memory of my friend,
rugby and sailing partner,
Paul Stevens

Grateful thanks to my longtime collaborator and friend, Richard Gardner, for his encouragement and many suggestions, and Anastasia Mann, Pamela Godfrey, Marion Rosenberg, Kevin Conner, Nicolas Hippisley-Coxe, Gavin Scott, Sheila Ghiraldo, Olaya Rivaya and historian Alfred Herbosa, for their time, thoughts and notes.

A SMUGGLER'S SONG

RUDYARD KIPLING

(Extract from *Puck of Pook's Hill*)

If you wake at midnight, and hear horse's feet,
Don't go drawing back the blind, or looking in the street.
Them that asks no questions isn't told a lie.
Watch the wall, my darling, while the Gentlemen go by!

Five and twenty ponies,
Trotting through the dark —
Brandy for the Parson,
'Baccy for the Clerk;
Laces for a lady, letters for a spy,
And watch the wall, my darling,
While the Gentlemen go by!

PROLOGUE

1803 found England in debt, exhausted from turmoil and wars with France, and having recently lost its American colonies. The king, George the Third, surprisingly well educated, passed in and out of madness. France financed the American colonies' war for independence from England and recognized the United States of America as a country in 1778. Soon after, France's King Louis XVI was overthrown and beheaded by the French Revolution. The revolution frightened the English establishment. They worried that they too might have a popular uprising. However, uneasy peace prevailed. People remembered England's own revolution of 1642, the beheading of the King Charles First in 1649, and unhappiness under the austere rule of Cromwell.

France's new revolutionary government continued the practice of kings. They developed armies to steal land and wealth from their neighbors. In 1793, the French won the battle of Toulon. Napoleon Bonaparte, a young artillery officer, received the credit and promotion to brigadier general. England entered the war against France to help its allies, but Napoleon took Italy and later Austria. In 1798, Napoleon traveled to Egypt with a large army and naval fleet. He captured Egypt and Syria. England had concentrated its war at sea and had won control of several Mediterranean ports, including Malta.

A young admiral, Horatio Nelson, commanded a section of England's Mediterranean fleet. The admiralty sent him on an impossible mission, to follow and attack Napoleon's French fleet. The French anchored in the River Nile close to the shore and moved most of the cannons to the side of the ships, facing the estuary. Nelson did the impossible and sailed his fleet between the shore and the back sides of the French ships, where they had few cannons. He destroyed them.

In 1801 Napoleon abandoned his army and returned to France, staging a coup to govern. He became first consul. A year later, England negotiated

15

peace with him. It was expensive. England had to abandon most Mediterranean ports, including Malta. They kept Gibraltar, guarding the entrance to the Mediterranean. The English Parliament cut back on military spending, laid up many of the ships, putting the officers and men ashore. Some were on half pay. The junior officers, the midshipmen, were unpaid and work was impossible to find. In the meantime, Napoleon persuaded his allies to stop trading with England. It put the economy into deeper trouble.

Rumors abounded about Napoleon's expanding military, including building a large, secret, army camp near the coast of France at Boulogne opposite England, to house two hundred thousand men. He thought about using hot air balloons, invented by the French in 1783, to take troops across the English Channel but the prevailing winds stopped that idea. So he settled on invading England using secret invasion barges, some powered by revolutionary wind machines.

The peace would not last long.

CHAPTER 1

March 1803 became one of the wettest and coldest in British memory. Farmers could not plough or plant crops, rivers flooded into the surrounding villages and towns. The economy failed, filling debtors' prisons and poorhouses. The poorhouses divided husbands from wives and children, and used them as slave labor. Expectations of continuous peace with Napoleon were low. The rumors of a pending French invasion caused the people to question why the politicians had mothballed most of the Royal Navy ships and laid off the crews.

A lonely fishing boat, *Sea Spirit*, battled its way across the stormy English Channel. The cold east wind and the rainsqualls drenched through the sailors' oiled smocks. Rain and salt-water ran off their sou'westers hats into their eyes. James Lancaster, captain, stood to steer while balancing himself against the wild motion of the boat and holding onto a line for safety. Like most of the Navy officers, he had been laid off, but he needed to earn a living. As second son from the second wife of Lord Lancaster, he returned home a hero from the sea to find his father dead and his elder half-brother having stolen his inheritance. The seventy-foot, twenty one meters, fishing boat, or it appeared to look like one, clawed up and over the waves created by the storm and wind that had been blowing for two days.

James scraped the salt from his alert but stinging blue eyes as he studied the white-topped seas, lit by the phosphorous in the water, breaking over the bows. Taller and broader than most men, his youthful, salt encrusted, red beard made him look much older than twenty-two. His high cheekbones, firm chin, war scarred left cheek, reddish-blond curly hair, his sense of humor and his wide mischievous smile attracted attention wherever he went. As he steered the boat to climb the next wave, the bow dipped into the sea and water rushed, tumbling down the deck towards him. The cockpit coamings diverted most to escape back into the sea out of the scuppers (holes) in the bottom of bulwark.

The light from a small crescent moon found its way through gaps in the rushing clouds, allowing James to see the waves. He hoped for enough moonlight to see the land ahead, yet not enough for others to see them.

To reap big rewards required taking proportional risks, but James wondered if this time he had chanced too much. Perhaps they should hove-to and wait for the storm to pass? But that would mean missing their smuggling partners waiting ashore. To get permission from Lord Rowley to marry his only child, Edith, James needed to show he could support her. That depended on getting paid for his cargo, wine and brandy. He pushed on.

Most sailors avoided storms, while keeping warm at home, or drinking in the local inn. At least James hoped that the Excise men followed that logic rather than chasing smugglers on a night like this. With luck, they were sitting in front of a log fire in the popular Swan Inn in Newton Creek and probably drinking the brandy James liberated two months ago from Napoleon's France. The Excise men tried to stop the smuggled brandy from entering England, but they had no trouble drinking it once it arrived in an inn. To avoid questions, the innkeepers gave them special prices.

James pondered on the irony of English laws. Excise men collected import taxes. They patrolled the coast in their cutters and reported to the local magistrate. Magistrates, normally the local lord or close relative, owned most of the local land and property. They leased out the farms, shops, mills, homes and the inns to the tenants. The inns needed game, spirits, ale and wine to sell to their customers, so they could pay the rent to the lord. The game, rabbit, deer, pheasant, duck and swan, all came from that same land owned by the lord. The lord employed the gamekeepers to prevent poaching. The poachers supplied the inns with game and shared the revenue with the gamekeepers. Napoleon banned trade between Europe and England. Smugglers, or free traders as they liked to be called, supplied most of the spirits and wines. Also many of the fine materials, glasses and other luxuries desired by the rich. Smugglers carried mail and people back and forth across the Channel to France. Sometimes even on behalf of the government.

The excise men or gamekeepers occasionally caught a poacher or smuggler. Unless they bribed their way out of it, the accused ended up in front of the magistrate. The magistrates knew popular sentiment to be against any taxes, especially on spirits. If the accused exercised their rights to be tried by a local jury *of twelve good men and true*, they normally went free. So the magistrate negotiated prison sentences, on average, six months to two years.

James found smuggling not to be as easy as the traditional tales suggested. The Excise complained that with hundreds of fishing boats, it became impossible to guard the south coast of England. There were many small bays hidden within cliffs that were easy for a smuggler's boat to enter. But a keg or barrel of brandy required two men to lift it. Not an easy item to carry up cliffs. To make smuggling economical and to pay the bribes, one needed a quantity of barrels for each trip. To get the goods to major towns James needed carriers with packhorses which were expensive. Avoiding paying the tax on wine and spirits of four hundred to six hundred percent of the value created substantial profits. Most fishermen only smuggled a few bottles at a time.

James's early Navy training under Captain Wilson taught him not to undertake minor projects with small rewards. The penalty for failure was the same as if you tried for the big reward.

He developed drop points near major towns where the customers lived, Falmouth, Plymouth, Poole and the Solent. Tonight was his first big shipment to the River Yealm, just outside Plymouth harbor. A difficult entrance with cliffs, rocks, sharp bends and a river that dried out at low tide. They planned to enter at night with the flood tide taking them up the river past Newton Ferris, to the Eastside. There they could load horses with manageable sized kegs and crates, and transport them to Plymouth through back lanes.

Five days earlier, they had left their home port, Beaulieu in the New Forest, on *Sea Spirit* pretending to be on a fishing trip. They rendezvoused in a quiet bay in Brittany, France, with Yvonne, a French fisherwoman, and James's French free-trader partner. Approaching France, one had to avoid the English frigates patrolling the coast, and Napoleon's inshore French patrols. If the French saw a strange ship, with no British Navy ships in sight, they rushed out to investigate or capture.

James spent three of his five years in the Royal Navy patrolling the French coast, so he knew the pattern of the patrols and how to avoid them. The wine and spirits were hidden in the false hull below a boatload of fish, purchased from Yvonne. James believed that if intercepted, their speed would outrun the Excise cutter. Of course, if boarded, they would protest their innocence, 'just hard-working fishermen'. He gambled the Excise men would not go into the fish-hold to search.

James passed the tiller to Tony, his childhood friend, and shouted over the wind, "Steer north, north-east, and keep a good lookout for the lamp signal off Swaney Head."

Tony, twenty-four years old, dark-haired, thick jawed, thin, mid-height, and from Norman blood, contrasted with James's mixture of Anglo Saxon and Viking. Son of a Buckler's Hard shipwright, Tony became prematurely bent from working over a carpenter's bench since a young boy, building Navy ships. Shaping logs into ribs and planks with an adze required powerful arms and enormous patience. Tony developed both. He worked in his father's yard helping build *Sea Spirit*. James needed his skills to assemble the false hull that hid the cargo. As the Navy had cancelled all their ship building, Tony thought himself lucky to be on the boat with James rather than unemployed on land. Now he worried.

"Captain, you know I cannot swim. How can any boat survive these waves?"

"Swimming would not help you. It just prolongs the agony. You'd best hope that you and your father built us a sturdy boat."

James thought of their carrier and Plymouth partner, Trevor, a retired Navy purser, jovial, short and round with a bulbous red nose, signaling his liking for Navy rum. Trevor promised to position a reliable person on the headland with a lantern. When uncovered, it showed a narrow beam of light confirming the river entrance, and to be free of Excise boats, safe to enter. Pursers handled the supplies for Navy ships and were often accused of syphoning off a percentage for themselves. Trevor survived by being efficient or lucky, perhaps both. He retired well off, the shrewd owner of a Plymouth inn, and still supplying Navy rum and spirits to other local innkeepers.

James climbed down the cabin ladder to call the crew back on watch and to check the chart. His height forced him to bend to miss hitting his head on the low beams. The dimly lit, hanging, swinging oil lamp showed the double tiered bunks with the wooden sides to keep the sailors from being tossed out, a wood-fired iron cooking stove, a water barrel firmly tied with rope, shelves with mugs, wooden plates and provisions, and a table with benches.

"Paul, Roger, Alan, on deck, landfall, hopefully, in twenty minutes."

The crew had protested when he sent them below to rest for four hours, especially Paul, who never wanted to leave James unguarded. James insisted they rest to be fresh for the river entrance and unloading.

They rolled out of their warm bunks, reluctantly pulling on their wet foul-weather smocks. The motion of the boat and oil lantern swinging above the cabin table made it difficult for James to read the chart and hold himself in position. Navigation combined science and skill. The five factors that James calculated as they spent sixteen hours battling the storm from Brittany in France to England were: tide direction, that changed every twelve hours; tide current, which changed speed each hour; leeway, how much the wind pushed the boat sideways while it traveled forward; boat speed; and the helmsman's ability to keep the boat on the compass course. For three years on the Royal Navy frigate *Defiance*, James studied the English Channel's tides and currents. He learned to calculate the ship's leeway by comparing the compass course to the wake, the patterns left in the water trailing behind the boat. To calculate speed, one threw a line with a small sea anchor over the stern, then counted knots in the line passing through one's hand during a minute. The science of navigation became an art when combining all the elements. Especially important in a storm when, on a dark night, the consequences of failure could be fatal. James's calculations put them two miles off the head and the outlying rocks.

Peering into the dark from the cockpit, ears alert for the sound of waves breaking on rocks, James still only heard whistling wind. The most dangerous time. What if he had miscalculated? They could be on rocks any moment. Despite the waves breaking over the bows, he needed a good lookout.

He called to Paul,

"P-p-p-p-p..."

God damn it, he thought. *I have not stuttered for ages*. He took a deep breath. The stuttering started with his brother's bullying and his father's indifference. He controlled it for years, thinking the sailors on *HMS Defiance* did not know. He called again, this time with bravado.

"Paul, up to the bows and keep a sharp watch for rocks and a lamp signal. For safety, tie yourself on to the Sampson post. Be prepared to gybe to port if we see any waves breaking."

Paul responded, "Aye, aye, Captain." In a low voice he said to Roger and Alan, "Our James is stuttering. He always does this before major events. He is more concerned than he pretends. Keep your eyes alert. God knows how he navigates in these conditions. He reckons we are about a mile from the headland. Not seeing fifty yards ahead, we could be on the rocks any moment."

James turned to Tony.

"Let's pray my calculations are correct. If we miss the signal, we'll have to stay out in the storm until tomorrow night."

James, as he often did, thought of Edith. Was she thinking about him as she lay in bed? He hated being unable to tell her the truth. She thought him a fisherman. For the thousandth time he regretted being at sea with the Navy when his father died. His inability to be present enabled his elder half-brother, Percy, to steal his inheritance. When young, James feared Percy. He was twenty years older, now shorter than James, but full of swagger and confidence. His ability to respond to others with a quick but demeaning retort caused polite laughter but discomfort for the onlookers. A person to avoid, especially by James while still a boy, Percy caused him pain when others were not looking. It might be a tug on his ear or a swift lash across his buttocks with his riding crop. It took James many years to grow tall enough to confront him and get over his fear. Percy inherited the title of lord. Lords had preferential laws not available to commoners therefore making it difficult for James to retrieve his inheritance. Percy owned all the estate and hired a conniving lawyer named Sweeney.

Enough of dreaming. James needed to concentrate and not let his mind wander into the agony of not being allowed to see Edith because of his apparent desperate financial state. It pained him to think of her mother busy maneuvering with other noble families to secure a 'suitable' fiancé for her.

Suddenly, from the distance, through the black night, came one long and three shorter light flashes. The signal confirmed the position of the river entrance and that no Excise boats were waiting.

James let out a sigh of relief. He enjoyed the feeling of the tension draining from his body, and checked the compass and the course to the river entrance.

Paul shouted, "Signal, fine on the starboard bow." His relief showed all over his face, and his admiration for James grew another notch.

"Thanks, Paul. Alan, give the confirmation."

Alan, a nimble seaman, uncovered their hurricane lantern, previously lit and blackened on three quarters of its glass. He held it up, shining the light towards the headland, giving one four second flash, confirming *Sea Spirit*'s presence, and that they intended to enter the river. They would have flashed twice upon seeing an Excise boat and then sailed off into the darkness to return the next night.

The signaler on shore also gave a sigh, relieved James's boat had arrived despite the storm. He waited alone, with the most dangerous and cold job. If Excise men on shore saw a light, he would be easy to capture. He signaled only twice, three hours and two and a half hours before high tide. If James failed to answer, the signaler would try again the two following nights, then leave. Now he could return to Plymouth to share in the bounty. That was, if Trevor managed to unload the boat and transport the casks past the watch positioned at most entrances to the town.

James called, "Tony, steer east by north."

Paul, James's stocky coxswain, and seamen, big Roger and little Alan, all laid off from *Defiance* by the Navy at the same time as James, hauled in the sheets (ropes) of the foresail and mainsail. As *Sea Spirit* came under the protective lee of the land, the wind diminished and the sea calmed. After sixteen hours of extreme physical effort it was an enormous relief.

"Paul, call out once you see the point."

"Aye, aye, Skipper!"

"Roger, get the scull oar ready!" James knew entering a river at night created tension, and the crew needed to be confident. He put on a brave face for them. It would shock them to know how nervous he had felt minutes before and still felt. He pretended to find it easy to approach a difficult entrance in the dark, and that he had confidence that Trevor's crew would avoid being arrested by the Excise men, and forced to give away their secret signal.

Paul called out, "Noss Mayo Point fine on the starboard bow."

Tall cliffs appeared ahead, and the night darkness created the impression they were headed into them. Slowly a crack appeared and they could make out the river entrance.

After struggling through the storm worrying about their safety, making such a landfall relieved Paul. He remembered James coming aboard *HMS Defiance* as a young midshipman. Too tall and skinny for his fifteen years, with his small chest, clumsy, and overawed by the ship, crew and officers.

Paul turned to the others. "We made it. Neptune looks after our James. That's why the crew on *HMS Defiance* called him Lucky Lancaster."

Paul went to sea on his ninth birthday when his mother sold him into the Navy. She loved him, did not want to lose him, but could not afford to feed him. The Navy fed their crew and it was better for him than the poorhouse. As a frightened Paul climbed into the longboat to be rowed out to the ship with the press gang and four men they had captured, she called to him.

"Be brave. Don't let them see you cry."

She stood on the wet dock watching as the boat disappeared into the waves, tears streaming down her face, regretting, and ashamed of the coins she clutched tightly in her hand. Paul determined not to let his mother down. They had survived so much hardship together. He resisted crying despite the wet, cold and rocking of the small boat. Once they arrived at the ship, the sailors helped him get aboard. The reek of the sewage living in the bilges of the ship sickened him. The shouting of the bosons and their liberal use of 'starters' intimidated him.

Paul became a powder-monkey, collecting the gunpowder from the magazine, a thick-walled storeroom at the bottom and in the middle of the ship, where it was most protected. He and other boys rushed powder up three flights of stairs to the gun crews. It would explode if banged or dropped. They ran behind the thundering and smoking cannons recoiling violently, straining to get free of the strong retaining ropes. A noisy and dangerous work. Paul served his two gun crews, collecting their food from the galley, cleaning up their mess and endeavoring not to attract attention. The crew looked after their own members, so the equivalent of twelve elder brothers protected and taught him. A tough life, but hard work, and learning about ropes, knots, sails, anchors, cannons and rowing got him promoted, first to seaman working on the decks. Then to top-man, and able to climb up the highest masts in all weathers, controlling the sails.

Later, Paul made coxswain, required to steer the ship and manage a ship's longboats. As he matured, surviving scurvy and other ship diseases, he developed a thick neck, big chest and powerful arms. His shipmates called him the Bulldog, quiet, dependable, sturdy, yet dangerous when provoked. Being beached and joining the many unemployed had been dramatic. Paul only felt comfortable on ships.

James shouted through the wind. "A half point to starboard."

The sails started luffing and flapping.

Tall cliffs, and rocks with the seas breaking over them guarded the entrance. As they turned into the bend, the wind shook the sails. The wind, now in front of them, stopped the forward motion.

"Roger, oar out. Scull long broad strokes. Main sail down. Let the foresail fly."

Big Roger lifted the twenty-foot spruce oar like a toy, and put it into the stern rowlock. By forcing the blade through the water from side to side, he drove *Sea Spirit* forward, giving them extra steerage. Roger, a farmer's son, handled a plough at twelve. Tossed a bale of hay onto a rick at fourteen. By sixteen, he kept up with his father with a scythe, cutting the grass for winter cattle feed. He grew big and strong, a perfect target for the press gang to force him into the Navy. It took three of them to subdue him and four days for the bump on his head to go down. Paul saw him board *Defiance* with the battered press gang and recognized Roger's fighting ability, so maneuvered to recruit him into his watch. Roger's strength, farmer's patience and readiness to learn made him invaluable.

Alan, blond hair, short, thin, agile, with darting eyes, nimbly dropped the boom and gaff onto the rest and secured the mainsail with rope ties. He had been a city street urchin, learning the crafts of lock picking and pickpocketing, before the press gang took him. Existing through his wits since escaping from the poor house as a child, he regretted his careless wallet snatching the night he bumped into a press gang while running away from the night watch. Bunched in close quarters on a Navy ship with three hundred men, all wanting extra food and rum, required stamina to survive. Paul remembered his luck having Roger and Alan in his mess — Alan as a watcher and Roger as the enforcer.

Cliffs and the tree-lined riverbanks now protected *Sea Spirit* from most of the wind. The constant motion and noise of the flapping sails vanished leaving only the squeak of the oar in the rowlock, and the wind in the trees. Calm. An eerie silence. No boats anchored in the river, no lights ashore. It looked as though they had entered unseen, but James remained alert and cautious.

They rounded the next bend in the river and used the jib to help them sail the last mile up to Wembury Wood. There they would anchor to ferry the goods ashore in the rowboat, now tied down to the foredeck.

In a low voice, James reminded the crew, "Speed is essential. We must leave when the tide starts going out, the ebb tide, or get stuck in the mud, aground. Easy prey for the Excise men in the morning. We need the signal from Trevor's shore party to confirm that they are waiting, and the Excise aren't present."

Sea Spirit drifted silently and slowly. Nothing stirred in the willows and old oak trees that hung over the riverbank. The trees with their black twisted branches, were ominous against the dark night's cloudy sky. James strained with nerves, waiting; still no signal.

"Be ready for a quick exit."

Were they at the correct place? At last, the signal came: one long, three short flashes. If the Excise men were hiding in the reeds, they would now emerge. James looked. Nothing moved. He must commit. Too late to leave.

"Tony, bring her about into the wind. Paul, be ready to drop the anchor. Roger, we'll need your oar to help on the turn. Alan, as we come into the wind, drop the jib."

Paul loved James's clear, simple orders, given with no fuss and quiet confidence. In case something went wrong, he always prepared a back-up plan. This Paul had discovered during their first boarding party on the French schooner, years before.

James's voice brought Paul back to the present, reminding him they were smuggling in the River Yealm.

"Bring her into the wind, steady now. Roger, stronger strokes on the oar. Alan, drop the foresail. Tony, steady as she goes. Paul, let go the anchor. Ease the cable, let her go back a bit on the tide. That's enough. Belay, make her fast."

Through the trees, James saw Trevor's team, at least twenty men each with two pack horses, slipping out of the woods and gathering by the water's edge. It seemed safe, with no signs of any Excise men.

"Paul, set up the mainsail top boom, as a crane to get the tender along the starboard side. Alan and Roger, push aside the fish in the hold and start bringing the cargo up on deck. Keep it quiet. You know how sound travels at night, though the wind should help hide our noises."

James rowed ashore. Trevor extended an arm to help him out of the tender and whispered, "Good to see you, Master James. If it were anyone else, I would not have come tonight. Only someone as mad, or lucky as you, would have crossed the Channel in this storm."

James grinned. "A bit more than luck, we built *Sea Spirit* to stand the worst, although at times tonight I thought we tested her limits. You won't mind me seeing the money before we start unloading?"

For two hours they hoisted the kegs, smaller and lighter than barrels, and crates out of the hold and into the tender. Once ferried ashore they were strapped onto the packhorses. Two kegs and a crate for each horse. Trevor, with his red face and even redder nose, but surprising agility for such a round man, counted the kegs and crates. His men worked silently, most with their faces covered to hide their identity. They looked more like a band of highway men than honest smugglers. They all had jobs in Plymouth and could not afford rumors connecting them to their night trade. The white patches on the horses had been painted dark brown, the bits, bridles, tack and pack saddles altered to eliminate the noise of jingling metal on metal, the typical noise of horses that carried through the night alerting Excise men. The constant watch for intruders added to the tension. They strapped the last keg onto a horse. The numbers were agreed, and the price paid in guineas and gold.

"Thank you, James. I hope to hear from you again soon. It's not easy to come by the likes of this cargo with so few honest smugglers left. There be a lot of hardworking thirsty fishermen and sailors in Plymouth, and the inns be wanting to sell them refreshments."

The men disappeared like ghosts into the dark, leading the horses towards Plymouth. Silence again.

James let out an enormous sigh.

"We did it. I hope we do not have many trips like this, or we will all die of tension."

James's face broadened into one of his famous grins as he produced a bottle of brandy.

"I think we deserve a small celebration. Now we have removed our cargo there is no danger from the Excise. We can anchor inside the entrance and get some rest. We'd better move quickly or find ourselves aground. Tides wait for no man,"

"Captain, I'll take first watch," Paul said.

It concerned Paul that James had been up for over twenty-four hours under the strain of navigating and running the boat. Paul watched out for James as one might a younger brother, determined nothing would ever harm him.

"Paul, that is a captain's privilege," James responded.

"Begging your pardon, sir, but captains must learn to trust their crews. Me and the lads feel you've done enough today."

The crew's concern secretly pleased James. He needed sleep. Paul was a superb seaman and James had learnt that when he spoke, which did not happen often, one could not argue with him. He earned the name Bulldog for a reason.

James gratefully collapsed into his bunk.

"Captain, with your permission, I am going to light the galley stove. Not only to warm the cabin and to dry our wet clothes, but to brew tea and make a hot breakfast in the morning."

The high-sided bunks kept the crew safe while the ship heeled and rolled at sea. James loved laying in the bunk after a rough, cold sail. Warm again, he listened to the wind whistling through the rigging, enjoying the mild motion of the boat and half dreaming before falling asleep.

CHAPTER 2

James, warm in his bunk, thought about the first time he saw Edith at his sixth birthday party.

"James, where's your mummy?"

James had been momentarily stumped by this nosey, confident little girl, so responded defiantly. "I have a nanny, not a mummy."

"Everyone one has a mummy and most have a nanny as well, except the farm workers."

For James's birthday, Nanny Jones organized a picnic party on the lawn in front of the mansion, a four story limestone building, a slate roof and countless chimneys. On the top of the tallest chimney was a bronze wind vane in the shape of old Father Time with his scythe and hourglass. Over to one side were the barns and stables. The French windows from the family main salon, dining room, and James's father, Lord Lancaster's study, opened onto the lawns. So Nanny Jones set the party away from the house and nearer to the river that ran though the estate, so as not to disturb James's father. It was one of the first times James had other gentry children to play with. The question from Edith, one of the girls, surprised him, making him uneasy. Had he done something wrong?

"What do mothers do, that Nanny Jones does not do?"

"Mainly scold us."

James felt relieved and vindicated. "I think I will stay with Nanny."

James liked Edith, even though she was a girl, and that for once he had boys to play with.

A year later, at the impressive age of seven, James received a New Forest pony with inexhaustible energy. To begin with he was on the ground as often as in the saddle. But with perseverance he learnt, and he and the pony and he became inseparable. It was hard to tell which one of them wanted to take the risks of crossing streams and jumping low hedges.

At the same time a tutor arrived to start his schooling and discipline. A large wood floored room was cleared and a school desk, master's desk, blackboard, bookshelf, world globe and an hourglass were added. It was initially frightening sitting all alone at a desk in the middle of the room trying to learn the mathematical tables, watching the sand slip though the hourglass, dreading the tests, and punishments if he did not do well. Nanny Jones was supposed to retreat into the background, but she kept a close eye on him. She did not indulge him when he came to her in tears for having to do one hundred lines, or stand in the corner for an hour after being caned, but told him the best solution was success. To learn things before he was tested, and bring them to her so she could help.

He was always in trouble outside the classroom. She had to grab him by the ankles and pull him down into the fireplace to stop him climbing up inside the chimneys when sweep sent his boy, an orphan boy, up into them to clean them. He climbed the scaffold the steeplejack erected when he came to repair the wind vane on top of the house. During the annual village fete he joined the tug of war contest and was dragged through the mud, laughing, by the winning team, in his new clothes. He played hide and seek with the milk maids in the cow milking barn and knocked over a whole pail of fresh milk. It never stopped, but she knew him to be special. When he needed comforting, food or biscuits, she provided it from her private parlor, off the kitchen.

James spent most of his playtime alone. Initially he rode the pony near the house, but slowly he explored further afield to search for adventure and friends of his own age. He joined with estate workers' children. They assisted their parents with the farm work, so often James helped. Then one day he found Buckler's Hard, a shipbuilding village on the banks of the Beaulieu River. The warships were built between the tradesmen's two story red bricked cottages. There were two rows of cottages and workshops facing each other with plenty of space between them, built on a slight slope that went down to the river. At any one time they normally had one boat in the water being finished and three in various stages of construction. The ships towered above the cottages. They used local oak from the New Forest created as a hunting reserve by William the Conqueror, nearly eight hundred years before, and one hundred years later extended by King John. James loved Buckler's Hard at first sight. Just looking at any boat, a small rowboat to a warship, excited him. Now he also played with boys.

At home, his elder half-brother, Percy, isolated and ignored him. The children of the estate workers or tenant farmers remained distant, reminding him that his father was their landlord. The shipwrights' boys inherited their fathers' streak of independence, and James had to earn the right to play with them. Soon he sculled small rowboats, or sneaked onto one of the warships being built, as fast as the others. They dared each other to climb up the masts via the shroud's ratlines (steps). James hesitated. He got vertigo even at home when looking over the third floor balcony, to the hall below. The other boys taunted him from above.

"If you're scared, go and play somewhere else."

For the first time, James experienced that inner sensation that later came in battle. By focusing on looking up, the climbing became less scary. That was until he got to the yards where the sails would be attached. He looked back at the deck below and froze. Something in him pushed him to jump, so held on tight, trying to calm the panic attack, by breathing deeply.

The other boys called to him again. "Come on up, James, unless you are a sissy."

By looking up, he continued. Two thirds of the way up the mast, he came to the look-out's crow's nest. He climbed up into it, through a hole in the bottom rather than climb outside, as the other boys did.

They laughed. "Are you scared?"

This was to be a defining moment for him. He sensed no shame in being scared. "Yes," he answered.

It surprised the boys. It scared them all when first climbing masts, but they denied it. Everyone knew the truth. They liked James's honesty.

"Going up is not so bad. Just avoid looking down, and especially when we descend."

It struck James that one gained more power by telling the truth, a lesson that paid him well later. It took him ages to go down. He never overcame his fear of heights, but learnt how to manage it when climbing to the top of the masts and out onto the sail yards. Strangely, when the boys challenged each other to jump off the lower yards into the river, he experienced no fear and preferred it to climbing down the ratlines. That way, he learnt to swim.

He also played with Edith, daughter of their neighbor, Lord Rowley, the local chief magistrate and who, along with the Earl of Southampton who owned the Beaulieu River, was one of the other big landowners.

James's elder brother, Percy, told him, "Only sissies play with girls."

James often found himself with her, having fun together. She was a fearless tomboy, and loved climbing trees, so he followed. He preferred playing hide and seek and pirates. It devastated him when, at twelve, they instructed him to no longer play with her. His older brother Percy continued to be particularly mean. Nanny Jones explained to James the genuine situation.

"When your father dies, by agreement at his marriage to his first wife, your brother Percy will inherit the title and estate. Your small inheritance will only last a short time. You might get a job as a tutor in a private house, or as a junior estate manager. Perhaps go into the Church as a vicar hoping to get a rich parsonage where you can live a modest life. An Army commission is too expensive. There are just no real paying jobs for impoverished gentry. To associate with the noble families, you need wealth."

James did not understand the real implications of the news. He liked Edith, so still secretly played with her in the woods behind her father's mansion.

At fourteen, James was tall for his age. Too big for his faithful pony, which they had traded long before for a horse. He followed the fox hunt, jumping hedges many would not try. Regularly, he got into trouble for disappearing and returning late from his adventures with dirty, torn clothes. He learnt to enter via the servants' door and slip downstairs to change into the spare clothes Nanny Jones kept for him. Every morning he studied under the demanding eye of his tutor, Mr Mason, doing well with arithmetic, geography and history but struggling with Latin.

Nanny Jones became James's surrogate mother. He recognized her differences from the rest of the servants. Tall, thin, always well dressed, her hair knotted tight at the back of her head, educated, a little imperious with a scary puritanical face, except with him. Then her smile radiated like a lantern. She refused to discuss her age but the staff calculated she was already in her eighties but still active. He learnt she came from an old Church family of bishops and clergy. Her father, the local vicar, fell on hard times. He enjoyed too much communal wine and drank away her dowry, thus stopping her from getting married. So, Miss Jones took the job as secretary to James's grandmother, newly married to James's grandfather. When James's grandmother became pregnant, and delivered the baby who became James's father, Miss Jones became Nanny Jones. Nanny loved looking after the children. Years later, when James's father grew up and married, she became a permanent family retainer.

Then came Percy, James's elder brother. Percy behaved so differently to his father and later, to James. He showed a malicious and selfish streak. As hard as she tried, Nanny found no way to connect to him. James naturally and generously interacted with people, including the servants and farm tenants. A surprise baby, he was not welcomed by twenty-one-year-old Percy, whose mother had died five years earlier. James's mother, his father's second wife, died giving birth to James, and Nanny Jones poured into James the love she missed in her life. But she did not spoil him. She ensured he focused on his education, on manners and not, as most boys did, just playing.

It came as a surprise when one day Nanny Jones said to him, "James, it's time for you to talk to your father about your future. Once your brother inherits the estate, you will have to leave. To buy a commission in the Army requires a lot of money. Gentry do not go into business. You're too high spirited to become a vicar, or an estate manager. Consider the Navy, as you are always playing on the boats at Buckler's Hard. Your father should be able to get you a midshipman's berth. Unlike the Army, where you buy promotion, in the Navy it is through exams and success. To become a captain, one needs luck, the death of one's own captain and/or serious connections and money to provision a ship and secure a crew. If you have a professional captain, good luck, survive scurvy and sea battles, there is prize money. Most goes to the Admiralty, the admiral and the captain. Little trickles down to the officers and crew. Even so, you should consider it."

James played on the ships at Buckler's Hard with his friend Tony and the other shipbuilders' sons, often dreaming of going out to sea, standing at the ship's wheel and heading into battle with cannons blazing.

"Talk to your father even though it is difficult."

James seldom talked to him, unless being reprimanded because his brother Percy reported his pranks, his playing with the farm boys or the boat

33

builders' sons. Leave the estate, his home, his world! A career never occurred to him. Now it looked as though he needed one. He hardly knew his father, and his elder brother Percy was a bully, so he avoided him. Luckily, Percy spent more time in London than on the estate.

As a child Percy wanted to be perfect. He hated it when Nanny Jones repeated how he had to tie his shoelaces. When his father took him out on the estate, he would explain about crop rotation to keep the soil rich, how they planned when to plant seeds based on the moon and weather. At home his father talked to him about politics, the new inventions and the industrialization of cottage industries such as weaving. He taught him whist and other card games of skill that would be socially useful. A music teacher tried and failed to teach him to play the piano. The hunt master gave Percy riding lessons so he could jump his horse over the fences during fox hunting. A fencing master came twice a week to give him lessons. But Percy loathed it when his father tested his knowledge and he could not answer, or when he lost at whist. He avoided jumping his horse over a big fence in case he fell and looked stupid. His fencing master always won, making it seem so easy. Percy became an expert at avoiding being embarrassed by avoiding participating.

As a teenager at the social events at the other big mansions he was not sure what to say. One time he gave a witty retort and everyone laughed, so he tried to copy the success. But his humor had a cruel streak in it, and the other teenage boys and girls avoided him. He became angry and failed to learn, except how to avoid learning. He found London, with the gentlemen's drinking and gambling clubs, easier.

Lord Lancaster, James's father, sat in front of the log fire in his private study. Even though spring had arrived, he found the weather cold. Montague, the butler, kept the fire full of logs, and roaring hot. When young, Lord Lancaster rode exceptionally well. Not tall, but thin and strong, rumored to read lots of books, an intellect. The reputation as an intellectual did not often make for a rich social life. Now gaining weight, his hair thinner, feeling cold most of the time, he seldom found the energy to join the hunt. Buried in books and news sheets, he kept to himself. Now James requested a meeting.

His father wondered if it were possible for him to remove the barrier he had created between them. He thought of his first wife's death caused by fever when Percy was already sixteen and he forty-five. Too old to consider remarrying, until he met Ann, thirty-five and youngest daughter of a large local family. The title and estate would go to her eldest brother. With no significant dowry, she did not attend the debutante year in London, so became a spinster. She lived at home focusing on being an efficient manager of the household. No one would call her pretty, but had a good frame, a strong face, almost handsome. She loved to read, paint, play music, have fun, having a whimsical sense of humor. They were always laughing. Lord Lancaster enjoyed the same activities and thus, they fell in love and married. She had no problem with the inheritance arrangement as she was too old to have children. Percy and the rest of the family did not approve, especially when, at thirty-eight, Ann unexpectedly became pregnant. Lord Lancaster waited downstairs during the birth. He paced up and down the long hall, listening, expecting the pain cries that happened during Percy's birth, but there were none. Nanny Jones carried his son, James, downstairs for him to meet. He already smiled and looked happy. Lord Lancaster was overjoyed, until he spotted the doctor, with a pained face, following Nanny.

"The delivery became difficult, the bleeding would not stop, we are so sorry."

It devastated Lord Lancaster. His love, James's mother, dead, and James caused it.

"Get that child out of my sight."

He ignored his new son, leaving him to be raised first by Nanny Jones and then by tutors. Now he regretted it. The boy showed talent. Seemed to be always in trouble, but because of his adventures and not poor character. Unlike Percy, everyone liked James, everyone except Percy. James's mannerisms reminded him of his mother, Ann. Nanny Jones often tried to talk to him about his son but he avoided it, first through anger, then through guilt of his neglect.

James knocked on the paneled oak door, and with trepidation, entered his father's study. His few previous visits were to receive a telling off, or a caning. Today, the study seemed to be a cozy room, lit by the last of the evening light filtering through the French windows that gave a view across the lawns down to their fishing stream. Oak panels, paintings, and bookshelves covered the walls. For the first time, James noticed the hanging paintings of ships, and of the farms on their estate. One of the river going through part of the estate caught his eye.

"Brought that at the Royal Academy last year. Young painter called Constable."

His father sat back in his green leather chair in front of the fire. James stood waiting, not knowing how to start the conversation. His father fidgeted uncomfortably.

"Sit down, James." He wanted to make the boy welcome. "Nice to see you."

James looked surprised. Lord Lancaster noticed the reaction and felt guilty.

"Have a sherry."

He suddenly realized what he had said. James was only twelve, or was it thirteen? He silently kicked himself. This would not be easy.

"Pour yourself a glass, and top mine up."

James looked around for the cut glass decanters. He hesitated to know which one to pick up and guessed the one at the front.

"Yes, that's the one."

It surprised Lord Lancaster how much his son had grown. Big for his age, good shoulders and strong chin, bright blue eyes, blond-red hair like his mother.

"What do you want to talk about?"

James hesitated and then blurted it out, stuttering. "M-m-m-m-m-my future, sir." He always called his father, sir, never being invited to do otherwise.

For once his father showed no impatience with his stuttering. James felt more secure.

"I would like to join the Navy, sir."

"The Navy?" Lord Lancaster experienced a sudden pang of concern. "You're more likely to die on a king's ship than in a Cornish mine or debtors' prison. If the French don't get you, Neptune or scurvy will."

"But sir, one can have success in the Navy. Look at Nelson."

"He is lucky. Nelson got the king's eye. Trained the prince in Navy ways. Now has Court influence. He is lucky to be alive after losing his arm and eye. As that cad Napoleon said, 'It is better to be lucky than clever.' Nelson has both."

36

"What else can I do? Percy is to inherit our estate and your title, and he has no time for me."

James's father responded sharply, "I am not dead yet."

James was embarrassed. "Sorry, sir. I meant no disrespect."

Once again, Lord Lancaster blushed with guilt. He knew that his elder son had hated the birth of James, and bullied him ever since. He regretted that he ignored it. Nanny Jones told him that James only stuttered through fear of Percy and knowing his father's impatience with him. Now Percy spent most of his time in London. The rumors were not good. Percy took no interest in the estate he would inherit, or in its people. Lord Lancaster needed to ensure James's future.

"If you want to go to sea, I will find you a midshipman's berth. We need to prepare you. I will hire an extra tutor for trigonometry, geography, and naval knowledge. Maybe a retired officer. Also a French tutor."

James stood. "Thank you, sir."

He headed for the door, hesitated a moment, and then left before his father changed his mind. For once, Lord Lancaster wanted to talk to his son, to learn more about him. He saw him hesitate at the door, but did not find the words to call him back. Then he missed the chance.

James left excited because he had actually talked to his father. He wanted to be invited to stay longer, to ask about the paintings, and about his mother. Maybe one day it would happen. Now he rushed down the servants' stairs to Nanny Jones's small suite, near the kitchen, to tell her the news.

First Lieutenant Langford became James's Navy tutor. He was a decorated veteran of the battle of Algeciras, a mid-sized man of forty-five with an unkempt beard and a wooden leg, with gruff persona, resenting not being at sea. His oak stump, pounding on wooden floors as he limped around the mansion, announced his pending arrival. His injury, acquired in the battle, still gave him nightmares. He remembered the intense pain and rasping noise as the ship's doctor used a carpenter's saw to remove his shattered leg while six seamen held him down on the surgeon's table. Luckily, he survived the infection. Later, he learnt to walk with the wooden peg-leg. Unable to secure a position on a ship, he took the tutoring job. He needed money, but resented training a lord's son to do what he used to love doing. Then he found James's longing to learn and Langford realized he enjoyed teaching and going into his memory, sharing his knowledge. After a month, he woke up, suddenly no longer angry, but looking forward to teaching James. He filled the classroom with models of all types of ships, insisted all communication was in naval fashion, and used the hourglass and a ship's bell to keep track of time, making the lessons fun.

Marie, a middle aged niece of a French noble family who had escaped from the revolution, was his French tutor. She only talked to James in French and spent most of her lessons walking around the house and estate making James talk. *"You can learn the verbs later."* Her unconventional teaching system raised eyebrows, but it did not take long to see the results. James rapidly learned by mimicking the sounds she made.

Initially, Nanny Jones wondered why Lord Lancaster chose Lieutenant Langford from the many retired naval officers living close by. She soon realized James's excitement and that he studied harder than he ever had. Lord Lancaster received regular reports. Some midshipmen started on ships as young as thirteen. He urgently needed to seek a ship for James. On his fifteenth birthday his father called him back to his study.

"I have secured you a position as midshipman under Captain Wilson of *HMS Defiance.*"

James's tutor had taught him the names of all the commissioned ships of the line, and of their captains, so he knew of *Defiance*, a frigate, a real ship of the line, with a famous captain.

"I will be disappointed if you are sent back after your three months' trial."

James understood the message. He spent a lot of effort trying to earn his father's respect. Even though his tutors were pleased with him, he never received a 'well done' from his Father. He would work hard to ensure he did not get dismissed from the ship.

"Next week, you will take the coach to Portsmouth. We will book and pre-pay for you, a room in the Swallow Inn for the night. The following day take a ferry out to the ship. We have a week to put together a small chest with uniforms, clothes and provisions for you."

The week flashed past. So much to do. He managed to meet with Edith in their glade in the wood behind her father's mansion.

"I have been appointed midshipman to the frigate *Defiance*. It's a powerful ship, with a famous captain."

"But the Navy is so dangerous, and…" She hesitated as though she were embarrassed to say it. "I will miss you."

James realized this moment defined that their relationship became more than just play mates. He did not know what to say other than the truth.

"I am already missing you."

He became so clumsy. Had no idea when he would return. Being young, it never occurred to him that he may never return. Finding courage, he bent forward to kiss her on her cheek. She blushed and pulled back.

"James!"

Guilt and embarrassment spread through him. He did not mean to upset her.

"Edith, I promise I will write."

The kiss excited her. For a long time she had waited for it, or something more than climbing trees and hearing of James's Navy tuition, but she kept a straight face.

"You'd better write, or I will never talk to you again."

With that, she turned and skipped away across the big stepping stones in the stream that protected their glade, but silently vowing never to wash her cheek again in order to preserve her first kiss.

James watched her leave, confused, stunned. Surely, a little kiss on the cheek should not have upset her so much?

It surprised James's father when Montague, their long serving butler with the dead-pan face, assembled all the servants in a line outside the front door to pay respects to James as he left. Maids were even crying. James became embarrassed by the attention, especially when the maids curtsied to him and he remembered playing hide and seek in the upper corridors with them just a few years before. Nanny Jones did not want to be seen crying in public, so said her goodbye downstairs. Then she discreetly entered the morning room, looking through a window from behind a curtain. James's father wanted to hug James, but ended up shaking his hand.

"Good luck, James. Protect our name and bring it honor."

As James stood on the step of the family chaise, it leaned slightly with his weight. He looked back at everyone and loneliness spread through him. His father slowly climbed the steps up to the front door, hesitated, turned around, wishing he could have said more, waved, and entered. For the first time, James saw how slowly and carefully his father walked. It worried him.

He scanned for Nanny Jones. The curtain in the morning room moved. He waved, took a breath, resisted tears, and pulled himself up into the seat.

The driver cracked his whip and the chaise took off down the long driveway, with the morning sun flickering through the branches of the avenue of oak trees. It scared him to leave home. He had never slept anywhere but in their own home. The twelve mile bumpy drive to the inn at Lyndhurst, where he would get the coach to Portsmouth to become a sailor, went by quickly. The coach inn's landlord was expecting him and had him bundled into the coach to sit by a window rather than be squashed in the middle between other passengers.

CHAPTER 3

As the coach pulled into the courtyard at the Portsmouth's Swallow Inn, the innkeeper saw James's age. He put him in the dormitory with fifteen other travelers. The boy would not complain, and he could get a second fee by re-letting the private room reserved and prepaid for the night.

James was confused then angry. He called as the landlord went down the stairs, "Landlord, my father paid for a private room."

The landlord, a big man, with a beer belly and strong arms from lifting barrels and wearing a leather apron, shouted over his shoulder as he walked away, "Take it or leave it. Your supper is paid for and you can have it in the bar."

James entered the bar intending to confront the landlord but it was impossible. The landlord never responded and just pushed past him through the crowd of people leaving him standing. A serving girl took pity on him, found him a corner table and served him a mug of ale, and a bowl of chicken and parsnips.

James sipped the ale which he did not like, but wanted to pretend to be sophisticated, while guarding his chest. He thought about the landlord's behavior and how difficult it was to argue with a man walking away. It was a lesson he would remember when he had to give difficult orders and did not want to discuss them.

The low, yellow, tobacco-stained ceiling, with beams taken from broken ships, trapped smoke from the large wood fire and the nicotine clouds from the sailors' clay tobacco pipes. The noise of laughter, shouting, arguing, the bawdy behavior of the sailors, the flirting of the buxom barmaids, and the officers in a corner aggressively playing cards intimidated James. He left after he had eaten, struggling up the stairs to the dormitory with his chest. The corner bunk, with its straw mattress, looked the safest. He put the chest behind his head. It made the bed space small and uncomfortable but allowed James to feel secure and fall asleep, with his knife under the pillow and thinking that one day he would return to the inn and pay the landlord back.

Early next morning the innkeeper advised James to have breakfast as it would be the last good one he would have for a long time. Then James put on his midshipman's uniform, and hired and prepaid a porter to carry his chest as he proudly marched through the small streets busy with people, carts and porters heading to and from the port.

The port seemed to stretch forever, on one side multi-story Navy warehouses, and on the other tall-masted ships towering over the docks, with a confusion of spars and ropes. How could anyone manage all the ropes, or even know their names and what they did? Each sail and rope, on ships they called ropes lines, had a specific name which his tutor taught him using a model of a war ship, but the reality seemed so different. He had a moment of panic. What if he failed? The ships at the dock were being serviced, and to stop the pressed sailors deserting, guarded by marines. Once the ships returned to ship-shape condition, they would anchor out beyond the harbor in the Solent at Spithead. It made it impossible for the press-ganged sailors to escape.

James's porter stopped halfway down the wharf, at the King's Steps, cut into the side of the dock leading down to the water. A cluster of piratical looking boatmen badgered James to use their ferry service to sail him out to his ship. He selected two muscle bound women whose smiles showed most of their teeth missing, and who looked less intimidating than the men.

"Your honor, wait here a few minutes and we'll be at bottom of the steps with our lugger."

A few minutes stretched into fifteen. James wondered if he had chosen well. Thank goodness the boatmen now ignored him, focusing on others who needed a ferry. At last, the ladies arrived in a small lugger sailboat with a single mast and four oars. James looked down the steep, worn, slippery, seaweed-covered stone stairs to twenty feet below, the sea swelling and swirling over the lower stones. He had a moment of vertigo, of panic, but his bigger concern was not wanting to arrive on the ship with his new uniform wet. Hanging onto a rusty chain, he climbed down the steps. At the bottom, the lugger rose and dropped on the swell, as did the water on the bottom steps. James timed his jump into the boat to keep his shoes and trousers dry. One lady grabbed him as he tumbled into the stern seat. The motion of the lugger felt very different to rowing on the calm Beaulieu River with his friend Tony. The porter passed the chest into the boat and the women put it in the bows.

"How come you ladies are doing this work?"

"Ain't been called a lady for a long time. We'll take the compliment. Our husbands were wrongly press-ganged into the Navy. To survive, we took over their boat. The other ferrymen did not like it, but after they received a few slaps they leave us alone."

The ladies sat on the two middle benches, an oar in each hand. They rowed out of the harbor past warships moored to the Portsmouth quay and the castle with its cannons, into the choppy sea.

James felt vulnerable being rocked and tossed by the waves. What had been a stout little boat in the harbor felt very fragile in the open sea. The ladies did not seem to notice. Once clear of the harbor entrance, they raised the lug sail and moved James into the center of the boat, while one of them moved back to steer.

"With the tide at half height, we can cut across the bank and save half an hour."

The bank, a sand bar to the side of the harbor entrance and blocking the direct course to Spithead, could not be crossed at low tide. At high tide, the sea level rose twelve feet. This provided enough water to sail over the bar, but as the waves rolled onto the shoaling sand bank, they broke up, making the seas rough. James had a scary fifteen minutes with waves splashing over the lugger's bow, keeping one lady busy bailing water out of the boat.

The sea became a little calmer once they crossed over the bar and headed out to the Solent and Spithead, site of the famous 1797 Navy crew mutiny. The Navy sailors were treated as slaves with terrible conditions, harsh punishment and a high death rate. They refused to sail unless the admiralty agreed to their demands, getting their confidence from the mutiny on the *Bounty* in the South Pacific eight years before. When the admiralty lost control of their ships, it frightened them. The king was concerned it was the start of a revolution like the one in France. They tried to bully the sailors into surrender. In the end, they agreed to the sailors' terms. The memory of it still made the captains nervous, but the sailors' lives improved.

Lots of small boats sailed to and from the ships with stores, people, and dispatches.

"With all these boats, how do you avoid crashing into each other?"

"Your honor, the boat with the wind coming from the starboard, or right side, has right of way. But ships do sink. We are sailing over the bones of Henry the Eighth's famous ninety cannon battleship, the *Mary Rose*. It capsized in fifteen-forty-five while protecting England from the French Navy during an earlier war. All except thirty five of the five hundred or more people on board drowned."

There were many impressive warships anchored, their sails tied on the yards, and flags and pennants streaming from the tops of the masts in the wind.

"That big ship, with more officers pacing the deck, is the admiral's."

Officers with telescopes watched the little lugger. They recognized a fresh midshipman by his crisp new uniform and the way he held onto the thwart (seat) rather than letting his body roll as the lugger healed in the wind, pushing its way through the small waves. They remembered their initial trip out to their first ship and how frightened they had been.

Defiance, painted black and white, with gold leaf on the stern, looked magnificent, but only three officers walked along her quarterdeck.

James's excitement at seeing *Defiance* diminished when thinking of all those poor *Mary Rose* sailors and knowing that even today, ships still sank. He arrived at *Defiance* wet, cold and seasick, a condition that would become very familiar. The officer of the watch, a midshipman, called out the formal request for identification, and the women responded, "Officer on board."

Midshipmen were technically officers, but those on deck saw a cold, wet youth in the boat. No one would lend a hand. The officers on watch rationalized that the boy had to learn. Bullying new midshipmen happened on most ships. They wanted to see how he would manage, and have the fun of watching him slip and perhaps even fall into the sea. Bullying happened to them, so why not to him? To James, the ship looked enormous, towering over the lugger, and he worried that at any moment they would smash into it.

"Jump for the chains," the women instructed. "But wait until the wave carries us higher."

The little boat rose and fell. James did not understand how the ladies remained so calm. How did they keep their little boat from crashing into the side of the enormous ship? The gun ports were open to get fresh air below decks. Sailors' faces stared out, causing James more insecurity. On the third rise, he leapt and found himself holding the shrouds, the thick ropes that supported the mast. He found it easier than it looked, climbing quickly onto the deck full of coiled ropes and busy sailors. He saluted the first person he saw and said, "Midshipman James Lancaster reporting for duty… sir."

"You report to the first lieutenant, you nincompoop."

Later James learnt he had saluted the senior midshipman, Jeffries, a soft, overweight young man bulging at his uniform's waistline, with shifty eyes, and old for a midshipman. He had failed his oral officer's exam three times, enjoyed his rum more than his studies, and seemed destined to remain midshipman.

James went to the oldest officer on the deck and likely to be the first lieutenant. Again James reported, handing the officer the letter addressed to the captain by his father. In contrast to Jeffries, the first lieutenant appeared tall and thin, with white hair showing under his cocked hat and his face weathered and wrinkled from many years at sea. His eyes were piercing, but kind.

"Welcome aboard, Mr Lancaster. Captain Wilson is ashore and will see you when he returns. We will bring up your chest. Mr Ratsey, show Mr Lancaster the midshipmen's mess, and get him settled in. Oh, Mr Lancaster, you are looking green. When you vomit, do it over side, or anywhere but on my clean decks!"

"Yes, sir, thank you, sir."

James noticed how spotless the teak decks were, as he rushed to catch up with Mr Ratsey, terrified that the rumblings in his stomach would cause him to disobey his first order.

The first lieutenant had seen many young men come and go, most still boys, wanting to be Navy officers. At least this one appeared to be agile and got on board effortlessly. They sent down a hoist for the chest and James wondered why he could not have used that to board the ship. Later, he found out they reserved the hoist for senior officers who often had gout and could not climb.

The midshipmen, when they were not on watch, ate, slept, studied and lived in a small cabin called the mess. The low beamed ceiling kept in the smoke. High sided bunks, one above the other, lined the walls. Being so small, only a couple of them could dress at a time. James would come to think of the bunks with fondness, and as the one place he could be private and warm after a cold watch.

As soon as he had stowed his trunk, Senior Midshipman Jeffries called James.

"Go to the top mast and tell the lookout to keep a sharp eye on the admiral's ship."

"Aye, aye," James responded.

Arriving on deck for the first time intimidated him. Teams of men working, the officers on the quarterdeck pacing, the luggers taking people and supplies from the port to and from the ships. The ship rocked gently. James had to concentrate to balance on his feet. Looking up, the sailor on the masthead looked minute. Now he must decide which of the shrouds gave the best access. He imagined everyone to be watching him. In reality, most were too busy. Then he started the loneliest walk in his life across the spotless white teak deck past the busy sailors, and they did start to watch him, a new young boy midshipman, who would have authority over them. Many of them had spent their lives on ships and knew more about ships than most midshipmen would ever learn. They realized he had been ordered up the mast, a typical bullying for a new midshipman.

Some justified to themselves that it helped him learn. But it surprised the sailors. They knew of the dangers of climbing the masts. Boys were not sent up the mast until a few weeks after they joined the ship. Many never made it to the top on their first attempt. James had spent years playing on the masts and rigging of the ships at Buckler's Hard, but heights still frightened him. Climbing these enormous masts was multiple times more frightening than the mast of a smaller ship in the calm waters of the Beaulieu River. Especially on a ship where the top of the mast swung in an arc of at least twenty feet.

Now, many of the ship's crew and officers watched as he climbed up onto the gunnel and started up the ratlines of the main shroud. The first lieutenant did not like it. Sending new midshipmen up the mast was a longstanding tradition. But not on their first day. Captain Wilson would be

46

furious if anything happened to the boy. However, it would be bad for discipline if he countermanded the order. Wilson walked up the deck to inspect a coiled line and motioned to the bosun.

"Have sailors standing by to bring Mr Lancaster down when he gets stuck at the first yard."

He would talk to Jeffries later.

James paused on ratlines. His legs did not want to move. He thought of Edith and following her up trees, imagining following her now. To everyone's surprise, James climbed, not fast, but steadily. He even passed on the outside of the crow's nest rather than through the lubber's hole, as many of the midshipmen still did because of their own fears. To suppress his fear, James focused on looking up, thinking of Edith, and taking his time. He arrived at the masthead, alongside the sailor.

"Well done, sir. Few fresh midshipmen make it to the top first time."

James mumbled, "Thank you. They told me to tell you to keep a close watch on the admiral's ship."

"Yes, thank you, sir, but Mr Jeffries, I expect he sent you, knows that those are the standing orders. He created an excuse to test you."

James, for a moment, relaxed, then made the mistake of looking down through the ropes, stays and yards to the small deck below and all the faces turned up towards him. The boat swayed from one side to the other, with the top of the mast going through a big arc. He hung on tight, having a panic attack, thinking he could never get down, his stomach churning.

"Sir, judging by your green face, you had best vomit when the mast is leaning over the sea. The first lieutenant has had midshipmen caned over a cannon for messing his decks."

James thought he would die. He had been told how bad sea sickness was, but not this bad. He held his breath and waited as the mast head travelled to an extreme and opened his mouth. A stream of vomit flew out down with his breakfast to the sea below. He regretted allowing the innkeeper to persuade him to buy such a big meal. As the mast swung back, somehow, he stopped the vomit flow until they were over the sea on the other side. He thought there could be no worse way to start his life in the Navy. Disgraced. Probably sent home. Perhaps he should end it all and just jump. The seaman interrupted his thoughts.

"Begging your pardon, sir. You should be keeping your eyes looking forward to the horizon, or perhaps to the admiral's ship. Take your time. Once the vomit is all out, you'll feel better."

From the decks below, the crew and officers watched the thin figure way above, clutching the mast and vomiting. The crew took bets on when the vomit would land on the decks. The first officer called, "Bosun, it looks as though Mr Lancaster needs help to come down."

"Aye, aye, sir. Smithers, Jason, up you go."

James saw the two sailors starting up the ratlines, realizing their intention. He could not stand further disgrace. Somehow, he started down the upper ratlines, feeling his way and looking ahead, but on the ratlines on opposite side to the sailors.

After a couple of minutes, the first office called out, "Bosun, you can stop the sailors. Mr Lancaster seems to have found his sea legs, already!"

The sailors settled their bets by swapping rum rations. Coxswain Paul later noted that betting James would not mess the deck became the first of many pieces of good luck he brought him.

By the time James reached the deck, he felt a lot better, but his initiation continued. They sent him to the sailors' quarters on the lower deck, a place most midshipmen avoided. Being dark, the only lighting and fresh air came from some of the gun ports that were open. The sailors could make comments without being identified, and they used the opportunity to let the midshipmen know how they felt. James climbed down and looked around. He went up to the first sailor and introduced himself.

"Good day. I am Midshipman James Lancaster. What is your name?"

Taken aback, the sailor responded, "Able-Seaman Jones, sir. You'd be the first officer ever to introduce himself, begging your pardon, sir."

James went around the whole of the quarters, and having shaken all hands while trying to remember names, delivered his message. Jeffries sent him to every part of the ship. He got lost a few times, vomited twice over the side and once through a gun port. By the end of the day, he was tired, hungry and relieved they had not sent him home.

At last, the midshipmen squeezed around the table for a meal in the confined quarters of the mess. Being anchored just outside Portsmouth harbor, they had fresh food, gammon, and boiled vegetables. It took time to adjust to the darkness of the mess, lit by one smoky oil lamp hanging above the table which swayed as the ship moved with the waves.

Senior Midshipman Jeffries sliced and distributed the meat, leaving James's plate empty. Everyone waited for his reaction. James had survived their game all day, but now the bullying had to stop. He needed to confront it. Long before, James had plucked up the courage to challenge his older brother's bullying by going nose to nose with him. It surprised him how quickly Percy had backed away. Now he needed to confront this bully.

Removing his throwing knife from his sock, he looked Jeffries in the eyes and lifted the knife. Jeffries showed fear in his eyes. James brought the knife down, stabbing Jeffries' steak, lifted it and drove the knife into the center of the table. It quivered and vibrated with the steak halfway up the blade.

"Mr Jeffries… it appears you miscalculated." James rose. The low-beamed ceiling forced him to bend towards Jeffries. Looking Jeffries straight in the eye, he said in a low but firm voice, "Should everyone cut off a piece of their steak and put it on my plate, or shall I keep this one?"

For a moment Jeffries thought to protest, to put the newcomer in his place. Then he noticed James's clenched fist and bent arm were ready to punch him on the nose. Jeffries, glued into his chair, squirmed, trying to think of a way not to lose face in front of the others.

"Mr Lancaster, your behavior is uncalled for. I am so sorry. I had forgotten we had an extra person in the mess. Everyone shares."

The mess steward watched the entire episode. By the end of dinner, the entire ship's crew knew that the new midshipman had passed the initiations during the day, with some difficulty, but with dignity. He had also bested the ship's most disliked person.

James found the first days on board chaotic. He had trouble walking on the decks as the ship rolled, keeping warm from the cold wind, and to avoid feeling sick. Slowly, he understood that the midshipmen's basic role provided communications or telegraph. Running messages from the officers on the quarterdeck to and from the action in the ship, such as raising the anchor, flaking the cable into the bowels of the ship, raising sails, turning the ship through the wind by tacking or wearing, exercising guns and much more.

A midshipman managed most tasks, often responsible for up to twenty men. James had so much to learn. He would not have managed without his home training, remembering with gratitude the tutoring that Lieutenant Langford gave him. Captain Wilson seldom talked to the midshipmen. James had been on board for three days, often standing at the rear of the quarterdeck behind the captain turning the hourglass, and watching for flag signals from the admiral's ship. Captain Wilson never even seemed to notice him.

Quarterdecks were positioned at the back of the ship and raised above the main deck, giving the captain, and helmsmen at the ship's wheel, clear views. Its narrow staircase to the deck also made it easier to defend from boarding enemies or mutinying sailors. Housed on the sheltered deck below were the captain's and officers' cabins.

Captain Wilson paced back and forth along the starboard side of the quarterdeck. The other officers and midshipmen clustered on the port side. Captain Wilson had bushy eyebrows that made him look fierce. He was not a tall man, but with big shoulders and legend to have a powerful swing with his cutlass when boarding enemy ships. He appeared impervious to the cold. While the midshipmen donned their heavy coats to keep the north winds out, their captain paced in a light summer coat, ignoring the weather. He had been lucky. Not born into a noble family, he gained promotion from the death of his seniors during battles. Winning good prize money enabled him to supplement the ship's stores. Once a week, the younger officers enjoyed a generous meal and wine in his cabin.

At the end of James's third day, Captain Wilson turned to the first lieutenant.

"Mister Stevens, I will see Mister Lancaster in my cabin."

"Aye, aye, sir."

The first officer waited for ages to inform James, but eventually turned to him.

"Mister Lancaster, get someone to relieve you on the hourglass, and report to the captain."

The prospect of going into the captain's cabin and meeting the great man made James nervous. Would he send him home? He passed the marine sentry at the companionway to the captain's quarters, who came to attention, but not as smartly as he did for the captain and the lieutenants.

The marines on board guarded the captain to protect him from mutiny. James descended the tight, steep steps to the corridor outside the captain's cabin. The captain's steward stood by his small pantry. He felt sorry for young gentlemen anxiously waiting for their first interview, and for others knowing they were in trouble. He tried to help them.

"Knock firmly, and when you go in, stand to attention and wait. He's not as stern as he looks."

"Come in!"

The captain, sitting at his desk reading newly arrived dispatches, initially ignored James. Ship's rumors predicted they were sailing orders from the admiralty. Captain Wilson had served at the battle of Copenhagen, becoming a favorite of Nelson. He worked his way up the ranks, fortunate not to be wounded, serving on ships that had lots of action and prize money. He did not tolerate idiots, had detailed knowledge of ship maneuvers, eyes in the back of his head and ears everywhere.

James glanced around the cabin. Beyond the captain's desk were windows and large cannons secured in front of gun ports that opened in the ship's stern to fire on enemy coming from behind. Canvas screens, which were dismantled in battle, divided the captain's day cabin from his bunk/night room, and his dining room. At the dining table, they conducted the rare officers' meeting, and more often, where they would have dinner. The chart room could be seen beyond the dining room.

Noblemen frequently asked Captain Wilson to accept their sons on his ship. He became an expert at making excuses for not taking them. Often, when he accepted a boy, he had to be dismissed early, or kept to the end of the voyage, then sent home with a letter of polite thanks, but never again to sail with Captain Wilson. The letter from Mr Forest had startled him. Twenty years before, he shared a carriage to Portsmouth with Lord Lancaster. Lieutenant Wilson, his rank then, used to be discreet talking to strangers about his personal issues, especially to a lord.

Lord Lancaster had been easy to talk to.

"Expecting to receive prize money from the Navy, I married my sweetheart, setting her up in a house prior to returning to sea. The admiralty announced a delay in paying the prize. I have only a month before we depart for a voyage to find someone to lend me the money until the Navy pays. The banks want extra property as security. The money lenders will take it

51

all in interest, even though everyone knows the Navy always pays, but often late."

"Hmm…" Lord Lancaster had said, appearing disinterested. "Tell me what you know about the rumors of the tests with iron ships and the idea of putting steam engines on wooden ships."

It had been an interesting conversation. A few days later a Mr Forest had found Lieutenant Wilson at an inn in Portsmouth and offered him a loan on reasonable terms.

"Our bank views naval officers as excellent investment, especially as you are due admiralty prize money. The house and the prize money will secure the loan. It will be repayable out of the prize money. If it does not come, then out of your future earnings. If wounded or killed in action, and you cannot pay, then you and/or your wife can use the house until you are both dead. After, it reverts to the bank."

"I cannot thank you enough. Can you tell me who recommended me? Could it be Lord Lancaster? I need to thank the person."

"Do not worry about thanking. Repayment, and our interest is enough. There may be a day when we ask a favor, but there is no obligation other than to repay the loan."

Wilson never heard of any other officer being granted the same loan. He paid off the debt but never forgot. Some months ago, he had received a letter from Mr Forest saying the bank would deem it a big favor if he would take Lord Lancaster's son as midshipman. It did not take him long to see potential or recognize a disaster in a young man. The information came to him from the lower deck via his steward, from the first lieutenant, and from his own observations. James had potential.

"So, you're the runt of Lord Lancaster's litter? Hmm… I respect your father. Met him twenty years ago. He asked the most detailed questions about the new inventions that are now just coming into use. Shame about the other part of the litter, your half-brother, and his reputation for gambling."

James had heard arguments between his father and half-brother Percy, but did not know the news had spread so far.

"But you come from another sow, so I hope you will be satisfactory. I have no favorites. Work hard and learn. You have the best teachers in the first lieutenant and the sailing master, so listen to them. On another

52

matter…" He looked stern, paused and James's heart skipped a beat. "I do not appreciate midshipmen damaging the mess furniture."

James turned red. How did the captain know about the knife and steak?

The captain paused, looked James in the eye, and broke into a smile. "Well done."

James rushed back to the quarterdeck to receive an enquiring glance from the first lieutenant.

"Meeting went well?"

"Yes, sir."

"Hmm… longer than usual."

First Lieutenant Stevens, older than Captain Wilson, had no interest in promotion and especially in a captain's responsibility of handling admirals. He had served under Captain Wilson for years, a solid seaman who prided himself on not wasting time imagining the future. How could one think of installing coal fired steam engines on wooden ships, or building ships out of iron? Iron did not float on water. Wilson stuck to proven systems. His duties were to run the ship and crew, including educating midshipmen, all of whom used family influence to be appointed. Only a few turned out to his exacting standards and stayed until they passed their board to be promoted to junior lieutenant. He wondered how James's father had persuaded the captain to allow James on board.

The next day, a rumor spread through the ship that they were joining the Channel patrol to keep French ships in their harbors, and to stop Napoleon's army invading England.

"Pipe hands to stations, shorten the anchor cable, loosen top sails, up foresails, up anchor, loosen the mains, steering west by south, signal to admiral 'Anchor clear, heading to station', tighten the starboard sheets, (sail ropes), wash the anchor mud off the deck…".

The orders were rapid and confusing to James. Over the next months, James understood the organization, in what at first appeared to be chaos. They rotated him to different positions to learn everything. The ship operated day and night. At night, they reefed sails, and the watches were easier. A watch lasted four hours, then four hours off, four hours back on watch, eight hours off to sleep, eat and study. When the ship had to tack or wear, or have gun practice, all hands participated. When they were not tacking, or wearing the ship, they were practicing with the guns, cleaning and more cleaning and constant maintenance. The British sailors' nickname, Jack Tar, came from the fact the sailors were forever painting the rigging with tar to keep the salt from corroding the ropes. The tar got into the sailor's clothes and the teak decks. As the decks had to be spotless, it became an endless cycle of work to keep everything clean or, as they called it, shipshape.

At last, in the afternoon, the sailors rested, but then the midshipmen started school under the firm hand of the sailing master. Captain Wilson informed the midshipmen.

"He has my permission to lay any of you across the cannon if you did not learn to his satisfaction."

James enjoyed learning. His home tutor, Lieutenant Langford, had prepared him well. James wrote to him, keeping him informed of what they were doing. He soon mastered the noon sights, chart plotting, dead reckoning, tide height, ship speed calculations, boxing the compass, and the normal flag signals. But he had much more to study. Admiralty law; battle tactics; replacing broken masts and spars; careening the ship to remove barnacles from the hull; victualing and supplying three hundred men with food, clothes and hammocks. Health and scurvy management; control and safety of gunpowder; determining the size of the powder charge, depending on the size of the gun; cannon ball projectile; and working the rowboats. The list seemed endless, and the attention to detail, exhausting.

The Navy rationed gunpowder for training. Victory and prize money required the ability to out-shoot the enemy. Captain Wilson used more of his limited wealth to buy extra powder for practice. He taught the gunners to aim the cannons by using old water barrels as targets, towed in the sea with long lines by the ship's rowboats or longboats. Target practice gave James the first chance to be in charge of a longboat. He had a sleepless night before. The midshipmen told terrifying stories of the cannon balls hitting longboats instead of the barrels, and how difficult the coxswains could be. His coxswain, Paul Sumners, immediately took charge.

"Begging you pardon, sir. As this be your first time in a longboat, and towing targets in front of cannons can be dangerous, perhaps you'd best leave it to me to give the orders. You let me know the captain's orders. I will do the rest."

As they rowed away from the ship James saw Captain Wilson pacing, seven strides each way along the quarterdeck. James wondered what occupied the great man so much. Later he learnt the captain imagined every maneuver, what could go wrong, and how to counteract the resulting problem. "I win battles with details, and with contingency plans for when things go wrong, and they often do."

He had the midshipmen offer their plans for different exercises and pounded into them, "Give me details. Details make for success. Success does not happen without effort."

There were six empty and corked barrels painted white in the bottom of the long boat. They rowed calmly for about five hundred yards until a flag was raised on *Defiance's* yard arm. Then coxswain Paul dropped the barrel in the water connected with a long line and commanded, "Row, you blighters, double pace before some enthusiastic gunner fires and hits us."

The men did not need encouragement as Paul called out, "In, out, in…"

The barrel followed at about one hundred yards behind, bobbing in the water.

It seemed they had only gone a short distance when the cannons started firing, one at a time. Splashes rose up from the sea all around the barrel, some further away. It was exciting to see the ship firing the guns, but not when a couple of balls landed close enough to splash them. Paul was not amused.

"Row harder. Sons of whores, that was the twelfth cannon. I will be having words later."

Finally the barrel was hit to a loud cheer from the ship. Paul commented, "That gun crew will get an extra ration of rum tonight."

More flags went up on the ship, and James checked his flag chart and said, "We are to head back to where the barrel was, and drop another one."

"Yes, sir. We will row steady to give the men a chance to gather their strength, so they can row hard once we drop the next barrel."

For James, it was a fun day and the first of many spent in a long boat with coxswain Paul. Midshipmen never handled ropes on board the ship so he used the time spent waiting for the gunners to hit the barrel to start learning about seamen's knots.

Supply ships delivered water, food and mail. James wrote to Edith and to his father describing all he learnt, praising the captain who had become his hero. He wrote to Nanny Jones, making cartoon pencil drawings for her to show the other servants how the ship lived and worked. She shared these not only with all the downstairs staff but with his father. He kept them on the table by his chair in the study so he could easily reread them, often falling asleep while imagining James's life on the ship.

James received letters from Nanny Jones, and sometimes brief notes from his father, but nothing from Edith. At first he blamed the Navy mail system until he had to admit she had not written. He could not understand it. She had promised. Laying in his bunk, he fretted over it, needed to hear from her. Had he upset her so much when kissing her? He kept sending his letters to her. James asked Nanny Jones to find out why Edith did not write. Nanny decided he must face the reality. She reported that Edith and her family were well. But with James having no future estate, her parents would never allow him to marry her, so felt it inappropriate for them to communicate. They should not have kept their childhood friendship going when her parents banned them from playing together. The news only made James more determined.

Other midshipmen received letters from their sisters, mothers and sweethearts, and sometimes from their fathers. Letters were read out loud so all could share. Midshipmen fell silently in love with their mates' sisters, and some plucked up the courage to write to them. Letters were reread many times.

When *Defiance* sailed back to Portsmouth, anchoring at Spithead to replenish, they did not allow crew ashore in case they deserted, and the midshipmen in case they became home sick. Being so close to home, and Edith, frustrated James even more. He loved the sea life, never thinking of leaving, but he needed to see her. At the end of three months, he nervously waited for his captain's interview, worrying that he would be sent home. A month later with nothing said, he relaxed. While anchored at Spithead, the merchants came out to the ship in small boats to sell much needed clothing and other personal items. Even though sailors' wives, girlfriends and professional ladies were forbidden on board, some clambered through the lower gun-ports for the night. As James had grown even taller, gained muscle, his midshipman uniforms were much too small and worn out. A large part of his meager pay went to buy new uniforms, a better foul weather oiled cloak, writing paper, quills and ink.

CHAPTER 4

Towards the end of their first year, as part of the English fleet patrolling the French coast, *Defiance* stopped a neutral trading schooner, flying a Swedish flag, to check her cargo. This happened at least once a week, normally resulting in the ship being sent on its way. The French had an army with already thirty-five thousand men assembling near the port of Calais, just opposite the English port of Dover, waiting to cross the Channel to conquer England. The English were desperate to keep them in Calais, so were suspicious of every foreign vessel.

The plump, red-faced captain objected to being held. He shouted through a speaking trumpet, "We are neutral! You English have no rights to stop us."

Captain Wilson turned to Lieutenant Stevens.

"Mister Stevens, I would be obliged if you would fire a shot across his bows to teach him manners and to remind him that our right comes with a frigate full of cannons."

The *schooner*, a handsome vessel painted green with a gold stripe, two masts leaning backwards, a long bowsprit, a mermaid figurehead and nine crew, continued. The cannon ball passed close in front of their bows, landing in the sea with a major splash and showering the *schooner's* deck with salt water.

Captain Wilson shouted, "Captain, perhaps now you will do us the courtesy of heaving to."

The *schooner* hauled their sails, but still drifted fast to leeward and away from *Defiance*.

Captain Wilson turned to the first lieutenant. "Mister Stevens, please hove-to and send two boats over to inspect her."

"Back the top sails, reef all other sails except main royals. Mister Jeffries, Mister Lancaster, take your boats and inspect the ship's cargo."

Sailors swarmed up the masts and out onto the yards.

57

The two coxswains heard the orders and Paul had already taken the covers off their longboat by the time James had collected their crew's cutlasses.

Jeffries called out, "Lancaster, give space there. I am senior and our boat goes in first."

Paul mumbled under his breath, "We will still get to the ship first, you little toad."

James pretended not to hear.

"Coxswain, our orders are to board the ship and search the cargo. First boat's crew on board has an extra rum ration. Make it happen."

"Aye, aye, sir. Give way together, pull on those oars."

Paul liked how his relationship with James worked. Simple orders and then delegation to Paul to run the boat and crew. Unlike most of the midshipmen, James did not run the boat himself. He knew the sailors' names, relaxed talking to them, seeking their advice on knots and all basic nautical issues. James's longboat normally carried mail to the flagship, or took officers ashore. He loved being in the smaller boats with responsibility, away from the discipline of the big ship. He heard from the other midshipmen how difficult the coxswains could be, but James found the opposite.

Once Paul trusted James, he became an amazing source of practical knowledge. On board the ship, the rules stopped officers socializing with sailors. Being in a small boat out at sea, with waves much taller than the boat, at first intimidated James, but he soon got used to it.

The *schooner's* captain appeared to be preparing a boarding ladder to make it easy for the British sailors to get on board.

James's crew were catching Jeffries' boat. Paul called out, "In!" to time the oars to strike the sea in the bottom of the swells.

"In... heave... in... pull harder Davis, all together, in..."

Even with the noise of the wind, Jeffries' voice carried as he berated his crew to row faster, ignoring the waves. Paul knew he could get alongside the schooner first if the other boat's oars caught a few more 'crabs', tops of the waves, and slowed them. Even after years at sea, Paul hated the Navy's meals of old salted pork and biscuits full of live weevils. The rum ration helped hide the rancid tastes. He wanted to win the bonus ration. James's voice interrupted Paul's thoughts.

"Coxswain, aim at the schooner's bows, not at the boarding ladder."

Paul reacted. Did the lad think himself a genuine officer?

"It is better if we keep on as we are." He remembered to add, "Sir." The Navy demanded that sailors call the midshipmen 'sir' even if they were still young, inexperienced boys.

James stared intently at Paul. "The bows, Coxswain."

James's intensity surprised Paul.

"Aye, aye, sir, but we don't want the captain thinking we're… er… disobeying his orders, or… we're afraid. And…"

For an awful moment, Paul wondered if he had overstepped the mark and he'd be reported. One should never answer back to an officer, not even a boy midshipman, let alone suggest he's a coward. Paul looked at the sailors rowing, for a reaction, but they kept their faces blank, not wanting to get involved, or let Paul know they had heard. Paul had to handle his own troubles.

"Apologies, sir, I did not—"

"Coxswain, look at the way they've hauled the sails."

"Sir, they are hove-to."

"Look up at the fore topsail. She has enough sail loose to catch the wind and their boat going at about two knots away from *Defiance*. They'll soon be out of range of our guns and close enough to the shore to seek shelter with the help of the French gun batteries on the cliffs. I keep seeing heads ducking down below the gangway bulwarks. They're up to something. Get us in front of the *schooner* and be quick."

"Aye, aye, sir."

Paul had been taken aback, and this time he meant 'sir', relieved that he had avoided being remanded, but wondering why he had failed to see how the *schooner* sails were catching the wind, and the captain up to mischief, when a young midshipman had.

"Heave-away, me hearties, more back into it, I want to see those oars bend, in… in…"

James sensed tingling in his stomach. Excited but concerned, a new feeling. He recognized adventure afoot, and the day special. They were now pulling past the Jeffries' boat and James called out, "The *schooner*'s captain is preparing something behind the bulwarks, be careful."

"Lancaster, remember I am senior, so back off. We are boarding first."

Jeffries knew Captain Wilson would have the spyglass on them. No junior would get in front of him. James, being the tallest, strongest officer on the ship, popular with the men and the senior officers, able to climb the mast as well as the sailors, irritated Jeffries. In one year, James had learnt to do noon sights, calculate them and looked ready for his lieutenant's oral exam. Jeffries had not forgotten the lecture he received from the first officer for sending James up the mast, or the meat episode. One day he would get his revenge. He still had the embarrassment of failing his exams. Now James wanted to trick him so he could get on board first. No way.

Captain Wilson looked through his telescope at the two longboats racing towards the *schooner* and took a bet with himself that James would win. Then he saw James's boat turn to the right. What the hell!

"Mister Stevens, it looks as though Jeffries is about to board. Let's get the topsails drawing and get closer."

At that moment, a cloud of smoke came from the *schooner*, and seconds later the noise of the cannon fire smothered Lieutenant Stevens' reply.

"Aye, aye, sir."

The gunfire happened just as James's boat crossed under the bows of the *schooner* and its sailors hoisted sails to escape from *Defiance*.

Jeffries ordered his boat crew to back away quickly, perhaps forgetting that it would take the schooner's crew at least three minutes to reload, probably much more, giving him time to board.

Captain Wilson let out an oath.

"Poseidon be dammed. That idiot Jeffries has put his boat between us and the schooner. We cannot fire. Now it looks as though Lancaster is about to have his boat cut in two. Get more sail on."

He regretted sending Jeffries. It seemed such a simple expedition. One that even Jeffries could not mess up. James needed experience. He would have to answer for disobeying orders. Shame, he showed promise.

As the menacing bowsprit of the *schooner* loomed over James's boat, Paul called out, "Double speed, pull, you dogs of mermaids! Pull. That is if you don't want to learn to swim, pull…"

Most sailors did not swim. Going into the sea meant drowning. As the boat passed under the *schooner's* bowsprit, James leapt up and caught the bobstay. He got a leg around the dolphin catcher and hauled himself up to the deck.

It horrified Paul. A midshipman going by himself onto an enemy ship? He dared not imagine the fury of Captain Wilson if something bad happened to the boy. Paul shouted, "Roger, Alan, follow the lad, er… I mean Mister Lancaster."

The forward motion of the *schooner* pushed the longboat aside and the smaller craft scraped its way along the *schooner's* hull. Paul's sailors grabbed the ship's chains and held on with all their strength. As they did, the *schooner's* captain's head appeared over the bulwarks. He pointed a blunderbuss straight at them.

Captain Wilson did not believe what he was witnessing. Jeffries' boat still backing away but in a direct line of fire. James's boat disappeared behind the *schooner*. He feared it sunk. Then a figure, James, climbed up the bow and over the figurehead, waving a sword.

"What in thunder is happening? Has the world gone mad?" He cursed because he was stuck on his ship and not in action.

The *schooner's* captain looked down on the boat crew. "Let go or I'll sink you."

Paul ordered, "Let go."

Then the plump captain heard running footsteps behind him. He looked up to see a wild young man charging towards him, swinging a cutlass. He swung the blunderbuss, aiming at James, and in a panic, he yelled, "Stop, or I will fire!"

James's feet kept moving over the deck planks, drumming as he ran. Unable to stop them, realizing he had misjudged and become a dead man running. The captain's chubby hand and swollen fingers tightened on the trigger. James's Navy career was finished, without even saying goodbye to Edith. Dying, saving his boat crew, offered its own reward. Suddenly, the gun jerked up and fired in the air. The lead pellets hit the mast, sending out wooden splinters. James felt a painful jab in his left cheek and something in his eye. He dared not hesitate, and rushed straight on, his left eye closed, and hacked at the captain's gun arm. The bone splintered with a terrible thud and crack, a sound James would never forget and that would haunt him.

"Aaaah… bon sang!" the captain screamed in French, grabbing his splintered and useless arm gushing with blood, as the gun fell clattering onto the deck, along with a marlinspike.

Even from that distance, Captain Wilson heard the shot. His heart sank. A dead midshipman, a prize lost, and a court martial or early retirement.

James's heart raced. What happened? He felt his eye, but could not open it. There was a big wooden splinter sticking out of his left cheek and blood pouring everywhere.

Paul clambered over the bulwarks, waving a cutlass. On seeing James standing, but bleeding, over the broken captain, his face spread into a grin.

"So at least you are alive, though it looks as though you need the ship's bone-smith as soon as possible. Always thought that one day, knowing how to throw the marlinspike would be handy."

Navy ships did not provide recreation, so sailors created it. Playing darts with the marlinspikes became a favorite. The real purpose of the spike, often nine to eighteen inches long and made of hard wood, helped loosen the knots in ropes. The sailors became accurate at throwing them, especially as they gambled on their success with their rum rations. They were not allowed to carry knives, so during the night watches, they used the spike as a weapon to settle personal scores.

With the captain screaming and bleeding on the deck, James turned to face the *schooner's* crew, bunched in front of the cannon. A motley, hungry looking group, gripping their spikes and old swords, forced into service, they were contemplating the consequences of losing life or limb to rescue a bullying captain. Seeing James covered in blood and looking vicious quelled any last confidence they had. James watched out of his good eye to see who would rush first. No one seemed keen. He guessed they would understand French, so he called to them.

"Arrêtez-vous la, hold up there. No need for more injuries. Put down your weapons. Go into the fore-hold and I will speak for you with our captain. He is a good man, and never hurt an honest sailor."

Paul guessed at what James said, but stood by to rush the French sailors with his boat crew. Like James, he felt relieved when the French studied the size of the opposition and their beaten captain, and after a brief discussion, they laid down their arms. Sad and defeated, they shuffled to the forward hold.

"So, Coxswain, you said you wanted our crew to be on board first to win the rum ration."

A lasting friendship started.

"Paul." For the first time James called his coxswain by his name. "Lock the French crew in the fore-hold. Reef the topsail so we do not drift away from *Defiance*. Put a guard outside the captain's cabin and warn our crew that anyone who finds and drinks grog will get the cat. Tie the captain to the mast and put a tourniquet on his arm to stop the bleeding. Raise our blue ensign to tell Captain Wilson he has a ship. Get the sails reefed so we are properly hoved to, and not drifting from *Defiance*. Then open the hatches to see what the schooner captain was scared we would find."

"Aye, aye, sir, but while the crew is working, let's get some bandages on you. You are also bleeding from your arm and chest."

The pain in James's eye was excruciating, and he wondered if he had lost it. But the adrenalin coming from capturing the ship helped him focus on taking control.

Captain Wilson looked at the figures on the deck. No sign of James or his boat. Then the blue ensign replaced the Swedish flag.

"Well I'll be dammed! Young James seems to have taken the ship. Mister Wilson, send Captain Smith with his marines and Lieutenant Jones, with a strong crew, to take command and get Mister Lancaster and Jeffries back here to report." His relief was enormous.

By the time Jeffries' crew climbed on board the *schooner,* James's crew had pulled off the tarpaulins and hatch from the main cargo hold. They found it full of cannons and ammunition intended for the French army. The schooner had hidden its French identity. In the captain's cabin, James found a veritable treasure, secret French signal codes, still in their weighted bag, and which the captain should have thrown overboard to sink. If he ever returned to France, he would be in trouble. Later, when the schooner, with its rich cargo, sailed to Portsmouth with the second lieutenant and a small crew, it earned the *Defiance* officers and crew good prize money.

Once James had the ship under control, the post shock set in. The pain in the eye was bad, but also his face, arm and chest felt like they had stabbing needles in them. He needed to hold the mast so as not to let others see his limbs shaking. During the action, he'd had no time to think. Now he understood how close his boat and men had been to sinking. Remembered the image of the gun barrel pointing at him. Sounds of the bones breaking as his cutlass shattered the captain's arm. The French crew had been ready to attack with their meager weapons. His concern was that his crew did not get drunk. Emotions whelmed up on him. They weren't the emotions that he read from other naval officer's descriptions of successful battles. Stories posted in the *Gazette* always made the victors seem so brave and unemotional. He liked it when his crew and those of Jeffries came up to congratulate him. All except Jeffries, who busied himself inspecting the schooner, avoiding James.

Defiance's second officer, Lieutenant Jones, boarded the schooner to take it back to England.

"Great job, Mister Lancaster, but I hope your injuries are not too serious. For a moment, we thought they had rammed your boat. Later, that they shot you, perhaps dead. I look forward to the full story. The captain wants you and Jeffries and your crews to return straight away."

On returning to *Defiance*, a stern faced first lieutenant confronted James.

"Mister Lancaster,.." Then he saw his face. "Neptune be dammed, are you all right? Never mind, tell me later. Report to the captain. Mister Jeffries, and Coxswain Sumners, wait here until he is ready to see you."

James wondered what had upset the first lieutenant. He expected everyone to be pleased with the prize and their success. The captain was looking out to sea. It seemed ages until he turned around and saw James covered in blood, bandaged and shaken.

"Good god, what happened to you?

"The captain's blunderbuss sent splinters off the mast."

"Is your eye all right?"

"I do not know. It is closed and bleeding, and hurts like hell."

"Purser, get a message to the doctor to stand by for Mister Lancaster. "But first, what were your orders when you headed to the *schooner*?"

"To board her as quickly as possible, sir."

"So, what happened?"

James took a deep breath and tried to get his mind in order. *Just telling the simple truth is always the best.*

"I ordered Coxswain Sumners to aim at the schooner's bow as I feared it might sail away. We noticed how the sails were not fully furled. The schooner's crew were hiding behind the gunwales doing something. It turned out they were preparing and loading a cannon. Once they had fired the cannon, they raised the sails, and the ship's bows almost cut our boat in two. I climbed on board via the bobstay and dolphin catcher. Then charged the *schooner's* captain, who tried to shoot me. Coxswain Sumners saved me by throwing a marlinspike, knocking the blunderbuss upwards, enabling me to disable the captain. After, I promised the French crew you are a fair captain, and persuaded them to surrender. That, for sure, saved lives and injuries. I respectfully request you take that into account when dealing with them. I did not want our sailors to find the captain's bottles of spirits and get drunk, so put a guard on the door. Then I looked in the captain's cabin and found the logbook and orders. As luck would have it, I also found the code book and charts. With the French crew in the locked forepeak, we hove-to so as not to drift from *Defiance*, and so Jeffries' crew could board. Once the hatches were off the hold, we found the cannons."

James's action and success impressed and pleased Captain Wilson, but knew it could go to James's head, and if it did, it would stop him learning from the mistakes.

"Did you try to warn the senior midshipman of your concerns?"

"Yes, sir, but... with the wind, I am not sure he could hear."

"Hm... Get to the doctor and tell him to report to me after. Ask my purser for some vinegar to get the blood off your uniform. Then get a good meal. If you shake, it often happens after one's first battle, retire into your bunk and sleep. You're excused watches. I will see you later. Send your coxswain."

He reluctantly dismissed him with no words of praise. But he also felt guilty. He had not trained him properly, and that would change.

James left, confused and dejected. Surely Captain Wilson understood that if he had not boarded the *schooner*, it would have escaped.

First Lieutenant Stevens wanted to hear the story and the captain's orders. For once, he smiled.

"Mister Lancaster, a good day's work, but you have a lot to learn. The captain let you off lightly. Get to the doctor and then rest."

The doctor was used to extracting wooden splinters. To help, he had his patients drink a mug of rum. It did not stop the pain, but made them sleepy and easier for his helpers to hold the patient down.

"You have a splinter through the eyelid. It does not seem to have touched the eye itself, so we may save it if you do not get infections. I have to cut the skin to remove it. It will hurt. You must not move, so we will hold you."

It took time to remove the splinters, exhausting James fighting the hands that held him still during the pain. The entire ship heard his yells. The doctor sewed up the wounds and doused them with brandy.

"All done. You will have some handsome scars. Get to bed and see me tomorrow. I will tell the first lieutenant I excused you watch keeping for at least two days. Seaman, help Mister Lancaster to his mess."

All the midshipmen off watch filled the mess, wanting a detailed account of the action, and wishing it had been them. Their steward served a splendid meal, making himself look busy so he could report everything to the lower deck. Someone found a hidden bottle of wine and they were celebrating when a long-faced Jeffries returned from his meeting with the captain. He did not look happy.

"Lancaster, you lucky sod. You disobeyed orders, got shot at with a blunderbuss, and got away with it."

It established James's nickname, Lucky Lancaster.

Everyone wanted Jeffries' side of the story. What happened when the schooner fired the cannon, and what did Captain Wilson say? Jeffries described what he told the captain.

"After the cannon went off, I wanted to board the *schooner*, but my first duty was to save the lives of my crew. I ordered us to back away fast. Then I signaled *Defiance* to get orders. The ship was too far off. Captain Wilson said, 'Well done,' and dismissed me."

Actually, what the captain said, as reported by his steward and known by everyone soon after, was, "Did Mister Lancaster try to warn you of his concerns?"

Jeffries paused, worried, not knowing what James, or the coxswain, had told the captain.

"He shouted something, but I could not understand."

"Did you calculate how long it would have taken them to reload? How long for you to board? Did you think to move out of *Defiance*'s line of fire?"

Jeffries' blank face answered the questions.

"I thought not. Get out."

For three days, routines continued as normal. Except for Jeffries, who as senior midshipman, kept the third officer's watch. The third kept the second watch, while the second officer sailed the *schooner* prize back to Plymouth, hoping to return on the next supply ship. James still had bandages and could not open his left eye, but after two days, insisted on doing his watch.

On the fourth morning, the first officer announced, "There will be no midshipmen lessons today. The captain wants to see Mister Lancaster and his coxswain at afternoon four bells of the middle watch."

Paul passed a message to James, via the mess steward, to find out why they were summoned to the captain. James did not know, and wondered why they were in trouble and not heroes.

CHAPTER 5

The morning took forever. James had the watch and gun practice. Later, at three bells of the middle watch he asked permission to change into his best uniform to meet with the captain. Just before four bells, Coxswain Paul approached the quarterdeck in his Sunday attire. They stood waiting, feeling like condemned men. The ship became unusually quiet. In the sailors' minds, both Paul and James were heroes who'd won them prize money. In fact, Paul now had the pick of any sailor for his longboat. They assumed Lucky Lancaster would be in the boat and wanted to be part of his future actions.

For James, the ringing of four bells did not have the normal cheerful sound, signaling that middle watch over, and the start of the relaxed afternoon watch. Today it sounded like a church funeral bell.

The other officers were looking anywhere but at James and his coxswain, embarrassed, not knowing what to say to them, as they started their lonely walk to the captain's cabin. The marine sentry came smartly to attention as though for a captain.

Captain Wilson stood with his back to them looking over the cannons, through the stern windows out to sea. He turned to them.

"I should put you both on captain's report."

The words sounded like a death knell. For James it implied no promotion, docked pay, and maybe dismissal. For Paul, as a sailor, fear of being whipped with the cat of nine tails.

"Your actions almost cost me the life of the best potential officer I have ever had."

James wondered which officer? There was no other officer with them, except Jeffries. Impossible for him to be the best potential officer.

James's face was a picture of confusion, and Paul wished to vanish.

"I mean you, Mister Lancaster, you idiot. If it had not been for your coxswain's actions you'd be dead, or worse, maimed for a short life."

Paul relaxed a bit. James became really concerned.

"Your ability to read the danger, make bold decisions, and take action marks you as a born leader. Your unthinking bravery partly makes up for your stupidity of charging a man holding a blunderbuss while you were carrying only a cutlass."

James became more optimistic.

"You, Coxswain, once the danger became apparent, should have used your experience to stop Mister Lancaster charging ahead. We send the midshipmen out with you to learn. This afternoon we are going to go through every step of the boarding, see what alternatives there were, and discuss what to do in the future."

It became the best afternoon of James's life. Understanding that warfare required science and tactics, not just undisciplined enthusiasm. Listening to the captain and first lieutenant dissect the events moment by moment was a revelation. Even Paul relaxed.

"Excellent decision to cut ahead of the schooner and to climb on board, but you should have called for support. A major mistake charging, with only a sword, an armed man. In the future, you always…"

They continued to seven bells, and the captain mentioned, "We will start new training, including hand to hand combat, shore expeditions and cutting-out parties. Oh, Coxswain," the captain added as they were leaving his cabin, "I have passed word for double rum for you and your boat crew tonight."

The ship's training changed. The French guarded their coast, but left long empty areas where there were no towns or villages. *Defiance*'s crew used those beaches. They practiced silent rowing with muffled oars; beach landings; ship boarding; fighting in small teams to charge the opposing crew while protecting each other; forced marches at night; scaling high walls; blowing holes in walls and gates with gunpowder; and towing the frigate with the ship's rowboats. All this, while patrolling the Channel, helping to keep the French warships in port and capturing the occasional coastal trader.

The activity confused the French who feared the English were planning an invasion. They sent more troops to guard the area, diminishing their own invasion army.

James's left eye slowly healed and he could see again. But he had a vertical scar going from his eyelid through his eyebrow and up to his forehead. Also one on his left cheek, plus those on his arm and chest hidden by clothing.

Captain Wilson set teams of midshipmen with their boat crews in competition. James treated it as a game, just as he had done playing pirates with his friend Tony at Buckler's Hard. Yet his crew always came out on top and ended up with the extra rum ration prize. The other midshipmen asked if he had a secret to ensure success. He did not have one. They wondered if the captain tipped him off before the exercises, giving him more time to prepare. He laughed at that idea. He had seldom spoken to the captain since his debriefing of the schooner incident. James found it so obvious. Define the objective of the exercise to the team and get them to suggest the best way of achieving it, or steer them to the correct one. Make them the authors of the solution and let them execute it. James had difficulty understanding why his fellow midshipmen had so much trouble talking with and taking advice from their boat crews.

James's ability to speak French made him the ship's interpreter, especially with the fishermen whom the captain paid generously for their catch of fresh fish, if it came with information. He wanted to know which ships were in the ports; those ready to sail; which trading ships were being loaded and what their cargo was; and were there any troop-carrying craft being prepared to cross the Channel. Also the names of the Navy boats and their captains, so he knew what he would be up against.

Captain Wilson emphasized, "Success does not happen by chance, but through information and planning."

While off-loading the fish onto *Defiance*, James boarded the fishing boats to chat to their captains. It enabled him to practice and improve his French, while gathering more information and developing good relationships with the fishermen, and especially Yvonne. She and her younger brother, Maurice, mainly fished herrings which the ship purchased for the seamen. But she also owned a few crab and lobster pots, and supplied Captain Wilson with his favorite meal at least once a week. Her boat seemed more professional than the others. There were more nets but neatly piled. The ropes were coiled. But most intimidating was the rack of vicious looking knives that she later claimed were for fish gutting, but looked very much like weapons to James.

At first James was surprised to meet a woman fishing captain. She reminded him of a younger version of the Portsmouth ferry women, but taller. She wore a fisherman's oiled cloth large apron, to keep her dry as they hauled in the net or raised the crab pots, showing she was very plump. Her long hair was bundled onto her head and held in a net. Her eyes were piercing and she answered with short sentences, making it clear she was independent and in charge. What was most startling was she wore trousers behind her apron That was a man's exclusive attire. Why did the French let her? As he learnt later, "A skirt on a boat in a storm is not practical. I do a man's job and no one dare try and stop me wearing trousers."

She had to deal with men's prejudices and learnt to cut them short when any made inappropriate remarks. Her face was almost handsome but with lines from the sun and salt. However, when she occasionally smiled, the lines disappeared and her face was remarkably attractive. James guessed she was about thirty.

Their first conversation was a little strained. She did not trust men, especially foreigners.

"What name do I call you?"

"Captain, of course. What else would you expect?"

James was a little intimidated. It was like calling a woman 'sir', something a man would never do. But he did.

"Yes, Captain."

So James asked about the blue lobsters. "At home, the lobsters we eat are red."

Yvonne laughed. "You must come from gentry with kitchen staff. All lobsters either side of the Channel are blue when they are alive. They hide during the day in rocks and come out at night to hunt for their food when their color keeps them safe. Once they are cooked they turn red."

On Yvonne's next visit James plucked up the courage to ask her about herself. "I have never met a fishing-woman before or a woman captain. Can you tell me how that happened?"

Yvonne was about to give her normal answer, 'Mind your own bloody business', but there was something about James, an innocence, no judgment but linked to an inner toughness.

"I am a fisherman. My father died of lung disease, and before helped build our fishing fleet. I want to be part of the fleet, respect his memory, and not separated from the other captains by the name fisherwoman. My eldest brother worked with my father and would have taken over the boat. But he was pressed into Napoleon's Navy and died at the battle of Aboukir Bay, you call it the Battle of the Nile. Your Admiral Nelson outwitted our admiral, François-Paul Brueys d'Aigalliers and destroyed the fleet. We, my mother, younger brother and I, have to eat, so I decided to take over the boat with my younger brother as crew. At first the fishermen objected, and made it difficult, and a few proposed marriage hoping to gain the boat. I said yes, if I could see their cocks to check that they were big enough for me, and they all fled. But they see I work harder, and catch more than they do, so now they leave me alone."

James was embarrassed. He had never heard anyone, even men, talk so openly.

"I am so sorry, for your husband. But it is not the English people who want war. It is always caused by the leaders. Typically ones who want more power and wealth."

"I do not blame you. My other elder brother is in Napoleon's army somewhere in Spain, and the information is the war there is barbaric. We had a revolution to remove a king and have replaced him with a genius, but also a dictator. But look, your men have finished unloading. Get me my money and we will leave."

Later, James was told to report to Captain Wilson.

"Lancaster, I watched you having a long conversation with the fisher-woman. Did you learn anything?"

"Nothing much yet. But she has lost her father and husband. Her elder brother is fighting in Spain. She has to work to live, and she blames Napoleon."

"I have a feeling she may become useful beyond her crabs and lobsters. Spend more time with her."

"Yes, sir."

Actually James was happy to have someone to talk to in conversational French and to learn more of how they felt about the war. Although he continued, with dying hope, to hear from Edith, he still wrote to her, and mentioned the fishermen, but failed to mention one was a lady.

During Yvonne's next visit Captain Wilson instructed Lieutenant Stevens.

"Do not hurry the unloading. Give young Lancaster time."

Stevens was surprised. Encouraging a midshipman to gossip with a fisherwoman, and one who wore trousers! What chaos to social order the war was creating? A woman on a boat was bad enough, but captain of a fishing boat!

On Yvonne's next visit James asked how the general population felt about the war.

"It is not one war, but continuous wars. On one hand people are pleased that there is work and the economy is good. But on the other, over two million men have died in battles so far, and every family in France has suffered. We got rid of the king and royalty but in reality they are back in charge. For instance, Admiral François-Paul Brueys d'Aigalliers was stripped of his noble titles by the revolutionary council and allowed to remain as a captain, but then Napoleon reinstated his titles when he put him in charge of the Mediterranean fleet."

"But why did you get rid of the king?"

"He lost touch with the people. Every summer, when the previous year's wheat crop is nearly finished, the price of bread always goes up. In 1789 the price went out of control. The king not only ignored it, but tried to raise taxes again. On October the fifth some ten thousand women marched from Paris and actually entered the Palace of Versailles by a side door to protest the price of bread. They left peacefully but it was the start. After that, it snowballed. The king was offered a compromise of a joint rule with parliament, but he refused. He insisted on absolute power and lost everything. Women played an important leadership role throughout the revolution. But Napoleon's new Code gives us no rights and puts us and our property back under the control of our fathers or husbands, who may have mistresses, but can send us to prison if we have a lover. It has also removed us from being part of the political leadership. But tell me about you."

"I am the junior midshipmen, second son of the second wife of a lord, but with no inheritance."

"How long have you been on the ship."

"Nearly three years."

"But you have a sweetheart."

"I thought I did, but she has not written to me since I left home."

"So you are eighteen and have never been with a woman?"

James blushed.

"Er... Captain..."

"You are so English. During the revolution men and women talked much more openly about love and sex. Now it is returning to as it was before, unspoken. But tell me, why does your captain allow you to talk to me? He pays me well to know about the boats in the harbors. What else does he want?"

"I am not sure. He stresses that information is the key to success, so I suppose he hopes that by talking to you I will learn more."

Yvonne liked James's honest answer. "If you want to learn more, come with me to the ports and see for yourself. Your French is good enough if we say you come from Marseille. We can start at a small fishing harbor without a fort or army, where they are building the invasion boats. It will be safe."

"My captain will worry it is a trick to capture me."

"A junior midshipman is hardly a prize, especially when I can earn so much more selling your captain fish, crab, lobsters and information."

"I will talk to the captain and hopefully next time you come I will go with you."

James reported to Captain Wilson that Yvonne had invited him to sail with her. "She proposes to try first a small harbor with little security, that dries out at low tide, where they build Napoleon's invasion boats. I think it is worth a try."

Captain Wilson did not agree. "What you are proposing is dangerous. If they catch you, the best you can hope for is prison. As you are not a full officer, you will be in the sailors' prison, forced into hard labor. However, it is more likely you will be tried as a spy and executed. If you are successful, the information about the invasion boats would very helpful and a breakthrough, but I cannot order you to spy. The decision is yours. I need it in writing, if you are volunteering."

James did not think of it as spying, but as an adventure. A chance to get off the ship for the first time for nearly three years.

"Sir, it will be a relief after spending hours at the mast head with the telescope working out what is happening in the harbors. Yvonne tells me that the French do not believe England has an army ready to invade, so security is very lax. It would be good to get a real look at the invasion craft, as there is so much speculation about them."

"Agreed, have the sailmaker stitch you up some fishermen's clothes, make them look dirty and worn, and prepare a bag with food for three days. I will give you some money for bribes, in case of emergency. Make sure that you account for it carefully. Take a good knife, a pistol and a ship's cutlass."

CHAPTER 6

Five days later James was up the mast when, through the telescope, he saw Yvonne's boat.

He descended and reported to the first lieutenant.

"Sir, the fishing boat is approaching. Permission to be relieved from watch and prepare."

"Go ahead, Mister Lancaster. Good luck, though I think you are crazy to go. Captain Wilson expects you back in three days. After, if you do not return, we will stay in the area two more days, then you are on your own."

"Yes, sir, thank you, sir."

Yvonne's normally serious face spread into smile as James climbed over the ship's side and down into her boat dressed as a fisherman and carrying a bag.

"So your captain trusts me?"

"He was not sure, so as insurance he will pay you a bonus when we return. He wants me back in three days."

"If he values you that much, I will have to look after you. What do you have in the bag?"

"A telescope, pistol, cutlass and food... Captain."

"The telescope may come in handy but if you need the weapons we are in big trouble, and there is no way we are eating English ship's food. Not only do we have fresh fish and crustaceans, but French cheese, pâté and bread. Even the poorest French eat better than the average English. We have five hours before we arrive and time for you to learn how to sail a smaller boat, which is different and more fun than your frigate. Take the tiller and head on a broad reach to that dark spot on the horizon, which is a small forest."

James loved steering with the tiller, learning to adjust the sails for better speed, and how Yvonne watched the sea surface for indications of wind and fish.

"We often stop in the harbor overnight and sell our catch before heading home and getting another catch on the way. Fish stay in certain areas, and the seas outside the harbor are a rich fishing ground. Unfortunately the harbor is small; most of it dries out at low tide and it can be dangerous in a storm. The shipyard is building some of the invasion boats and a couple are moored in the middle of the harbor where there is normally water. If all goes well we will stay the night, and tomorrow we will fish and return you to *Defiance* with a fresh catch."

Once away from the frigate, Yvonne removed her fisherman's apron and let her hair out of the net. James was startled to see her robust figure. She looked taller, and her ample breasts, strong arms and shoulders, made her look like the plump figures of mermaids sculptured onto the bows of ships. Yvonne smiled as she caught James staring at her. He looked away in embarrassment.

Yvonne's younger brother, Maurice, a little older than James, was short, thin and an excellent sailor. He made adjusting and raising sails, furling the lines look easy, and he basically managed the boat on his own while his sister, or now James, steered. He said little, but when he did it meant something. He put up with Yvonne's bossing with humorous disrespect, but they were clearly very good friends. Maybe he noticed James's reaction to Yvonne's femininity.

"You're the first man she has allowed on this boat since she frightened all our local men away."

"How did she do that?"

"Maurice, keep quiet."

"It is only fair he knows. We were moored by the quay close to a café. A number of the suitors she said yes to, if their cocks were big enough and if they would show them, were drinking. They were a little drunk and boasting. One said he was big enough, and intended to show Yvonne, and staggered on board. As he took it out to show, she grabbed it with her right hand, burst out laughing, picked up the filleting knife and said she was going to cut it off and nail it onto the cabin wall to show what small was. The man tried to pull way but fell over onto his back trapped. He squealed like a pig until all the others came to see what was happening. Eventually she let him go and washed her hands for ten minutes. Ever since they keep away."

James determined to be even more respectful. This was not a lady to upset. But he enjoyed looking at her as she laid down in the cockpit while he steered.

They sailed into the small harbor with a stone quay, houses and a couple of bars. The village was on the slope of a hill behind. At the end of the harbor were big boat sheds and a number of what looked like flat bottom barges. In the middle of the harbor there were two vessels moored. One was a flat bottomed rowing barge, and the other an extraordinary barge with paddle wheels on each corner and windmills to drive the paddle wheels.

"What are they?"

"James, stop staring and assist Maurice to tie the sails and tidy the nets. Otherwise you will attract attention to yourself. You can study Napoleon's boats later."

A fish merchant arrived with a barrow with metal rimmed wheels making a noise as it bounced over the cobble stones. Yvonne argued for the price, and then they unloaded the balance of the fish that *Defiance* did not buy. The local gendarme came by.

"Good afternoon, Yvonne. A small catch today?"

Although everyone knew the local fishermen sold to the English, it was illegal and Yvonne had to be careful.

"When it is sunny like today the fish go deeper. We will make up for it tomorrow. Would your wife like a few fish for supper?"

Finally the boat was tidy and Yvonne turned to James.

"Maurice and I will go to the bar where we can watch the boat and anyone who approaches. You can pretend to be asleep in the nets with your back to the quay and study Napoleon's boats."

James laid in the nets and took out his telescope to look at the flat bottom rowing barge. It seemed to have twenty rowlocks each side for a total of forty oars and rowers. He estimated it must be one hundred feet long and twenty feet wide and could carry about one hundred men and their equipment. There was one cannon each on the bow and stern. It seemed perfect, for a flat lake with no wind. James could not imagine it rowing into waves. The water would splash over the bows and fill up the boat in no time. He could only see one side of the inside of the hull, but there was very little longitude bracing, so as it went over waves it would flex and possible break up.

The second vessel was a much stronger looking barge, nearly square in shape, rather like the barges used to hoist masts onto ships with big cranes. But they stayed in the harbors. On what appeared the be the front and rear sides of the barge were big paddle wheels attached to conventional windmills. So this was Napoleon's secret ship that caused so much speculation. They would use the windmills to drive the paddle wheels and could even go into the wind. But how could they control the speed of each paddle wheel to keep the ship going straight? What would the effect be of the big windmill buildings as they went into the wind? Surely they would create a lot of wind resistance. James pretended to wake up and look back to Yvonne and Maurice sitting at a table outside the bar. They indicated for him to join them.

"Would you like an ale or wine and some cheese?

In a low voice Yvonne asked, "What do you think of the boats?"

"I would not like to go out in one of the rowing barges in a rough sea."

"That is what the fishermen who tested them said. The harbors up to Calais are crammed full of them, and they say there are two thousand to carry over twenty thousand men. There are so many that they could not get more than half out of the harbors on one tide. If they launch them they need two days of flat water, no wind and little tide current to get them to England. That seldom happens. Napoleon watches the troops, practicing landing on the beach and storming the cliffs, from the cliffs of Boulogne. He uses real cannon balls firing over their heads to train them not to be scared. The fishermen in the boats report they spend more time bailing than rowing. Villeneuve, the admiral for the French Navy's main fleet, is supposed to provide protection. But he has been reluctant to let the ships leave harbor. Unless he does it will be easy for the British Navy to sink the invasion boats."

"What do they say about the windmill ship?"

"Impossible to steer. It does not go into the wind and it does not like waves. Let's have supper and get up early for the tide to take us out to sea."

Yvonne and Maurice had bunks in the cabin and said for James to sleep in the cockpit. He used the net to make the hard wooden bench a little more comfortable and to create a pillow when Yvonne came up from the cabin with a blanket for him. She was just wearing loose underwear. James tried to look away.

"What, have you not seen a lady before? Stupid question. Of course not, you are still a virgin. Feast your eyes, as from what I hear most English ladies stay covered, even on their wedding night."

"Captain, you are not behaving as a lady."

"James, that is exactly what I am doing. The name gentleman is made out of two words, and you are obliged to live up to the first, 'gentle'. Lady is one word, and it gives me the freedom to behave as I choose. I have a lot to teach you, and it is not only about Napoleon's boats."

James had a troubled night. Yvonne appeared at sunrise wearing just a loose fitting blouse and trousers, but seemed very distant.

"James, get up. Maurice will show you how to use the sculling oar and you can scull us out of the harbor."

The oar was long and fitted into a rowlock in the transom at the back of the boat.

"You move it side to side, forcing it through the water and pushing the boat forward."

It was hard work and took James's mind off the images of the previous night and generous glimpses of Yvonne's breast that her blouse failed to hide. Once out of the harbor they raised the sails and sailed to the headland.

"Fish seem to like the headlands. Maybe it is because the current is faster and they have more plankton to eat."

James thought that there was so much to learn. Each trade had layers of detail. Every day was an opportunity to gain experience, never knowing when the knowledge might be useful. Yvonne made no reference to the previous evening, in fact hardly talked to, or acknowledged James. He presumed it was because he had looked at her in her slip and embarrassed her. He tried to be very polite and avoid her, but in a small boat that was difficult. They put out the net and trawled for two hours. The boat slowed down and was barely moving.

"It seems the net must be full. Now the hard part, retrieving it and extracting the fish."

They dropped the sails and started to pull in the net. Maurice laid out six fish boxes. As they pulled in the net there were fish caught in the mesh.

"We extract them carefully as the wives will not buy damaged fish. Then each type of fish is put in a separate box."

Finally they were near the end of the net where most fish were. It took all their strength to haul the net and fish up the side of the boat, over the bulwarks and onto the deck.

"I was told they call you Lucky Lancaster. You have brought us luck as this is an exceptional catch. Let's empty the net and get it back in the water."

Whatever tension had been passing between James and Yvonne all day, vanished. Yvonne and Maurice were excited, and James had trouble keeping up with them as they sorted the fish. In the early afternoon they had the net back in the water and started gutting the fish from the first catch. Early evening they pulled in the net and once again they had a good catch. It was night and dark by the time they emptied the net.

"We will take shifts to sail through the night to rendezvous with *Defiance*. We have a small hand-held compass and an oil lamp. Check the compass every few minutes and steer by feeling the wind on your face, and listening to the sails. They will shake if you go off course. Keep a sharp watch for other boats and regularly call out ahoy. We cannot afford the fancy bell the big ships have."

Dawn came and James was on watch. The sea was empty. James was both concerned not to see *Defiance* but relieved. He was not in a hurry to return to the strict formality of naval procedures. He had hoped for another view of Yvonne's glorious body but that had not happened. She and Maurice came on deck wearing fishing aprons and started gutting the fish. The boat was surrounded by seagulls which retrieved the fish entrails from the sea, but unfortunately covered the boat, and them, with their droppings.

Mid-morning *Defiance*'s sails appeared on the horizon. It would take two hours for them to meet.

"James, if you, and more importantly your captain, think this trip was useful, next time we can go to our home port where there is a frigate and merchant ships converted into troop carriers. You should be able to work out how close they are to being ready. However, the port has a fort with big artillery and guards at the dock."

"I will discuss with the captain and let you know on your next visit."

Yvonne had enjoyed the conversations with James. When she suggested he join them, she saw it as a way to earn extra fees from *Defiance*'s captain. But she found James to be very knowledgeable and interesting to talk to, and at the same time innocent and shockingly honest.

His views about women's rights were very liberal. He talked about his love, Edith, like the ancient knight Sir Lancelot talking about his queen. How could he be so naive to think a woman who had not answered for three years still loved him. But it was so refreshing. Even though he was ten years younger than her she found him very attractive. Tall, strong, with an athletic body, and without the macho attitude of so many older men. She felt a little ashamed that she had shocked him, but delighted by his reaction. She liked his blushes and that his manhood had grown.

On drawing alongside *Defiance*, Yvonne sold half her catch and received payment for returning James. With most of the ship's crew watching, and some hauling up the fish, James was unable to say a proper goodbye. Just a, "Thanks,", and "We will see you in five days."

Lieutenant Stevens was shocked by James's smell of fish and the state of his fishing clothes covered with fish scales and stained in blood.

"The captain wants you immediately, but first get rid of that smell and into uniform."

As Yvonne sailed away, her last image was of James standing naked on the deck, with two seamen on either end of a long pump handle, rocking it up and down and causing a heavy stream of sea water to wash over him. It was a view she wanted to see again.

James reported to captain Wilson all he had seen and heard, and provided crude sketches of Napoleon's two vessels.

"No seamen would go out into the Channel in these rowing barges unless it was guaranteed to be flat as a lake. It will take them more than a day to get all the boats launched and filled with men and equipment. With normal channel waves they will fill up with water and the boats will bend going over the waves letting more water in, or breaking them. Their cannons are small and no match for a frigate. If they do have perfect weather and tides, they will spread across the Channel and be easy to sink. Most can be sunk just by ramming them. Napoleon hopes Admiral Villeneuve's fleet will provide protection, so him trying to leave Toulon harbor will be the first sign of an attempt to invade. Napoleon is training his troops near Boulogne and it might be good to send a spy to watch. The windmill barges can never work."

"Are you really confident in your report? Is there any chance the French organized this to make you believe their invasion fleet is in such difficulties?"

"I am absolutely confident."

"Then I must get this information to the admiral. Well done."

"Sir, Captain Yvonne suggested that I go with her next time to her port. There is a frigate and four merchant ships converted to troop and equipment carriers."

"Mister Lancaster, it will be much more dangerous, but after this first success I will let you try."

It took over a week to beat up the Channel to join with the admiral's ship, and for Captain Wilson to report. Signals flew from the admiral's ship instructing Midshipman Lancaster to report to with all speed. By the time James was dressed in his best uniform Paul had their whaler in the water waiting. James was led by a lieutenant to the admiral's conference room where Captain Wilson and other senior officers were looking at charts. There were no pleasantries or introductions. The admiral peppered James with questions, had him draw more sketches of the invasion craft, wanted details of his conversations about them with Yvonne and then dismissed him.

Defiance returned to their normal area and Captain Wilson gave a 'well done' to James, but nothing more. The admiral dispatched a fast cutter to take the news to Portsmouth. From there it was rushed to Whitehall by courier. Little did James know the importance of connecting Admiral Villeneuve to the invasion plans.

Defiance stayed in the area where they normally met with Yvonne's boat, but for four days she did not appear.

"Mister Lancaster, this is concerning. Perhaps she was a spy and is now keeping away."

"I am confident she will return."

But inside he worried that he had been duped.

CHAPTER 7

On the morning of the fifth day Yvonne's boat appeared. James changed into his fishing clothes.

The boat came alongside *Defiance* and Yvonne and Maurice were wearing their fishing aprons.

"James, I am glad to see your ship is back. You were away over a week and I thought you had been sent elsewhere. I have fish. I see you ready to join us. If you can get the fish unloaded quickly we can get back to our port for this afternoon's flood tide. Otherwise we will have to enter tomorrow morning. Is it the same deal as last time? Payment for your safe return?"

"It is the same deal, and my captain wants me back the day after tomorrow."

"OK, tell him depending on wind and tide, mid-morning."

Once they left *Defiance*, Maurice took off his apron.

"Maurice, why do you wear that in hot weather when you are not hauling the net or filleting?"

Maurice glanced at his sister. "Yvonne… I mean our captain, insists we wear them when we go to naval vessels."

James looked at Yvonne. "But why?"

"It is tough being accepted as a woman captain. Men get excited and make crude comments when they see a lady with a figure or that I wear trousers. It is not pleasant and diminishes my authority as a captain. So I hide mine. You can take the tiller, while we rest. Then we need to prepare the net and catch fish before we get home so they don't suspect us of selling to the English."

Maurice turned to James and with a grin said, "It is good to have you back on board. It helps to have an extra person to absorb some of Yvonne's bossing and to share the work. She will not pay for another crew."

Yvonne jokingly responded as she took off her apron, "Maurice, be careful what you say."

James focused on steering but also enjoyed seeing Yvonne's plump figure in her light summer blouse and trousers.

After a lunch of bread, cheese, pâté and red wine they put out the net and an hour before arriving at the port pulled it and the fish on board.

They entered the French harbor, under the shadow of the towering fort and its cannons, with two French soldiers patrolling the quay. At the back of the quay were multicolored two and three story houses, workshops, fishermen's warehouses and a couple of cafés. The main town was beyond and only visible by the chimneys. James remembered what happened to the captain of the French schooner, for being out of uniform. For sure, the French had seen the schooner's captain hanging from the yard of the admiral's flagship. If they caught James in civilian clothes, coming from the same fleet that hung the captain, he could expect 'Madame la Guillotine'. But James rationalized that a young man, dressed in smelly fishermen's clothes, did not look like the English officers they trained the French guards to look for. Day after day they stood at their sentry box, marched up and down the quays, watched, waited, trying to keep warm or cool. Nothing ever happened, especially in the winter. It left them bored, cold, often hungry, and more interested in getting to the end of their watch to consume their spirit ration. The English showed no intention of ever invading France. The French had strong forts and powerful guns, making a frontal attack by an English ship impossible. James learnt that the French gun crews practiced their gun drill every day, but seldom fired the cannons. Gunpowder and cannon balls were needed by Napoleon's Army, and were in short supply.

Rocks and sandbars littered the approaches to most of the Atlantic and Channel ports. As soon as war started, the French removed all the buoys that marked the route into the harbors. So did the English. James made charts of the courses taken by Yvonne. He marked which land based transit marks she used, such as a white cottage coming in line with a church spire. Once in the harbor, he would list and count the different boats, and look to see if there were more of the troop-carrying invasion barges. As Yvonne's fishing boat came under the fort's guns, the soldiers raised flags on a tall pole with a specific code. Yvonne hoisted answering flags. The code changed often. The wrong reply signal meant a boarding or, for bigger boats, cannon fire.

On arriving in port, James stayed in the hold, filling up the wicker baskets with fish. They hoisted the baskets up to the dock and loaded them onto carts to take to the market. The port guards had to be bribed. Once they had their fish, they left. After, James worked on the deck cleaning and repairing fishing nets, while watching and learning.

He became confident, perhaps overconfident.

"Who are you?" barked a guard who had approached silently. James reacted slowly, looked around to see who the guard wanted to talk to, realizing he had to answer.

"Ramon."

They planned that in the unlikely event the guards question him, James would be Ramon, a distant cousin of Yvonne from Marseille, exempted from the army because of his 'slow reactions'. Dim-witted.

James grinned at the guard. He wanted to avoid talking. Yvonne was negotiating with the fish merchant at the end of the quay. James extruded a lot of saliva as he twisted his head and muttered, "Ramon," and grinned again.

Then he returned to repairing the net but showing difficulty in passing the fisherman's 'toggle' with the repair line through the holes in the net. The guard became impatient.

"Papers."

James created more saliva and apparent distress. He retreated into the center of the boat.

The guard shouted, "Come with me."

James knew his luck had run out. Should he make a run for it? Perhaps he could knock the guard out and escape in a small mackerel boat. He backed further away towards the outside edge of the boat, feigning madness and fear, showing that he would jump into the water. The guard did not know what to do. He called for help, and the other guard started running over. James could not keep the pretense up much longer.

Yvonne arrived and shouted, "You should be ashamed of yourself, frightening Ramon. That is how people who God made different were treated before the Revolution. He is my cousin from Marseille. Despite his impediment, he is helping to feed our armies."

She went to James, who shied away in apparent fear.

"Do not worry, Ramon. No one is going to hurt you any more. You're safe. Carry on with your nets,"

James gave a disturbed grin and carefully picked up his net toggle while keeping one eye on the guards in apparent fear.

The guards looked embarrassed. "Captain Yvonne, it was a misunderstanding."

Yvonne's tough reputation came in handy.

James stayed on deck, slowly repairing the nets. Maybe he still had his luck.

"James, I will stay at our home with our mother this evening and I expect Maurice will be with his girlfriend, so you can sleep in the cabin. You can finish repairing the net, then wash down, brush and clean the deck and cockpit using a bucket and sea water. Keep a low profile. There is food and wine so help yourself. Tomorrow afternoon we will take the tide out of the harbor, catch some fish and then meet your ship the following morning."

"Yes, Captain."

James was a little surprised to find himself working as common sailor and obeying Yvonne. However, being on his own and working on the deck gave him time to study the harbor; the frigate and merchant ships; and the fishing boats returning with their catches, and loading them onto merchant's barrows to take them to the market.

The frigate and merchant ships were attaching the last sails to their spars and loading barrels of water. Military tents in neat lines covered the hills beyond the port. The ships were obviously preparing to sail and to carry a lot of troops. The Royal Navy did not have enough fighting ships to guard all the ports all the time. What if the French slipped out? Even if *Defiance* was there they could attack the frigate, but the troop carriers would escape. They could probably land a thousand soldiers on the south coast of England and set up as support system for Napoleon's invasion. How could they stop them? With all the rocks littering the harbor entrance, and the cannons on the fort, there was no way to send in a fire ship.

James focused on cleaning the boat and at dusk opened a bottle wine and settled into the cockpit. As it became dark it was difficult to see the big ships anchored in the middle of the harbor. A plan came into his mind, a crazy plan, but one he intended to present, even though he expected Captain Wilson to reject it. It required rowing boats. There were many mackerel fishing boats tied to the dock. James calculated how many men could hide for seven hours in the hold of Yvonne's fishing boat. He needed a dark night with no moon. If possible, during a celebration or holiday, when most of the French ship's crews would be ashore, and the fort gunners warm in their barracks. James planned to capture the French frigate, cut the anchor cable and tow her out, past the fort, with row boats, aided by the ebbing tide.

James suddenly realized it was nighttime. He had spent hours imagining his plan in detail while nibbling on the cheese and pâté and sipping the wine. He went down into the cabin and climbed onto Yvonne's bunk. It was more comfortable and much wider than his on *Defiance*, and had her lavender smell. He fell asleep thinking about her blouse and how inefficient it was at hiding her bold breasts and proud nipples.

It was the slight movement of the boat and soft footsteps on the deck above him that woke him. Had they found him? He pulled his throwing knife out of his sock and laid very still. A dark figure descended the companionway steps and crept across to Maurice's bunk. So, they were searching for him. How many more would be on the dock? He felt confident he could manage one, but then what? Could he slip out of the cabin and into the water to swim looking for a boat to escape in? The figure moved backwards from Maurice's bunk towards James; he leant forward and covered the figure's mouth with his hand, and holding the intruder firm, put his knife to the throat.

"Mutter one sound and I will slit your throat. Nod if you understand?"

The figure nodded in agreement. James relaxed his hand.

"James, it is me, Yvonne."

"Yvonne, sorry, Captain, what are you doing?"

"Trying not to get my throat cut. But call me Yvonne this evening. Move over, I am coming into my bunk"

James could just see that Yvonne was wearing a dark hooded cloak, and when she slipped it off, just a white slip, and nothing else. She nestled into him and James felt her soft voluptuous body against his. She pulled his face to hers and kissed him. Her lips were soft, searching, demanding. He responded but she cautioned him.

"Slow and gentle."

"But is this not dangerous? What if the guards find us? What if Maurice comes?"

"We are in France and there is no crime in having a lover unless one's husband objects, and I lost my husband, and told Maurice to take tomorrow off to be with his girlfriend."

"And what about my Edith?"

"James, one of the things I like about you is you are a romantic. But face reality. Your Edith has not written one letter to you in three years. But even if she had, the present I am going to give you is for both of you. You must learn that women have as much need for lovemaking, and often more, than men. And I am in need, it has been many years. But many men just enter the bride, satisfy themselves and fall asleep. English wives are taught that is how it should be, and put up with it as their duty. I will teach you how to make a French woman happy before you receive your pleasure. We will start with kissing, then I will run my hands and fingers all over your body teaching you where it is sensitive. After we will progress. We have a lot of time until the next tide. Now get undressed. Do you normally sleep with your socks on?"

"On ship, it makes getting up in a hurry easier, and it holds my knife."

It was embarrassing undressing in front of Yvonne, even though it was dark and hard to see. She pulled her slip over her head and crushed her breasts into his chest. They were soft and sensuous and he wanted to put his face into them.

"Kiss me. Let your lips search mine. Let them tell me how much you want me. Be gentle but demanding. Move your hand down to my breast and hold it. Kiss my ears, eyes, neck and then my breasts. Use your lips, not your teeth, to press the nipple and suck it. Now my lips again."

James was beyond excited and his physical reaction embarrassed him. Her hand went down and held him.

"Do not be shy. I am pleased I excite you. All men have one and they grow when excited. You will hear a lot of nonsense about the importance of size. It is not size, but how you use it that matters."

She squeezed him and electric shocks passed through him, taking his breath away.

"Now kiss me again and explore my body with your hand. Use your fingertips. Touch me behind my ears, my neck, my lips, my breasts. Gently drag your fingernails down my back. Explore my bottom, the inside of my thighs, massage my feet and kiss them. Move your hand up my leg and gently touch my womanhood. Put your finger, a little higher, yes, touch there. That is wonderful, In a moment I will guide you into me and you must push powerfully when I say."

James was in a complete confusion of erotic tension. He was about to explode when he felt her hand guide him. Her body welcomed him as she started moaning.

"Now, now."

He respond to her hips moving by thrusting and as she let out a yell he erupted. An extraordinary feeling which he knew he would never be able to explain. He searched for her lips as her body continued with a series of volcanic eruptions that died down slowly. She rolled him off her and pushed his head into her breasts and held him tight.

"I knew you would make a great lover, but you have a lot to learn. Sleep for a while, and we will start again."

He suckled her breast, wrapped his legs around her, and fell asleep.

James woke to find the sun streaming though the cabin companionway hatch and Yvonne standing gloriously naked. His reaction was immediate, and she noticed and smiled.

"I went to the baker for fresh bread and jam for breakfast. You slept well. Get up and come and hold me."

He rolled out of the bunk and held her in his arms, kissing her lips.

"Yvonne, you are amazing. I had no idea lovemaking was so fantastic. But is there not a danger of making a baby?"

"James, we learnt from the aristocrat ladies who used to marry for convenience and had lovers. They taught us how to use half of a lemon. There is no risk. Put me down and kiss my breasts. What we have is mutual affection and sex. Imagine this with someone you really love, Edith for example. It will be ten times better. Do not confuse what we are doing into thinking you love me. You are still a boy. This may be our only chance for this. So enjoy it to the full. I certainly am, as I needed it. It has been four years since they press-ganged my husband. Have breakfast as I want you strong, then you may give me a massage and get to know my body better."

Yvonne laid on the bunk on her front and James ran his hand over her back and down to her bottom.

"Your body is so beautiful. I would like to kiss it all over."

"Most people call me plump, but beautiful will do. First a massage. Start with my head then neck and shoulders, arms, lower back, then go down to the feet and work your way up to my bottom."

His hands worked on her powerfully but gently. She had not been honest, she could easily fall in love with James. His hands and eyes explored her body. She wanted him, but restrained herself. James, standing naked over her, exploring every inch of her, was having to use every ounce of self-restrain. His hands moved between her legs and she groaned. James rolled her over, kissed her as he eased himself onto her. She felt his weight and strength.

"Yes, now."

This time he entered by himself. He membered that she had stressed he must restrain himself until she started to come. He moved in rhythm with her with powerful strokes and feeling her tightening, her leg becoming taut, her nails digging into his back, biting his neck. It was difficult to control so he slowed a little.

"Faster, harder, do not stop." He obeyed and she let out a cry, "Oh yes, saints alive, this is unbelievable."

All of her body trembled. He joined her. The feelings were much more powerful than the first time. They kept coming. She continued after he stopped, her body giving involuntary jerks accompanied by cries.

"It is too much, but I want more."

She hungrily kissed him, biting his lips, his neck, crying, laughing, holding on tight.

He found her breasts and suckled them, holding her, never wanting to let her go.

"James, during the Revolution I heard women talking about their new freedom to find a lover and how wonderful it was, but I never expected this. So few women actually experience what we just had."

"But do you not want to cuddle?"

"James, remember you are on my ship, so have to obey or face consequences."

James grinned. "Yes, Captain."

Yvonne liked being the boss. She had loved her husband but lovemaking had never satisfied her, and after he always made her get up to fetch wine and cheese. Having a younger lover who obeyed had its advantages. As this was probably the only time with James, she wanted to explore everything she had heard the revolutionary women leaders talk about.

James kissed and gently bit Yvonne all over while she lay enjoying and dreaming of how she could suggest more trips to other ports. She pulled his head down towards her. James hesitated, and she pulled harder.

"They say in a man's lips and tongue there is magic. I want to experience it."

Her body shook and kept shaking until finally she pushed him back.

"Now it is your turn."

They kept exploring each other and Yvonne coached James as to what she enjoyed while showing him the pleasures men can receive.

It was late afternoon when James looked out of the cabin hatch.

"Yvonne, Captain, the tide is fully out."

Yvonne looked.

"So it is. What a shame. Another twelve hours to make love."

"But you do not understand. I have to be back for the rendezvous with *Defiance*. It is impossible for a midshipman to keep a whole frigate waiting. If I am not there tomorrow morning they will return late afternoon for two days and after presume I am captured. I will be in terrible trouble."

"There is nothing we, or even Napoleon could do about the tide. You will have to blame the port security for the delay. In the meantime, as we cannot solve the problem, let's use the time, or I could just shackle you and keep you."

"The idea has merit, but I think we will follow your first idea and make love for twelve hours."

"First let's go ashore for some food. This is the best place for oysters, crab and all seafood. Perhaps the Navy might pay. The bar will be full of soldiers and you might learn something. Though it will be hard to keep my hands from touching you."

It was Jame's first French fish meal and he wondered why the English, who had the same raw food, did not prepare it as well. After Yvonne continued with Jame's training and they resurfaced in time for the high tide and slack water at four a.m.

"James, it will be just you and me, Maurice is not coming. We will need the scull oar to row us out to sea and hope there is a morning breeze."

James lifted the long oar and put it in the stern rowlock. It was hard work. He had learnt a lot from Yvonne. Not just lovemaking, but about handling smaller sailboats, fishing, entering harbors, onshore transit marks and much more.

"Stop dreaming and skull harder."

"Yes, Captain."

Yvonne had to focus on getting them to the rendezvous and catching fish on the way, but it was hard. She had fallen for James and knew it would be difficult to find anyone like him, not just his lovemaking, but his sense of humor, and gentleness. It takes a strong man to be gentle.

It was early afternoon, having worked hard to fish, when they spotted *Defiance* on the horizon.

"James, tie the tiller and make love to me one last time."

James stripped, laid a sail on the cockpit seat, and undressed Yvonne.

"Yvonne, I will always love you. A man or woman can surely love more than one person, all a little differently."

James was powerful, but gentle. As Yvonne climaxed she cried.

"Yvonne, what have I done wrong?"

"Nothing. It was perfect. I can think of nothing nearer to heaven than making love to you, at sea, on my boat. I am so happy, but sad as I know this may never happen again. I will remember it for always."

James put on his fishermen's trousers, but left his shirt off. Something he could never do on board *Defiance*.

Captain Wilson was relieved to see Yvonne's fishing boat. He worried himself sick that James had been caught. Now he was angry at the delay. He looked through his telescope and saw a shirtless James at the tiller and Yvonne sitting close with her hand on his leg. There was no sign of Yvonne's brother.

"Mister Stevens, as soon as the boat is alongside have Mister Lancaster wash and change and report to me post haste. Here is payment for the fish, if they had time to catch any!"

Lieutenant Stevens was confused; what did the captain know that caused him to think they had no time for fishing?

James noticed the flash of sun reflecting off glass coming from *Defiance*.

"They are watching us with a telescope."

"James, fortunately, they are too late to see much. Once the war is over, and if your Edith does not want you, come back to me."

It was hard not being able to give Yvonne one final kiss so James busied himself preparing the fish for *Defiance*.

As he climbed on deck Lieutenant Stevens was aghast. James smelt of fish, had even more fish blood over his shirt and trousers, and with marks on his lips he looked as though he had been in a fight.

"Mister Lancaster, glad to see you safe. The captain wants you to report post haste, as soon as you have washed off the fish smell and are in proper uniform. We will handle the fish unloading."

CHAPTER 8

"Come in."

Captain Wilson was looking out of the window watching Yvonne sail away.

"She is a good captain, so tell me why you are over twelve hours late?"

"Well, sir—"

"But before you do, answer carefully these questions."

James became very nervous. This was unlike Captain Wilson, who was normally very direct.

"Did you get the cut on your lip from a fight?"

James had not seen his lip and had no idea the love bite was so obvious.

"Are the marks on your neck and lips in any way connected to your failing to be here on time?"

James had no choice but to confess and try and divert the questions.

"Yes, sir, they are connected, but you warned my spying was dangerous and one had to be ready to make sacrifices."

Captain Wilson smiled to himself at James's attempt to justify being late. If he had achieved the same result, but returned on time he would have celebrated with him. For any man sexual baptism is a defining moment in his life, and especially with someone as attractive as Captain Yvonne. He hated to admit it, but James had become his favorite, and he had to show the ship he had no favorites.

"Mister Lancaster, I need your report, but first we must deal with this issue. To be late with no acceptable reason is inexcusable. To delay His Majesty's ship and three hundred men unforgivable. However I also recognize you undertook a dangerous mission. So I give you the option. Captain's report in the logbook and extra watches, which will be seen by the admiral who may add discipline. Or, lay over the cannon for caning of six of the best. It will be recorded in the log as a separate incident from your trip and as 'youthful exuberance'. Your delay will be credited to the winds."

James was shocked. A captain's report could be the end of his career if the admiral investigated further. But the whole ship would know he had been caned, so he would not only have the pain but the humiliation.

"S-s-s-s-s-sir…" James started to stutter and took a deep breath. "I will take the caning, sir."

Captain Wilson opened the door and called, "Send for the bosun at the double, and tell him to bring his cane."

As James suffered the humiliation of bending over the cannon, he heard the shouts for the bosun. Now the whole ship knew someone was to be caned and in a few minutes they would know it was him. The ship would go unnaturally quiet as everyone would listen to hear as he yelled quietly or screamed.

Midshipmen Jeffries was at the back of the quarterdeck with other midshipmen. He thought that at last the captain's favorite was being brought down to size. He wondered what James had done to receive such a tough punishment.

"I will bet a shilling we will hear him screaming before the sixth stroke."

"You mean like you did when the sailing master caned you for your noon sights?"

"Watch your mouth. James no longer has the captain's confidence, so be more careful."

"I will take your wager."

Three of them took him on. Not because they were confident of winning, but just to show support to their favorite who had stopped Jeffries bullying them.

James waited, realizing the ship was silent except for the pounding of a pair of feet across the deck, up the steps to the quarterdeck, and down the stairs to the cabin.

"Bosun reporting, sir."

"Kindly give Mister Lancaster six of the best. I mean, best."

The captain knew that the men liked James and the bosun might hold back a bit.

"Yes, sir, six of the best, sir."

The bosun had to make it look the very best for fear of going on report himself. But he also knew the crew, especially Coxswain the Bulldog Paul, would not take it kindly if he was too enthusiastic. He moved over to check James was in the correct position and slipped him a piece of leather to bite on.

"Are you ready, Mister Lancaster?"

"Yes, thank you, Bosun, carry on."

Captain Wilson loved James's spirit. He hoped the caning would not break it.

The bosun tested the cane in the air, making a terrible swish noise, startling the captain and frightening James. The officers on the quarterdeck above heard it. The bosun hoped that the violence of the test swishes would distract from what he hoped would be the softer real strokes. But even so, they would hurt and he had seen many grown men break down and having to be held in place.

James took a deep breath and bit hard on the leather. The cane landed with a cruel blow and James bit harder and kept quiet. After the fourth blow tears were coming to his eyes. He thought of Yvonne and Edith. What would they say if they learnt he yelled out?

The bosun was surprised. Not even a shout. He made the next one a little harder. James gasped, nearly dropped the leather but shoved it back between his teeth. One more to go. He would do it.

The last switch. James had to dry his eyes before he stood up and showed calm.

"Six of the best, sir."

"Thank you, Bosun. Mister Lancaster, you can get up."

The captain was very surprised and proud for James.

James was thinking that he would have taken the double for having had the chance to spend the time with Yvonne. He got up slowly.

"Would you like time to gather yourself before giving your report?"

"No, thank you, sir, but I would be grateful for a glass of water."

"Steward, two waters. I would offer you a seat but I guess you will be more comfortable standing."

"Yes, very considerate of you, sir."

Jeffries was not happy.

"The bosun went soft on him, it does not count."

"We all heard the swish and the cut as the cane landed. It was tough. Pay up or we will take it from you."

"Captain, there is a frigate and four merchant ships converted to troop carriers preparing to take one thousand soldiers, all a few weeks from being ready. The troops are camped behind the town and I sat next to some in a bar and listened. They expect to sail in about four weeks and land near Folkestone, and march to support the French troops coming from Calais to near Dover."

James explained to the captain the difficulties of the harbor entrance, making a direct attack impossible.

"You sat in a bar with French soldiers? An excellent job, Mister Lancaster. The Navy does not have enough ships to let us sit outside every harbor. Even if we are here when they come out and we engage the frigate, the troop ships will escape."

Captain Wilson acted as though the caning had never happened.

"Thank you, sir. Permission to speak, sir?"

Captain Wilson was worried that James wanted to discuss or protest the caning.

"Permission granted, what is it?"

"I think we can capture or sink the French frigate anchored in the harbor, and blow up the other four transport ships as well."

The captain, relieved, listened intently as James laid out his plan.

"Worst case is we sink one or more of the French boats and escape in the mackerel boats. The best case is we capture the frigate and sink the rest."

"The worst case is we lose part of our crew and get nothing in return. Tell me more."

Captain Wilson's response made James pause for a moment. He had not thought of failure. With a renewed interest in details, and thinking out loud, he drew out the plan in ten-minute sections with chalk on the captain's blackboard.

"Let me think, but not a word to anyone, I mean anyone. You may tell your fellow officers what you saw."

Captain Wilson was starting to regret that he had been so tough. James was special but required careful grooming. His youthful enthusiasm needed to be balanced with caution. He had conceived an outrageous plan, one Nelson would be proud of. They had spent months watching the French stay safe in harbor while building up their invasion army. This would be a brilliant blow, if it could be achieved. Wilson wanted to lead it himself, but the admiralty never allowed a captain to leave his ship for such a dangerous expedition. The caution and experience of Stevens, the first lieutenant, mixed with the enthusiasm of James's youth, should bring the correct balance.

James emerged from the captain's quarters onto the quarterdeck, embarrassed not knowing where to look. First Lieutenant Stevens approached.

"Handsomely done, Mister Lancaster. You will want to rest after your…" He was about to say caning, but caught himself. "Fishing trip. Excused next watch."

As James went to the main deck to enter the midshipmen's mess, the seamen were working but were silent and watching. The bosun was talking to a group and looked up, feeling a little guilty. James went over to him. He drew back defensively. James extended his hand.

"Good job. Thank you, Bosun."

"No hard feelings then, Mister Lancaster?"

"On the contrary. You did your job as ordered. I was grateful for the leather bite, but would have preferred that the fifth one was not so hard."

"Yes, sir, sorry about the fifth one. As you made no noise I was worried that the captain might think I was being soft."

James grinned. "I would not call it soft."

The bosun turned to his mates, including Coxswain Paul. "That is the first time anyone has thanked me for using the cane or cat. And the first time a midshipman has not screamed for mercy."

When James returned to the midshipmen's mess, there was silence. They wanted to know about his trip and the caning, but were embarrassed to ask.

"OK, here is the news. The canning hurt. I got it for youthful exuberance. I cannot tell all, but in France my lip was damaged, and the other person did not get away lightly. Now for the trip. We approached the harbor at the start of the flood tide, at its lowest, using the current to help us in. There is a maze of rocks sticking out of the water, some twenty feet high. The tide height, from low to high ranges between twenty and thirty feet, covering many rocks at high water. To hit them would be fatal. To navigate through them, the locals use a series of land based objects that create transit lines. One is a barn coming in line with a rock painted white. A granite fort with narrow windows and a gun terrace guards the port. Powerful cannon muzzles peep out between the buttresses. Fishing boats have to fly signal flags to be allowed to enter. Anchored in the harbor are a frigate and four troops carrying cargo ships getting ready for sea, plus many fishing boats. The harbor quay is well constructed, and the houses surrounding it neat, and painted in multi-colors. Soldiers guard the quay and check everything. On the hill behind the town are rows of army tents and a thousand men training to invade England while waiting to embark on the ships. One good thing, the brandy is cheap, and I have a couple of bottles to prove it."

James's mess mates showered him with detailed questions while enjoying the brandy. The mess steward listened and reported to the lower decks.

Next day James resumed normal watches that continued relentlessly seven days a week. On Sundays, Captain Wilson ordered the sails reefed, and after a small church service, the crew relaxed.

CHAPTER 9

Percy, James's brother, enjoyed the London life but was frustrated as he was never fully included with the top families. It was hinted that it was because he was yet to inherit his title, and as he had not purchased an Army commission, he was little more than a dandy, and not dressed as well, so none of the debutantes encouraged him. It was not because he did not go the best tailors in Saville Row, Gieves, but the clothes just did not make him look good. He was therefore very pleased when his friend agreed to sponsor him to join White's club, and he was accepted. It was the oldest and most prestigious club in London and his father was a respected member. The members voted in secret using white and black balls, and one black ball stopped one becoming a member and damaged one's social standing.

His first evening at the club, the famous Duke of Wellington was playing hazard and there was an empty seat at the table. Percy asked to join.

"Are you Lancaster's son?

"Yes, my Lord."

"Haven't seen him for a while. He plays a mean hand of whist. How is he?"

"He is basically well, but has to be careful."

"Send him my regards. Hazard is a man's game and we play a version called chicken with our own money, not our father's. I play like I fight my battles, to win."

"I can assure you, my Lord, that my father would approve me playing with you."

Percy started well. The dice were lucky for him and very soon he was up nearly three thousand pounds. A year's allowance. He became more confident and increased his winnings. Then the duke started individual bets with him. He started to lose but then his luck changed again. His winnings increased to four thousand and people collected around the table to watch.

The duke leant back and surveyed the table. He was famous for big bets and he had been known to place ten thousand pounds on the table for one bet.

"You can double your winnings on the next throw of the dice, if your luck holds. I will add to that with a wager that you will miss the numbers. Ten thousand guineas."

Percy hesitated and started to sweat. If he won, his debt problems were over and he would be known as the man who stood up to the duke. He would be made socially. Even his father would be proud of him. If he lost? He could not think of that.

"Of course, if it is too rich for you, we will say no more."

"My Lord, it will be an honor to win your wager."

There was a low murmur of admiration and Percy glowed inside. He might even make it into the newspaper gossip column. He focused on the numbers he needed, rattled the dice in his hand and threw. He dared not look but he did not need to. The crowd groaned.

"Hard luck, young Lancaster. I will take the cash on the table and you can draw a note for the balance, to be paid within two months."

Percy left the table penniless. He had already written a number of notes for debts, but if he did not pay the duke within the allotted time he would have to resign from the club and society.

James with a spyglass was swaying at the top of the mast, counting the boats in a small French harbor, when he heard the first officer's call from the deck far below.

"Mister Lancaster, report immediately to the captain's cabin."

The Navy seldom used 'immediately' unless urgent. James tried to think about what more he had done wrong, but had no time to consider it now. He called down, "Aye, aye, sir."

Climbing down the ratlines would take time. James wanted to try the old sailor's trick, used in battle to get down from the mast quickly. It required an excuse to do it. Removing a leather patch from his pocket, he wrapped it around a back-stay that led to the deck.

With both hands, he held onto the patch and jumped, accelerating towards the deck. He squeezed the leather around the rope stay and his descent slowed. The leather became hot, but manageable. He landed on the deck to the amazed looks of the officers and men. Before the first officer said a word, James saluted him.

"Reporting immediately to the captain, sir."

He marched past the sentry to the captain's companionway.

While waiting outside the captain's cabin for permission to enter, the first officer arrived, his face with his normal stern look.

"Sailors may not use that trick in case they get injured. The same goes for officers. As I ordered you to attend the captain immediately, we will have to forget that you did it." He gave one of his rare grins. "Wanted to do it myself, while a midshipman. You took quite a chance there, Lancaster. Even with your lucky record."

The captain's voice summonsed them. He stood at his desk, studying charts.

"Mister Lancaster, please be kind enough to explain to Mister Stevens your crazy plan."

James was relieved. As he talked through the plan, Captain Wilson asked lots of detailed questions such as which sailors and midshipman James recommended for each section of the plan, and the backups.

Stevens' questions showed him to be less excited, but protocol required he support his captain.

"Mister Stevens will lead the expedition, with you as back up Mister Lancaster."

The plan accepted! A glow and tingling passed through James, the same feelings he remembered from just before he boarded the *schooner*. A chance for a real adventure, and if the action succeeded, excitement. After explaining the plan out loud, he had more ideas. He hoped to offer them. In the Royal Navy, junior officers waited to be asked to give ideas. Their superiors received the credit for the successful ones.

"You will work with the first lieutenant to develop the plan and report back. Use the chart room. We have fifteen days until the next new moon and dark nights, and that coincides with the French July fourteenth celebration. The ebb tide starts at one a.m., which should help you sail the frigate out of the harbor. Everything must be ready by then. I hope your fisherman friend makes contact so we can schedule her. She'll never agree, so we will 'borrow' her fishing boat. Leaving her and her brother tied up so they can claim innocence, but hiding a generous payment where the authorities cannot find it."

That afternoon, at eight bells, the captain called the crew on deck.

"We are planning a dangerous cutting out expedition and need forty volunteers."

The crew knew of the expedition. The captain's steward overheard the discussions, and as usual, traded gossip for shares of the crew's rum.

"Those willing, step forward."

The entire crew moved one step forward.

The captain turned, smiling at the first lieutenant.

"Select the teams and let's get training."

"Aye, aye, sir."

Over the next ten days, the teams practiced boarding and capturing the frigate, using *Defiance* as the French ships. Cutting the frigate anchor cable. Hoisting towing lines from the captured row boats onto the frigate to tow her out of the harbor. Placing the bomb boats under the sterns of the four other ships anchored in the harbor. Collecting the crews from the bomb boats to join the captured frigate or, if disaster struck, rowing out to sea to be rescued in the morning by *Defiance*.

James expected most of the French frigate's crew to be ashore, celebrating July Fourteenth, Bastille Day, leaving a skeleton crew on board who would probably be in their bunks or hammocks. Four teams, boarding two from the bow and two from the stern, planned to knock unconscious the on-deck watch. Capture any officers in their bunks. Seal the companionway gratings to trap the French crew below. Silence was essential so not to alert the gunners at the fort. They made sand filled canvas cudgels to stun the watch. Scarves to gag them, stifling any cries. Once they secured the frigate, they would connect the towlines to the rowboats and get ready to raise the sails. Even in the dark white sails are easily seen. They would not be raised until they maneuvered the frigate past the fort, or until the alarm sounded. They would depend on the tide current and rowboats to propel the frigate for their escape out of the harbor.

The sailors found that cutting a three-inch tightly wound hemp anchor rope under tension is not a job for a sailor's knife.

Erik, the aging ship's carpenter, stepped forward.

"Begging your pardon, sir, but me and my saw can cut though that massive cable in no time."

Lieutenant Stevens did not imagine taking the aged carpenter on the expedition, so responded, "Erik, lend your saw to Philips."

"I am sorry, sir, but me tools are precious. I don't want them destroyed by a clumsy sailor."

A delicate moment for Stevens. A man's tools belonged to him. Captain Wilson intervened.

"Erik, we can always replace a saw. If it is damaged, we shall. We cannot replace your experience as a carpenter. Let Philips try."

Erik reluctantly handed Philips the saw. Everyone watched as he pushed hard, fumbling, bending and nearly ruining the blade.

Captain Wilson spoke up.

"Philips, stand down. Now, Erik, show us how it should be done."

In no time, Erik cut through the cable and turned around, clearly satisfied.

"Mister Stevens, I recommend you consider Erik to join the team."

"Aye, aye, sir."

It thrilled Erik. At last, a real adventure to boast to his grandchildren, if he got back home. The rowing teams planned to take the towing cables with them. They could not risk searching for lines once they were on board the French ship. Erik made spare oars in case the French rowboat owners took theirs home with them.

James teamed with Paul, his coxswain, and three men to board the French frigate via the starboard stern, with First Lieutenant Stevens boarding to port. Two more teams trained to board the frigate's bows. In case the French crew were not in their bunks and stormed the quarterdeck, they would take a battery of pre-loaded pistols, creating a firewall to stop the French at the quarterdeck steps. The French sailors would not have cutlasses or pistols as they were always under lock and key, for fear of a mutiny, and only issued for battle.

Midshipman Brown had responsibility for the towboats, and Smithers for the bomb boats and for getting the bomb crews out safely.

James would sail the fishing boat into the harbor, make the correct signals to the fort and handle the French guard. On the frigate, he had responsibility for piloting it out of the harbor. Plotting the course out of the

French harbor in the dark, past a series of sand bars and rocks, created James's biggest concern. Captain Wilson spent time with him developing charts, calculating courses, distances, and times based on different boat speeds. He let James practice using *Defiance* and altering course, and calling out sail changes, based on the boats estimated speed and timed with sand glass. Captain Wilson privately thought it impossible to sail the frigate with a small crew out of the harbor at night. He rationalized that when it ran onto the rocks and sank, the French lost it, and the *Defiance* crew hopefully could escape in the rowboats. If they did not escape, sacrificing forty men would be considered by the admiralty a small price to pay for destroying an enemy frigate. In a sea-battle with a French frigate the deaths and injuries would be more.

The bomb boat crews practiced in *Defiance's* rowboats, using empty gunpowder barrels, covering them with tarpaulin and lighting the ten-minute slow burning fuses. When the bomb boats exploded while attached to the French ships' transoms, they would hopefully breach the hulls, sinking them, or at least start fires and destroying the ships' rudders.

The more the teams practiced, the sorrier James became. If one French person saw them and raised the alarm, they might be caught. In the event they were successful, and escaped past the fort, James had to navigate out of the channel in the dark, passing through the maze of rocks. Expecting the night to be pitch black, he memorized the route based on the compass settings, calculating the distance for each section of the channel. Their freedom depended on correctly estimating the frigate's speed, and then timing each leg of the complex route before the turns. They were taking a sand minute-glass to help. A good thing about the difficult entrance and the dominating fort was that the French did not raise chains across the harbor entrance at night.

First Lieutenant Stevens started the training as a skeptic, but the more they trained, the more he believed their plan might work. He began to enjoy himself.

A week into the training, the fishing boat with Yvonne appeared. Captain Wilson purchased her catch of fresh fish at a generous price. James told her he could go with her if she returned in one week. She blushed.

"James, that is good news, but one week is July fourteenth, our national holiday. No one fishes then."

"Exactly. It will be a safer day to enter the harbor and look more closely."

"James, it must be the thirteenth or the fifteenth."

Now James had a problem. If he pushed too hard she might back out. But if he gave in to her dates the plan, which was already dangerous, might become impossible."

"I had to argue with my captain as he was reluctant to let me go again with you. Finally he agreed to the fourteenth. I really had hoped we could have at least one more sail."

Yvonne did not want to let the chance of being with James again, slip away.

"Agreed, the fourteenth, but early morning. The tide will take us in late evening."

"Thank you," James said, relieved but also feeling guilty. He had no idea how he would tell her the truth on the 14th.

CHAPTER 10

The day arrived and the cutting-out team was treated to a special breakfast. They dressed in dark canvas cloaks, made by the sailmaker, to cover their uniforms. Their faces darkened, and they were issued with cutlasses and knives which they sharpened on the ship's grinder. Some wrote, or officers wrote for them, a last message to their loved ones. Now, the long wait.

James wrote to Edith, Nanny Jones and his father. Waiting made him even more nervous than the battle itself. During battles, one did not have time to think.

Midmorning, the fishing boat appeared, and moored alongside *Defiance*. James called down, "Bonjour, Yvonne, Captain. We are in a hurry. May we come down to help you unload?"

Yvonne's face showed she was pleased to see James dressed in his fisherman's clothes and started thinking of lovemaking that evening.

"Of course."

Coxswain Paul, and two other men followed James down into the boat.

"Yvonne, we need to borrow your boat today."

"Saints alive! Are you crazy? No way."

"Yvonne, it is not a request."

She looked at James, and then Paul, realizing this was not negotiable. "Shit."

"I should have said, we will rent your boat today."

James opened a small leather pouch full of gold coins. Yvonne was incredulous.

"Are you serious? Why did you not say? That is a small fortune. But there must be a catch!"

"It will be yours, but there is a certain amount of adventure, or perhaps danger. You and Maurice need to wait on board *Defiance* until we are ready."

James's team cleared out the fish hold and cabin to create maximum space to pack everyone in. Erik, the carpenter, installed benches to seat the crew, expecting them to be hidden for seven hours. They required water and food, and a bucket to pee in. After loading the weapons, towing lines and supplies, they very carefully secured the gunpowder on deck under the fishing nets.

"Yvonne, we are taking some sailors with us. We will not need a ride back. It must appear that you were forced into letting us take the boat. We will leave the bag with the gold below the anchor cable. I am afraid you will have to be tied and gagged once we are close to the harbor."

"James, I do not know how I fell for your seduction. I am getting soft. I had thought the only person being tied would be you, next time we made love."

"I promise you it was not planned. I will always love you."

"One day we will meet and you will pay for this, the French woman's way."

They set sail, with Yvonne and Maurice below.

No one talked. Silence, except the gurgling of the wake against the hull. Finally, First Lieutenant Stevens spoke.

"If another sail comes in sight, all on deck dive below. We hope to arrive at dusk, an hour before sunset, to get permission to enter the port, with a flood tide and current helping us. The west setting sun behind us will only allow the soldiers at the fort to see silhouettes, no faces. Mister Lancaster will be steering. The harbor guards know him as Yvonne's cousin from Marseilles.

The French coast appeared as a smudge on the horizon. They needed at least four hours to arrive. The wind started dying. Perhaps they should row? Then, a slight ripple on the surface of the sea appeared, showing the arrival of the late afternoon sea breeze, with luck, driving them all the way. A perfect sail on any other occasion, but with the growing sense of anxiety, it seemed to take forever. Thanks to the July Fourteenth holiday, all fishermen were ashore celebrating, so no other boat could be seen.

"Sir, may I suggest some low-voiced singing might help boost morale?"

"Good idea, Mister Lancaster. Coxswain, pass the word, and start with my favorite shanty, *Blow the Man Down*."

Other than rum, there is nothing a sailor likes better than a fiddle, song and dance. Packed into the hold of the fishing boat, they only had songs, *Drunken Sailor*, *The Cabin Boy*, *The Mermaids Singing*. An endless list and they continued until within five miles from the shore. The boat returned to quiet again, and First Lieutenant Stevens and Paul retreated into the cabin.

The flood tide carried them towards the port, and the breeze pushed them along. As they were making good speed, James eased the sheets, so the sails were a little loose and the boat slowed. The sun would dip over the horizon at nine, but the sailor's sunset, dusk, gave light for an extra hour. James aimed to be at the fort at eight-thirty. Yvonne, before being tied and gagged, confirmed the current signal code.

James tied the answering code signal flags on a halyard ready to run up to the end of the gaff. He would navigate by using the shore markers he had learnt during his earlier visit. With twenty foot tides, at high water the sea would cover the rocks that they were sailing between, making them invisible. Hitting a rock just below the water line would sink any boat. The castle, with the grey granite walls, looked bigger than James remembered. The ominous cannons on the castle battlements all seemed to point at them. Fewer soldiers patrolled the ramparts than normal, showing that most were in town celebrating. If they saw a British ship, the castle bells gave French gunners at least two hours' warning.

They sailed under the high wall of the castle and guns. James scanned the castle flagpole. Still no signal! Perhaps because of the holiday and the fort having fewer people? Maybe the soldiers who were left behind, drank and celebrated? Or did they know something? James waited anxiously. Finally, a signal raised on the castle flagpole. Not the one James expected. His heart sank into his boots. He cursed Yvonne for tricking them. He called the first lieutenant to get Yvonne so he could talk to her. Then, the flags lowered to be replaced by the ones James expected. What a relief. Holding the tiller against his leg, so the boat sailed straight, he stood up and raised the answering flags. No response. A small group of soldiers with a book surrounded the flagpole. Hopefully the signal book. Were the regular signal people away? Then the castle signal flags lowered, allowing the fishing boat to enter the port.

James called out, "All's well."

Boats filled the harbor, with fishing boats tied up two or three abreast. The harbor seemed to be deserted of people, except for the two guards leaning and watching cats foraging for discarded fish pieces. James planned to moor on the outside of three fishing boats, as far from the dockside as possible, making it difficult for the guards to see into the boat.

Leaving the tiller tied, he dropped the mainsail and gaff. The boat drifted past his chosen berth. He turned the boat back into the flood tide current, slowing it. He let the jib fly and flutter. The boat came to a stop alongside the outside fishing boat.

"Good evening. Where is Yvonne?" barked the guard.

The guards wanted their usual 'present' of fish. James held up an empty bottle of brandy and another, a third finished, while pretending to be impaired.

"Yvonne and Maurice started celebrating while we were out at sea, so will sleep it off. The market will open tomorrow. We have plenty of time to offload the catch."

Yvonne, tied and gagged, listened to the exchange, wanted to be rescued. Being tied up was more uncomfortable than she imagined. What did the English hope to do? She was starting to realize the seriousness of the situation. This was not just the crime of selling fish to an enemy. They had come to do serious damage. She was facing Madam la Guillotine. Even worse, she needed to pee.

"Perhaps you would take care of the rest of the bottle?"

The guards gratefully accepted the two-thirds full brandy bottle, thanked James and left.

Waiting for the dark took patience. Especially for the team packed into the hold in absolute silence. James reconfirmed the positions of the French ships and the fishing rowing dinghies. Sentries guarded the ships' quarterdecks and bows. Most looked bored. After all, nothing ever happened.

James whispered the information to First Lieutenant Stevens, who passed it to the crew, telling them, "Eat, and sleep, but wake anyone who snores."

James, back on deck put away sails, worked on repairing the nets, kept watch, occasionally reporting below. The noise of the July Fourteenth celebrations came from the town. He experienced anxiety when the guards strolled past, and the occasional reveler used the dock to relieve himself. The harbor cats searched for fish heads and fought over them. Except for tension, the hours of confinement in dark cramped quarters, and the need to remain still and silent, the adventure had, so far, been easy.

First Lieutenant Stevens whispered, "It is time."

In pitch black, it was hard to distinguish between objects. James checked the guards were in their sentry post, enjoying their brandy, waiting for the morning to finish their shift. He showed Paul the direction of the ships that were invisible in the dark and the steps to the mackerel rowboats, which were secured on long lines between the dock and an anchor.

James went to Yvonne who was tied and curled up on the anchor cable. No one could see them. He took off her gag and kissed her. At first she resisted, but then surrendered and responded with passion.

"James, you must give us both black eyes so they know that we tried to fight you."

James passed the word for Paul.

"Give them black eyes and mark them so it looks as though they fought."

Paul slapped Maurice, who was gagged, with his hand back and forth across his face. His lip and nose bled and his eyes swelled up.

"Begging your pardon, sir, but I ain't going to hit a woman."

Yvonne whispered, "But you must."

"Then Mister Lancaster has to do it. Gag her first, sir."

Paul left.

"Come on, James. Otherwise I will not survive, and I need to so I can repay you for this."

It was the hardest thing James ever had to do. Unlike Paul, he started softly and she shook her head indicating she wanted more. He gave her four hard slaps, causing her nose to bleed and blackening one eye. The blood covered her blouse making it look much worse than it really was. James kissed her forehead.

"Yvonne, I will always remember you."

The crews climbed into their boats with their equipment, put mufflers in the rowlocks to silence the noise of the oars. One by one, they rowed to the far side of the harbor by the seawall to wait unseen. The first six boats had the job of cutting the frigate's anchor cables and towing her out of the harbor. Then the four bomb boats, with two rescue boats, headed into the dark. Last, the four boarding boats, with James and coxswain Paul taking up the rear.

As Paul and three others rowed into the dark, James steered while guessing the direction to the frigate by keeping the slight wind on his right cheek. The slack tide helped. The frigate loomed in front of them. James turned the tiller hard. They stopped rowing, drifting silently to the stern.

A lonely voice above them complained, "Why am I always on duty during holidays? The lieutenant is a son of a bitch."

The action was to start precisely five minutes after the church bells rang midnight. James wondered if the other boats had found their targets. To coordinate the timing, a person in each boat would count to three hundred.

As the church bells rang, the sky filled with celebration rockets exploding with loud reverberating bangs and lighting up the harbor. James saw several of the other rowboats getting into position. He prayed the watch-keepers were well lubricated and focused on the sky.

As fast as they appeared, the rockets now spluttered towards the ground, plunging the harbor back into darkness and silence, except for the distant sounds of celebrations in the town.

James felt that nervous feeling in his stomach again. He maneuvered the rowboat alongside the frigate's stern mizzen chain, checked his pistols were secure in the holsters, that he could draw his cutlass, clutched his cudgel and hauled himself up. Paul and their three men followed to the quarterdeck rail. Two French officers stood by the ship's wheel. James and Paul slid over the rail and tiptoed forward.

One of the French officers half turned. Had he heard something? James froze. The whole adventure might be discovered. He prepared to rush forward but the French officer said, "With the rest of the crew ashore, drinking, we should have a measure."

His companion handed him a flask.

"Thanks, I need this."

First Lieutenant Stevens appeared and climbed over the port rail. Paul and the first lieutenant's coxswain held the ends of their scarfs in their hands. The French officer took the flask away from his mouth. The coxswains looped the scarfs over the French heads and into their mouths, gaging them. First Lieutenant Stevens and James knocked them out cold with well-aimed blows to the side of their heads using the sand filled cudgels. Two sailors tied the first prisoners, while the others went below to the officers' quarters. The three officers were soon subdued and tied.

Noises came from the bows. First Lieutenant Stevens stayed with five men and pistols to control the quarterdeck. James, with Paul, rushed forward to check and help capture the foredeck.

The sailors who boarded from the bows had bolted the hatches, locking the French crew below. Lines were thrown down to the row boats, then towing lines hauled up to the frigate's bow. Erik's carpenter's saw made a low vibrating noise as he cut through the first anchor cable. Then, with a twang, the cable parted. The rope's end made a splash as it fell into the water. Then he cut the second cable.

They all held their breath. No one seemed to have noticed. The sailors in the six towboats pulled on their oars. Moving the dead bulk of a big ship with small rowboats requires enormous effort. The *Defiance*'s sailors bent their backs, pulled hard, bending their oars with the strain, but the rowboats stayed still. They needed no extra motivation to avoid years in a tough French prison. They had to leave the harbor. The rowers pulled even harder. Assisted by the now ebbing tide, the frigate moved slowly forward, heading towards the exit channel.

Paul organized the sailors, sorting out ropes and lines to set the royals and mainsails, and angle them to the wind. He positioned men up the mast hanging on the yards, ready to release the sails.

First Lieutenant Stevens couldn't believe their luck. When he first learnt of James's plan, he thought it crazy. Tradition required that he 'volunteer' to lead any off-ship expedition the captain wanted. James's detailed planning impressed him, as did the men's improvement after their first rehearsal. He had expected failure. In another ten minutes they would be at the fort. If they passed without being blown up by the cannons, they only had to navigate through the rocks. 'Only' was an understatement. When they entered the harbor at low water, he peeped out of the cabin, alarmed by the number of rocks towering over them they must pass to escape. With the moonless dark night, rocks would be hidden under three fathoms or eighteen feet of tidewater, some close enough to the surface to rip out the bottom of the frigate.

The frigate moved forward, like a ghost ship.

James sprinted, on his toes so as not to make a noise, back to the quarterdeck.

"Sir, French crew secured. Our boats have the frigate moving. One of the bomb-boat crew is catching up from behind, but not Smithers."

It took all First Lieutenant Steven's composure to calmly, in a low voice, order James, "Mister Lancaster, please take over the con and navigation," when he wanted to shout, "Damnation, get us out of here, and quickly!"

"Aye, aye, sir. Coxswain, a point to starboard."

Stevens's calm voice reassured James.

Bang. A mighty explosion shattered the silence, and hot air rushed past from behind them, making it hard to stand. Flames shot up, illuminating the harbor. One of the bomb-boats had gone off early, putting on fire a transport ship. Flames were already leaping up her mast, igniting the sails bound on the yards. After a moment of silence, shouting came from everywhere. Bells started ringing. The French crew, battened in the frigate's forecastle, were also shouting and trying to break out of the hold.

First Lieutenant Stevens issued orders,

"Fire a warning pistol shot into the hold but miss the men. Tell them, unless they are quiet, the next shot will kill one of them."

One of the bomb-boat crews arrived and four much needed men came on board.

With the fort alerted, they were in real danger.

"Release royals and mainsails. Sheet them well on a starboard tack. Bomb boatmen, watch over the sides that the French crew do not escape through gun ports to get onto the deck. Take pistols and shoot the first one who tries. Get the tow boat crews back on board and tow the boats tied on long lines behind. Where is the other bomb boat rescue team?"

Stevens issued orders rapidly. The Navy James loved. He focused on navigating them out of the harbor, his first time navigating a big ship, and at night by dead-reckoning. Thank goodness for the practice. He found himself surprisingly confident.

"Helm, two points to port. Coxswain Paul, adjust the sails."

The fort ramparts were full of running figures. Torches being lit, highlighting the groups around the cannons. The fort's gun crews were assembling, still dressing as they ran. But many were in the town. Boys rushed down multiple flights of stone stairs to collect the powder stored in vaults below the castle. When powder arrived, they had to load, run out the guns, aim and then fire. James calculated it would be another ten minutes. After which, all hell would break loose. Their lives or liberty depended on how good the French gunners were at aiming in the dark.

James heard Paul issuing orders to sailors working on lines and sails. They had the towboat crews available to help now. More sails were opening and drawing.

First Lieutenant Stevens stood by the rail at the front of the quarterdeck enjoying the command but dreading the coming cannon ball battering. Had he been hasty in starting to enjoy the action? At least they were in uniform. If caught, he could expect prison or parole until he could arrange a swap. He preferred parole as once he gave his word not to escape, it allowed him to rent rooms in an inn and live a reasonable life until he was swapped for a French prisoner. Conditions would not be so pleasant for the men or James.

The flames from the ship on fire illuminated the other three ships still at anchor and untouched. Had the bomb boats been discovered? They were due to explode in one minute.

Stevens called out, "Strike the French colors and run up our ensign."

James listened to the gurgling of the ship's wake. The speed must be three knots, plus a knot of tide. He rethought his calculations. Timing of the navigation through the rocks, and out to safety, started in front of the fort. Another two or three minutes. He looked back. Still no sign of Midshipman Smithers and his bomb-boat crew. Had they had been caught, or blown up by the premature explosion? A real reminder of the responsibility of committing other people to action.

Boom, boom, boom.

Three ear shattering explosions shook the air. Another rush of hot air pushed them forward, and for a moment caused confusion for everyone. The explosions coincided with the first broadside from the fort. The flashes from the gun barrel, and then multiple bangs, confirmed they were under fire. They were followed by the swish sounds, as cannon balls rocketed across the ship, creating holes in the top sails.

A well-trained gun crew needed three minutes to swab out a cannon, reload, and run it out. James guessed they had at least five minutes before the next salvo. If only they had more sail and speed. With forty men, minus the three missing, instead of two hundred and fifty manning a frigate, they could not set all the sails. Now they were abeam of the fort with its flickering torches lighting the cannons pointing at them and making them seem even more menacing. James set his sand glass, estimating the ship's speed at five knots. In four minutes he would have to wear ship. He hoped he did not have to maneuver it while receiving a battering from the big guns.

Behind, James saw four ships on fire. Even if he could not navigate the frigate to their freedom, they had caused immense damage. He tried to imagine his actions as if he were in command of one of those ships. No time now, he would think of it later.

The castle, except for the torches, disappeared into the darkness.

James called to First Lieutenant Stevens, "Sir, we need to wear ship in two minutes. Coxswain, it will be four and a half points to starboard."

Stevens looked ahead into the black abyss strewn with jagged rocks. Turning around, he gave James a look that said, I pray you know what you are doing.

"Carry on, Mister Lancaster."

"Hands to wear ship, lively now."

The crew did not need encouragement. The explosions and gunfire filled them with excitement and fear.

On the fort ramparts, the junior French officer paced with frustration, surprised to find himself in charge of the fort while his seniors were celebrating. He had the chance to be a hero and get promoted, but he was short of men, reloading taking too long and despite practicing nearly every day they seldom had used gun power or fired the cannons. At last the gun crews reported their cannons ready. The French officer had the guns run out, aimed them, ordered a ten second fuse so the gun-crews could get back to safety.

"Light the fuses."

The fuses lit, the crews ran clear of their guns, the ship with those bloody Englishmen disappeared into the dark, and worse, turned right. The guns fired. The young officer could do nothing except watch the phosphorescent splashes caused by the cannon balls as they hit the water where, moments before, the frigate had been.

While wearing ship, most of the sailors had half an eye on the fort, saw flashes of the guns firing, and waited. They had been trained not to hide behind the bulwarks, equivalent to a wooden fence going around the outside of the deck. A cannon ball hitting the bulwarks turned it into flying wooden splinters. Sailors had more chance of being injured by them than from being hit by a cannon ball. At least being hit by a ball resulted in instant death.

Cannon balls passed very close to the ship. Everyone expected havoc, but were happy to be soaked by the spray of water when the cannon balls hit the sea.

The fort's guns were still within range. The night had no moon, so the ship had become invisible.

A cheer broke out.

"Silence there. Stand by your stations."

First Lieutenant Stevens needed to keep the men focused on handling the sails for the next few turns, hoping James calculated accurately.

"Sir, wearing ship. Coxswain, three points to port."

The flames of the burning vessels backlit the castle, turning it into a silhouette. First Lieutenant Stevens and the crew watched the flashes of the castle guns as they fired, and moments later, they heard the boom of the cannons.

The young French officer had done a good job of getting the guns reloaded in record time. He could not see the ship, so aimed based on guesswork.

Crash!

A violent splintering sound as a cannon ball hit the mizzen topmast. The topmast, yard and sail were falling. A lucky shot, but one that could sink them if the sail and spar fell into the water acting as a sea anchor, pushing them onto the rocks. Lieutenant Stevens leapt into action, organizing the top men to cut away the rigging and lower the spar to the deck.

"Sir, we need to wear ship."

"Carry on, Mister Lancaster, give the orders while I deal with the top mast."

"Aye, aye, sir."

James took a trumpet. "Stand by to wear ship. Helm, two and half points to starboard."

Another round of cannon balls from the fort, but it passed to port.

There was a bump and the ship slowed. The grating noise confirmed the keel was rubbing along the tops of rocks. There was nothing James or anyone could do. To get so far and to be stuck on a rock! Except for the scraping noise there was silence. James called out, "Open more sails."

Paul started giving orders but the men were already swinging to the yards where sails were still furled and releasing them. The frigate ground to a halt. The rowing boats they had been towing behind, now carried by the tide current, started hitting the hull. As more sails opened the scraping noise started again. They were moving forward very slowly. Everyone waited anxiously. Then suddenly the ship lurched forward. They were over the reef. The crew cheered and First Lieutenant Stevens called out, "Well done, Mister Lancaster. Do you anticipate any more rocks?"

"I think we have had enough for now, sir. Coxswain, west by north to join *Defiance*. Sir, may I suggest we check the bilges in case the rocks created any leaks?"

They sailed off into the dark night, safe, while the fort still fired cannons into the dark.

Now James could relax but he was still worried about the missing bomb boat crew. He thought of the sailors on the ships they had set on fire, hoping they escaped. Also that Yvonne was safe and would not be blamed or punished, and wondered what revenge she was planning. He was tired, but had to stay awake. The excitement of the crew gave him fresh energy. Paul led them with, "Three cheers for First Lieutenant Stevens and Mister Lancaster, hip, hip hooray."

It took a moment for First Lieutenant Stevens to realize the enormity of their achievement. No one had ever stolen a French frigate, sunk four big transport ships and stopped one thousand soldiers from being able to invade England. He knew it would be the pinnacle of his career. Headlines in every newspaper, and of course, the *Navy Gazette*. The expedition had been stressful, something he had always avoided, as much as the Navy permitted. But the excitement and sense of satisfaction went beyond anything he had ever experienced. Perhaps he had lived too cautiously? It took imagination and bravery to come up with a plan like this. Stevens knew he did not have the imagination. James had the gift and this action would be one of many he would experience. Now Stevens had to ensure the French were safely locked into the hold, check the bilges, and prepare gun crews in case any French ships found them before they reached *Defiance*.

As dawn rose, *Defiance* sat silent with reduced sail, and her guns ready. During the night, they waited ten miles out at sea. Hearing the explosions, seeing the cannon flashes and flames from the burning ships, brought a sense of dread. It had been a long night, not knowing if their comrades had escaped. Wilson regretted that as captain he could not have led the action. Through the morning haze, backlit by the first rays of sunrise, the French frigate emerged. It amazed Captain Wilson.

"Well I'll be dammed."

At best, he hoped for small mackerel boats with survivors. *Defiance* remained at battle stations in case the French still had control. Then the signal flags confirmed that the French frigate was now part of the Royal Navy. Wilson relaxed, jubilant. The long night of waiting and tension had exhausted him. A shout went out from the crew. For once, he allowed it. They deserved a moment of victory. Through a series of signals, Wilson learnt that the frigate had five French officers and about seventy French sailors imprisoned below decks. Stevens needed extra help to manage them. Also, Midshipman Smithers and his two men were missing.

"Ship's boats away, with boarding parties."

It took a day to organize the French frigate. First, to separate the real French crew from the foreign conscripts. Many conscripts volunteered to join *Defiance*. British naval ships seldom had a full crew. Now Captain Wilson had a few extra men. The French officers accepted parole. They were transferred to *Defiance* and packed into the first lieutenant's cabin. He remained on the frigate with James as his first officer.

Captain Wilson inspected the ship, looking through the captain's cabin and taking the papers and charts. Debriefing First Lieutenant Stevens and James, he made detailed notes for the log and the official report. The purser and gun captain did a rough inventory of the ship's stores and ammunition.

In case the French sent ships to rescue it, Captain Wilson wanted to get the frigate back to Plymouth as soon as possible. He had to wait forty-eight hours in case Midshipman Smithers escaped from the French port and made the rendezvous. He did not like having fifty-five French sailors locked in the hold, probably conspiring to retake the ship. They had another long night with the ships sailing within hailing distance, every half hour calling to confirm 'all's well'.

Dawn, and with it a spot on the sea heading out from France. A small boat, and in it, Smithers with his men rowing. Their boat had capsized from the shockwave caused at the first premature explosion. They struggled onto a fishing boat to hide. With confusion and panic caused by the four ships on fire and the stealing of the frigate, no one searched for English sailors. After a nervous day, with no food or water, they stole a rowboat and headed out into the moonless night.

The frigate set sail for Plymouth with First Lieutenant Stevens as commander, James as first officer and Paul as bosun, with forty sailors and the blue ensign flying above the French tricolor. *Defiance* accompanied her sailing a mile up wind, providing protection.

As they sailed into Plymouth harbor and dropped anchor, the guns of the fort fired, signaling the capture of a French ship. The admiralty would buy the ship for a handsome price. With no other British Navy ships in sight of the action, *Defiance* did not have to share the reward with other crews, and they were buoyant.

It took a few days to hand the frigate over to the admiralty. They dispatched the French prisoners to a new prison built at Princeton on Dartmoor.

Captain Wilson called for James. "We have a new assignment. It will take at least three weeks to get the ship ready. *Defiance* will be careened at low tides to be scraped clean of weed and barnacles, then covered in the newly developed thin copper plates. They are believed to stop the worm entering the wooden hull, and the weed and barnacles sticking to it. The *Navy Gazette* reported our action. I thought you would like to read it."

James scanned the long article, which detailed the brilliant action as conceived and managed by Captain Wilson, after instructions from the admiralty. It credited First Lieutenant Stevens with leading the expedition and made special mention of the outstanding contributions of Midshipman James Lancaster. It also named the other midshipmen, including Smithers, who managed the bomb boats, and who, two days later, they found thirsty and hungry with his two men in a small row boat.

"Very generous of you, sir."

"Generous be dammed. The ship's logbook details your full contribution. The admiralty likes to publish their own version to make it sound like it was all their idea. We know better. There is an extra copy for your father. If you take tomorrow's early stagecoach, you can be home in two days to give it to him yourself."

It left James almost speechless. He thought of Edith, hoping to see her.

"Thank you, sir."

"Thank me by being back in two and a half weeks. Now go, and on your way, ask Mister Stevens to see me at his convenience."

CHAPTER 11

After three years, James landed on English soil. The quays were busy with merchant ships unloading and the pubs filling up with lunch time customers. The ground seemed to move the same way the ship did, making walking difficult. He found his way to the coach inn and bought the last ticket on a six-horse cramped Portsmouth coach. Nearing the top of the Downs, the male passengers walked to help the horses. James looked down at the Plymouth Sound with the ships at anchor and the French frigate with the blue ensign over the French flag, her new captain and crew working to get her ready to join the English Blue Squadron. James wondered if he should have remained on *Defiance* to help the preparation, but then Edith came back to his thoughts. He hoped she would meet with him.

Plymouth being a naval town, everyone learned of the captured frigate. People loved news, but few could read. Newsreaders earned their pennies by standing on street corners, and often inside inns, reading out loud the latest news sheets and the *Navy Gazette*. Good news seldom came, especially after so many years at war. The occasional victory received rapt attention.

Once the coach passengers discovered James came from *Defiance*, they insisted he tell the frigate story. It was the first of many times he told it. The coach stopped at inns every two hours for fresh horses and some new passengers. They, too, wanted the story. It embarrassed James to receive so much attention, but earned him a free dinner and bed when they stopped overnight at the Rock Point Inn, Lyme Regis. At least it shortened the journey. His anxiety increased when thinking of seeing his father and hoping to see Edith. Despite his monthly letters, she had never responded.

James left the coach at Lyndhurst, the so called capital of the New Forest, famous for its hill, where legend recorded that a local knight killed a dragon controlling the forest and intimidated its people. King George owned a house in the town, which he rarely visited, so the town received the privilege of being called Royal. Once a week, it hosted the best market for sheep, cattle and horses. It housed the law court where Edith's father sat as chief magistrate.

Normally a member of the Lancaster family would have stayed at the inn while a messenger rode the ten miles to call for the family coach to collect him or her. Too excited to wait, he rented a horse, but found it difficult to leave. The innkeeper had read the *Navy Gazette*, recognized James as he got off the coach, and insisted he retell the adventure.

Lord Lancaster sat in his favorite chair in front of the study fire, even though the summer sun had warmed the air. His cough continued to worsen. He had been sipping his brandy and trying to read the *Navy Gazette* when his elder son Percy returned home, wanting to talk. Percy only returned from London when needing more money. His generous allowance did not cover his mounting gambling debts. Lancaster looked at his son, medium height, weak chinned, with a stomach, and shifty eyes. How, he wondered, could he have been his father? He put all his paternal effort into his firstborn, Percy, and now regretted ignoring James. Percy refused to involve himself in the estate, the tenant farmers, the fox hunt, or to marry a local woman from a good family with a decent dowry. There were enough local daughters available, as more girls survived early childhood than boys. Lord Lancaster saw no point in pretending to believe Percy returned to pay a social visit. After his death, Percy, as first son, would inherit everything and probably ruin the estate.

"How much this time?"

Percy squirmed, not knowing that his father wanted to get the money agreed, so he could return to reading the *Gazette*. On the table beside his father's chair were still the pile of letters from his brother James. During his last visit, Percy slipped into the study to read them. They chronicled James learning to navigate, his 'luck' at capturing the *schooner*, and his admiration for the damnable Captain Wilson, who also sent confidential reports praising James. It made Percy jealous. On his way from London he read the *Gazette* report boasting the capture of the French frigate, giving James a lot of the credit.

When Percy asked for money for his ventures, his father urged caution, but gave it to him. Percy never apologized for his sure investments failing and losing so much money, nor for his ongoing run of bad luck at cards.

He passed forward copies of debt notes he had signed.

"I have to pay these as they are threatening to put me in debtors' prison, and if I do not pay the Duke of Wellington, I will be thrown out of White's and lose all social standing."

Lord Lancaster looked and gasped. "You had a wager with the Duke of Wellington for ten thousand at White's, in front of everyone. How could you be so stupid? He nearly always wins, and if he loses he doubles until he does. He is so rich that he can outlast nearly anyone. Off course you must pay him immediately. And these other debts? It's a year's revenue for the estate. Maybe debtors' prison is the best place for you. Thank goodness you have not yet inherited my title, as after you have it, you will be protected from prison. This is the last time. Next time you can learn how ordinary people live."

"Father, I had unusual bad luck. I promise never to gamble again. The duke sent you his regards. He said you play a good hand of whist."

"Don't waste your time promising, or asking for more, if you gamble. You should have learnt whist when I tried to teach you. It is a game of skill rather than dice, which is one of luck. One makes one's own luck."

Lord Lancaster wanted Percy to leave and free him to read of James's latest exploits.

"I will transfer the money next week. Now get out."

It surprised and relieved Percy that his father had agreed so easily. *Silly old fool*, he thought. *You won't live long, then I will have it all*. Rather than having a boring night at home, he went to the coach inn at Lyndhurst to drink and buy comfort from Jenny. But Jenny was cosseted in a booth with one of her regular travelers and pleased not to be available to Percy. So he drank, and when drunk picked a fight with Jenny's regular. It was a mistake. Next morning, with a black eye, he took the first coach back to London, and real life.

Lord Lancaster eased himself back into his leather chair, reading the *Gazette*'s description of the capture of the frigate. He tried to imagine himself as James, steering the small fishing boat crammed full of *Defiance* sailors towards the French harbor. Sailing under the granite castle walls with the cannons. Sitting, waiting for the dark. Rowing out to the frigate and capturing it. Then the explosions. The cannon fire from the castle and the escape. In James's last letter, he had mentioned a plan to capture a French frigate he presented to Captain Wilson. The *Gazette* credited the captain. Lord Lancaster realized the truth, feeling proud. Why had he not written more often to James, and bonded with him better? Nanny Jones asked if he would like to read the letters and drawings that James sent to her. He felt jealous of their relationship.

"He's coming."

Lord Lancaster woke out of a dream. Montague, the butler, rushed in.

"Excuse me, my Lord. There is a man on a horse entering the lodge gates. The junior staff with good eyes, say he has the profile of Master James."

Lord Lancaster bounded out of his chair, forgetting his cane and gout, and rushed to the front door to look. A half mile away, a horse trotted up the long drive. Even with his poor eyesight, he recognized James. Without his cane, his legs let go and he stumbled. Montague extended his arm to support him. The staff gathered at the door.

Montague told them, "Line up. Let's give Master James a hero's welcome."

Lord Lancaster reflected the last time this happened was when James left to go to sea. They never did it for Percy. James noticed the staff assembling at the door, recognized his father, and urged the limp livery horse into one last effort to canter the final half-mile.

There could be no doubt how James had grown. Even on the horse, one could tell that he had become taller and broader. His red-blond hair blowing in the wind, the midshipman's uniform, saber at his side and pistol in his belt, all helped him look so handsome. But there were the scars he had written about. In a way it made him look more handsome and experienced.

James looked ahead at his father waiting on the steps, supported by Montague. He looked so much older. Nanny Jones stood just behind him, her normal regal self. It surprised him to see the staff all lined up, a ceremony reserved for estate owners. How had they expected his arrival? What should he say to his father? He had received so few letters from him since he left.

Leaping off the horse to the staff's applause, he passed the reins to the stable boy. The applause embarrassed him, but he smiled and greeted them one by one. He wanted to rush up and hug his father, but he walked steadily, holding out his hand. Lord Lancaster had hoped his son would run up the steps to hug him. He thought of going forward himself, but then hesitated, and extended his hand.

"Nice to see you, sir."

They shook hands. Nanny Jones wanted to strangle them both. She knew how much time Lord Lancaster spent reading James's letters. He paid for the *Naval Gazette* to be delivered post haste, in case it mentioned *Defiance*. Yet they would not hug. She understood, from the effort James made to write to his father, how much he wanted his approval and love. After three years of absence, they were greeting each other as strangers. They were strangers. This had to stop.

"Welcome home. Congratulations on the *Gazette*. Every time it mentions *Defiance* and her actions, starting with your schooner escapade, you are in the thick of it."

James grinned. "Thank you, sir. More luck than judgment."

"I understand they call you Lucky Lancaster."

"Yes, sir, you told me to protect our name. The luck continues as Captain Wilson gave me leave. I can stay ten days."

"It's great to have you home, even for a short visit. Freshen up for dinner. We will have it in my study. I cannot wait to hear all your news."

It was James's first invitation to dine in his father's study.

"That would be wonderful. But I have not enjoyed a hot bath for three years, so with your permission will do so first."

"A hot bath it shall be." Lord Lancaster looked at his son. "I can't believe how big you have grown. You left as a boy and returned a man. Your uniform is worn out, and your old clothes won't fit. The tailor will be here in the morning."

Nanny Jones smiled. James turned and gave her a hug.

"Good to see you, Nanny. I will come to chat. Montague, how have you been?"

"Very well, Master James, welcome home. We'll have hot water ready in no time."

"I rented the horse from Lyndhurst Inn. A groom will collect it and deliver my valise."

Few people bathed, it being considered dangerous to health. Louis 14th of France only bathed twice in his life. To avoid smelling body odors, the French used perfume and the British snuff. James, who washed most days on *Defiance* using a bucket of cold seawater and a flannel, dreamt of sitting in the copper tub full of hot water. On the ship, they only used fresh water for drinking.

When James entered his father's study, a feast awaited. Such a contrast to ship's food. The candles, and flames from the fire provided light. It surprised James that his father needed a fire in the summer and saddened him seeing how his health had declined. At least his mind seemed as sharp as ever.

"Start at the beginning, when you left for Portsmouth."

James's father wanted every detail. His questions showed his knowledge of the Navy, of the war with France, of Napoleon's battles and his new laws, and of the new British industrial inventions. They talked into the night until Lord Lancaster's eyes closed.

Montague coughed.

"Master James, it will embarrass your father to wake up realizing he fell asleep while talking to you. Perhaps you might retire and I will tell him you were tired."

"Very considerate, Montague, he is lucky to have you looking after him. Thank you."

"It's my pleasure. He is very special."

James popped into Nanny's suite, hoping she was awake. Her smile, on seeing him, lit up the room. They talked until she said, "James, I need to sleep. We have an entire week to chat."

"One thing, Nanny, what news of Edith?"

Nanny had been dreading this question. Information passed between the downstairs staff of the local mansions, so there were no secrets. Edith's mother insisted on her marrying well, and James did not fit the mold.

"She is in good health. They are taking her to London for the winter, and introducing her to Their Majesties, in Court for her 'coming out'."

James's stomach churned. He had no expectations. She had not written. Even so, he still had held onto unrealistic hope.

For the next three days, James spent his time with his father or Nanny Jones. His father talked about the estate and their tenant farmers. He could not ride so they used a small two-wheel trap, drawn by a pony, and toured the estate. The tenant farmers stopped working to greet their lord. He used to visit more often. On seeing James, they cheered. Word of his exploits had spread, and they embarrassed him by calling him a hero.

James plucked up the courage to ride to Edith's father's mansion. Bigger than theirs, a small stone fortified house built in the fifteenth century, extended into a limestone palace.

Capability Brown, the famous English landscaper who revolutionized estate gardens and designed on a mammoth scale, had planned the lawns, flower gardens, woods, rolling landscaping and the lake. Beyond were fields, the New Forest and the Beaulieu River. Even before James raised the big brass knocker, Morgan, the butler, opened the solid, tall oak door, greeting him with a smile.

"Master James. Welcome back. Good to see you, we heard you returned. Congratulations on all your mentions in the *Navy Gazette*." The butler's voice dropped to a whisper. "His Lordship gets the *Gazette* and always checks for mention of *Defiance*."

"Really, thank you, Morgan. May I see Miss Edith?"

The butler's face changed to the official butler stoic, 'no emotion' look.

"I am sorry, Master James, Miss Edith is not available, and will not be receiving you."

"Morgan!"

In a confidential tone, the butler told him, "I really am very sorry, Master James, but it is Her Ladyship's instructions."

It staggered James. Not even allowed to make a social visit! For sure, Edith knew he had returned home. Could she be that heartless? He left, dejected, and retrieved his horse. What to do? He rode to their secret glade in the wood behind the mansion, where they played as children.

The dense trees forced him to bend low in the saddle to avoid the branches. He jumped the horse across the small stream that acted as a barrier to their glade. It looked smaller than he remembered. The tall oak still occupied the center of the clearing, but the branch he used to climb, which had been near the sky, seemed lower. Now he could easily climb onto it by standing on his horse's saddle. He used to sit on the branch waiting for her, jumping down to surprise her. Nostalgia and the pain of being rejected by her overwhelmed him.

He was sitting on the branch with his eyes closed, remembering, when a voice called, "James. You frightened me, riding into our secret glade on a horse."

Her voice! He opened his eyes, turned around to find Edith coming out of a bush. No longer the tomboy he played with, but a beautiful, tall, full-figured girl. Her long brown hair, penetrating green eyes, wearing a white dress, and backlit by the sun that filtered through the top branches of the trees. His heart skipped two beats. Waves of emotion flooded through him.

"James Lancaster, you promised to write. How could you fail me? Those scars are worse than the *Gazette* reported."

James became tongue tied. He leaned forward, trying to respond and fell off the branch, falling onto Edith in a heap in the thick carpet of leaves. She looked at him, shocked, as he moved his face closer to hers and kissed her. The kiss she dreamed of. Soft lips caressing hers. Shivers of electricity running through her body, his fingertips touching her face. James could not believe such emotion existed, but as he pressed her lips, she pulled away.

"James Lancaster, what do you think you are doing? You ignore me for three years and then leap off a tree, knock me over, and kiss me. My dress is all messed up. How can I go home?"

Edith had dreamt of having a kiss from James, but now it scared her. Her mother said kissing led to having babies and shame. When she returned home, would they recognize she had been kissed? How would she explain the condition of her dress?

"Edith, I fell off the tree in excitement at seeing you. I sent long letters at least every month for three years and never received a reply."

"Impossible, you're fibbing, I didn't get one from you, but I wrote many to you."

"My father and Nanny Jones received all my letters. Nanny told me your parents did not want me writing to you as I am not worthy of you, having only a small inheritance."

"Worthy! One of the few war heroes, and my best friend. My inheritance will be sufficient for two. That means my parents, no, my mother, intercepted all our letters. But you are presumptive, Mister

Lancaster. Kissing me without first declaring your intentions, or asking permission. You've been at sea too long and have forgotten your manners."

"I dreamed of you every day, thinking of you as my playmate. Now I find you are a woman. Let me ask your father."

"James, you can't. Even if Father agreed, Mother does not want us to meet. She makes the rules. She wants me to marry someone with a title and money. We go to London for the Season. She will hunt for my husband. She controls everything. As a child, she controlled me with the fear of the birch. Now she threatens to reduce my allowance or inheritance. Daddy promised he will look after me, but he fears her wrath. We must win with cunning. You were lucky only to have Nanny Jones who spoiled you. I am so relieved that you wrote. I also wrote to you. I will discover how Mother took our letters, find and read them, and then find a new way to correspond.

"Edith…"

"James, you are again too presumptuous."

Edith looked serious, but inside she was flirting and playful. Her mother had always told her that unless you train your man from the beginning they will take you for granted.

"I inherit my father's title. You may call me Lady Edith, which is easier than Lady Rowley.

"But—"

"No buts, other than you may give me another kiss."

She leant forward and ran her fingers over the scars as he closed his arms around her. For the first time, Edith felt the joy of being held close to his powerful body, relaxing into his strong arms. He had become a man. The kiss, long and gentle, sent a shiver of joy through her, stirring emotions and physical feelings she had never imagined. He let go and looked at her.

"I always loved you."

"James, I want to believe you. Let me check on the letters. I must go or they will send someone looking. My father gets the *Gazette* and loves reading about the *Defiance* and all your exploits, as do I. You are a local hero. Can we meet here tomorrow? Be careful not to be seen."

"Of course I will be here. But I am not a hero. The dispatches make it sound so easy. I wrote telling you how scared I became on the schooner, thinking the captain's blunderbuss would kill me. How awful it is to slash someone with a sword, hearing the bones breaking and seeing blood gushing out. I am lucky to be alive because of Coxswain Paul."

Edith went cold. "You actually wrote and told me you were scared?"

"Yes, most of us are, despite what the *Gazette* reports."

"When father read the admiralty reports out loud, telling us how brave you are, my mother said, 'In reality, he is scared.' My father scolded her for talking nonsense. Now I realize Mother not only intercepted our letters, but read them. I will have to fix this."

"You're so beautiful."

She smiled, leaned forward, kissed him on the cheek, and then left, skipping through the trees.

Now his emotions were confused. His legs had turned to rubber, his tongue tied as she pranced away. He wanted her back. Wanted to be her knight and needed another kiss. As Yvonne had told him, kissing was so different when one was in love.

In her room, Edith looked at herself in the mirror. Did James truly love her? Had he really written to her? Perhaps he did not have a girl in every port. He had grown so handsome. Her feelings for her childhood friend, her distant hero through the admiralty reports, had turned into an unfamiliar emotion. A tingling throughout her body. Not one she experienced before. It excited her, but made her a little ashamed. No one had told her that women reacted to men the way she now experienced it. She needed to find the letters and pulled the bell rope for her maid.

"Mary, what did you do with the letters I wrote to Master James?"

"Oh, miss, I gave them to Woodsman, the under-butler. As you instructed."

"Please send him to me in the morning room."

Edith's mother would be in her room preparing for the evening, while Morgan, the butler, served her father brandy in his study. It gave her the chance for a quiet moment with Woodsman, without being seen.

Woodsman arrived in a hurry. Midsize, a little plump, very hard working and a little too submissive. The family seldom called for him, so something important must have happened. Finding himself alone with Miss Edith, he became nervous and embarrassed, and bowed. Even though they lived in the same house, they seldom interacted, unless Woodsman served

132

at table or family picnics. Edith's mother ran the staff, communicating through the butler, Morgan, the head housekeeper and cook.

The morning room had windows looking out at the mile long oak lined drive that led to the lodge and main road. It had sofas, chairs, a writing desk for letters. Pieces of partially finished embroidery lay around, and a piano, which was mainly used by women and their guests who stopped by for morning tea and gossip. Most of the paintings on the walls were of spring and summer flowers and family picnics. Edith sat in her mother's chair, trying to look calm and collected, yet nervous inside.

"Woodsman, what happened to the letters I wrote to Master James? I instructed you to send them to admiralty in Portsmouth. Did the Navy send any letters to me here?"

Woodsman broke into a sweat, concerned. "I... er... could not say, Miss Edith."

He had grown up in the house beginning as a kitchen helper, and then being promoted to upstairs footman. Morgan, the butler, noticed his potential and trained him. He loved his work, trying hard to learn about cleaning silver, wine, spirits, how to serve at table, to run a household along with the chief housekeeper and cook, to keep the accounts and cross check the deliveries and bills of the shop keepers and tradesmen. A neighbor's chief butler planned to retire in a year, and the family had asked Woodsman to take his place. It was a smaller household but a major promotion and one that allowed him to marry. He had his eye on Mary. A career upset would be a disaster. The staff lived vicariously through the successes and downturns of the masters and mistresses. They discussed everything that happened, including, over supper one evening, about Edith writing to James. Later, as Woodsman left to deliver the mail to the post in Beaulieu, Edith's mother called him aside. She instructed him to deliver all Edith's letters to her, swearing him to secrecy on pain of dismissal. Woodsman guessed that Agatha, Her Ladyship's maid, informed on Edith.

"Woodsman, do you mean you do not know, or cannot say? I will not report you, but I need the truth."

Edith often sat in court with her father, the local chief magistrate, and learnt his questioning skills. She watched Woodsman break into a sweat and recognized that he was hiding something. She got him to confess, learning that her mother had collected all the letters.

"Woodsman, I will make a deal with you. What happened is not your fault, but you should have told me. If you promise to deliver the letters in the future, I will make sure you keep your job and are rewarded. Otherwise…"

She had no need to explain more. Woodsman would receive a full shilling for each of James's future letters he delivered. For the next two years Woodsman became postman using Tony's father, who had his workshop at Buckler's Hard, as postbox. Woodsman delivered the mail to Mary, who took them to Edith.

Now Edith trusted that James had told the truth and did love her.

Time flew past. Just three more evenings before James started the return journey to *Defiance*. The tailor had made his clothes plus new midshipmen's uniforms.

He met Edith each day. Their kisses became bolder, but Edith thought carefully. She wanted more, but put firm limits. Even so his gently touching of her neck and behind her ears sent electric shocks through her.

"Edith, I am anxious about you going to London."

"There is no reason to be."

"No reason! You're going to meet the most handsome, rich and eligible young men in England and Europe. I will be out at sea. Of course I am worried."

"Daddy likes you. Eventually, Mummy might give in. If you ever propose to me."

James blushed. "I cannot propose without your father's permission and that will not happen as long as your mother says no. She will never agree to you marrying a pauper."

"My dowry is enough for us both."

James would not be a kept man. "We have to wait and hope that *Defiance* captures some rich French prizes."

Their visits were brief. James found himself impressed at how mature and organized Edith had become. No longer the playmate he climbed trees with.

Edith listened in admiration to James's stories, which he told with such vigor and confidence. But he was still shy with her. Such a strange contrast to his natural self-confidence, but also endearing as she would not like him to be overconfident and pushy.

They had to part.

"Mother says that most sailors die of scurvy and battle wounds, and others because their ships sink in battles and storms. You are always taking such risks. How do I know you will return?"

"With my love for you nothing will stop me, not even Napoleon himself."

Edith turned to leave, hesitated. James wanted one more embrace. Edith said, as one used to being in charge, "I expect a letter next week."

And then she skipped away, out of their clearing.

Later, it pleased Edith's mother that James had given up writing to Edith. His infatuation with her must be over. It made it easier to get Edith a quality husband.

There were two more evenings for James to spend with his father. He found his father's knowledge of politics, new industries powered by the steam engines, and general finance impressive. How did he learn all this? Country squires with tenant farmers knew about horses, farm animals, the hunt and social gossip. His father used to spend time in their London home, as did most of the gentry. However, they did not have his knowledge. Percy spent all his time in London learning nothing. James's father did not discuss Percy except to say they must have passed each other as James rode home from Lyndhurst.

Lord Lancaster became more and more convinced he had to make bold decisions. He heard of Percy's behavior at the Lyndhurst Inn, and to protect the Lancaster name, sent money to repair the damage from the brawl Percy started. He had not changed, and never would. Should he tell James about his ideas? Had he matured enough? James made him proud with his Navy successes, his appetite for learning, and his openness to new inventions. This age of invention had led to many new opportunities for trade. But 'gentlemen' did not trade. Trade belonged to the new class of nouveau riche who developed companies, financed inventions, traded overseas for tea and minerals. Merchants and businessmen were not invited to join the best gentlemen's clubs. Lord Lancaster regretted all those years he had ignored James. Yet James did not seem to resent him for it. Now Lord Lancaster felt a bond with James that he never had with Percy, or in fact, with anyone except James's mother.

"James, what will you do when the war is over?"

"The war has lasted so long no one thinks it will end soon. They say that in Egypt Napoleon spent a night alone in the pyramid's king's chamber searching for the secret of eternal life. He will keep fighting forever. I hope to stay with Captain Wilson. It is my best chance for prize money and promotion."

"Even kings die, so I doubt Napoleon will escape the inevitable. Tomorrow is our last evening together and I want to start early as we have a lot to talk about."

James went to bed, intrigued about the prospects of tomorrow's conversation and thinking of the return journey to Plymouth to rejoin *Defiance*. Another bouncy coach ride, though coaches were not as uncomfortable as storms at sea. He looked forward to learning from the other midshipmen about the careening and refurbishing of *Defiance*, and their future assignment.

The sound of pounding horse hooves on the long gravel drive woke him from his dreams. It was still pitch black and night. Then the distant echoing of banging at the oak front door. No one came at night. The sound of door bolts being drawn, voices, and then a breathless under butler rushed into James's room holding a candle.

"Mr Montague says there is a messenger with a letter from Captain Wilson."

James sprinted downstairs and opened the envelope.

James, you must return. The admiralty advanced our sailing orders. You have until the afternoon tide on Thursday, or we will have to leave you behind.

James's father arrived downstairs supported with his cane in his nightshirt.

"What the devil is happening?"

James explained. "My ship leaves Plymouth in two days."

"Damnations, we needed one more day. The coach will never make it. Take two of our best horses, and our senior groom also with two horses, and ride to Plymouth. Montague, get cook to prepare pack meals. Fit James's new uniforms in saddle bags. James, get dressed and start straight away. You have enough light from the moon. Once you're ready, come to my study."

James made a quick mental list of the things he needed, got dressed, prepared his pistol and saber. After the *schooner* boarding, he learnt always

136

to have a loaded pistol ready for danger. Riding at night left one vulnerable to highwaymen who, because of the economic crisis had proliferated. He said goodbye to Nanny Jones, realizing she had done more than spoil him. Her doting hid how she kept him focused on his studies, while allowing him to explore, play, and grow into an athletic man. Nanny, as always, kept a straight face, hiding her disappointment that James had to leave, but happy when he hugged her.

His father stood in front a furious fire with fresh logs.

"James, I have a lot I wanted to say. I am sorry it took so long for us to get to know each other. It is my fault."

"But sir—"

"James, let me take responsibility, and if you don't mind, I would be pleased if you called me father."

A lump came to James's throat.

"Mind? Father, I would be very pleased."

Lord Lancaster glowed at the response.

"I am also sorry that our English title and estate inheritance laws are so rigid. Our estate cannot give you the living you need. Your brother gets both the title and estate. I have other ideas. They may shock you a bit and I need time to explain. I had hoped to do so tomorrow night. Now it will have to wait. While you're away, I will prepare my ideas in more detail and discuss them on your return."

It perplexed but fascinated James that his father turned out to be such an interesting man, equal or perhaps better than Captain Wilson. Lord Lancaster approached his son, hesitated, and then gave James the first hug they had ever had. It embarrassed James, but thrilled him.

"I have a small present for you."

A superb cutlass made from Damascus steel. James looked; it was a thing of beauty, engraved, and with a razor edge. Damascus steel was rare. Famous for being strong, sharp and flexible, so it did not break, an important attribute in battle. It must have cost a fortune.

"It is fantastic. I do not know what to say."

"Also a small pouch to supplement your midshipman's pay. Now be off before I become sentimental. I will look for your letters, and in the *Navy Gazette* for your actions."

CHAPTER 12

The horses were lively. James and the groom were well past Lyndhurst when the sun rose. They stopped by a brook to water, rest and swap the horses. No highwaymen bothered them. James had not ridden while at sea. After twenty-four hours, his thighs were sore and stiff and he kept falling asleep in the saddle. They pushed on. At noon on the second day, they crested the Downs and looked towards Plymouth Sound below full of anchored ships and small boats going to and from the shore. The French frigate had left. *Defiance* rode at anchor, the cable short, the sails on the yards in stops, ready to be released. *Defiance* would leave on the afternoon tide. James spurred his horse forward, and the groom kept up with him. They arrived at the admiralty docks just as the tide changed. James hired the largest ferry, and paid for two extra rowers, grabbed his bags and dived into the boat.

"There's a guinea if we get to *Defiance* before she sails."

Even as they cleared the dock, Defiance released the first topsails. James heard the fiddle and voices of the men as they sang a shanty. It gave them rhythm to push, step by step, against the bars that turned the windlass, bringing up the cable and anchor out of the Plymouth mud.

Captain Wilson stood on the quarterdeck of *Defiance*, disappointed. Maybe his messenger did not get to James's home in time. Having dismissed Jeffries, and now without James, he would be two midshipmen short. He had hoped, and felt sure that James would arrive, but could not delay sailing. After capturing the frigate, and despite their differences in rank, they had developed a new unspoken bond, helped by the handsome prize money and career credit they all earned. The anchor cable came vertical. The next few heaves would wrench the anchor out of the mud, freeing *Defiance*, allowing her to sail out to sea. Captain Wilson had expected the admiralty to transfer some of his well-trained men to other

138

ships, but luckily, because of the urgency, it did not happen. He had a full crew.

His orders were to carry important dispatches to the governor of the Caribbean Islands, to report to the English admiral and join his small fleet that protected the British merchant ships from the French Navy and pirates. They rushed *Defiance*'s refit. The hull was cleaned and covered with new copper plates which stopped seaweed growing that slowed up the ship's speed. The ship did not get new sails but received the canvas to make sails, cord to replenish the rigging, food, water, cannon balls and gunpowder. Captain Wilson expected to arrive in the Caribbean in eight weeks, enough time to get *Defiance* ship-shape again. He had everything they needed, except his best midshipman.

He made a last sweep with his glass, looking at the shore, docks and Plymouth Hoe. About to put the glass away, he noticed a ferryboat and a figure with arms waving. He took a second look. A bare-chested man in civilian clothes waving his shirt with blond-red hair. James, but out of uniform, and coming out to His Majesty's ship? He would sort that out later.

"Belay on the anchor, Mister Stevens. Hold as we are." Captain Wilson grinned at his first lieutenant. "Stand by to receive an officer."

The news delighted First Lieutenant Stevens, the midshipmen and coxswain Paul. It relieved the sailors at the windlass, enabling them to rest. It required enormous power to break the anchor out of the mud. The bosons produced it with liberal use of the rope starters that stung the sailors into action, leaving welts.

James saw the anchor cable stop moving. He could make it. To miss the ship would be the end of his naval career. At his age, impossible to get a midshipman's post, and a captain as good as Wilson. Officers could not board a Royal Navy ship out of uniform. He stripped off his riding clothes and by the time the ferry arrived at *Defiance*, he was dressed in his new midshipmen uniform, wearing his father's sword. He leapt for the ship's chains and as he did, he heard Captain Wilson say, "Mister Stevens, I would be obliged if you would raise the anchor and get us underway."

"Aye, aye, sir."

Moments later, James reported to the quarterdeck in front of Captain Wilson. "Midshipman Lancaster reporting for duty, sir."

Captain Wilson smiled to himself. He had known James would arrive, even after a difficult, non-stop journey. He arrived in uniform, a new smart one that fitted. James had grown out of his old one long ago. No need to write him up.

"Carry on, Mister Lancaster. Next time try not to arrive at the last moment."

"Aye, aye, sir. May I send a line down for my saddle bags?"

"Mister Stevens will arrange it. Get to your station."

"Aye, aye, sir."

The fiddle, shanty, and the sailors' footsteps pounded in unison on the lower deck as the men pushed against the windlass bars, shouting a loud hooray when the anchor freed. First Lieutenant Stevens shouted, "Release the royals and main sails, lively now."

The noise of the flapping sails and the thud as the wind filled them confirmed *Defiance* to be alive and sailing again.

CHAPTER 12

Lord Lancaster's time spent with James had thrilled him, but he was disappointed not to have the chance to talk to him about his future. James might be away for another three years. He would use the time to complete his plans. He hoped Percy would learn from his current crisis, but did not think it likely. How could two boys from the same father, home and nanny be so different?

James made Nanny so proud. She secretly thought of herself as his mother. They had talked a lot during his visit. She promised to send any news she found about Edith, telling James not to fret. Word filtered down from Edith's maid that she only had eyes for James, rejecting all suitors her mother tried to introduce.

Edith's mother planned a season in London to open her daughter's eyes to the reality that mothers arrange the best marriages. She lined up some husband candidates.

Edith doubted her mother knew she'd seen James. She would have mentioned it and punished her. Through Mary, her maid, she learnt a messenger arrived at James's home in the middle of the night, and of James leaving in a hurry. She could not wait to receive his first letter, learn about the emergency, but more, she wanted to read that he loved her.

For days after she thought of the kiss, concerned she might be pregnant. Finally she plucked up the courage to ask Mary if she knew how women created babies. Mary blushed deep red and explained, using the farm animals as the metaphor.

"You mean, it is not through kissing?"

Mary tried to hide her laugh. "Oh lordy, no. Begging your pardon, miss. Though kissing can lead to other things." Mary smiled remembering her secret meetings with Woodsman. "You can get a sore lip, but not babies."

Relief spread through Edith, but she wondered what other misinformation she had learnt from her mother. What consequences did come from kissing? She planned to have Mary sit down and explain it all to her.

Defiance, with her clean hull, made fast speed in the summer winds as she sailed full pressed down the English Channel. Then across the Bay of Biscay, past Portugal, the Straits of Gibraltar to the Canary Islands. After that they turned to starboard and used the trade winds to cross the Atlantic to the Caribbean, the same Atlantic route Columbus took when he discovered America.

Captain Wilson worried. The hurricane season had started, a three-month period when the admiralty sent no ships across the Atlantic. *Defiance*'s orders instructed them to deliver the dispatches to the governor, with all haste, which, for the admiralty, justified the risk. Wilson prepared the crew for extreme conditions. Assuming they arrived in one piece, with the masts intact, he looked forward to joining the fleet with a mission to seek, capture, or sink the French and pirate ships. He hoped to get on with the admiral, known as a stickler. Everyone reported to someone. Even kings reported to God. Admirals could make one's life hell if they did not like you.

James returned to the rhythm of watch keeping and gun practice. Installing new sails made by a team of sailors sitting on the deck, stitching away. Replacing running rigging, sheets and lines. They would replace the fixed rigging once they were in Antigua's English harbor. Keeping rigging tarred and the decks clean. Compared to the stress of patrolling the English Channel, they had almost a relaxing voyage with warm winds and gentle seas. That changed after heading west across the Atlantic, with the trade winds behind them and big sea swells. *Defiance* rolled from side to side, making it difficult to stand, walk, and sleep. The roll traveled so far the crew thought that *Defiance* might capsize. Captain Wilson assured them it was normal, but they were still frightened.

The closer they got to the Americas, the stronger the winds became. They reefed the top sails, and then the royals. Still, they surged forward through the tall Atlantic swells, and *Defiance* rolled even more. Extra lines secured the cannons from breaking loose. James wondered how the masts stayed put with such strain on the rigging. The watch kept a careful eye to the south east for high whirling clouds, which warned of a hurricane. If one came, they would reef all sails, lashing them to the yards, so they did not shred to pieces, then run before the wind under bare masts.

As the winds increased, waves broke over the gunnels and seas washed over the decks. The water found all the deck leaks. For the unlucky seaman in a hammock underneath, it became a nightmare. The cook extinguished his fire. They ate cold food. Jack lines were secured along the deck to avoid seamen being swept overboard. More sails were reefed. It required three seamen on the wheel. The high winds lasted for ten days, but did not become a hurricane. Then they declined, and *Defiance* arrived in Antigua to perfect weather.

As *Defiance* entered English Harbor, her guns fired the salute to the admiral on his flagship. Three other Navy ships were at anchor.

Captain Wilson turned to James. "Mr Lancaster, I would be obliged if you would have your boat crew assemble in their best uniforms and have the boat ready the moment we anchor."

"Aye, aye, sir."

James sent word to Paul while he changed into his best uniform. The captain wanted to impress the admiral.

As *Defiance* anchored, signals were hoisted on the flagship, ordering *Defiance*'s captain on board with all haste.

James launched the boat even before the anchor line became taut, knowing the fleet's eyes would be on them. If delayed, Captain Wilson would be furious. He boarded the flagship with all the dispatches, and James delivered the fleet's mail to each ship, knowing many were waiting for news from home. How long would it be before he received a letter from Edith? James liked to be assigned boat work. But taking the captain to the flagship meant sitting in the boat for hours, waiting until he finished with the admiral, often until after they dined. Not all midshipmen's life could be as exciting as capturing enemy ships.

Defiance started two years of cruising in the Caribbean with its many islands, white sandy bays, palm trees and blue sea full of fish, hunting French ships, searching for pirates, normally with friendly winds and weather. During the hurricane season they kept close to the islands with safe harbors. Otherwise, they sailed on long trips, searching for pirates from the Bahamas to Trinidad, and into the Gulf of Mexico. Captain Wilson informed the midshipmen that he expected them all to use this time to study to become officers.

"Next hurricane season there will be a board with the admiral and captains for promotion to lieutenant."

The admiralty based one of the captain's grades on how many of his young gentlemen became officers.

CHAPTER 13

Edith had waited a frustrating three years for James's letters. She needed to be careful before searching her mother's room. She paused until her mother visited a neighbor, and Agatha, her mother's maid, went to lunch. Her mother's room was big with a four poster bed, a big vanity table with mirrors, multiple wardrobes, two sofas and an antique gilded French writing desk. A door, not often used, connected to Lord Rowley's rooms.

Edith checked the cupboards and desk drawers, but found nothing. Then she remembered that as a young girl, she had watched her mother open a secret compartment in her desk. Edith pressed every knob, and turned every piece of sculptured decoration. Nothing moved or opened. Time slipped away. She pulled out each drawer, but they only came three quarters of the way. Then one came fully out. Inside, she saw a button and pressed it. A section of the desk opened, revealing a secret compartment and all of the letters bundled in date order. Taking a few, she closed the desk, slipped the letters into her bodice, and headed for the door just as Agatha returned. She gave Edith an inquisitive look. "Is there anything I can do for you, Miss Edith?"

"Nothing, thank you, Agatha."

Edith had no intention of staying to talk. Agatha gossiped to Lady Lancaster, getting the staff in trouble. Below stairs, the staff were careful of her. For sure, Agatha would tell her mother.

With her mother or Agatha nearly always present it took weeks for Edith to get and read all James's fascinating letters. He described his exploits, such as capturing the *schooner*, but from a different perspective than that described in the *Navy Gazette*. He explained that when the *schooner* started moving forward, he had ordered Paul to maneuver their rowboat to go in front of it. Then he realized his mistake and his blood boiled. He had responsibility for fourteen seamen's lives. The ship would ram and sink them. The men could not swim. Anger rather than bravery propelled him to climb up the bowsprit and charge down the deck. When he smashed the captain's arm with his cutlass, the sound of the breaking bones shocked him. The sight of the arm dangling sickened him. Blood flying everywhere made him nauseous. The reality of sword fighting had nothing to do with the galant stories told in novels, nor anything like the practice he had at home with his older brother's fencing master, when Percy failed to turn up for his lessons. To survive, one had to be quick, skilled and violent. The first hit won. He felt sorry for the schooner's captain being hung from the yardarm. He must have obeyed orders when pretending not to be French.

Now, when they had to board a ship, James prepared and loaded three pistols which he wrapped in waterproof cloths, ready to use. Contrary to standing orders about not arming seamen, he gave a pistol to Paul, not wanting to rely on his ability to throw marlinspikes. James used a sword as the last resort, although he practiced the short-cutlass, knife fighting and boxing with *Defiance*'s marine officer, and became more than competent. The short cutlass was easier to use in close combat when boarding a ship. They also practiced with rapiers which were still popular with gentry and military on land.

Edith laughed when she found a letter assuming that she was upset with James because he had kissed her on the cheek. He asked if that was why he received no letters from her. It surprised her that pretending to be shocked at the kiss had been so effective. In fact, too effective. If only he knew the truth! James also told her how he lay in his bunk, after a tough time on watch, dreaming of her.

James's first letters from the Caribbean arrived after four months. They thrilled her. She had almost given up hope. Her mother insisted they prepare to go to London for her coming out, and as was her right, to be introduced at Court to Their Majesties. It kept her very busy and concerned. There were ballroom dresses to be made. Dance lessons with a teacher who came from London, for the latest versions of the country-dance, cotillion, quadrille and the Scottish reel.

Her mother complained, "The modern dances have too much skipping and jumping. Ladies should limit themselves and be careful not to perspire. Edith, you must learn the names and family histories of the young people who will take part in the season."

When the first batch of Edith's letters arrived in English Harbor, James read them many times, thrilled by the confirmation that she remained his sweetheart. He read parts to his fellow midshipmen but kept the most sensitive passages for himself, then stored them at the bottom of his trunk.

Having suffered the cold weather of the English Channel for three years, they never tired of the Caribbean wind and sun. Still, the ship's routine continued day and night. Even when at anchor, midshipmen kept watch. They searched for French and pirate ships, sometimes chasing distant sails for days and nights. James became used to the relentless four hours on watch, and while off watch, being called with all hands to wear ship or shorten sail. The midshipmen took noon sights with the sextant, keeping their own logs, and studied for the exams and admiral's board. Even if they passed the board, they were unlikely to be promoted unless lieutenants in their small fleet became sick or were killed in action.

James's father's health was no better. Percy had not changed his ways and so he needed to protect James's future. He did not look forward to the journey to London, swaying in his coach, bumping over the roads full of ruts and holes. The inns on the way had fresh horses ready to minimize the delays. London used to be fun: the streets full of busy people; fashion; attending Court and Their Majesties; lectures at the Royal Society about the latest science discoveries; the annual Royal Academy of Art Exhibition, where he supported young painters including Turner and Constable; gossip; politics; news; and the parties. But that no longer interested him. He owed it to James to cope with the journey and make arrangements.

CHAPTER 14

The hurricane season came again with *Defiance* back in Antigua's English Harbor, along with the other four ships of the fleet. The flagship summoned midshipmen who thought they were ready to be examined by the board. First Lieutenant Stevens and the sailing master tested the *Defiance* midshipmen in mock interviews. Captain Wilson told them only to attend the board if they were confident of being ready.

"The admiral fails young midshipmen if their answers lack detail. I will not be happy if any of you return without passing."

The board, the admiral and five captains ate a hearty breakfast. Seventeen midshipmen sat on benches outside the admiral's quarters, talking in whispers. Screens in the admiral's quarters at the stern of the ship had been removed, and the rooms converted into one for the meeting. Board members sat behind a long table, their backs to the stern windows that gave a view out to the ships anchored behind, and beyond them, the harbor buildings. They summonsed the first midshipman who entered the room, stood to attention and gave his and his ship name. They divided the questions into groups: navigation; ship handling; fighting tactics: signaling; artillery; aiming; powder; shot; distance; ship provisions; and admiralty law. Each board member asked one question.

The first candidate took forever. He exited with a long face. They admitted the second candidate. The remaining midshipmen gathered round and asked the first, "What happened? Which questions did they ask?"

"I am having trouble remembering. It is nerve wracking standing before an admiral and five captains. Trying to explain trigonometry, cannon ball velocities and distances based on the size of the gun and the amount of powder. Remembering which order to give first, if a ship is locked 'in irons' near a lee shore. It was terrifying. The admiral advised me to study more."

Over the next three hours they examined nine of the candidates and only four passed. The board announced a break for lunch. The remaining candidates could lunch in the officers' mess before being examined in the afternoon.

Over lunch, the midshipmen asked each other taxing questions. They were not confident, especially as they expected the board members to wash down their lunch with generous glasses of wine, and become more critical.

After lunch, the admiral's aide called the first *Defiance* candidate. He stayed a short time and left dejected.

"They must have drunk too much as they asked an impossible question: giving longitude and latitude, barometer reading, and August as the time of year. Then they wanted the ship's location, and asked what would I be doing. I guessed the ship just passed the Canary Islands and I would add more sails to take the trade winds to the Caribbean. They laughed and said I could leave, failed."

James thought that, based on the longitude and latitude given, he would have answered Malta. The glass, being so low in August, forecast a Mediterranean storm. He would add another anchor and more bindings to keep the sails from getting loose from the yards.

They called James next. The board members looked tired. James introduced himself. The admiral, sitting in the middle seat, smaller than Captain Wilson, sitting on his right, looked up. He had earned his nickname, the Ferret, by being small and full of frenetic energy and sarcasm.

"Ah, Mister Lancaster, you're the *Defiance* midshipman who has had so many mentions in the *Gazette*. I hope your naval knowledge is as good as your luck getting mentioned in dispatches."

James knew his apparent confidence made some people, such as the admiral, aggressive towards him. He credited this to his height. He could not afford to have the admiral as his enemy. The way he spoke sounded to James as though the admiral thought that his success came from luck, rather than him making the luck.

"Based on the last *Defiance* midshipman's performance, you will need more than luck."

Captain Wilson showed no facial emotion, but by the way he lifted his shoulders, James knew him to be unhappy with the admiral's comments. James remembered Captain Wilson's warning. He did not want his midshipmen to fail. But James could not let the admiral intimidate him.

"Thank you, my Lord. I hope I will not need luck. I have already been lucky to receive Captain Wilson's training."

Captain Wilson smiled. The admiral did a double take. *A midshipman speaking up! Interesting!* He told the first captain to ask a question. Every board member, other than Captain Wilson, asked a question and James answered them all. The admiral did not seem satisfied.

"Mister Lancaster, you are the senior surviving officer of *Defiance*, which just engaged the enemy and shot away her main mast. The enemy has struck her ensign and appears to have surrendered, but is drifting away fast. Her crew is clearing away the mast. You have seventeen dead, including all your senior officers and fifty-three wounded. Your carpenter reports the ship's pumps are not keeping up with the water entering the hull, and the pump crews are exhausted. The carpenter cannot get to the leaks caused by cannon balls. The cargo will take a couple of hours to remove. Give your orders."

James paused a moment to think:

"Appoint officers. Give orders to position *Defiance* up wind and close to the prize. Send two armed boat crews to take possession of the prize. Have lookouts warn if anything unusual happens on the prize and a cannon ready to fire a warning shot. Instruct the sail maker and boson to haul a large canvas or sail under the hull and over the holes to reduce, or stop, the leak or leaks. Rotate the pump crews. Check the wounded are being looked after. Secure powder back in the hold, and when safe, have the cook start fires and prepare meals. Collect the dead. Make a quick note in the logbook of the situation and decisions."

The admiral looked at the captains. Based on this midshipman's notoriety for getting mentioned, the admiral anticipated they would be reluctant to promote him. They also knew of the admiral's prejudices. But they all nodded yes.

"Mister Lancaster, you are ready to be a lieutenant. Congratulations."

As James left, relieved and pleased, he noticed Captain Wilson beaming and heard the admiral say, "Wilson, after that first idiot of yours, I expected more of the same, but Lancaster lives up to your stories. Well done."

Passing the board made no difference to James's role on the ship; he remained junior midshipman. He wrote a long letter to Edith explaining the board and saying he hoped that his promotion would soften her mother, and hoping Edith was actually receiving his letters.

CHAPTER 15

Edith was facing her own ordeal at the Royal Court. The debutantes were young ladies of noble families who the king and queen agreed to meet. The season started at the palace reception in a large room but nearly empty of furniture with two thrones on a dais, where the queen insisted the debutantes wore old fashioned hooped dresses. It made walking very uncomfortable. It was also difficult to sit, but as they were not allowed to sit in the presence of the king and queen there were no chairs. They stood for hours waiting for the lord chamberlain to introduce them one by one, to curtsy to their majesties and exchange a few polite words. Edith felt they looked her over as they did their horses, matching her for mating prospects. Then there were balls in large private houses or hotels, paid for by the parents, for the girls to get to know each other and form lifelong friendships, but mainly for young men to survey the girls and select potential brides.

The *Morning Post* reported Edith's ball to be one of the season's best. It cost her father a fortune. Edith had fun going to the other debutantes' balls and parties, until pathetic young men, urged by their mothers, approached her father asking for marriage. Her mother pushed her to consider the most incompatible offers. She refused, causing her mother to have a rage and cut the visit short.

They returned to their New Forest estate in almost silence after Edith's mother asked furiously, "Edith, how could you? Your father spent a fortune on your season, and you made no effort to attract a husband. You will become an aging spinster like your aunt."

"Aunty is fun, and it is preferable to be a spinster than married to a bully or wimp."

Her father tried to be neutral, but Edith had the impression he agreed with her, and not her mother. She and her father had become close. She told him about James, how her mother had intercepted the letters, and she read parts of them to her father.

Other than James's letters, Edith enjoyed reading her father's law books and discussing them with him. He had one of the biggest local estate and loved his role as chief magistrate. Edith liked to sit in court with him. At home, they debated the cases, especially the lawyers' arguments and how they could have better defended their clients. It gave her an in-depth understanding of human nature and about the lives of the ordinary people, which few aristocrats ever got to see. It shocked her to learn how vulnerable they were to weather and crop disease and she looked more closely at helping their tenants while she assisted her father administering their estate. As women could never become lawyers, and many husbands did not want clever wives, her mother disapproved of her interest. Her father encouraged it, becoming more and more impressed by her knowledge.

During the five years James was at sea, Edith grew from a girl into a woman. In all that time, she had seen James only one week, yet their letters made her feel connected to him. She had inherited her Italian grandmother's looks, long brown hair, penetrating but alluring eyes, an impressive figure, her father's intelligence and her mother's cunning, presenting herself with apparent confidence and style, intimidating many would-be suitors.

Like everyone, she'd heard of the continuing horrors of Napoleon's exploits. His taking of countries, stealing their wealth and art, dismissing their rulers, of enormous battles with the fields covered with the wounded and dead of the conquered and his own French troops. He started a trade blockade of England, intending to starve the English into submission. England's population of nine million was outnumbered by France's thirty million. Napoleon had bigger armies, more wealth, plus all the wealth he stole from other countries.

Edith also read of the benefits of Napoleon's administration. The reduction in corruption. Of the Invalids' Hospital, the first to specifically look after injured soldiers. The rebuilding of Paris with grand streets. Most interestingly, of the new commercial and civil law system, Code Napoleon. The Code replaced all the local feudal laws, developed over a thousand years by the previous aristocrats, and for their own benefit. Now the whole of France, and many of the conquered countries, had one legal system for everyone and required the judges to enforce it fairly. Napoleon felt that history would credit the Code as his major contribution to France. Perhaps more important than the forty plus battles he had already won. Edith had a secret admiration for most of the Code.

In Edith's letters with James, they discussed the Code, but not with others. The English, living under the threat of invasion, considered everything Napoleon did as bad. Edith felt one could learn from his military success and his civil achievements. James grudgingly admitted the French ships were better built than the British and lasted longer. Some British ships fell apart in two years from the mistake of using iron and copper fastenings close together, causing the copper to dissolve away. The British were lucky. Napoleon had trained in the Army, and not the Navy. He did not know how to manage his Navy.

Edith's and James's secret correspondence turned her affection and childhood admiration into a deep love. But she wanted James to respect her as a person. It came as a shock to find English women such as Mary Wollstonecraft wrote about and advocated full women equality. It had never occurred to her that women were treated as second class citizens, effectively belonging to their fathers then husbands. Most women she knew were actually cleverer than their husbands. She had studied the law better than most male university students, though she could not attend university. Edith wrote about her thoughts to James and was pleased and relieved that James agreed with her.

Captain Wilson's training sessions had turned James into a very efficient fighter, not just with pistols and cutlasses, but also with knives and fists. He learnt how to lead small teams to board ships; to land ashore through surf; to penetrate forts by scaling walls, blowing up doors and picking locks. Several seamen, including Alan from his boat crew, were ex thieves and lock pickers who traded prison for life in the Navy. Captain Wilson used their skills to train the midshipmen.

Otherwise, life at sea became monotonous, with *Defiance* seeing little action for two years except for capturing three small pirate boats which they delivered to the admiral in English Harbor. He hung the pirates and sent their boats to England for the prize money, with crews from other ships. James spent his spare time writing to Edith and rereading her letters.

When passing a headland, it surprised the crew of *Defiance* to see a large pirate schooner anchored in a bay. Most of her ship's long boats were deserted, on the beach. Her rigging, sails and hull were in good condition, but not the paint and varnish. She looked a mess, intended to disguise from merchant ships the danger she represented.

Captain Wilson called out, "Clear for action, reef the top sails, load and run out the starboard guns, boarding parties prepare."

They had rehearsed these maneuvers countless times, but Captain Wilson turned the sand minute-glass to check how long it took before First Lieutenant Stevens confirmed the ship ready.

"Only six minutes, not bad Mister Stevens."

Through the spyglass, they could only see a few men on the deck of the schooner.

"The rest of the pirate crew must be ashore on a raiding party, stealing from unprotected plantation owners. Let's take the ship."

With a British war ship bearing down towards them, guns ready to fire and obliterate them, it did not take the eight or ten pirates on schooner long to surrender by dropping their skull and cross bone flag.

It pleased Captain Wilson that he did not have to waste ammunition, nor risk the life of his men.

"Mister Stevens, I will be obliged if you would send Second Lieutenant Bishop with Mister Lancaster and four boats to take command of the schooner. Sail it out just beyond the bay and hove to. Leave the skull and cross bones flying. When the pirates return with plunder and hostages, they will have to row out to the schooner. *Defiance* will be out of sight behind the headland until the pirate rowboats are out at sea. Then we will swoop to capture them. Judging by the number of boats on shore, there must be at least fifty of them. I do not want to let pirates escape back onto the island to wreak havoc with the plantation owners, forcing us to send the Army after them."

Action at last! The adrenalin rushed through James as he prepared his pistols and cutlass. Paul had their boat in the water first.

Lieutenant Bishop called to James, "Mister Lancaster, you board by the stern. My three boats will board at the companionway and bows."

"Aye, aye, sir," James responded, though disappointed that he would miss the action, and wondering if Bishop wanted all the glory. He ignored

154

the enquiring look he received from Paul. James preferred even the smallest action to watching from onboard *Defiance*.

Lieutenant Bishop's boat pulled ahead, and as he approached the schooner, he called to the pirate crew, "Assemble at the mast and face it, with your hands on your heads."

Bishop planned to board the leeward side of the schooner, protected from the wind and waves. The pirates had their backs to James as he rowed along the windward side, out of sight. Boarding a strange ship could be tricky. Especially with pirates who expected to be hanged, so had little to lose.

Lieutenant Bishop shouted instructions for the *Defiance* seamen to board and form up in two lines on the foredeck. As they climbed on board and lined up forward of the mast, ready to take the pirates' surrender, the pirates rushed towards the stern. Then they jumped into the ship's hold, leaving the deck clear. Lieutenant Bishop was aghast. What had happened? Why had they fled into the hold, with no escape? Unless they had a way to get out. If they had intended to flee, why, as soon as they saw *Defiance* approaching, had they not taken their last boat to the shore? He moved aft towards the hold hatch, took off his hat and put the brim over the hold to see if they intended to fire a pistol at him. Silence. He looked into blackness, seeing nothing.

A voice shouted, "Stand where you are."

Lieutenant Bishop looked up towards the stern and quarterdeck. Pirates were removing a canvas covering a newly invented swivel gun, a giant blunderbuss that fired lead balls to stop boarders. Behind the gun were at least twelve pirates. How had the pirates acquired such a modern weapon? It swiveled forty-five degrees to the left and right, aimed up and down. There was no dodging the lethal volley of one hundred small lead balls. It would kill or maim all his men.

"Avast there. We loaded the gun with grape shot and if you advance, I will blow you away. Put down your weapons."

It had been a trap. The *Defiance* seamen looked to Bishop, knowing his career was finished. An English naval officer never surrendered, he expected death or court martial. Bishop thought living to be the best decision. At least he could argue he had no choice. Hoping that Captain

Wilson, with *Defiance*, would rescue him, he looked back to his seamen. "Do as they say."

As he lowered his pistol and sword to the deck, he called out to the pirates, "You cannot get away with this. The Royal Navy will track you down and *Defiance* will never let you leave. It will blow you out of the water."

"On the contrary. Your captain might sacrifice thirty-six seamen. But he will respect and care for the wives and daughters of the plantation owners we have on board. We want free passage and ransom payment for the lives and virginity of the hostages."

James heard this while hidden in his boat behind the Schooner's stern. He and his crew had practiced boarding and fighting as a team. He indicated for them to follow him up the transom of the ship. The transom leaned out, making the climb difficult, but the gilded ornate wooden decorations gave them hand holds. Paul, Alan, Roger and the rest of the crew followed James as he leapt over the bulwarks and charged towards backs of the pirates with the swivel gun pointing away from them. James held two pistols and Paul one. Without warning, they shot three of the pirates. The others tried to swivel the gun, but it would not turn that far.

James dropped his two pistols onto the deck. If he survived, he would collect them later. He pulled the third pistol and his cutlass from his waist and shot the leader. The pirates turned in shock, pulled out their swords but James's team came as one, hacking with their short naval cutlasses on the joint between the pirate's shoulders and necks. Blood spurted everywhere, coupled with screams and shouts.

Bishop, seeing the swivel gun pointing away from him, grabbed his sword and rushed forward, followed by his seamen. They trapped the pirates between two efficient forces. Before they could surrender, many were dead or wounded, the deck covered in a mess of bodies, limbs and blood. James surprised himself, in the middle of the action, thinking how much work it would require to get the decks clean to Navy standard. But enough of day dreaming, more pirates were hiding below decks.

Those aboard *Defiance* heard pistols shots and shouting. Captain Wilson was responsible for the safety of his men and the capture of prizes. If something had gone wrong, he faced court martial.

"Mister Stevens, bear down alongside the schooner, and be prepared to give a broadside with our starboard battery and then board her."

Stevens did not envy the decisions Captain Wilson faced. A full broadside would ruin the schooner and kill many on board, including their own seamen. The admiral might forgive the dead and wounded, but not the loss of prize money, if they destroyed the schooner. Would Wilson sacrifice his own crew to regain control? One more reason Stevens had not wanted promotion.

It relieved them that, as they bore down towards the schooner, the blue ensign rose above the pirate's skull and crossbones flag. Lieutenant Bishop stood on the shrouds waving and shouting that they were in control. With the pirates shackled and chained in the hold, they searched the ship. James discovered half a dozen young ladies with their mothers locked in a cabin. They huddled together weeping, first in fear and then in relief realizing they were safe. Saved by a young, handsome naval officer with battle scars.

Lieutenant Bishop called out, "Mister Lancaster, well done, and thanks. Please raise the anchor, put up the skull and cross bone flag again and get the sails pulling while I interrogate the pirates. Keep the ladies out of sight."

Captain Wilson's first assumption about the pirates raiding the plantations proved correct. There were over forty of them ashore.

An hour later, the schooner hove-to out at sea. They positioned two pirates as though they were on watch, and told them that if they warned their comrades, they would be whipped around the fleet before being hanged. Bishop and James hid themselves so they could watch through the telescope for the returning pirates.

Late in the afternoon, they arrived, leading a band of reluctant hostages and stolen packhorses with looted bounty. Upset to see their ship so far offshore, they waved and fired pistols, demanding that the schooner go back into the bay to collect them. When the ship showed no sign of returning, they loaded into their boats and started rowing out. Arriving at the bay entrance, they again fired their pistols, demanding the schooner sail towards them. The pirates on the schooner, with knives in their backs, waved back, insisting they row out. It made the pirate leader furious, planning, once they were back on board, to punish his crew. The rowboats were about two miles from shore when *Defiance* sailed around the headland and separated them from the beach. One boat made a run for freedom, heading down the coast. Bishop put the schooner after them and they were soon captured.

It thrilled Captain Wilson and the crew to have captured the pirate schooner, its crew and also rescue the plantation hostages with their possessions. They expected good prize money for the schooner and the plantation owners typically gave generous rewards when helped by the Navy. Wilson ordered *Defiance* and the schooner to English Harbor and from there they could return the plantation hostages to their islands. He needed Lieutenant Bishop to return to *Defiance* to provide the information for the admiral's report, leaving James in command of the pirate's ship.

Bishop reported to his captain all that had happened. It did not take long for *Defiance*'s crew to learn, via the captain's steward, that Lucky Lancaster, and his Coxswain Paul, had once again saved the day.

On board the schooner, James enjoyed commanding a ship for the first time, but had discipline problems. He had dreamed of his first command. He had no trouble controlling seamen or pirates, but young ladies? He could not manage the six plantation daughters now falling in love with him. Giggling and standing at the ship's wheel, wanting to learn all about him, refusing his request to go below.

He called to Paul. "Coxswain, remove these ladies from the deck."

"Come on, ladies, follow the captain's orders."

The ladies giggled. "Are you going to put us in irons?"

"Captain?"

James had never been called captain before. He was in command, but out of control. This would not do.

"They are refusing to go below."

"Coxswain, six seamen, six buckets of fresh sea water, one for each lady who is still on the deck three minutes from now."

Once the seaman approached with the buckets, the girls ran away laughing, but not for long.

They soon returned. In retrospect, James remembered his first command as fun. They had two days and nights of sailing in perfect weather, with the company of the grateful girls, and their ever-watching mothers. James took brief naps on deck but otherwise stayed awake the whole time, concerned that the pirates did not escape. They were going to hang, and desperate, so were put in chains. James did not have a big enough crew to manage them if they escaped. He worked out the crew watches, kept in exact position behind *Defiance*. Then planned the entrance into English Harbor with coded flag signals for the fort, rehearsed the gunfire to salute the admiral and the anchoring procedures. Everything they did would be watched, discussed and criticized, with perfection expected.

CHAPTER 16

Both *Defiance* and the schooner fired the salute on entering English Harbor. *Defiance*'s flags signaled they had a prize ship, prisoners and rescued hostages on board. Signals from the flagship showed where *Defiance* and the schooner were to anchor, and requested Captain Wilson on board. James turned the schooner in front of the flagship, proud of the fact they had their ensign flying over the jolly roger. They came head to wind, stopped, and dropped the anchor with a splash.

Soon after Captain Wilson reported to the flagship, the admiral's ship signaled *Defiance* and the schooner that boats were being sent to collect the hostages and their possessions. The girls were reluctant to leave without James promising to write to them.

"But I have a sweetheart."

"You can have more than one."

Their mothers were keen to get off the ship, leaving James in peace, but now he did not want that. He enjoyed the company of the bright young ladies, but it made him miss Edith even more.

Another signal from the flagship informed them that shore boats would collect the prisoners. Once collected, Lieutenants Stevens and Bishop, and Acting Lieutenant Lancaster, were required to report to the flagship for dinner. *Acting Lieutenant!* A strange way to be informed of promotion, but an exciting one. Plus, dinner with an admiral on board his flagship. James's luck continued, but he needed a lieutenant's uniform. He sent a boat over to *Defiance* to ask Bishop if he had a spare one he could borrow. Sometimes the Navy etiquette created problems, and officers needed to solve them. James would use his savings to buy new lieutenant's uniform, while hoping to have enough left to buy Edith a very special present.

A boson's whistle saluted James as he stepped onto the flagship's deck, a new experience for him. He found it embarrassing, as they normally reserved the ceremony for captains, senior visiting officers and dignitaries.

This time it was to show James respect for the capture of the pirate ship. The admiral's staff officer escorted him to the stateroom where the admiral and five captains were enjoying rum punch. Lieutenants Stevens and Bishop, already there, looked uncomfortable in such distinguished company.

The admiral turned. "Ah, Lieutenant Lancaster, again the lucky hero of the day."

James could not tell whether the admiral was being sarcastic or genuine but Captain Wilson's smile reassured him.

"First, I have to thank you, my Lord, for my promotion. But I also must say that luck is created and not given. Captain Wilson's training gave us the skills we needed. The command of Lieutenant Bishop, who had us board the schooner from both ends, enabled us to overcome the pirates' trap."

Captain Wilson smiled and Lieutenant Bishop beamed in gratitude. Bishop worried he might be court martialed for surrendering to the pirates. His plan to earn all the credit by isolating James from the action had, in retrospect, saved the day and his career.

"Hmm. You earned your promotion. Captain Wilson told me you are modest, as is proper. Now to dinner. The captains and I want to hear, in your words, the whole adventure."

Late in the evening, just before the port passed, the Admiral announced, "Lieutenant Lancaster, Captain Wilson has agreed to release you to take command of the schooner and deliver her to the admiralty in Plymouth."

James could not believe his luck and spluttered, "Thank you, my Lord, and also Captain Wilson, I am speechless."

Captain Wilson interrupted. "You had best find words quickly as a commander has to sleep on his ship. You can have Coxswain Sumners and your boat crew. Other ships will provide two midshipmen, promoted to lieutenant, and additional crew. You have a week to get the schooner looking like a Navy vessel, provisioned and to get under way."

James, turning to the Admiral, said, "My Lord, I would like to thank you for your generous hospitality, and with your permission, leave to get my trunk and move over to the schooner."

"Shame to miss my excellent port, but yes."

The following morning, the two acting lieutenants and the crews assembled. James read them his orders to take command of the ship, then delegated the work to remove blood stains from the deck, spruce up with paint, and get supplied with provisions, water and charts.

It took four days before they were ready to leave and James used the fifth day to do basic training to ensure the seamen had assigned jobs and knew how to do them. He sent a boat to collect the admiral's dispatches and mail from each of the other ships. Then he visited *Defiance* to say goodbye to his shipmates, and to thank First Lieutenant Stevens and Captain Wilson.

"James." It was the first time Captain Wilson had called him by his name, rather than Mister Lancaster. "The way the Navy works, there is no guarantee of us serving together again, but I hope we can. I will do my best to get you back with me as a lieutenant. Good luck, not that you need it as it comes your way. Please pay my respects to your father and thank him for sending you to me."

The voyage across the Atlantic passed by quickly. James enjoyed his first command, made more exciting by being away from the fleet and the continuous signals from the flagship. He reveled at watching the sun come up each morning, with the ship ploughing through the friendly seas while he drank tea standing by the quarter-deck rail. James hoped to avoid any confrontations especially as his small crew were just enough to manage the sails, but even so he trained them with the guns as a precaution. They would be returning to Plymouth as a heroes, and James anticipated receiving permanent promotion. Before being assigned to a new ship, he hoped to be granted a few weeks to see his father and Edith. Perhaps now her mother would allow him to propose.

With the ensign flying over the jolly roger, they sailed into Plymouth Sound flying signals informing the admiralty they had dispatches from the Caribbean. Guns fired a salute from the fort to congratulate the crew for delivering an enemy ship. They informed the Admiralty, and the town's people, who rushed to see the ship, and learn the news.

Signals from the admiralty port office told them where to anchor, and for the ship's captain to report ashore. It surprised James to see so many Navy ships at anchor with only skeleton crews, and not ready for sea. What had happened while they were away? Once James was ashore, the admiral's secretary took the dispatches and James's report, leaving him to sit and wait.

He thought he had been forgotten. The secretary returned and took him into the admiral's office with its view out over the harbor, and a chart of the harbor painted on a large wooden board. Circles painted on the chart showed the anchorages, each one with a small ship's model and ship's name.

"Excellent report, and you made good time from English Harbor. But I have bad news for you. The politicians agreed peace with Napoleon, though many doubt that it can last. Most Navy ships have been mothballed, and the crews laid off. When war starts again, there will be problems to get crews, and ships recommissioned. We will put your schooner out to auction. The admiralty is not buying ships so it will not get much. I am sorry, they will not confirm you as lieutenant until you get a new ship. You will go ashore as a midshipman. Unlike full officers, midshipmen do not get half pay while on shore. You can apply to the admiralty in Whitehall for a ship, but it is unlikely. The good news is, when the war starts again, you are senior for promotion. We will write up your recent exploits in the *Navy Gazette*. The admiralty wants to let the politicians and public learn of Navy successes, so they will publish the story within a week. Now, report to the harbor captain for orders to get your ship handed over for auction. In two weeks, you and your crew will be paid off, and you can head home."

Going home to see his father and Edith made James happy. He thought the rest of the news very sad. He had expected to return home in his lieutenant's uniform instead of dressed as a midshipman. So, he said what one always says to Admirals.

"Thank you, my Lord."

After a busy two weeks, there were laid off, and Paul approached James.

"Begging your pardon, sir, it is unconventional, but me, Alan and Roger wondered if we could buy you one last grog before we all go. I ain't been ashore for many years, but an old purser of mine has an inn where you can find real Navy rum. It seems unlikely we are to be shipmates again, and we wanted to thank you."

"Coxswain Paul, it should be me thanking you. Not only for saving my life, but also teaching me so much. What do you plan to do ashore?"

"I have saved a little. Me mother left two acres of farmland on the way to Dartmoor. Enough to keep one family, so I thought I would try to learn to farm while keeping my eyes open for a wife. Not that I would know what to do with one, after all these years at sea."

"From what I hear, you do not have to worry about what to do with wives. They manage husbands. We just follow."

Trevor, the round, red nosed, rather jolly, but sharp-eyed landlord, owned a busy inn with the best Navy rum. James wondered how Trevor managed that, but concluded he best not know. James, Paul, Roger and Alan enjoyed a few grogs then James said, "Paul, I have to leave. But I promise, if I ever nominate a crew, you will be my bosun."

CHAPTER 17

The journey to Lyndhurst took three days. It rained. The roads were full of puddles and holes. On hills, the men descended to lighten the coach. Their boots became clogged with mud. Not the glorious trip James imagined. He could not wait to be home to see his father, wondering what he wanted to talk about, and to hug Nanny Jones and ask Edith's father for permission to propose. Edith's last letters took four months to get to the Caribbean. She told him how cross her mother had been with her for avoiding all suitors. She had little hope of being allowed to see James. Her mother refused to let her go for walks in the woods on her own. James became insecure. How would he get to see her? The *Navy Gazette* published the story of the capture of the pirate schooner. He hoped his father, Edith and her father had seen it and read that he was captain while bringing it to Plymouth.

The coach arrived at Lyndhurst at night. James found they had the *Gazette*. Too late to go home, he stayed at the inn and enjoyed an excellent dinner of New Forest deer roasted on a large spit over a wood fire. Everyone wanted to learn about the pirate incident, but the locals seemed hesitant to talk to James. He could not put his finger on it, but something had changed.

He wanted to arrive home after his father's breakfast, so he left the inn on a livery horse at nine a.m. The rain and cold dampened his excitement. He hoped his father had read the *Gazette* and would guess that he was returning soon. He rode up the long drive with bare branches of oak trees seeming to claw at the sky, as though in agony. James had the rumblings he always felt before battles, but he ignored it, expecting his father and the staff at the front door to greet him. Only one person appeared, a tall, trim figure standing in a long black dress, hair pinned back and looking pale and ashen. He could always rely on Nanny Jones.

James jumped off the horse and saw Nanny crying. She never cried.

"Nanny, what on earth is the matter?"

"Oh, Master James, it is so good to see you. Have you not heard the news?"

"What news?"

Nanny sobbed. "Your father died two weeks ago."

James could not understand what she said. He stood still, trying to cope with the pain that shot through his body. The realization he would never talk to his father again nor find out what he had wanted to tell him. So sudden and final. He had missed him by only two weeks. He probably died as James arrived in Plymouth. Perhaps, if he had not stayed to hand over the schooner, he might have been on time to say goodbye.

Nanny saw the shock on James's face. "Master Percy is now lord of the manor. He told me to leave. I have some savings, but your father made me a family retainer and this is my home. Where can I go? Once my savings are finished, I will be a pauper."

"Leave! Percy said that? Nanny, that's impossible! I will sort this out."

It filled James with anger. How could Percy disrespect his father's wishes so much? To dismiss a retainer, with the prospects of the poorhouse, and Nanny Jones of all people.

Montague, the butler, stood in the hallway, as always, with his solemn face, but his red eyes showed his genuine feelings of loss.

"Welcome home, Master James. I am sorry you returned to such bad news. Your father would have been so proud to read the *Navy Gazette* that arrived yesterday. Master Percy, I mean Lord Lancaster, your brother, is waiting for you in the study."

"I will be there as soon as I change my wet clothes and muddy boots."

It shocked James to see Percy in his father's study, slouching in his chair, drinking brandy so early in the day. In the corner, looking like a bodyguard, stood a caricature of an ex-army sergeant with an exaggerated moustache and a fat stomach. Did Percy fear James would attack him, or were there others that scared him?

"So, you're back! Sorry you missed the funeral. People came from all over. Our new lawyer, Mr Sweeney, in Southampton, has your inheritance. What there is. You can stay until Monday, then you find your own way."

James was speechless. He had to hold himself from hitting Percy, who said nothing about their father. No kind words. This was, had been, James's home. He never had a close relationship with his half-brother, but to be thrown out.

"Who is that man?" James asked, pointing at the sergeant.

"He is an insurance policy. You can ignore him."

James looked him over carefully, concluding that the sergeant's best days were well past, and in a fight, he could be beaten. The sergeant recognized the confidence with which James's eyes scanned him, saw the battle scars, and hoped he would never have to confront him. He found it easy to frighten away Percy's city creditors. But this man had seen action, and judging by the way he carried himself, was not someone to mess with.

James smiled. "Not much of a policy if you face real trouble."

Percy cringed in his chair, having witnessed the silent exchange and James winning it. How did James become the man he wanted to be? As he had watched James grow he was envious of his ability to get on with everyone, to laugh when he fell off his pony, or made other mistakes. Percy had always done his best to show his father James's irresponsible behavior, and enjoyed getting him punished or whacking the back of his bare legs with his riding crop, making him suffer. That was until that terrible day when James was only fourteen and confronted him nose to nose with his fist clenched ready to hit. Percy had never had a fight and was scared, so backed away. He vowed then that one day he would repay him.

"You can throw me out, but why would you do this to Nanny Jones?"

"Father's sentimentally cost too much. She hasn't had a job for years. With the war, we must be economical and make changes. Anyway, I never liked her."

Percy had wanted to say this for ages. He had never liked Nanny and always hated James. That Nanny doted on James drove him crazy. It also upset him that during the last few years, his father had grown to like his brother. Thank goodness James had returned after their father died and the will had been read. He coughed for ages but lingered on longer than most people, enraging Percy by saying, "I want to live to see James one more time."

Finally, the old man died, leaving Percy to inherit the title and estate, and hiring a new lawyer to handle the tenants.

James realized he would not change his brother's mind. Laws, not available to the common man, protected lords. Hopefully James's inheritance was safe, but with Percy, you could never be sure. Rather than wait until Monday, James departed the next day with Nanny Jones. A sad occasion. So much left unsaid. Leaving his home forever. Not knowing what the future held. But then he became angry. No one had the right to throw out loyal staff into a life of poverty, nor to gamble away generations of hard work that had created the estate. At least his father had left him an inheritance. He once hinted at a farm with a good yield. One way or the other he would be back.

The staff lined up to say goodbye, many in tears. For James, the staff were his family and losing them more painful than losing his home. Nanny Jones had only lived in two homes. Now, late in life, heading into the unknown with little money and no work or prospects was frightening. It scared the rest of the staff that James and Nanny were kicked out. They were both liked and a major part of the household family. There were few major changes in the big households, except births, marriages and deaths. If Percy could dismiss someone as important as Nanny Jones, how secure were their jobs?

James turned to the butler. "Montague, please have my things packed, and hold them here until I send for them."

"Of course, Master James. I don't know what to say. Your father would never have wanted this."

"Things will work out. I will be in touch."

Montague did not share the same confidence. "I hope so, Master James. We will miss both of you."

They piled Nanny Jones and their little luggage into the family carriage. James rode his horse. He booked rooms in the Master Builder Inn, a short walk from Buckler's Hard. Being Saturday, he would have wait until Monday to see the lawyer in Southampton to sort out his inheritance.

Montague would miss his regular card games with Nanny Jones. Although he guessed her age was in her late eighties, she refused to say. He was at least twenty years younger, but they were good friends and she was the one person he could confide in. A butler's life could be lonely.

James thought how quickly life changed. Last week a ship's captain, today homeless, no work, with no prospects and the awful shadow of the debtors' prison. Many poor gentry ended up not coping, having no practical qualifications.

To clear his head, he walked to Buckler's Hard to find his friend Tony, son of the shipwright. Instead of a vibrant shipyard, there were a couple of deserted and half-finished ships standing in between the shipbuilders' cottages. He found Tony at home, with his parents, his young wife and children around a small wood fire, watching a stew cook in a hanging pot. It embarrassed Tony. His father had always been employed. Now they were struggling to survive. With one meal a day, they were hungry.

Tony explained, "Our situation is terrible. The Navy stopped all shipbuilding. It left us shipwrights with all the timber, fastening and building materials we purchased for the Navy. The Navy refuses to pay until they can order the ships finished. You can see the river full of laid-up ships. The craftsmen's shops are empty. Many shipwrights left to find low paid work on farms, or went north to work in the new factories."

"I cannot believe it. What happened to England while I have been at sea? How could King George and the government abandon the people who built the ships that stopped Napoleon's invasion? I want to help, but the Navy laid me off and now I am homeless, so it will not be easy."

CHAPTER 18

James was desperate to see Edith, but first he needed to know his financial situation. On Monday, he rode to Southampton to meet his brother's lawyer. The law office occupied a three-story house on Bugle Street, a narrow road near the port. An expensive property for a local lawyer. It looked as though the upstairs provided the living quarters. James joined three strained looking people in the waiting room. He reflected that people seldom hired a lawyer unless they experienced problems, and then the exorbitant legal fees added to their stress. They could see through the glass window into the general office, six clerks busy writing behind tall desks, their quills scratching on the paper as they looked up to see visitors, but not so the senior clerk noticed, in case he reprimanded them for slacking. He took James's name, kept him waiting for over an hour, before inviting him into Sweeney's office.

"Good morning Mister Sweeney."

James stretched out a hand. The pudgy, bulbous nosed man in front of him, protected by his desk, made no effort to get out of his chair. He seemed reluctant to extend an arm, as though fearing losing his small weak hand.

"I understand you are my brother's lawyer and have information about my inheritance."

"I am lawyer to your brother, Lord Lancaster's estate. Your father willed you an income of seventy pounds a year from the estate, as long as it remains in the family."

"Seventy pounds? No farm? No house?"

"Seventy pounds. Not a penny more."

It shocked James. The estate received a substantial revenue from the tenants, plus profit from their own farms. Percy inherited the estate. James's inheritance was more than a midshipman's pay, but less than a first lieutenant. No house, nothing to offer Edith. Over the last few years, he had become close to his father, and they wrote often. He knew he would not have left him penniless.

"I would like to see the will."

"That is not possible. You should have attended the reading after the funeral."

"I was serving in the Navy. I will go to court."

"Try, but it will take years, and you will fail. I have practiced law in Southampton for a long time. I know how to make things work."

"You are a crook."

"Guard your tongue, young man, or you will regret it. Your father left this envelope for you."

James's anger built up. Family members are entitled to read the will. He thought of shaking the nasty little man. But that would cause more problems. He would get his own lawyer. Maybe the envelope would explain things.

Sweeney held up the envelope but did not pass it over. He had read the will at the estate with few witnesses, leaving out various items, including what Percy felt were over generous gifts to the staff and a farm and five hundred pounds a year promised to James. The envelope seemed unimportant, so Sweeney had listed it as belonging to James. Sweeney had become adept at taking legal short cuts, but having mentioned the envelope, it would have been dangerous not to have given it to James. Anyway, an inexperienced youth should not be a problem. Sweeney would soon learn about its contents. He held out the envelope and James saw the wax seal, in fact, three seals and they were intact.

Sweeney asked with a sly smile, while clutching the envelope in his chubby hand, "Shall I open it for you?"

As James's father had left him a sealed envelope, and with three seals instead of one, James did not want the lawyer knowing its contents.

"No, thank you."

James stretched out his hand for the envelope, but the lawyer drew back into his chair.

"I must insist on opening it. Lord Lancaster is entitled to know anything regarding the estate."

James leaned over the desk. Sweeney, frightened by the piercing eyes and scarred face, leaned back away from him and tilted his chair. James pushed his finger into his chest, and as the lawyer toppled back, removed the envelope from his hand.

"How dare…" Sweeney toppled back onto the floor, and because of his round shape, had trouble getting up.

"Good day, sir. I will send you my bank information for the inheritance income."

The clerk helped the struggling Sweeney to his feet. He shouted after James, "I'll get you arrested for assault."

James left. He had intended to go to the Dolphin Inn for a pleasant lunch. With the terrible financial news, he needed to get used to a poor lifestyle and start immediately. It was time to revisit the Swallow Inn where he had stayed the night before he first boarded *Defiance*. The landlord still wore his leather apron but no longer looked so big. James ordered the best lunch. Once secluded in a corner, he opened the envelope, wanting to preserve it and the seals. He pulled out the one sheet of paper. It was blank, except for an address.

Mr Forest.
Lawyer.
62 Inns Court, London.

A lawyer in London! Maybe his father had anticipated his problems. The lawyer could get the will.

The landlord interrupted his thoughts. "That will be two shillings"

"Does the name Lancaster mean anything to you."

"No, other than a lord near Beaulieu has that name."

James rose and looked down on the landlord.

"Yes, my father who paid for my room five years ago, and you stuck me in the dormitory. You can take the two shillings from the room price and keep the change."

"Who the hell do you—"

James took a step back. It was then that the landlord noticed James's fist clenched, his battle scars and the eager look in his eyes and he remembered the boy. But this was not a boy.

"It was a misunderstanding, your honor. Let's call it even."

Once again James had to delay seeing Edith. He reluctantly sent her a letter saying he had returned to find his father dead and his brother with all the estate. "I have to go to London, but will return in a week."

The journey to London took two long days. The roads were terrible, the coach small and full, and it swayed. James did not want to be crammed inside. He called up to the coachman,

"May I ride with you? I hate being cooped up."

"If you can use that pistol and sword, you will be welcome. Brazen highwaymen are now robbing coaches."

The stories about London, its size, the confusion, the dangers for strangers, were legend. James's imagination did not expect the reality. The coach dropped him at Whitehall. People pushed each other to get to him. They offered their services to find him a room, carry his bag, find him a companion, female or male, in fact, anything he wanted. He selected a dirty faced young boy with a wide smile, Jimmy, to guide him to the Inn of Courts.

Jimmy might have been twelve or fifteen, and looked undernourished and short. What he lacked in size, he made up for in personality. He looked James over. A gentleman from the country and not used to London. He had an air of confidence and authority and could look after himself. Shame that he wanted to carry his own bag. Jimmy charged extra for it. *He's scared I might steal it.*

"Your honor, that'll be a shilling. Six pennies now, and the balance on arrival."

If clients would not pay money up front, they would not pay at the end.

James dodged through the maze of pedestrians trying to keep up with Jimmy. He seemed to recognize half the people of London and called out to them. His hat and clothes, an assortment of pieces he had stolen, were as colorful as his quick-witted answers. James's height gave him a view over the heads of the people rushing and pushing in all directions. It helped him dodge the coaches whose drivers shouted at the pedestrians making no effort to avoid them, the handsome carriages with starving looking horses, and commercial carts that wound their way through the cobbled streets and chaos. That they ran no one over amazed James.

The smell of the people, and horse droppings and the dirt on the road made him hold a handkerchief to his nose. Now he understood why so many people used snuff to hide odors. An army of people made a living by collecting and selling horse manure. For a small fee, they cleared paths through the mess for gentry to cross the road.

He found the noise deafening. The iron rims on the wheels of the coaches rumbled and horses' hoofs clip-clopped on the stone cobbles. Coachmen shouted at the pedestrians. Street merchants advertised with their cries and songs. It all combined to make a searing racket. How could people live like this? James remembered standing on the quarterdeck of the pirate schooner as they crossed the Atlantic, enjoying the sunrise, wind, surge of the boat over and through the swell. Checking and adjusting the sail trim, and thinking that he wanted to spend his time at sea as a captain.

"'Ere you are governor, sixty-two Inns Court."

They were in a small square, much quieter, with neat white regency styled houses designed by John Nash, columns outside and steps leading up to the front door and brass plaques announcing the names of the lawyers and barrister inside. A couple of handsome carriages were waiting. Clerks hurried with bundles of papers. Barristers in wigs walked with that air of superiority they felt entitled to.

CHAPTER 19

James paid the boy the second half of what seemed an exorbitant fee for a twenty-minute walk. London lived up to its reputation of being expensive. *If a street runner's fee cost so much, how can I pay a lawyer to get to see the will?*

He pushed the door open into a small, quiet waiting area. A bell, attached to the top of the door, rang. White painted wooden panels covered the lower part of the walls. The upper parts had hanging paintings of ships, including, to his surprise, *Defiance* under full sail passing the Needles. He looked closer, and the artist had even included a midshipman on the quarterdeck.

A small, neatly dressed, thin-faced man, with twinkling eyes peering over his spectacles, entered from the back offices. His face broke into a broad grin.

"Master James, I would recognize you anywhere. You are the spitting image of your father, sorry, late father. We are so upset. What a tragedy. What a fantastic man. There is much to talk about. I am Richard Forest, your father's lawyer and agent. Did you arrive this morning? Do you need lunch, a hotel? But you will want information. There is so much to tell you."

James, lost for words, followed Mr Forest down corridors to a big paneled office. More paintings, an imposing desk and with French doors letting in the light and opening onto a walled courtyard garden.

"Your father's office, when he came to London. Before we start, let me ask you, who gave you our address? I had planned to seek you out soon. I read in the *Gazette* that you just returned from the Caribbean with a prize. What a shame the admiralty will not buy her. I am very pleased to see you."

James explained about meeting with his brother, and then his lawyer Mr Sweeney, about his small inheritance, and taking the envelope with just this address.

"Not good. I will explain all. You should not contest the will now as your father had much bigger plans for you. We have a lot to discuss. Your brother will not think of it, but Sweeney will have you followed. It will not take them long to describe a six-foot young man, and track you to Inns Court. We do not want that. Your father kept us private for excellent reasons."

Mr Forest opened the door to the corridor and called, "Albert."

The man, average height, dressed in dull clerk's attire hiding his powerful arms, wide shoulders and a very thick neck, was not a city wimp. He grinned on seeing James tugging at his forelock in respect. One could imagine him being able to disappear into an open square and be invisible in a crowd. The arms of a Cumberland wrestler, and the intelligence and cunning of a poacher, he did not belong in a normal lawyer's office. Not a person to upset.

"Albert, track down that young villain, Jimmy, who guided Master James here. He will hang out at Whitehall, waiting for coach passengers. Persuade him of the financial rewards for keeping us informed about any enquiries for Master James, or a six-foot young man who arrived on the Southampton coach today. Tell Jimmy to inform anyone who asks that the tall man went to Squire's Bank in Fleet Street. On the way, go to the White Hart Inn and tell them to deliver a grand lunch for two. Only the freshest oysters, game that has hung long enough to give it full flavor, and to wash it down, a good bottle or two of the best wine."

"But I cannot afford—"

"Don't worry about that, Master James. There is so much to talk about. It is a long story. Your father has left you the details in an envelope in the desk drawer."

As much as James wanted to read the message left by his father and hear the 'long story', he had to show restraint and patience. This little man, bubbling with enthusiasm, understood the ways of London. He seemed to have been fond of his father and had secrets about his father's life that James did not know. Why did his father support a separate office in London when they had the house in St James and the estate in Hampshire? What did Mr Forest act as 'agent' for? Why was the painting of *Defiance* so prominently displayed? Since his return from the sea, and learning about his father's death, he had only received polite condolences from friends, abuse from his half-brother, disrespect from Sweeney. Now this unknown lawyer called his father 'fantastic'.

"Perhaps you would like to take a seat while I cancel my other appointments?"

James checked the office, sat in the leather chair behind the desk and wondered how often his father had used it, enjoying the view of the garden, full of roses. On the office walls were landscape paintings of their estate, and unusually, with the farmers working. Portraits of his father's first wife, and James's mother. *Defiance* under full sail. The French frigate escaping past the fort with guns blazing and with the ships behind on fire. There were two paintings by Turner, a young painter with romantic views of boats and the sea, that James especially liked. They captured the energy and spirit of the sea more than the normal formal ship's paintings. It struck James that his father had created a small sanctuary of things important to him.

Over the next few hours, first in the office, then over lunch in the garden, and afterwards back at his father's desk, reading his letter, the story unfolded.

Since you're reading this letter I must be dead, having given in to my cough before you returned from the sea. Years ago, a prominent friend of mine got into gambling debts. His estate would have paid off the debts, but not the expanding interest payments the money lenders wanted. He came to me as a last resort. I had used Mr Forest, then a young lawyer, on a small transaction, and he impressed me. I asked him to check into the debt. We found things about the lender he did not want society to know and threatened him with a usury lawsuit. So he sold us the debt at his cost with only a small profit. Rather than admit to being involved, I told my friend that a private bank run by Mr Forest had agreed to help. In reality, we set up a business. Titled gentlemen, do not involve themselves in ordinary business, nor lend money. I always kept the bank hidden and never merged the business into our estate. Over the years, we made many loan transactions with modest interest rates. Most of the debtors repaid their loans and the goodwill I received for the introductions to the bank repaid me multiple times. My friend introduced more of his friends and by handpicking them we helped many gentlemen and widows. Sometimes by putting a manager into their affairs, or just by providing a bridging loan, as happened to your Captain Wilson. When still a lieutenant he bought a house for his new wife expecting to pay for it with prize money from the admiralty, that was delayed. Other times, when the client could not repay, the bank ended up with property, including a great vineyard and distillery in France. Alas, with the war, and Napoleon forcing the vineyards to sell wine and brandy to the Army, the wine prices in France are very poor. Even if it gets past Napoleon's trade blockade, we may not import wine or brandy into England without paying enormous taxes. Because of the shortage, the prices here are exorbitant. Once the war is over, there will be a flood of wine, so prices will reduce.

We also made investments in new industries such as steam and coal mining. For twenty-five years, I kept our family name separate from the bank and had planned to merge them a few years ago, but then I realized the gravity of your brother's gambling problems. At first, I tried to help him, but I found him so deep in debt that I doubt, once he inherits it, our estate can survive. It breaks my heart. Captain Wilson sent reports as to your substantial progress: 'His best officer prospect ever'. I hoped that you would return in time to protect the estate, by putting you in control while leaving Percy with the title. That has not happened.

I have also became concerned at Percy's choice of lawyer and if you would even receive Apple Blossom Hill Farm and five hundred pounds a year, that I left you. I therefore instructed Mr Forest to keep the bank secret for at least five years, or until such times as your brother cannot claim it. If you are interested, Mr Forest will teach you how to manage it. The cash, mostly in gold, will not be available to you until you are thirty, but you may make investments if Mr Forest agrees. If your brother finds out, he will take it all and gamble it away. Therefore, you must ensure he does not get wind of the situation. It would be disastrous for you and the bank. You must live off whatever inheritance the Hampshire estate is going to give you, and from your Navy salary. Trust Forest. Tell no one. Secrets always get out.

In closing, I should say how proud I am to learn you have passed the board to become a lieutenant and hope you get posted before the war ends. My biggest regret is not being able to stay alive until you returned.

178

Tears came to James's eyes.

"There is much to read and think about. May I stay a few days to absorb all this?"

"Your apartment is upstairs. It's best if you do not go out. Before you leave, we will teach you a few of the city crafts, so on any future trips, you are not followed. We will also get you a tailor, so your clothes blend in. Yours show you come from the shires. We do not want you to stand out, but look like a Londoner."

For two days, James read through the record of over one hundred and fifty transactions, some tiny, others quick bridging loans for a few weeks. Occasionally there were very large ones, and long-term investments in new technology. Most ended with mutual satisfaction. A few resulted in his father gaining property such as the vineyard in France, a haunted isolated estate on Dartmoor and a couple of townhouses in London. All, except the vineyard, provided modest income. According to records, the vineyard had a small fortune of wine and brandy, but due to the war, it had not been checked for a number of years. James started dreaming of finding a way past Napoleon's blockade and getting it to England.

It surprised James to learn that many people in high and influential positions, including members of parliament and the admiralty, had been helped by the bank. They would consider any favor asked for by the bank. An amazing opportunity. His luck continued. He had to sit, think, and learn from Mr Forest. Follow his father's way of doing things, keeping his name out of the transactions. The sad thing was that he could not even tell Edith's parents.

James realized the incredible power a debtor's note gave the holder, especially when they had no ethics. His father and Mr Forest had worked out how to buy the notes from predatory lenders at reduced prices. Most lenders preferred a percentage of the debt paid in cash rather than fight in debtor's court, often against influential people. Even worse, against a lord. They were exempt from debtors' prison, and could appeal to the House of Lords. The lords seldom found one of their own guilty.

The next afternoon, Albert turned up and whispered with Mr Forest. Albert nodded in agreement and slipped away.

"That young scoundrel Jimmy reported that there were two men asking about you. Jimmy protested he did not remember anyone matching your description. Then he remembered, but would not tell, dare not tell. He even allowed himself to be clipped around the ears, and protesting, accepted a shilling for informing them he escorted you to Squire's Bank. The lad then rushed here for his reward. Albert is going to watch the bank."

Jimmy, nursing his sore ear, wondered about James. He had brought him luck, having earned a shilling from him, three shillings from Albert, and a shilling from the men looking for James. Albert had just paid him another two shillings and told him to wait for another job. More than a good month's income.

Mr Sweeney hired two Southampton enforcers to track down James, former seamen whose scruples had long vanished. The hustlers at the Whitehall coach inn remembered and identified the boy who James picked to guide him. It did not take long for the boy to be persuaded to identify James's destination, Squire's Bank. They were finding London less difficult than they expected. They had yet to learn who they were dealing with. Albert watched them storm into the bank and stood close enough to the door to hear them demanding who James Lancaster had met with. The bank clerks protested that they had no record of a James Lancaster. This only made the enforcers more aggressive. They threatened the clerks who called the watch. The enforcers found themselves being manhandled to the lock-up. They were no match for the London Watch.

Albert let them cool off in the jail for an hour. A cramped basement jail cell full of London's worst criminals, with hard wooden benches, and a shared bucket, would humble the hardest man. Then Albert talked to the watch, vouching for the men, explaining the misunderstanding. Silver passed hands, and they released the enforcers. He took them to the Ship's Anchor, a small sailors' inn by the Thames, overlooking the Pool of London and the Medieval London Bridge, marking the end of the Thames navigation for big ships. Merchant ships were unloading and smaller sail barges were taking the tide current under London Bridge to carry goods further inland. A few beers later the enforcers felt more at home and Albert had learnt all he needed. Before long, they were singing and then fell asleep, drunk. Albert sent Jimmy to fetch Mr Forest and Master James.

"Master James, look at the men, so you recognize them if they turn up again. Landlord, turn these drunken strangers out into the back alley to sleep off their hangover."

They woke up later, but without their shoes, coats, or money. Jimmy's fortunes were growing, and he kept low and far away from Whitehall for a few days.

James decided that if the Navy did not want him, he would not sit idle doing nothing until his thirtieth birthday, when he inherited the bank.

"Mr Forest, do you think the bank would like to own a fishing boat? Well, a boat that looks like a fishing boat, which can also transport wine and spirits? One that is faster than an Excise cutter?"

James laid out the business case.

"With all boat building stopped, shipwrights unemployed, and with the shipyards full of material for unfinished Navy boats, we can have a new boat built at a reduced price. Just two trips with wine and brandy would pay for it. In between trips, we can fish. Many consider smuggling, or free trading, as most smugglers like to call it, a respectable trade. We English hate taxes. The taxes on tea caused the Boston Tea Party and loss of the American colonies. Most people feel the government has no right to impose them, especially the four hundred to six hundred percent they charged for importing wine and spirits."

For two days James impressed Mr Forest with his ideas and questions, demonstrating that like his father, he too thought like a businessman. This free trade project, came with the added value that James understood boats and had the skills to be the boat's captain.

"I would like to hire a crew, my coxswain, two key men from *Defiance* and one local lad from Beaulieu."

"Master James, say nothing I should not know. Napoleon stops wine and spirits leaving France, but there is nothing wrong with preparing for the day when it is possible. The bank will contract with another company to build and own the fishing boat. That company will pay you a tiny fee to manage the boat building, run the boat, and to hire the crew. No one will connect the company, the boat or you to the bank."

"While we are preparing the boat, I would like to charter a real fishing boat. I can use it to slip into France and visit the vineyard to verify they still have the wine and brandy. If it is there, I will find a way past Napoleon's coast guards and set up contacts with free traders to transport the goods from the English coast, inland to the customers. I noticed there are some wine merchants on our list of those people the bank helped. Perhaps we can contact them? Now, Mr Forest, I have ideas about my brother's debts for you to consider."

Mr Forest listened with growing amazement and a widening grin.

"Your father would have liked that idea. We will start tomorrow and keep you informed."

CHAPTER 20

While James was away at sea, Edith had spent a lot of the time learning the law. She acquired, from the newly formed first English law faculty at Oxford University, a law syllabus and studied using law books from her father's vast library. She found it fascinating. Every Tuesday she accompanied her father to the magistrates' court in Lyndhurst, much to her mother's displeasure.

"Edith, we have a difficult case today as the Buckler's Hard boat builder is being sued for non-payment of timber supplies, and I fear he may go bankrupt."

The court was unusually full, with local people supporting Alfred, a fourth generation ship builder, and his wife Isobel, parents of James's friend Tony. The timber merchants were suing for payment of wood delivered to build the Navy ships. Alfred had used some on the partially finished Navy boats standing forlorn at Buckler's Hard. That wood could not be returned. The merchants understood Alfred could not pay until the Navy ordered the boats to be finished, which eventually they would. But they used the delay to try and take possession of his valuable yard and slip.

Mr Finch and his colleagues, the merchant's barristers, all the way from London, presented the contracts to Lord Rowley. Alfred's local lawyer was clearly out of his depth. Every time he tried to raise a point Mr Finch objected on a point of law. The public in the court booed Mr Finch when he objected even before Alfred's lawyer finished his question. Lord Rowley was not amused. "Silence in court. Mr Finch you will pay the courtesy to Mr Davis, the defendant's lawyer, to let him ask his questions, before you object."

The public cheered.

"I said silence in court."

Even so it looked as though the merchants would win. But Edith, sitting by her father, noticed an attachment to the contract between Alfred and the Navy.

Edith whispered to her father, "Can we take an adjournment?"

Lord Rowley pretended not to hear. He busied himself with the papers for a couple of minutes, and then said, "Mr Finch, we will take an early lunch and reconvene in two hours."

Mr Finch, the London barrister, tall, confident, used to winning, wearing the latest fashion under his court gown and wig, called out, "My Lord, it is most unusual to have court in the afternoon. We have a coach waiting to take us back to London for important cases. This case is so simple. Can we not have a judgment?"

Up to that moment, Lord Rowley thought the merchant's case sound. He could not imagine what Edith wanted to talk about. But he did not like an overpaid lawyer from London thinking the prospects of a local man losing his yard and livelihood, and whose family had built ships for generations, was unimportant. He sat back and his normal permanent smile turned into an intense stare, making them wait.

"We do not want to inconvenience you. Especially as three important barristers have traveled so far for a simple, unimportant, case."

Edith tried not to look aghast. The barrister, his colleagues and merchant looked at each other with smug expressions. An amateur, part-time magistrate in a small town was no match for them, even a lord.

"Mr Finch, if this afternoon is inconvenient for such eminent barristers, we can adjourn, say, for a month or perhaps two?"

Mr Finch and his team, winced, not wanting to waste more time on this case. They would retire to the inn and enjoy a good lunch, to be paid for by their client. Clearly, they had the upper hand.

"We will be back in two hours, my Lord. We meant no disrespect."

Lord Rowley banged his gravel. "Court adjourned."

Then left without a glance at the barristers. Edith followed, clutching all the papers.

As they strode into the Inn, Lord Rowley called out to the landlord, "Mathew, we will lunch in my room. As quick as you can."

Once they were alone, Edith's father looked at her with an exasperated expression.

"Edith, you cannot be champion for all the local people. It is tragic. The Buckler's Hard boat builders are victims of the war, like so many."

"Daddy, I think the merchants made a mistake. They were worried that if Alfred went over budget he would have no money to pay them for the timber. So they asked the admiralty to pay them direct. Alfred agreed. The admiralty deducts the timber cost from the money they owe Alfred. According to the contract, payment is only due when ships are delivered. The admiralty has not canceled the order, just delayed the delivery. Therefore there is no breach of contract. There was a similar case in 1773. I read about in one of the books in your library. Between the Ropery and Portsmouth Shipyard. The Ropery delivered all the anchor cables, rigging, rope and cord for the ship. But the admiralty ordered changes to the ship, delaying delivery. The Ropery wanted payment. The Ropery, not trusting the builder, had a side agreement that the admiralty would pay them direct, once the ship was delivered. The court decided that the builder was not responsible."

"I have told your mother many times, one day your reading would help. Can you find that book?"

"I think so."

"Take our carriage. But be quick. I cannot delay too long. I will save you some lunch."

On her way out, Edith spotted Tony's mother, Isobel, in tears.

"Dry those tears. There is hope. Sit tight and say nothing."

Donald, the carriage driver and his son David, the backstepper/footman, were sleeping, not expecting to leave for at least two hours.

"Donald, my father needs a book from his library for today's case. He instructs that we are to go as fast as is safe, to get back here before lunch finishes."

Donald was never allowed to drive the horses at full speed, something he had always wanted to do.

"Hold on tight, my Lady"

The horses, on hearing the crack of the whip, took off. For once not restrained and heading home for food, they stretched their necks and ran. Edith did have to hang on, as did the David, the backstepper, standing at the back of the coach. The coach rocked, rolled and bumped at high speed and

185

was back at the mansion in record time. Edith rushed through the main hall to the library and mounted the step ladder to look for the book on the upper shelves. It was not where she expected it to be. It took time to find it, precious time as it would be difficult to get back before the two hour lunch break finished.

Donald cracked his whip again but the horses were not as enthusiastic. Even so, they made good speed until they found the lane blocked with sheep. Sheep on roads were a normal part of country life, and one accepted them and waited until the shepherd led them to a new pasture. But not today. Edith yelled for the backstepper.

"David, instruct the shepherd to move them into the next field, and quickly."

But David, had trouble pushing his way through the tightly packed herd blocking the narrow lane, while worrying about damaging his white silk stockings and blue breaches, so it took twenty minutes before the coach could pass.

Lord Rowley delayed as long as he could, but finally had to reconvene the court. He needed to slow down the proceedings. Had Edith not been able to find the book? Was her memory faulty?

"Gentlemen, perhaps you would be kind enough to remind me of the legal principles governing this simple case?"

Mr Finch rose, putting on a condescending air, as if talking to a student.

"My Lord, this is a simple matter of contract law. Our clients delivered the timber, and the purchaser has to pay. Under the King's Court ruling, 1798 Albany versus Bromhead..."

Lord Rowley let him talk on. He quoted numerous cases, many of which he reminded his Lordship that he had won, and was clearly showing-off that he could remember so much detail thinking himself the expert in contract law.

"So, my Lord, you can see that the defendant has to pay."

He sat down with a satisfied smile.

"Very impressive, Mr Finch."

Tony's mother was in tears at the back of the court. Mr Finch rose, his left hand holding the lawyer's gown, looking very much the senior scholar.

"It was pleasure to be able to brief your Lordship on the major cases that form contract precedent."

There was still no Edith.

"Tell me, Mr Finch, do you, or your colleagues, consider that the attachment to the contract requested by your client, and agreed to by both the admiralty and the defendant, has any bearing on the case?"

Mr Finch paused, turned a little red and whispered to his colleagues.

"How did this local magistrate spot it? I thought it was hidden in the back of the contact." He turned back to the court. "My Lord, under English law, the buyer cannot take refuge behind a backup guarantee to make payment. In London we deal with this type of contract all the time. I doubt that Lyndhurst has ever had such a case. There is no legal precedent to the contrary."

Now Lord Rowley was in legal trouble. He either backed down, or trusted his daughter. But he had one more escape route.

"Another question. Did you check that your client owns the timber in question?"

"I do not understand, my Lord. He sold it to the defendant."

"But where did your client get the timber from?"

"He is a woodcutter, and has a saw-pit to turn the trees into planks."

"And which forest did he cut the trees in?"

Mr Finch turned back to his client and then responded. "The local forest."

"You mean the king's, New Forest. Does your client have a copy of his license to cut the king's trees?"

Mr Finch conversed with is client again.

"My client has been cutting wood in the forest all his life, and mainly for the king's ships."

"Interesting. Since most of the king's foresters were press-ganged into the Navy there has been a lot of tree poaching. It appears that he may be one of them, and therefore may not own the wood he sold to the defendant, making it stolen property."

"My Lord, I am sure it is a misunderstanding we can clear up."

"You seem to have concluded that Lyndhurst, as it is not in London, needs legal advice. You bring a suit against an honest ship builder without first checking if your client owns the timber. And as you have reminded us many times today, English law and our constitution are founded on precedent. The King's Court's, in Portsmouth, decision of 1773, Ropery versus Portsmouth Shipyard, is the precedent. Therefore, the overriding law."

Mr Finch was dumbounded. How could a local magistrate know so much about contract law? He must be bluffing to protect a local merchant. He would not be able to produce a copy of the case. He doubted that it even existed, as he had never heard of it and did not have a copy in his own vast law library.

"My Lord, with the utmost respect, we will have to check my client's rights to fell wood, which we are confident can be resolved with the proper payment, and I have never heard of the 1773 case. That is over thirty years ago. Do you have a record of the ruling?"

Lord Rowley thought through his options. He could rule with the hope Edith was correct, but if she was not he would be retired from the bench. He could call for an adjournment. At that moment an out of breath and rather disheveled Edith entered from the door behind the bench and whispered, "Sheep blocked the road, but here is the book with a marker for the case."

Lord Rowley scanned it.

"Mr Finch, having given such a scholarly lecture, with the assumption we needed it, it is hard to believe you did not know about such an important precedent. Or perhaps, you failed to mention it to help your client?"

"Your Lordship, I must protest—"

"Protest all you want. The case is dismissed and defendant's legal costs are to be paid by the plaintiff. Of course, you can appeal our decision, if you want to waste more of your clients' money. But I expect we will see him here in court soon on account of his felling the king's trees. Court adjourned."

Lord Rowley left the court room with the barristers stunned, Their client shouting they had guaranteed he would win. Tony's mother and father were crying in joy. After the case Edith's legal reputation increased. As much as she insisted it was her father, the people at the courthouse knew differently.

CHAPTER 21

James kept a careful watch to see if anyone followed him as he boarded the coach in Whitehall to return to Southampton, and from there to Beaulieu. He paid for the lower cost outside seat, complained about the price, and behaved frugally during the journey, a lifestyle that he now was forced to adopt. The coachman was pleased for him to ride up front. Thank goodness the bitter winter cold had gone, but the thaw had flooded the roads. Mud and stones came up from the horses' hooves, spraying the heavy canvas blanket the coachman covered them both with. The narrow-rutted roads made the journey bumpy.

James enjoyed the English countryside. The rolling hills covered with woods. Small hedged fields with farmers ploughing with shire horses or oxen. Farmers weaving the new thorn growth into the hedges to strengthen them. Sheep, with lambs suckling, and cows grazed off the spring grass. Thatched farmhouses with orchards, vegetable gardens and chickens running around the farmyards, pecking at the ground. The occasional foxes darting across the road making the lead coach horses shy. Smoke rising from the chimneys of manor houses sitting on hills surveying their owners' estate. The distant church spires showed the route from one small village to the next. Every two hours, the coach stopped at an inn. The passengers downed refreshments while the hostlers took five to ten minutes to change the tired horses with fresh ones that were waiting, already in harness. One inn boasted the record of three minutes to change the horses.

James made a mental to-do list. First to see Edith. Then to find cheap accommodation for himself and Nanny Jones. To work with the Buckler's Hard boat builders get a boat designed and built. Rent a fishing boat to sneak into France and check if the vineyard still had a cellar full of wine and spirits. If so, to find out how to get it from the vineyard onto his boat without being caught. Then to cross the Channel without being stopped by the Excise boats. The hardest task would be to identify safe English landing spots, to find trustworthy customers and organize the goods to be transported to them. He needed to find out the Excise men's schedules. Paul, his coxswain from *Defiance*, had told him he lived outside Plymouth on a farm, ten miles on the road to Dartmoor. James would take a trip to find him and Roger and Alan, two of his best boat crew.

Nanny Jones received the brief note from James, sent from Southampton after his meeting with Sweeney, saying he would be back in a week or two. Then rumors started that James had fled, bankrupt. The Master Builder's landlord heard, and asked about James's whereabouts. Who was going to pay for their rooms and board? Nanny Jones used her savings to pay an advance, knowing James would never run away. She was proud to confirm her faith in him, and relieved when James returned. She informed him about the rumors he was bankrupt and how the landlord insisted on being paid. The rumors shocked James. He was poor, and had to project that, but not bankrupt. How did the rumors start? Humbled by Nanny Jones risking her savings for him, it bonded him to her even more.

"Nanny, I cannot thank you enough. We are going to be safe, but for the time being you must just trust me. Here is your money. For a while, we must look poor. We are going to supervise the building of a fishing boat. I hope you will act as my secretary and bookkeeper."

"James, my first job at the Lancaster estate was secretary to your grandmother. I would love to do that again."

The innkeeper at the Master Builder Inn complimented James for his mention in the *Navy Gazette*.

"Master James, it is a pleasure having you here. You being a hero and all that. How long do you intend to stay? Can you pay in advance for the rooms and board?"

The innkeeper's attitude, and his bullying of Nanny Jones, infuriated James, but he needed to appear poor so did not confront him. That would happen later. No one would get away with upsetting Nanny. He handed over an advance and the innkeeper's attitude change.

"How long will you be keeping the rooms?"

James needed to advertise his poverty. "I cannot afford your rates. We will move as soon as I find suitable cheaper accommodation."

Discovering that James really was poor, the innkeeper felt pleased that he secured the advance.

Percy's day did not start well. Creditors demanded payment and his debts were mounting. His luck at gambling had not improved. No one had bad luck forever, so it must change. On top of the bad luck, Sweeney reported James had snatched the sealed envelope his father had left for him with the will, before Sweeney could see the contents. Then James took the coach to London. Sweeney had him followed, discovering that he visited Squire's Bank. The bank refused to admit they knew James, but for sure, his father left money there for him.

"You're a fool to let him take the envelope without reading the message. I thought it was just a sentimental goodbye note from my father. But James has never been to London before, and as he rushed straight to a bank, and one we have no relationship with, there must be money there. I wonder if my father hid an inheritance for him. I want you to find out, and if there is money, it is mine and I want it."

"My Lord." Percy enjoyed being called 'my Lord'. "It will take time, and we will use the law to get it."

"Did you inform the tenants about the new rents, and that we need an advanced payment?"

"Yes, my Lord. They are not happy about it, and we may need to give one or two notice to leave, to frighten the rest."

Percy needed money. He also wanted to destroy James and get him out of the area where people liked him and might help, so Percy spread the rumor that James had become bankrupt. Percy's quickest way to raise money would be getting a wife with a good dowry. Their neighbor, Edith, met that criteria. She was already twenty-one and still unmarried. It should please her parents to receive a proposal, and from a lord. At the Sunday church service, he would approach her mother. Everyone said she wanted her daughter to have a lord as a husband. Edith was beautiful and full of confidence, and they also said that she was very independent and difficult to manage. But once wed, she would have to obey, and her dowry would be his.

James sent messages to Edith, via her maid, that he had returned from sea. Edith already heard that Percy had forced him to leave home. He had moved into the Master Builder and then disappeared. Then rumor claimed

191

he had run away, bankrupt. Edith did not believe it. His being so close, but unavailable, was unbearable. Why had he not visited before he left again? Did he still feel for her? She received the letters he wrote before and after the pirate schooner adventure, and the ones he wrote as he crossed the Atlantic, in which said he loved her. While reading the pirate story in the *Navy Gazette* with her father, her mother commented, "Edith, you are lucky that I stopped you from seeing James. He is poor as a church mouse, did not get promoted to lieutenant, and has no prospects. People say he is close to bankruptcy. If he visits us, you will not be available."

Edith was shattered, but she would find a way to see him. Edith and her father did not know that Percy authored the rumors. Everyone would know James was poor, but bankrupt was different. He would be a social outcast and forced to leave the area. Edith's father responded, "They mention him in the *Gazette* more than most captains, and he is a hero. He will find an opportunity somewhere."

"Hero, or foolhardy and lucky? There is not much difference between them."

It made Edith furious, but knowing the best reaction to be no reaction, she kept silent. She did not want her mother to guess she had managed to keep in touch with James.

Her father commented, "What I do not understand is why James's father made no provision for him, especially knowing Percy's reputation? He liked the boy."

CHAPTER 22

Sunday church involved more than a religious ceremony. It became a social gathering. People were expected to walk to church to show reverence. The tenant farmers and workers did. Major families came by carriage. Ladies arrived in competing hats and dresses. Attendance became an unspoken, mandatory event. If someone missed a service, people gossiped. If a tenant missed too many, they found difficulty renewing the lease. Landowners learnt that the fear of God helped discipline the tenants and workers.

Every Sunday the congregation contributed money to pay the church costs. In reality, the major families financed it and ran the church council. The bishop appointed the vicar, but the church council controlled the vicar's stipend and therefore decided who to appoint. Edith's father, the chairman, left the running of the council to his wife. Lady Rowley controlled it, with an iron fist.

On Sunday mornings, weather permitting, the vicar stood outside the church on the village green to welcome the full congregation. Gentry and the church council received most of his attention; the vicar lived in fear of being fired by them. The Normans, after they conquered England in 1066, built the original church with the typical Norman square tower, that still existed. After Cromwell's death in 1658, and the restoration of the monarchy with Charles II in 1660, they enlarged the church. Stained-glass windows now filled it with colored beams of light. A cemetery surrounded the church. Gravestones dated back centuries, but many were broken or covered in moss, making the names of the dead unreadable. The path from the wrought iron entry gate passed through the cemetery, a reminder to the congregation of mortality, and to be in good grace with God, and the Church, while living. After the Sunday service, during clement weather, people gathered on the grass between the graves. They exchanged pleasantries, complimented the vicar on his sermon, and caught up on gossip.

The noble families occupied their own pews in the church. Nothing formal, but everyone understood that Edith's family sat in the front right pews, and the Lancaster family in the third row on the left. The Sunday church service gave James his chance to see Edith. He got there early, keeping in the background, observing the families arrive.

Percy waited outside the church gate, greeting the leading families and being congratulated on inheriting his title. Percy's bodyguard lurked in the bushes. What, or who, scared Percy so much? It would have shocked James to learn Percy feared *him*. If Percy died without an heir, James would inherit the title and estate. Accidents happen. Percy did not want to give James the chance to make one.

Edith, and her father and mother, Lord and Lady Rowley arrived in an open carriage, with their driver in full livery. Percy rushed up to it, to offer Lady Rowley a hand as she alighted.

"Thank you, Lord Lancaster."

Percy felt excited. Lady Rowley liked him and would encourage his advances.

As Edith stepped down, Percy smiled and said good morning, but she seemed not to see him. James slipped into the church through the vestry and stood by Nanny Jones in the Lancaster pew. Edith followed her parents into the church and walked down the central aisle to their front pew. It surprised but pleased her to see the back of the tallest man in the congregation, with broad shoulders and blond-red hair, standing in the Lancaster pew. She willed him to turn around, but he did not. Percy followed a little behind Edith. Seeing his brother standing beside Nanny Jones, with that attitude of confidence, irritated him, as did James's new clothes. Modest, but the height of London fashion. *He must have purchased with my money from Squire's Bank. The affront of the man to bring Nanny Jones and use the family pew when they are no longer part of the family.*

James watched out of the corner of his eye as the congregation entered. As soon as Edith's parents passed the end of his pew, he turned to look at Edith. Her heart skipped a beat. During the two long years since seeing him he had grown into a real man. Tall, strong, confident and so very handsome. She smiled back and went happily to her pew. James glowed inside. The exchange of looks infuriated Percy. Once again, his brother was interfering

194

in his plans. How did he even recognize Edith? They had stopped playing together years ago, and James had been at sea for five years.

Lady Rowley turned around pretending to view the congregation. But what she really wanted to see was James. She had noticed the back of a tall younger man in the Lancaster pew and guessed it was him. He had grown so handsome, his mentions in action were exemplary, and the affections and openness of his letters to Edith made her realize how much she had missed in her life. James was so unlike his elder brother who was untrustworthy and who would make a terrible husband. She thought back to her youth and her feelings for the hunt master's son. Her mother noticed how she conspired to ride near him, and arranged for him to go to another hunt to learn his trade. Her arranged marriage to Lord Rowley had been successful, though she felt guilty that she had not responded to his affectionate advances as much as he wanted. Her mother never discussed love making, other than to say men were "vulgar beasts" and "to close her eyes and suffer, so she could have babies." She asked her mother what it was she had to suffer, and her answer was, "It will be obvious."

Lady Rowley did as she was told by her mother and Lord Rowley was disappointed. When she started to enjoy making love to her husband she was embarrassed to tell him, and so after Edith was born they did not try very often and were not successful. She turned to whisper to her husband, "Do not say a word to Edith, but I feel it is such a shame that James is so poor, as they would be a handsome couple. For her sake we must be strict and find her a good husband. Hopefully one as good as you."

It surprised Lord Rowley. His wife seldom paid him compliments, and he thought she disliked James. Even though Lord Rowley had been a rich young bachelor he had been very shy at the debutante's balls. He had secretly fallen with Elizabeth, despite the rumors about her interest in a huntsman. When his mother confirmed Elizabeth's parents would approve his proposal he was thrilled. He knew her reserved and sometimes aggressive posture started when they first married. She was scared of making love and she suffered it so they could have children. As a young wife with no household management training, she had been scared of the staff, so developed a cold and critical communication style. He felt that inside she really wanted to be cuddled, but never allowed herself to let go. Maybe it was too late, but he would keep trying to get her to relax.

The church service took forever. The vicar prepared the congregation for Easter, reminding them to be generous to the Church's needs. He wrapped it in a never-ending sermon. James thought back to Captain Wilson's short Sunday services on *Defiance*, except once a month, when by naval law, the entire crew had to listen to him reading the Articles of War that gave captains almost unlimited rights to impose barbaric punishments. Thank goodness Captain Wilson seldom used the cat. He always found a short section of the gospel that related to their life on the boat. Sunday afternoon, the ship reduced sail, and after lunch and rum, the seamen were free to rest, wash and repair their clothes, dance to the hornpipe, play dice, but not officially to gamble. Captain Wilson talked little. The vicar should learn from him.

Edith also felt the service lasted too long. She had looked back and across to James and instead found Percy staring. It unsettled her. She thought back to her first kiss with James and the feelings it created. She did not understand how such a beautiful emotion could be a sin. Thank goodness they were not Catholic. She would hate to confess her feelings to the priest. Why did her mother insist on her marrying into more money? What did it matter that James had no estate? She had a rich dowry, more than enough for both. She had no brother or first cousin, so later she would inherit her parents' estate.

Edith had looked back again, but did not catch James's eye. Instead, Percy smiled at her, interpreting her look to mean that he should make advances, along with the support of her mother.

Once the service had finished, protocol still allowed James to join the social gathering outside the church on the grass between the gravestones. He exchanged pleasantries and gossip with the other senior families. They had not seen him for years, so offered condolences for his father's death and congratulations on his Navy actions. Many heard of the rumors about James's dire financial situation, but said nothing about it, as they did not understand why. His brother had inherited a rich estate, so why did he not look after him? The younger people, especially the girls, wanted him to call. There were few local war heroes, and none as handsome and single. He received many invitations.

Edith and Percy listened to James's conversations. Edith was concerned at the attention James received from the other young ladies.

Percy grew angrier, as despite the financial rumors that he had spread, the top families still invited James to call.

While Edith waited for James to come and pay respects to her parents, she developed a plan to see him. James approached. Her mother was polite, but distant. Her father congratulated James on his exploits, surprising him by knowing so much about them. Then James greeted Edith. She quivered inside, pretending not to know him, trying to keep a serious face.

"Mister Lancaster, welcome home. Is it really five years since you left? I am told you are often mentioned in the *Gazette*. Congratulations."

"Thank you, Miss Rowley. Would it be convenient if I visited you, to catch up to date?"

Edith saw her parents listening.

"I am sorry, but this is a busy period when I help my father with the estate and on Tuesdays accompany him to the Lyndhurst Magistrates Court."

James understood the message.

"Perhaps when you are less busy. I am going to Plymouth this week so will get the coach in Lyndhurst."

Edith's face showed her disappointment. "Are you returning so soon to a ship?"

"No, the Navy has laid up a lot of the ships and there are no appointments, so I must find work. My inheritance is not what I had hoped for. Life is going to be difficult."

It relieved Edith to learn that James did not plan to go back to sea, and she would see him in Lyndhurst.

The exchange delighted Edith's mother. Her daughter had learnt well how to reject unwelcome advances. It surprised her father, as he knew about James's letters and Edith always rushed to check the *Gazette* every time it was delivered. Percy was very pleased. He interpreted Edith's rejection of James as his opportunity to request to visit.

As James left under the watchful eye of Edith's mother, Percy approached.

"Miss Edith, I wonder if I might call on you this week?"

Edith wondered at the impudence of the man. What gave him the impression she would welcome his advances? He was already forty with a terrible reputation, but manners required that she answer politely.

197

"Lord Lancaster, that would be nice, but unfortunately, it is not convenient."

The stock reply for 'no', and it shocked Percy. What had happened? He was now a lord, and local. She, unmarried at twenty-one, should be honored by his attention. Did James once again get in first? How much of his inheritance had his father transferred to James at the Squire's Bank? It belonged to him and he would get it, then put James in prison for fraud.

Nanny Jones watched the whole encounter. Edith's body language with James said yes, while her formal but gentle response, was no. With Percy, her body and verbal language were defiantly no. Percy had never shown interest in Edith before. In fact, in any gentle women. The London house staff gossiped that he had professional ladies call, and did not treat them well, many leaving in tears and with bruises. Was he looking for a trophy wife or a rich one? Perhaps both? In any event he was going to continue to be a problem for James.

First thing on Monday morning, James met with the naval architect and chief builders at Buckler's Hard, including Alfred, the father of his friend Tony.

"I want you to design and build a fishing boat, but not just an ordinary fishing boat."

Builders of big warships did not undertake such small projects. But they had no work and the yard full of unpaid materials. Any work was better than unemployment. They respected the Lancaster family and liked James, a naval hero who had played in the yard when a boy with their sons, but was now rumored to have financial problems.

"Master James, we might fit this project into our schedule, but who will pay for it?"

James looked around the empty shipyard and smiled to himself. "Will this advance get us started?"

He produced a draft from a Scottish bank for the deposit. An advance; the Navy never paid advances.

"However, there are two conditions. First absolute secrecy. Second, we need it finished in not less than four months, with a bonus if you can build it in three. Now, about the design, we want a hull shape based on the new

Republic of Genoa concept of a thinner and deeper keel, which is much faster than the traditional round hulls.

"By the way, we expect competitors will send people to spy on the design and work. Please keep them away from the boat. Your customer is the bank. I am simply their low paid local supervisor."

As James laid out more details about the boat the bank wanted, his knowledge, the design innovations and his enthusiasm excited the boat builders. They politely did not question why a fishing boat needed to be so fast, or the reason of the double hull. James had developed so far from being the young boy they chased away for climbing onto ships. He exhibited confidence, authority and businessman skills.

Nanny Jones also met with them.

"Master James wants the boat finished in no more than four months and I am going to help you do it in three. I want to see your schedule and will monitor it as we go. Also your list of vendors and materials, and I want to meet them all to check their ability to deliver, on time and their prices."

The ship builders were not used to being supervised, especially by a woman. Ship and boat building normally went at its own pace which was why so many boats were delivered late. At first they resisted but when they realized Nanny Jones was the key to their payments, they cooperated and actually appreciated her help. For Nanny it was like preparing for a banquet at the mansion. Everything had to be delivered on time. Boat building was not much different.

CHAPTER 23

Edith did more than just accompany her father to the magistrate's court. She watched the unfortunate locals, most unable to read and write. They did not understand how to manage the system, sometimes facing eviction from their farm or shop, or being sued over the sale of a sheep or cow. Even minor infractions such as trapping a rabbit on the lord's land, stealing fallen New Forest tree branches or being drunk and disorderly, could result in prison or deportation. Edith noted how frightened the men were, coming into the court, especially having to sit in the defendant's box with upright spikes around its edges and guarded by the bailiff. They were often too frightened to argue their case with the lawyers of the landowners, or the local watch. The magistrates, who were also landowners and friends with many of the litigants, sat high above them in their wigs. Sentences, or decisions given by the magistrates were not always impartial.

"Father. There is something wrong with the system. Often, we can tell the defendant is poorly represented and is really innocent. Also, the wives and children become victims of the husband's mistakes, and through no fault of their own, sometimes end up homeless, in the poorhouse, separated from their children. The men go to prison, but the wives also face years of trying to survive."

"Edith, we try to be fair. The law requires us to consider only the evidence given. We may not guess what they forgot to say."

Edith, having watched the proceedings for over five years, anticipated the arguments being used. When she felt the law did not give justice, she would discreetly give advice to the wives. It frequently helped the case. Word traveled around and now wives often sought her advice before the proceedings. Edith and her father had rooms in the inn by the court for them to refresh, and where Edith secretly met the wives. Women could not become lawyers, nor go to university. Society assumed that complex concepts, such as the law and science, were too difficult for women to understand. So Edith kept her activities secret. She smuggled a note to James to meet her in the room on Tuesday, before the court session.

James arrived early in Lyndhurst to book a seat on the coach to Plymouth. He ordered breakfast in the inn, keeping a low profile, not wanting Lord Rowley to see him or Sweeney's thugs to follow him.

For Edith, the trip in the carriage to Lyndhurst took forever. Her father tried to make conversation but gave up.

"You seem distracted today. Is there a problem?"

"No, Daddy."

"You have behaved strangely since Sunday. Did Lord Percy Lancaster upset you?

"No, Daddy, just thinking."

"Then perhaps James affected you? He is a real hero."

Edith kept quiet. Her father knew her too well. She dare not tell him she had been thinking about nothing other than James, and desperately hoped he would come to her room. She had not one thought about Percy.

"Tell me if you need to talk."

James saw Edith and her father arrive in their coach and enter the inn. He slipped out of sight and waited a few minutes. When everyone seemed distracted, he sprinted upstairs.

When Edith entered the inn she was disappointed not to see James. She went to her room, anxious. What if he did not come? She waited, checking herself in the mirror. Her heart leapt at the gentle tapping on the door. She opened it a little to check. It was James. Her legs felt like jelly and her tummy full of electricity. She let him in, locking the door. He took one look at her dancing eyes, drew her to him, and kissed her. She had thought of this moment, thinking they would only talk. She resisted the kiss, then melted into his arms and her lips locked with his. His hand slipped up her waist to cup her bodice and shocks of excitement ran through her. She wanted more, but had no time.

"James, I am ready to elope with you. Then they cannot stop us."

James's heart raced. The most wonderful offer any man could receive, but he must not accept it. If she married him, it would destroy her life, if the Excise caught him free trading. He would become a social outcast and probably go to jail.

"Edith, my love, trust me. There is nothing I want more. I have dreamed about it for two years. Please wait. What appears to be my chaos will change. You will learn I am now poor, and am becoming a fisherman to survive. Please let everyone, including your father, know you believe it. I need my brother and his lawyer to think they have destroyed me."

James's rejection devastated Edith. Eloping was the biggest gift she could offer James. Him becoming a fisherman would not get her mother to allow them to marry. Gentlemen did not take menial jobs. She tossed her long hair, pretending not to care. She really wanted him to take her to the stable and escape on his horse. After, Father would have to agree to their wedding, or face a family scandal. It made her angry.

"Forget I ever mentioned it. But what you are up to?"

"I will never forget you made such an offer. I would accept it in an instant. But my problems must not ruin your life."

The hallway floorboards creaked and someone's knuckles rapped on the door. They froze.

"Edith, I hope you're not having another of your meetings?"

Her father's voice had humor. Her unconventional legal activities made him proud. He heard voices. She must be with the wives of today's hearings.

James looked for somewhere to hide.

"Daddy, just a few minutes. I'll meet you downstairs"

"Don't be long."

James let out a sigh of relief and drew Edith into his arms for another kiss. He put his hand on her back, and pulled her body into his. Even though he had rejected her offer, she allowed herself to mold with him, her body tingled all over. No wonder her mother had kept the joys of kissing so secret.

"I must go. Please wait a few minutes before coming down. When will I see you again?"

"It may be a couple of weeks."

"Two weeks! James, we must fix this problem, and quickly."

Her tone was that of a person used to being in charge. She left.

James found himself both elated and sad. She loved him, but he had to wait until his plan worked. If it failed, he would not let her suffer because of him.

Just before he boarded the coach, the innkeeper took James aside.

"Master James, there is a man asking if you are taking the coach. He has booked a ride. A stranger, and judging by his appearance, ex-army and not a gentleman. I'm concerned he may be a highwayman. Shall I call the watch to find out?"

After five years of action under Captain Wilson, and training to fight with the ship's marine officer, James felt confident that no normal thug would best him. He had his cutlass, pistol, a knife in his sock and his fists. If the stranger had ill intent, he would wait to attack James when they were alone, which would not happen. It would make for an interesting journey.

"Mathew, thanks for the information. It is much appreciated, but I will manage."

New Forest had few local heroes. The innkeeper would not let a stranger molest James. He supervised the coach loading, holding his cudgel that he used on unruly customers.

CHAPTER 24

The journey seemed uneventful. Passengers exchanged names. A tall, weathered man with a battle scared face introduced himself.

"I am Sergeant Stratford. Retired from the Guards regiment."

James kept up light conversations, responding to questions about some of his adventures on *Defiance*, giving no importance to the sergeant.

Two days later, they arrived at the Plymouth coach inn. The sergeant had been frustrated that at the coach stops James never went off on his own, but he was confident that James did not suspect him. James spoke loudly while booking a room for four days, and paying in advance. He watched the sergeant order an ale and settle to monitor the stairs and front door.

"Innkeeper," James said again in a loud voice. "I'm tired, I'll be going to bed early and will sleep late."

"Yes, sir, but you'll be having supper first?"

Supper and the drinks made the inn's profit.

"Not tonight, but I will look forward to a handsome lunch tomorrow before my meeting at the admiralty."

So, thought the sergeant, young *Lancaster is trying to get back onto a ship.* Despite the bench being so uncomfortable, he determined to sit through the night and keep watch. He had been told what happened to Sweeny's men in London. That would not happen to him. Sweeney promised generous pay for reporting every one of James's moves, and for 'persuading' him to give information about Squire's Bank.

James locked the room door, placed a bench under the handle to make it difficult to break in, then left through the window onto the slate tiled roof. He crossed over the roof, jumped into the back alley, then went to the docks to book into Trevor's inn.

"Master James, good to see you again."

The Navy discouraged officers from becoming friends with the seamen. But James had befriended Paul, who told Trevor all about their adventures.

"Are you joining a new ship?"

"No such luck. Just here on a little business that needs your local knowledge."

Trevor poured a generous glass of spirit out of an anonymous bottle. "Best savor this. The Excise has dried up the supplies of Napoleon's wines and brandies."

James sipped the drink, recognizing it as the best Navy rum, and grinned.

"I won't ask how you still get Navy rum, now you are no longer a purser. I have missed good rum since being ashore. Tomorrow morning I will need a horse and directions to Coxswain Paul's home. On another matter, there is a Sergeant Stratford, ex Guards, staying at the coach inn. He has an unhealthy interest in my activities. Please do nothing before noon tomorrow, when he will discover I am no longer there, and will search for me. If he had bad luck, or was pick pocketed and parted from his cash, it would be appreciated. Now, how about one of your famous meals?"

So, thought Trevor, *Lucky Lancaster is living up to the reputation that Paul described.* The seamen of Plymouth looked after their own, and did not take kindly to disruptive strangers.

"The Guards' regiment often patrols the ships in port to stop the press-ganged sailors from escaping. They are not popular. Your Sergeant Stratford may regret his visit to a naval town."

James found Paul on the edge of Dartmoor digging up rocks to make a vegetable and fruit garden by his small thatched cottage set in two acres of land. He looked up and grinned.

"Avast there, Master James, sir. What are you doing here?"

"Finding out if you are enjoying being a farmer."

"This digging is back breaking work, not that I mind work. But I prefer being on the top yard in a gale, struggling to reef a topsail with the ship rolling and pitching, rather than trying to dig rocks out of moorland. Do you have a ship?"

"Not a full ship. It's a long story, Paul. If you own a cider vat, and put down your hoe, we can discuss it."

"There is one sure thing about Devon, with so many apples, every farm has its own cider vat."

Paul's farm worker's stone cottage comprised of two rooms,: a kitchen/family room and a bedroom, plus an attic for children, or for laying out the apples to preserve them. Paul, still a bachelor, kept the cottage spick and span, a product of his Navy training. James noticed, even though Paul did not read, he had copies of the *Navy Gazettes* mentioning their adventures.

James told Paul the basic plan so he could decide if he wanted to take part. "I must send a discreet message to Brittany in France. I am supervising building, and am captain of a fishing boat, to be ready in four months. I need a crew I can trust, and who can handle difficult situations. There will be risks, with handsome rewards if we are successful."

Paul knew that because of the war, they built few new fishing boats. A Naval officer did not make a good fishing captain. Difficult situations and Navy crews did not go with fishing. Lucky Lancaster had an adventure, and Paul would be part of it.

"You can count on me, sir. This farming can wait a bit. As far as getting messages to France, Trevor knows all the free traders, and can advise us and be trusted."

Late morning, Sergeant Stratford still waited for James at the inn, trying to keep awake.

"Innkeeper, the gentleman who booked last night said he wanted lunch. Do you think we should wake him?"

Trevor supplied spirits to most of the local inns and had passed the message to the coach innkeeper that the sergeant was up to no good.

"What's it to you? He told me let him rest."

Early that afternoon, the sergeant was falling asleep. He went outside for fresh air, looked up and saw an open window with roof access. He rushed inside and upstairs, banging on the door. No answer. He tried to break the door down, but it would not move. The innkeeper pushed the sergeant away.

"Hold up there, or you will pay for the damage."

"He's gone."

"So, why are you so interested? He paid for four nights, and the rest is his business. Now you leave. Out, and you best be careful. You never know what happens in naval towns."

The sergeant let out oaths. He hated being fooled. It made him furious. He would search every inn in the town, starting down by the port where sailors stayed. James would suffer for this. It did not take him long to get to Trevor's inn.

"I am looking for a tall red-haired midshipman named Lancaster?"

Trevor took his time. "What's in it for me?"

"Would a shilling help your memory?"

"Hmm... that would help."

Trevor paused, forcing the sergeant to hand over the coin.

"He came in yesterday, looking for a cheap room. I sent him down the wharf beyond the fish market, to the Happy Mackerel Inn."

The sergeant walked down the busy wharf where fishermen were gutting fish and throwing the entrails into the water. The wharf, covered in blood and fish-scales, smelt disgusting. He congratulated himself. *The lad might be big, but he is not as clever as he thinks he is. Gentry do not fight.* The sergeant would find him, and when they passed a lonely alley, 'invite' him into it, to reveal everything about the Squire's Bank account. The bonus Mr Sweeney promised for that information would keep him for a year.

Up ahead, a group of fishermen were arguing, and pushing each other. An Army sergeant did not alter his stride for a shoal of fishermen. He marched through them. Someone bumped into him. He tripped, stumbled and slipped on fish scales, then tumbled onto his rear and slid across the wharf. Unseen hands pushed him to fall feet first, twelve feet into the smelly harbor water full of fish entrails.

"Help!"

No one heard him. Not being able to swim, he sank. His hand found a line, which he grabbed. He hauled himself towards the dock wall coughing out the water he had swallowed. With exhausting effort, he pulled himself out of the water and up the stone steps. Laying on the quay drained of energy, wet and smelling of rotten fish, he put his hand into his pockets for his money. It was full of water but the money had gone, as had the fishermen. They had robbed him.

"God damn Lancaster. Wait till I get hold of him."

He needed money to get home, after which he would face a difficult meeting with Sweeney.

Trevor agreed to send James's letter to France.

"Several people must be paid to get secure letters into Napoleon's land. Once I have an answer, I will hold it for you, rather than forward it by coach. You can never be too careful. A letter from your Aunt Maria saying that she misses you will signal your need to return to Plymouth."

James returned to Buckler's Hard. Work had started on the boat, Nanny Jones had set up her office and James was impressed that everyone seemed to report to her. Tony and his family were again eating well.

A few days later Sweeney reported to Percy.

"My Lord, most of the tenants have agreed to pay the increased rents, with down payments instead of the usual end-of-harvest full payment. A few have been difficult but the eviction notices cured most of that. I will threaten the ones still resisting with the court. If they do not agree, they will be out by the end of the year."

"What did my brother do in Plymouth?"

Sweeney could not believe it. Percy did not even say thank you or well done, even though he had increased the estate's annual income. Percy fixated on his brother. Sweeney expected information from a Squire's Bank clerk he had bribed, but needed a little more time.

"We think he met with the admiralty, but our man experienced a minor accident and lost contact."

"Our man? You hired him, telling me he was the best. What happened this time?"

"He slipped on the fish entrails in the fish market and ended up in the harbor."

"When did you ever hear of anyone slipping into the harbor unaided? You'd better find competent people if you want to remain our estate lawyer."

How Sweeney hated the aristocrats who thought they could hire and fire at will. They always wanted him to sort out their financial mess and produce more money for their estates. But they never gave him credit or paid him well. This time, he intended to get his fair share.

"Your Lordship, it is becoming obvious that your brother has access to help. That costs money. Our job is to track down that money. Squire's Bank is our starting point."

"Our job? You said you could do it and so far you have failed. Bank clerks are not paid much so find one of the Squire's clerks and buy the information."

"It is already in progress."

CHAPTER 25

After returning from Plymouth, James focused on getting the 'fishing boat' built. He joined the shipwrights, learning about their craft, enjoying the work and the good company. With no other projects around, they attracted plenty of skilled labor, so the boat and mast progressed rapidly. Some were insecure about the latest Genoa underwater design that the bank wanted. They argued that the thinner keel section and external ballast on the bottom of the keel would create too much strain and reduced the cargo space in the hold.

Others were skeptical when James told them the French warships lasted much longer than the English ones. They only used bronze nails and bolts. Unlike the English, they did not mix them with iron fastenings. The iron seemed to eat away at the bronze. It was strange as it did not happen on land. James insisted they must not use iron fastenings in the fishing boat hull.

The small sail lofts that James and Nanny Jones rented were next to the boat building. Nanny did the housekeeping while acting as the boat project bookkeeper/secretary, much like her original job at the Lancaster estate so many years before, but this was more challenging and exciting. The Scottish bank required all the bills for the labor and materials. They kept her busy asking for details, living up to the Scottish reputation for being frugal. James did not write to Mr Forest. Instead, either he or Albert would pay a visit to the Master Builder inn for discreet discussions in a private room.

Before sending the letter to France, James thought long about how to approach the vineyard. Even though a peace treaty had been signed, Napoleon imposed travel restrictions and Harold's name was still associated with the stealing of the French frigate. For sure if caught he would disappear into to one of Napoleons labor camps. If he sent the vineyard a letter by courier announcing his intention to visit, the manager might warn the local French magistrate, especially if he was embezzling the wine and spirits. If he arrived unannounced with the manager away, James's dangerous trip would be for nothing.

He left all his father's papers safe in London, but he remembered the notes. His father had an uncanny knack of selecting honorable customers. He left glowing notes about the manager, the original vineyard owner. During the French Revolution, the gentry escaped or were imprisoned and beheaded, so in either case they did not pay their bills. That left the merchants, who supplied the aristocrats, in debt. The vineyard owner supplied the king and other top aristocrats, so was left deep in debt and needed to sell his vintage wine and brandy. But during the revolution, the government would have confiscated it, paying nothing. James's father purchased the vineyard, and under his guidance, Mr Forest had them hide and store the wine, increasing the stock each year. But they could not sell it at real prices until the war was over. The original owner received a job for life, with a bonus based on sales. James chanced it and Trevor arranged for a smuggler to deliver a letter. Now he must wait.

Sweeney sent people to spy on James, his lifestyle, and his work in the yard. The men were always spotted. Tony and the shipwrights allowed themselves to be plied with ales in the inn in exchange for confidential information. The reports sent back to Sweeney were that James could not make ends meet, and even did manual labor on the boat. The young gentleman had become a common worker. Sweeney especially wanted information about the boat's financing. Rumors credited a Scottish bank fronting for a company that owned a lot of ships. They were taking advantage of the low costs because of the Navy cutbacks, and testing a new boat design. Sweeney expected information from Scotland including the name of the shipping company. One of the boat builders became an informant for a substantial fee. The informer, Tony's father, rehearsed what to say with James.

Something still troubled Sweeney. What did James do at Squire's Bank? Sweeney bribed one of the bank clerks. He reported that unless James's account was handled by a partner, he did not own an account at the bank. So why, Sweeney asked himself, did James enter the bank? Why were his enforcers seduced and robbed? He sent them back to London to track down Jimmy. The other street kids said he had disappeared. Albert and Mr Forest had organized a job for Jimmy in a big London house as the coal and candle boy, after the housekeeper had scrubbed him clean, and continued to do so once a week. For the first time, he ate regular meals and slept in a warm bed. He often said, "The luckiest day in me life, seeing this tall country bumpkin get off the Portsmouth coach."

Sweeney also worried about James's visit to Plymouth. If he was just going to the admiralty, how did he identify Sergeant Stratford as a spy? Why slip away from him? Did he organize to dump him in the fish harbor and have him robbed? Sweeney did not pay Stratford, even for his coach fare. But he thought him to be a competent thug. It took a sharp mind to identify and then best him. James must not be underestimated.

But Sweeney's chief preoccupation focused on the Lancaster estate, Lord Percy and the unhappy tenant farmers. Sweeney found that tenants, who for generations had farmed their land, possessed rights. They may not be able to read and write but had a knowledge of their families' ancient rights acquired through generations. They also had the sympathy of the local people and magistrates. They resented an outside lawyer forcing more money out of them. The farmers had always dealt with their lord, not a lawyer. They did not like the intruder.

For the next few Tuesdays, James traveled to Lyndhurst to meet with Edith.

"Is it true you are working as a ship builder? When do you plan to talk to Daddy?"

"It is going to take a little time. I will soon be captain of a fishing boat."

"But a fishing captain earns even less than a tenant farmer!"

"That depends on the type of fish you catch. Trust me a little longer."

They spent little time together, but their kisses became stronger and she folded into his arms, pressing against him. She understood that there were limits, as did James. He did not want to compromise her. He felt his plan to earn enough to satisfy Edith's parents was excellent, but dangerous. Just as was stealing the French frigate. The rewards could be substantial, but failure meant prison and ruin. He could not propose to Edith until the danger was past.

Edith found it hard to believe that James wanted to be a fisherman. What did he mean by, *"That depends on the type of fish you catch"*? He was up to something.

She helped many local women in the court. One was the mother of James's friend Tony. "Mary, get a message to Isabel, wife of Alfred, the boat builder and mother of Tony. If she is in the area, late one afternoon, I would like to see her and invite her to tea."

Mary said nothing. But what was Edith up to? Working-class women were never invited to visit, let alone to tea.

Isabel would have walked to Land's End for a chance to thank Edith in person for saving them. The next day, she timidly approached the tall front door. Morgan, the butler, showing by his body language he did not want to be contaminated by her, escorted her into the small day office off the reception hall.

The size of the reception hall and the sweeping staircase intimidated Isabel. The simple elegance of the office and the beautiful flower paintings on the walls amazed her. She curtsied as she entered and saw Edith.

"Your Ladyship, it's such an honor to see you. Me and Alfred will be forever in your debt."

"It was my father who helped you by knowing the law. Please take a seat."

The chairs were thin and elegant, made by Chippendale, unlike the ones her Alfred made out of offcut timber. She sat on the seat edge, scared to break the chair.

"Would you like tea?"

Isabel had never tasted tea. It was the drink of the rich.

"How do you take it?"

"Er… the same way as you, my Lady. Begging your pardon, Your Ladyship. It leaked out of the court, and every villager knows you did it. They say you can read books, have read more than any lawyer, and that you have an amazing memory. There are many families who have received your help and are grateful."

It surprised, but pleased, Edith.

"Thank you, Isabel. But women may not be lawyers. It will cause my father trouble if it leaks out. So please keep it confidential."

"Yes, ma'am, but there's many who think its women who should be educated and leave the men to hunting, fishing and shooting."

"It may happen one day, but in the meantime I have a small favor to ask."

Isabel wondered how she could help such an exalted person. "Anything for Your Ladyship."

"I am sure you have heard of my… interest in James Lancaster."

"Ma'am, rumor has it…" Isabel hesitated a moment, choosing her words carefully. "That your ladyship's mother refuses to let you marry Sir James."

"That may be true. But he is not a sir."

Isabel became quite agitated. They had known him since he was a boy and they all felt proud for him. "There be some who are born with a title and others who are natural gentlemen and our James is one of them."

Edith was amused by Isabel's passion but it also made her proud of James. "Tell me what you know about the boat James is building and him being a fisherman."

Isabel did not want to be disloyal but what harm could there be in telling her ladyship. After all, women had to stick together and she and Alfred owed Lady Edith so much.

"The men keep everything secret but we overhear things. They say the boat is being built for a bank, though Sir James makes all the decisions. It is different and bigger than a normal fishing boat and will be faster than even the revenue cutters. The crew are ex-navy men, one they call the bulldog, plus our Tony. They have hired extra shipwrights to build it quickly so they can go to sea this summer."

So, thought Edith, a fast boat with a navy crew and James' famous coxswain. What was James really up to? "Thank you Isabel. I hope you will keep me informed and come to tea regularly."

CHAPTER 26

James needed the charts of the French coast, and the maps of Brittany. The admiralty kept a close control on them. Mr Forest's naval connections solved the problem.

While in Plymouth, James discussed with Trevor about his inn's need for wine and brandy. His sources had dried up and an alternative would be welcome. On top of that, he had a network of inns also wanting supplies. James secured his first customer.

They provisioned the rented fishing boat for a week's trip. While sailing out of Plymouth, James thought about Sir Francis Drake, admiral of Queen Elizabeth the First's small Navy, and a privateer. He was one of Queen Elizabeth's favorites and rumored to be her lover. Plymouth Hoe is the hill above the town, overlooking the harbor and the English Channel. In July 1588, while playing bowls, Sir Francis watched King Philip of Spain's immense fleet of ships, the Spanish Armada, sailing past and intending to invade England. Philip intended to convert the religion back to Catholic and punish Queen Elizabeth for refusing to marry him. The advisers urged Sir Francis to sail out and fight. He insisted on finishing his game. Later he sailed, winning the sea battle, with a lot help from a storm. People thought Sir Francis showed enormous confidence, waiting to finish his game. Sailors knew he could not sail out of the harbor until the tide current left the harbor or ebbed, so could not have departed. Today James had waited for the ebb current to carry them out into the Channel.

As they left the harbor, Paul began organizing the fishing nets.

"So, Captain, but I have never fished before. How do fishermen know where the fish are? How do these nets work? I heard that off Start Point, outside the Race, is an excellent location."

James wanted to get to sea before discussing the actual plan with the crew.

215

"Fortunatly captain Yvonne taught me. I think our best catch will be in France. Gather around. I need to talk to you. I am actually visiting Brittany, but will understand if you three do not want to join me. I need your word that what I tell you will remain secret, even if you do not want to be involved."

So now the truth would come out. Paul had wondered about the boat they were building, with its double hull, a cannon with an ingenious wedge and tackle, allowing it to be ready on deck in minutes. Who had ever heard of a fishing boat having a cannon? The new, thinner hull shape was radically different to the tried and proved round hulls they were used to. The sails were being made from the best marine canvas with narrow panels so they would keep their shape. It was nothing like a normal fishing boat. When asked, James said the owners wanted more power than normal so they could use bigger nets. No one knew who the actual owner was, and spies were constantly checking on Master James. It seemed strange that James did not mind the spies, nor being left so poor. In the daytime he worked with an adze to shape a ship's beams and ribs. In the evening, with the help of candles, he spent hours studying the detailed admiralty charts that mysteriously appeared.

Paul had watched James grow up from a shy fifteen-year-old boy into a twenty-one-year-old man with the maturity of an experienced captain. Thank goodness Captain Wilson had teamed them early on and that James had kept them together. Besides their first capture of the *schooner* there had been numerous boardings and the occasional capture of French boats. Then the taking of the *frigate* and later the pirate schooner. James had more action experience than even Nelson. Helping capture the French frigate was the most exciting thing Paul ever did. When the Navy laid him off, his modest share of the prize money allowed him to move onto the two acres of land left by his mother. But he still missed the sea. James offered him a job helping build and crew a new fishing boat. He received a basic wage and a share of the earnings from the catch. What more could a seaman want?

Paul wondered if the admiralty was paying for the venture. Or if James had become a foreign agent and the spies were from Whitehall. It must be a secret Navy thing, otherwise how could he have obtained the charts?

"I have agreed to help someone move some fine wines from France to England. The hardest part will be to get them out of France. Importing wine into England is technically illegal. As you know, wine and spirit smuggling avoids the taxes that the government should never have imposed. We know this as free trading. The English have never liked taxes. Even the American War of Independence started over the English tea tax. The tea ended up in the Boston Harbor. Smuggling is only considered a crime if you get caught and cannot afford to pay the bribes to escape prosecution."

Paul was suspicious of the smuggling story. He wondered what James was really up to.

"The admiralty is not hiring. With no paid work, a seaman must survive. We will get paid and well. I hope you will join me, and if you do, you must swear on what is most valuable to you, to secrecy. If we get caught, I will swear you know nothing and are just hired hands. Over and above your wages, you will each get five percent of the profit. That is after I deduct the French value of the wine, all boat costs, your wages, payments and bribes made to agents and petty officials in France and England. Do you want to join me?"

Paul asked, "May we have a few minutes to discuss it?"

Not that he really doubted, but he wanted the others to agree. Paul took Alan and Roger forward out of earshot of James.

"I remember that we thought the frigate adventure would be easy until we entered the harbor. This already seems to be a high risk and complicated venture. The weak link will be the minor officials."

Alan spoke up. "Minor officials all over the world are the same. Underpaid and they survive off bribes. I am sure James can manage them. The boat at Bucker's is built to hold many cases of wine. This is big, and our share might be enormous. Roger, what do you think?"

"Whatever Paul agrees, so will I."

Paul paused before talking. "The builders say the boat will be the fastest and most maneuverable on the south coast. It should escape the English Excise cutters and any of the smaller French patrol ships. But most important, we have been with Lucky Lancaster for five years and he has never failed us. Very few normal people like us ever get the chance to get rich. I am not going to miss it. What do you say?"

It was a unanimous yes.

"Good, but I want no complaints if things go wrong."

James watched them talking while steering the fishing boat with its long tiller. He looked back at Plymouth, disappearing into the background, and lit with long shadows by the late afternoon sun. How did Drake feel when chasing after the Armada, and with so few boats? Had he been as nervous as he now was, heading to France? Or as he had been when sailing Yvonne's fishing boat into the French port under the enormous guns? The admiralty reports all made the actions seem so easy, the outcome almost predetermined. If the Spanish Armada had sailed into the Solent, instead of trying to go to Flanders to collect an army, they would have landed at Southampton. Unstoppable by Queen Elizabeth's small army and Sir Francis Drake's ships. Sir Francis's smaller fleet, helped by a storm, destroyed the Spanish fleet.

When James went to capture the frigate on Yvonne's boat, he had been scared, and a bundle of nerves. Now he looked at the group at the bows, forcing a smile, pretending not to worry. What if he had misjudged his crew, especially Paul? With Paul twenty years older than him, and able to survive on his small farm, would he be willing to take the risk? He'd mentioned that he'd met a lass who might become his wife. After spending all his life at sea, and single, he dreamed of sharing a bed on a frosty night with a kind, warm person instead of being bent and cold in a hard-swinging hammock, dreading the next call for, "All hands on deck." Struggling out into the freezing wet night, climbing the mast while the ship pitched and rolled. If he had misjudged Paul he would have to cancel the trip to the vineyard and rethink the whole plan.

The crew elected Paul to give James the news.

"Master James, I mean, Captain, we are with you, and accept the terms"

"What?"

"We will sail with you and keep the mission secret."

Why did James have doubts? Paul spoke.

"I never did like the idea of fishing, hauling in the nets, cutting, filleting and salting fish. I even prefer going up the mast in a storm. But if we have to catch a few fish as a cover, we will cope."

James's face expressed his pleasure. He had three highly trained sailors and fighters.

"Paul, take the tiller. Course, south by south east and keep an eye out for sails. I will open a bottle of Navy rum to celebrate and we will swear an oath to our venture. With this wind, we have an eighteen to twenty hour sail to France, and I want to land tomorrow night."

Paul never doubted James. After the schooner adventure, he had determined to nail his sail to James's mast. The capture of the frigate and the exploits in the Caribbean confirmed it. Since returning from the sea, he seldom paid for his ale. People always wanted to hear about Lucky Lancaster's adventures. They kept Paul's glass full to keep him telling the stories, which he sometimes exaggerated. With his first look at the new vessel's plans, he knew it would not be an ordinary fishing boat.

Sweeney's spies lost track of James again. He did not take a coach to London or Plymouth. The London boys in Whitehall reported that no one had seen him. For two weeks, he disappeared. Even if James's father had left James an inheritance, Sweeney thought Lord Percy's obsession with it to be stupid. A young man like James would want a fun life and would spend. Then they would track down the payment sources and claim it. Managing Lord Percy's finance allowed Sweeney a lifestyle he had always wanted and felt he deserved. Thank goodness Percy did not understand accounting. Sweeney would not risk upsetting Percy and losing access to his money. So, in order to keep reporting on James, he made up stories.

CHAPTER 27

James and his crew arrived off the Brittany coast in the late afternoon the next day. He checked the charts to confirm their location and then kept out of sight of land until dusk, and darkness arrived. Paul stayed on the fishing boat and kept it a mile offshore. Roger used his muscles to row the tender towards the beach with Alan steering. James in the bows positioned himself to jump ashore, with his pistols loaded and ready.

They selected a small beach in a rocky cove within a twenty minute walk from the main road. Problems would begin at the main road. The damnable Napoleon created a superb bureaucracy and one needed permits for everything, especially travel near the coast where there were checkpoints at regular intervals. The vineyard manager arranged a travel permit for himself and his son of similar age and size to James. They would meet at three a.m. His son would swap places with James and spend two days on the fishing boat. The swap also ensured James's safety.

Roger stopped rowing close to the shore. They listened and looked towards the moonlit beach and sand dunes to see or hear anything suspicious. It seemed safe. The boat grounded on the sand with a grating noise. James jumped ashore, followed by Alan. Then Roger rowed the boat away from the beach, one hundred yards.

If the French were expecting him, James anticipated they would watch the beaches closer to the rendezvous point which was a couple of miles to their left. James had chosen a small beach hidden from the road by trees. He and Alan worked their way up and over the dunes and into the woods, planning to arrive two hours early than the appointment, checking for an ambush. At nearly every step a twig broke, creating a noise. James stopped often to listen for noises of other people.

Paul kept the fishing boat hove-to out at sea. He preferred action to waiting. He did not like James being ashore without him. But if they caught

James, Paul knew how to get the boat and crew back to England. Amazing how unconcerned James behaved when he, Paul, was always worried.

Roger waited close to the shore for Alan to return with a young Frenchman. James kept the information about the vineyard a secret.

As James and Alan exited the woods, one of Napoleon's signal towers, lit by the moon, with its articulated signaling arms, was in front of them. It impressed James. At night, the family operating the tower would sleep, but they probably owned dogs. James made a detour to avoid waking them. The towers were used to pass coded messages along the chain of towers back to Paris, keeping Napoleon advised of English activity. Messages arrived in a few hours, instead of the days that couriers took. Invented during the early days of the French Revolution, it was a breakthrough in communication technology. Napoleon built over five hundred, covering France. The English copied and improved the invention and the admiralty built the Murray shutter towers. They passed coded information from the major Channel ports to London.

James planned to approach the rendezvous from the landside so crossed the road, actually little more than a cart track. A French ambush would expect him to come from the sea. James and Alan crept forward through the bracken and raw countryside until they came close to the crossroads. Behind, the sea glimmered in the moon light. To their left and the other side of the road, closer to the sea, the signal tower stood quiet and still. There was absolute silence. Even the wind died down to a gentle flutter.

They sat in silence, waiting. James thought of his last meeting with Edith in her room at the inn a week ago. Her father had called her faster than normal, giving them little time together. She was insecure, not understanding James becoming a fisherman. He sent her a love note via Woodsman before he left for France. How he wished he could tell her his actual plans.

From their left, sounds of distant horses' hoofs galloping penetrated the still night. The vineyard manager was not due for an hour and unlikely to make so much noise. The sounds came closer and James and Alan flattened themselves behind gorse shrubs. Would they be caught? James prepared his pistol. The rider, a Hussar, did not slow, his big leather saddlebag flapping against the flank of the horse indicated he carried dispatches. Dogs from the signal tower barked. The sound of hooves faded into the distance. Satisfied with their work, the dogs returned to sleep. Then all became quiet again. James and Alan let out sighs of relief.

A horse drawn open carriage arrived with little noise and stopped at the crossroads. Two people sat on it waiting, silhouetted by the glistening sea and the moon. James waited five minutes to be sure they were alone and then stood up and walked towards them, hoping it was not an ambush. Alan remained hidden, giving him a chance to escape, if it was a trap. James spoke in French.

"Good morning, I would like to learn about vineyards."

"We are here to teach you."

The response to the password was correct.

"My sailor will take your son to the safety of our boat and we will return him here in two days."

James climbed onto the carriage and Alan guided the boy into the woods and to the beach.

"Welcome to France. I am Phillipe Valente and manager of the vineyard. There are lots of checkpoints these days. The soldiers are nervous. My son, Armand, kept his face in the dark and did not talk, so if we are stopped the soldiers will not realize that I have swapped passengers. Please wear his cloak and hat. And if soldiers stop us, please keep quiet."

James did not see his host very well in the dark, but liked his rich, deep, experienced voice.

"Driving at night draws attention. We will go inland, hide in a wood until daylight and then continue."

James admired Phillipe's ability to drive down the narrow lanes in the dark. The tree branches on both sides created the illusion of a tunnel as the horse trotted ahead. After ten minutes, he drove the carriage off the road deep into a wood and stopped. Silence. They waited a few minutes in silence and then Phillipe gave the horse food and water and offered James a blanket. Phillipe spoke in a low voice.

"You should rest and sleep. One of our best brandies will help. Napoleon commandeers all wine and spirits at low rates, so many vineyards and distilleries have not survived. Thanks to Mr Forest's English bank, we preserved a large percentage of our best wine and brandy. They should fetch a good price once this damn war is over. Try this."

James sipped at the offered flask. It was amazing. His father's excellent cellar, and schooling from Morgan the butler, had taught James to distinguish the good from the bad. This was better than excellent. He calculated the sale price.

"How many barrels do you have?"

"Of this quality, about one hundred. A lot more of a lower quality, plus, the wine."

James realized his father's genius. There was a real fortune stored at the vineyard. Once the brandy and wine were in England, he would be wealthy, very wealthy. He needed to be careful and not show excitement, and remember all the obstacles that were waiting to trip him up. He wrapped himself in the blanket. Sea training had taught him to snatch sleep. Having slept in tossing ships, it would be easy in a carriage, even with the horse scraping at the ground, and letting out wind.

Philippe's family had farmed the vineyard for generations, but the revolution and the debts left by their main customers, the gentry, put them in financial trouble. A friend directed Philippe to the bank and Mr Forest. He had no idea that Mr Forest worked for Lord Lancaster. It turned out to be a blessing. He stayed on as manager and having a share of the profits, once they could sell again. When hearing of the possibility of smuggling the wine and brandy to England, he became optimistic. But now the bank had sent a young man.

James woke with the low sun sparkling through the trees and with a covering of wet dew on the blanket and carriage. He looked at Phillipe, still fast asleep with his long, weathered face and big working hands. Evidence of a lifetime of farming. His large red nose showed he had sampled a lot of wine.

Phillipe's horse scrapped at the ground, wanting to move. The carriage looked functional, but not one that would draw attention to the owner. France's revolutionary leader Robespierre no longer ruled. He had joined his many victims under madam guillotine's blade, his 'Reign of Terror' stopped. Code Napoleon now provided protection for individuals from being arrested for no reason other than someone on a political committee not liking you. But in France, one still kept a low profile. Phillipe woke up with a start.

"Good morning James, I hope you slept well."

"Very well, thank you."

"Hmm, I expected an older man to represent the bank. We are dealing with a valuable asset and major difficulties if we hope to ship it to England."

Phillipe, a careful man, survived the Reign of Terror by avoiding confrontation. He provided just enough wine and brandy to the local revolutionary leaders to keep them happy, but not enough for them to think the cellars were full.

"Monsieur Phillipe, you know the bank well. They would not have sent me without having absolute confidence in my ability."

"That you speak French is an asset. Your understanding of brandy at such a young age is also encouraging. I have cheese for our breakfast with a short measure of brandy, which will set us up well for the morning."

The horse, eager to move, set off through the wood and out onto the narrow road. He pulled at the reins, wanting to go faster. Soon they were traveling at a fast trot through high hedged lanes and past farmland with vineyards planted on the upper hills.

James noted how different the French landscape and houses were to those in England. Many houses were built out of grey dressed stone or red brick with slate roof tiles. Thatched roofs covered most English farmhouses, which were wooden framed using old ship timbers, the walls, between the wooden frames, filled in with brick or mud, and painted white. The French buildings seemed more robust, but not as pretty.

Phillipe avoided the villages. They had been driving and talking for an hour when, rounding a corner, they found the path blocked by soldiers.

"Good morning, Sergeant, what are you looking for today?"

Phillipe handed over the papers and waited.

"Why are you so far from home?

"To find unsold wines in the vineyards. Most claim to have sold everything to the Army. It is a difficult time."

The sergeant looked at the papers, then at Phillipe and James.

"Young men should be in the Army. Get down."

James climbed down slowly, as though suffering from a bad back. Phillipe noticed the sergeant watching.

"This is what comes from working on the steep slopes carrying the grape baskets. My son asked to join the Army, but they wanted fit men."

"Bad back or not, he should be in our troop. Do you have his papers?"

James felt his luck had run out. To be caught on his first trip… Phillipe took charge, worried that James's French accent might give him away.

"I keep his papers because of his… impediment."

James heard 'impediment' and guessed this meant he was a little crazy. The ruse worked for him before. He remembered the stories about mad King George so wandered up to a tree and started talking to it with his head bent to one side, slobbering from the mouth, arguing with the tree. Telling it he should be in the Army. Why did they not let him join?

Phillipe touched his head with his finger, indicating to the sergeant that James was a little crazy.

"He'd be no use to you, but he is a good grape picker, and I cannot manage on my own."

The soldiers searched the carriage as James became more and more cross with the tree. They found nothing except cheese.

The sergeant smiled at Phillipe. "You must be a partial saint to look after a boy with such problems. You may leave."

James heard Philippe's voice calling, "Armand," and remembered it to be his name. He looked around cautiously, and reluctantly shuffled sideways, while looking back at the tree, then returned to the carriage, climbing up onto it. Philippe consoled him and said the man did not mean to upset him.

Once clear of the soldiers, James commented, "Wow, that was close!"

"What an amazing performance. Where did you learn to act?"

"I have only learnt to survive. Once before, I pretended to look crazy. It embarrasses people. Perhaps they realize how lucky they are to feel normal. So they leave you alone."

They left the main road and headed into the hills, and then turned into a hidden valley full of cultivated grape vines, all with fresh leaves. The house and winery were not visible from the road, escaping the casual attention of passing troops who often helped themselves to farm food and especially wine.

A worker opened heavy wooden gates set in a two meter high red brick wall leading to a large cobbled courtyard with a well in the middle and chickens pecking at the ground. To the left, green ivy covered the grey stone house with a red tiled roof. Stables and a barn filled the end. Opposite the house was the winery, a tall, imposing, functional looking building with iron grills and heavy oak shutters protecting the windows from light and thieves, and at the front end a pond with ducks and geese. Dogs ran up to greet Phillippe.

"This is much bigger than I expected. May we see the winery?"

"First you must freshen up. We will have a light lunch. After we shall inspect."

Phillipe's wife, Jeanne, a round cheerful lady, accompanied by five children, with ages ranging from twenty to twelve, greeted them at the door, eager to meet the rare visitor.

"This is Monsieur James, visiting us from Marseille."

Phillipe had previously discussed with his wife the reason for his visit, but they dared not let the children know in case they accidently mentioned something in the village. She curtsied, but James's age surprised her.

"I am pleased to meet you all," James said.

After introductions, James washed off the sea salt and road dust in a bucket of cold well water, then sat down to a lunch of cheese, dried meats, and red wine.

James tasted the wine. "This is very good."

Philippe protested. "An ordinary wine, but we will do better this evening. Now let's visit the winery."

They entered through solid oak doors which Philippe unlocked with two separate big iron keys. James immediately smelt the aroma of wine and spirits. Philippe took pride in describing the process.

"Grapes are tipped off the carts, slide down a chute into vats. First, we crush them with paddles and then by many feet. We have a fiddler to play music to encourage the feet to move fast. Unfortunately, as we stamp we occasionally tread on drowned rats that jump into the vats at night. The grape juice drains into tall oak barrels for the initial fermentation and from there into smaller oak barrels for the final aging."

They then climbed down steps into an arched underground cavern lit by shafts of lights coming through windows high above them.

"The grapes and the liquid travel by gravity from one stage to the next. There are three tall barrels, about eight feet in diameter, and about fifty finishing barrels. As soon as we have the wine, and before it is ready, they force us to sell it. This is why these barrels are empty."

James noticed some brass piping and examined it.

"We distill the poor wine into brandy and then it is barreled and aged."

James saw another cavern beyond the distillery, with about thirty barrels.

"Those too are empty."

"Monsieur, I expected to see a vast store of wine and brandy. What has happened?"

"Patience."

Phillipe closed and bolted the main door, then lit two lanterns.

"Here, take this."

Phillipe moved to the last of the tall barrels. He pulled at some rivets holding the strong iron hoops that kept the barrel staves in place. The front of the barrel opened, revealing a passageway into a dark cavern.

James waited for Phillipe to lead the way. He wanted to trust him, but caution told him to be careful and to avoid becoming trapped.

Phillipe lifted his lantern, entering into a vast cavern full of doubled stacked barrels that were lined up on either side, each marked with their year dates in chalk.

"You will sample both the wine and the brandy."

"Are all these full?"

"Yes, and aged to premium quality. We used to sell most of our wines to the palace at Versailles. It should get top prices from the English aristocrats, clubs and restaurants."

Phillipe tapped three barrels and poured first red wine then white wine, and finally the golden brandy into glasses.

James tasted. "Incredible."

"I am careful. I only keep domestic wine in the house."

James's head was spinning from estimating the fortune in front of him. His father had been a real genius. But how could they transport it to the coast, load the heavy barrels onto his boat and then unload them in England? He took his time counting the barrels, while looking and thinking. A plan began forming in his mind.

"Phillippe, it is impractical to move these barrels. They are too heavy and bulky to transport them to the coast."

"James, you are correct, and in any event you cannot load these barrels onto a boat, off a beach. A port will be difficult. Two years ago, the English stole a frigate and set on fire four other vessels at a port not far from here. You cannot imagine the consequences that English raid caused."

James now remembered how dangerous it was for him to be in France. The French would not forgive him, even after he left the Navy. Their spies read the *Gazette* and knew of his involvement in the raid.

"Can we transfer the wine and brandy into smaller kegs that can be lifted?"

"That is practical, but will take time and money."

"We can arrange the money and we have time as the boat is not ready yet."

Back in the house, they talked. James surprised Phillippe with his creativity. They had three months to get everything ready. Then two months during harvest time when the roads were full of carts carrying hay and produce, usable to transport the hidden kegs to the coast.

"At the same time it will also be harvest in England, with farm carts heading to London to feed the one million people who live there."

About six trips across the Channel in their new boat would transport the bulk of the wine and brandy. If all went well, it would make him rich, in addition to the bank inheritance. Then he would ask for Edith's hand.

When the war eventually finished, he would bring Edith to the vineyard, maybe during harvest time. He imagined her treading the grapes, with her dress hitched up, the red grape juice staining her legs, while she laughed with excitement and the fiddle played. James wanted her so much and it heightened his determination and willingness to take risks.

Then he remembered he could not admit to smuggling for fear of being prosecuted, nor declare this source of wealth, as the Excise would take it. A problem still to be solved. James told Phillippe that he would report back to Mr Forest at the bank and recommend the plan for shipping the wine, purchasing the kegs, renting carts and money to pay for it all. They agreed on a code system, using the letters from alternative pages from *Beauty and the Beast*, by Madame de Villeneuve, for their correspondence via unofficial couriers.

Dinner, modest by French standards according to Phillipe, comprised pâté, roast baby pig, venison and cheese.

Next morning James walked briskly to recover from the large dinner, touring the hills and the vines. In the afternoon, they headed to the coast, stopping in the woods at dusk. When it got dark, they met up with Alan and Phillipe's son at the crossroads.

Paul, with Alan, Roger and Armand, had kept the fishing boat just out of sight from the Brittany coast. They were the longest days of Paul's life. When James returned on board, relief swept over him, followed by disappointment on learning that the crates of bottles were samples for potential customers and not to be consumed.

CHAPTER 28

Sunrise revealed a red sky and dark streaky clouds, a northwest wind and the sea building into waves. It looked as though they would have a fast, but choppy, ride home.

To the right of their direct course were three French fishing boats, dragging their nets. The English and French fishermen enjoyed mutual respect. They shared a high risk profession and helped each other in emergencies. They also traded and conducted their minor and time-honored smuggling, ignoring the war. Their common enemies were the English and French Excise cutters which were constantly checking on fishing boats. The cutters were armed with short cannons and sometimes a bow chaser. Much faster than the average fishing boat.

James turned to Paul. "Let's bear-away and buy fish to take back with us."

As they got closer to the French boats, Paul said, "You'd best use your glass and inspect. I seem to recognize that boat. It may be Yvonne's. Who knows what she will think of us after we left her tied up when we stole the frigate."

James studied the boats. If it was Yvonne it could mean trouble. She would never forgive him for using her boat, tying her up and giving her a bleeding nose and a black eye.

"I think you are right. Let's see if Yvonne is on board. If she is, then she was not arrested for helping us steal the frigate. They would have guillotined her if they suspected she was involved. Hopefully they considered her a victim. Which means she recovered the gold we left. But we must be careful. She threatened revenge. Tony, you take the tiller. Paul, Alan and Roger, load our pistols and collect the cutlasses, but keep them out of sight."

The French fishermen watched the unknown English boat approaching them. While their nets were in the sea catching fish, they trawled slowly and could not maneuver. If an enemy boat approached it would take over an hour to haul in the nets. To defend themselves, they would have to cut their nets free, losing them, and costing them a fortune. It looked like an English fisherman wanting to buy the few bottles of brandy.

As they came close to Yvonne's fishing boat, James called out, "Hi, Yvonne, Captain, it is me, James, James Lancaster."

"James Lancaster? What the hell are you doing here? You have a nerve."

Yvonne had often thought about James, never expecting to see him again, but she wanted to. Now she had a problem. She had enjoyed having a younger lover, so she had replaced James with Léon who fished with her and Maurice and was obedient. He was not the same as James, but it worked, and she did not want him learning about their time together.

"I am a fisherman now."

Yvonne did not believe it. An English naval officer and son of an English lord, a fisherman? The man responsible for the raid on their port and stealing of the frigate? Her memory went from their lovemaking, to being bound, gagged in the dark hold of her boat. Then the slaps James gave her to get the black eye resulting in her nose bleeding over her blouse. She had vowed to get her revenge. After he left her she heard the explosions, cannon fire, shouts, orders, marching feet and thought she would be sent to hard-labor or madam la guillotine. It took two days to get rescued. The Army closed the port to everyone. No one thought about how the English entered the harbor. By the time they found her, she and Maurice were in desperate need of water, looked close to death, the blood from the nosebleed made it look as though they had been badly beaten, and they looked and smelt foul, regretting ever selling fish to the English. They expected the worst. Instead, were called heroes. The authorities wanted at least one person to praise in the debacle.

It took a few days for Yvonne to recover and collect the gold. After, all the cafés served her free wine, and she repeated the story of how they fought off the English until overpowered, and were beaten, tied, and left to die.

She and Maurice used the gold slowly so as not to show their sudden wealth. Yvonne paid off her debts, purchased a small house by the port, bought her mother some new dresses, and the boat a new fishing net that did not need repairing every time they used it.

"Yvonne, Captain, do you have any fish that we may buy?"

A fisherman buying fish? The men with James looked very familiar. Yes, the coxswain, Paul, who gave Maurice the black eye. Perhaps an English Navy boat in disguise? She would be careful. It had been three years since James had last kissed her and left her tied and gagged. Her initial anger and thoughts of revenge had slowly been submerged under her memories of their day and a half together and the gold. She was excited to see him again, but cautious.

"Yes."

"Captain, may I come on board?"

"You may, but alone and no weapons, and I want you to meet my new friend, Léon."

She would not let James steal her boat again.

James saw the younger man about his age, fit and tall, behind Yvonne and understood that this was her new lover. It relieved him as he could be faithful to Edith and not have to fight Yvonne away.

"It's good to see you, and that you have a friend. When I returned to England, Edith was waiting."

James wanted to establish that he was not available.

Yvonne was relieved they had cleared any potential romance out of the way, but also a little jealous.

"You have a nerve coming to see me. For a long time I thought of castrating you. But in reality, meeting you was the best thing in my life. Not just the day together, the best catch ever, the gold, and now the fishermen have elected me leader of our local fleet."

"Yvonne, I am relieved your news is so good. Mine isn't. I was laid off by the Navy, my father died and I have to work, so am starting a small free trading business. Would you like to help?"

Yvonne turned to Léon.

"Léon steer the boat while we discuss this at the bows. Maurice, please join us."

Maurice extended a hand to James.

"Maurice, it is good to see you, how have you been?"

"Also good to see you, despite the black eye and forty-eight hours of hell, we are well. The gold allowed me to buy a house close to Yvonne's in the harbor and has made me an eligible bachelor. We had a message from our brother in Spain that he still lives, but fighting the Spanish is the hardest ever. He is a co-inheritor of our boat so we have saved his share of the gold for him. Fishing is going well but Yvonne is bossier than ever. For the first six months after you left she spent all her time describing in detail how she planned to castrate you. Then she admitted she missed you. Her having hired a younger fisherman has helped a bit."

"Maurice, I am still your captain, so watch yourself."

"As I said, she is still bossy."

James explained his plans and the help needed on the French side to transport the goods and load them onto the boat.

A couple of hours later, with a deal struck, and James's wicker fish baskets were full of mackerel. They headed to the Needles, the rocks off the end of the Isle of White.

Paul asked, "Captain, why do you feel safe to trust Yvonne?"

"Because she would not dare turn us in to the authorities. She knows we can tell of her involvement with the frigate. She and the other fishermen will make more helping us than they do by fishing, and despite everything, she is a friend."

James was staring to like the life of a fisherman. An exhilarating sail across the Channel. The freedom, excitement of passing and saluting the patrolling British warships. Then he remembered they had not spent hours working heavy nets, taking the fish out of the net and filleting them with freezing and stinging hands where the saltwater enters into the cuts fishermen always get.

CHAPTER 29

Back at Rowley Hall, Edith spent a lot of time in her room dreaming of James. He had said he would be away for three weeks. Ten days had passed and they seemed like months to her, especially as she had received only one brief message from him, once again assuring her everything would be all right. Why did he pretend to be so confident? He did not make enough to survive and lived in a converted sail loft. Fishermen did not fish for three weeks. The fish would rot. What was he really doing? It seemed impossible for him to become wealthy in his own right. Even if he was working secretly for the Navy, his salary would be small. Why would he not accept his new status and elope with her? Eventually, her mother would forgive them. Their secret meetings, short but intense, caused Edith so much confusion. They evoked such strange new feelings and emotions. Her mother refused to discuss what being in love felt like, or how women really make babies.

"Edith, there is no need to know about such things until you marry. Then it will be obvious."

Since Edith had been a child, her mother taught her how to dress and undress, insisting that she was never to be naked and able to see herself in a mirror. But now she did. She liked her body, even without the corset that, when she wore it, tightened her waist to the point she nearly fainted. One day, laying on her bed, she imagined James looking at her naked body and caressing her. It shocked her but felt wonderful, arousing emotions that startled and shamed her. She did not dare do it again. A knock on her door interrupted her daydreams, and her mother burst in.

"Enough of mooning around. Get practical. There's more gossip about you providing legal advice to our local women. Also, I know that you have been in contact with that fisherman, James."

Edith cringed as her mother used the word fisherman, making him sound like the devil. How had her mother found out?

"We go to London the day after tomorrow."

Edith's hopes sank.

The fishing-boat made a fast sail back across the channel. They stopped at Lymington to sell the fish to authenticate their trip. Then on to Beaulieu, keeping the fishing boat at Buckler's Hard until they launched theirs. James had gained confidence that his crazy plan might work. He would soon see Edith.

For days Nanny Jones looked from her loft to the Beaulieu river, watching for James's return. He would not enter the river when the tide, with its strong current, was ebbing, running out, so she only had to watch while the tide flooded up the river. Relief spread through her on seeing his tall figure and wild hair visible from afar. What would happen to her if one day he did not return? She knew he had special plans for the boat, but would not discuss them with her.

While he'd been away, the work on the boat progressed. Nanny loved the accounting and writing to Scotland to a Mr MacAngus, a clerk she knew only by name, to report on progress and to ask for payment. She did not know that Sweeney bribed a courier to intercept and read her mail. He found nothing in it to help him. The correspondence seemed genuine, especially as the bank asked for justifications for all expenditures, and James's fees were ridiculously small.

CHAPTER 30

James saw Albert, Mr Forest's 'assistant', waiting in the shadows, as they stepped ashore at Buckler's Hard. It seemed a long time since they had first met at the encounter with Sweeney's men in London. Albert often turned up unannounced. James checked to see if Sweeney's thugs were watching. The boat's progress pleased him. He joined Albert under the wooden scaffolding that held the boat up. Tarpaulins, hanging off the scaffold, hid the underwater hull shape from prying eyes.

"Master James, good to see you looking so well. The boat seems to be nearly finished. Mr Forest asked me to report back to him the moment you returned safe from France, and to brief him on what happened."

"Albert, it was an excellent trip, better than expected."

With the excitement of the journey James had forgotten he worked for the bank. Before James left for France, Mr Forest had queried every step of the plan, making valuable suggestions and recommending caution, often insisting that James go into more detail. He reminded James of Captain Wilson in the way he dissected every action. James reflected on how much he had learnt since his first stumbling climb onto *Defiance* as a midshipman.

"You need to rest and wash up. I am staying at the Master Builder. Let's meet tomorrow morning for breakfast and go through the details so I can return."

James sprinted up to his loft, finding Nanny Jones waiting for him.

"James, I am so relieved to have you back. I always worry about you."

James hugged her. "No reason to worry, but we have reason to celebrate. Everyone one else can think we are celebrating selling our first catch to the fish market."

Nanny loved seeing James so happy. "When will you tell me what you are really doing?"

James grinned. "Why, Nanny Jones, I hope you are not suggesting that I am anything but an honest boat builder and fisherman?"

"You can fool others, but not me. But I can wait. For sure, one day I will learn. In the meantime, the new boat is nearly ready to launch. Oh, there is a perfumed letter for you."

James recognized the handwriting and opened it with excitement.

My Darling James, my love, my Sea Spirit.

Sea Spirit, she never called him that before.

Disaster! Mother has found out we are in contact. We leave for London tomorrow. Father is not happy and says Mother is going to select a husband or disinherit me. If you can live as a simple fisherman, I can live as your wife. However, my female instincts tell me you have plans other than fishing. Let me help. Are you taking gigantic risks? I am very practical. My parents have taught me to run the estate and I have an expert knowledge of the law. You say that you cannot ask for my hand until your circumstances have changed. Your brother is unlikely to increase your inheritance. From what we hear, he will soon not be able to. My father is fond of you, especially after all of your Navy success. He says the best you can hope for is that the Navy is recommissioned and they promote you to lieutenant. But that is not a living wage. I will make myself disagreeable to any suitor and keep myself free. What are you planning? I pray it will work. But even if you are poor I am yours to take. It will be difficult to write as Mother controls anything coming to the house in London. Love Edith.

All James's excitement vanished, leaving him with a cold sweat of anger. He felt like rushing to the family mansion, and confronting Percy to obtain the will. Percy's bodyguard did not concern him, but if he attacked Percy, that would play into his hand. If a lord accused a commoner of wrongdoing, every court in the country would support the lord. No, he must calm down and plan.

"Nanny, what is for supper? I am starving."

Nanny Jones was never taught to cook, but she had lived by the kitchen for years and watched. Now she enjoyed cooking, especially for James.

"All we can afford is rabbit but thanks to friends we have at the Lancaster mansion, we also have a pheasant."

Nanny could see that the letter had upset James. On one hand she was frustrated that James had refused to stop writing to Edith. It was bound to end in heartbreak, and she suffered for him. On the other she was proud that he still never wavered his love of his childhood playmate, despite all the obstacles.

Sweeney's spies reported that James arrived back at Buckler's Hard in a chartered fishing boat, having sold their catch at the Lymington market. The meager payment James received would not support Sweeney in his new lifestyle for even a few days. Still, something was wrong. A midshipman being hired by Scottish bank to manage building a fishing boat? His bribes to the clerk at Squire's Bank should soon deliver results. In the meantime, the report that James had returned, and was under observation, should satisfy Lord Percy.

The next morning, over breakfast at the Master Builder, James briefed Albert.

"There is a fortune of wine and brandy stored and hidden in the winery vaults. I have brought samples. To move it from the big barrels to England, it needs to be transferred into dozens of smaller kegs which we must buy. This summer we will rent space on the harvest farm carts to transfer the kegs to the coast. A fisherman I trust will provide the labor to carry the kegs from the road across the beach and into our boat. There are customers waiting near Plymouth with transport available. Now we need to manage the shipments to London."

"Mister Forest reminds you that we must not connect the bank to your escapades. However, it has many friends, and we've made enquiries. Two of the biggest wine merchants are waiting for samples. They expect to buy everything you can deliver. Once the wine is in England and stored, the transport to London is ready. It will travel in small shipments, so if any are found we do not lose everything. The bank has purchased, through other names, Ginn's Farm located just inside the Beaulieu River. The new tenant farmer is improving his barn and dock. You can offload and hide the kegs there, and then bring your boat upstream to Buckler's Hard."

"Mister Forest is an amazing man."

"Your father appreciated him, as will you."

"Albert, may I ask a personal favor?"

"Of course."

"There is a lady in London with whom I need to correspond, but her mother will prevent it."

"Master James, it will be my pleasure to give this small service."

"It will be a great service, if you can do it."

"If I can do it! No one in London is better able. Have no doubts."

James had no doubts. He left the meeting relieved.

Early next morning, Paul and the team found James at the boat early, with a list of things to do.

"I want the boat finished within four weeks."

They sensed his mood had changed. He was more business-like, and serious.

"By the way, we are calling the boat *Sea Spirit*. Paul, have the name painted in bold letters on her transom."

It took two weeks and true to his word, Albert delivered the first letter back from Edith.

My darling, I have much to tell you. But first, how did you find Albert? He appears and disappears, as if invisible. A man of amazing resources and a big fan of yours. It is wonderful you found a way for us to communicate. Though I must be so careful. Mother even intimidated my maid Mary into being one of her spies. Mother has a series of husband prospects calling at the house. I am very nice to them. She sits with us as we chat about the current social gossips, sipping tea. But then mother leaves us alone for the customary ten minutes, "So you can get to know each other." This is when I talk about my enthusiasm for politics, the law and women being allowed in universities, and the French woman politician, Olympe de Gouges who writes that true equality makes women equal to men. Few men seem to enjoy such conversations. So far none have returned.

A mental rock lifted off James's shoulders.

It took the full four weeks to get *Sea Spirit* finished, the mast up, the sails fitted, then the anchors, lines, blocks, shackles and fishing gear installed. A long-range bronze bow cannon arrived from the Scottish foundry. They unpacked it at night and lifted into the secret deck compartment with derricks. The foundry had been hard hit by the Navy cutbacks. Selling the cannon to a Scottish bank, with delivery to a London dock, helped.

Paul commented, "I have never seen a cannonade like this."

"It is a new design by the famous Scottish Carron foundry. This is one of the prototypes. It is much lighter and the tests confirm it fires further. Once the war starts again the Navy plans to order them to install on *HMS Victory*. We are lucky to have one, though I hope we will never have to use it."

As *Sea Spirit* slid down greased planks and launched into the Beaulieu River, James stood on the deck, holding onto the mast. He was overjoyed and let out a big hooray, as did all the builders and their families. New wooden ships take in water until the hull planks get wet and expand, tightening up the joints between the planks. James rushed below to find a little water in the bilge. They had built a sound boat.

Paul and the crew wanted *Sea Spirit* to be painted and varnished, Navy style. James told them it had to look practical for fishermen, nothing fancy. The builders wanted the traditional launching party, but James had asked them to wait. He did not want Sweeney turning up before they were ready to sail. The Scottish owners would organize a party after the test sails. But no one could stop the blessing by the local vicar. He left with his customary guinea. Then the builders insisted on the traditional sacrifice of alcohol to the four winds and Neptune, asking for safe passage. Nanny Jones asked to pour the rum onto the bow. The boat builders were adamant. No women on board at the launch. It brings bad luck. No arguing would change their minds. James heard Nanny's opinion of this in no uncertain terms.

CHAPTER 31

Sea Spirit took off for her maiden voyage, using the ebb tide and current down the Beaulieu River with Roger on the stern skull and Tony and Alan on the side oars. On reaching the last section of the river that runs parallel to the Solent, they raised the sails. *Sea Spirit* came alive. James felt the energy through the long curved tiller as she sped up. Sailing close to the wind, she was balanced. Just enough weather helm to keep her heading up into the wind. Out in the Solent, they passed the normal fishing boats and coastal traders.

"Paul, ease the sails and slow down, or people will talk. She is fast. Everything we hoped."

They took the tide current west out past the Needles. Once out of sight of other boats, they pressed on the speed. With the topmast and topsail raised, they soon were doing nine knots and pointing close to the wind. They stayed away for two days. The sail training James had with Yvonne helped him understand sailing on a smaller boats. They adjusted sails and made notes of minor items that needed improvements, or that were to be fixed when they returned to the shipyard.

James still only had modest cash, so he did not have to pretend to be poor. The Scottish bank sponsored a party. Even Mr Forest and Albert attended and inspected the boat. It impressed them, but Mr Forest declined a trip.

"I cannot swim and do not even take the Woolwich ferry across the Thames unless urgent."

Building the boat involved many trades and people. All had relatives. Over two hundred turned up. A couple of ex-Navy ship fiddlers provided the music. A New Forest deer, provided with the help of the king's gamekeeper, roasted on the spit and the Master Builder Inn provided the ale. The party gave *Sea Spirit*'s team one last night to relax before they started the actual mission.

James enjoyed the evening, but watching the young couples dancing the reels made him wish he could dance with Edith and show her the boat. Despite his planning, he had concerns about free trading. So many things could go wrong. If the French caught them, he faced execution. If caught by the English Excise, prison. The older men sat back and watched the dancing. They reminded him of his father. He would have enjoyed the gaiety of the celebration. The artisans who built *Sea Spirit* were as proud of their work as if they built had *Victory*, Nelson's flagship.

The next day, Sunday, James went to church. In Edith' family pew sat a couple of distant aunts, but no Edith. James slipped into his family pew, shocked to see his brother Percy looking so thin, his face drawn, eyes red and coughing into his handkerchief. Percy hated to admit to himself that James scared him. What if he found out about his real inheritance? What if James caused an accident, to kill him? He knew that James would do nothing in a church. Percy had his bodyguard waiting outside, also in case any of the creditors arrived. Sweeney assured Percy that they would soon penetrate Squire's Bank, get the money and put James in prison.

As always, the sermon went on forever. Afterwards, the other leading families greeted James warmly. He did not realize that his bronzed look, uncut hair, ever-widening shoulders, infectious smile, Navy heroics and indifference to his supposed poverty made him a topic of gossip and interest. Once again, he received invitations to visit. This time, he had a genuine excuse.

"I'm so sorry. I will be fishing for the next three months."

Back on *Sea Spirit*, it surprised Paul to learn, "We are off for week's fishing tomorrow."

"Fishing! I had hoped we could avoid that."

"We will sell the first catch in Lymington to help with our cover, then head out for our rendezvous with Yvonne and the vineyard manager, Philippe."

Fishing meant hard and wet work. With their bigger boat with more sail, they could trawl a bigger net and catch more fish than normal boats. Three days later, they had sold their first catch in Lymington and headed across the Channel.

They met with Philippe from the vineyard. He traveled with Yvonne on her boat, to the south of Lihou Island, just to the west of Guernsey Island, off the Cherbourg peninsular of France. An area full of rocks, powerful tides and currents, and avoided by most boats. The back of the island provided shelter from west winds and Atlantic waves, so they could anchor.

Yvonne inspected *Sea Spirit* carefully.

"This is a beautiful boat. When you have made me rich, I will have a similar one built so I can use bigger nets."

It took them the best part of a day to complete all the details of the operation. Phillipe had not waited for the plans to be finished.

"I started transferring the wine and brandy into kegs and secured the transport. You can ship in two weeks."

Yvonne grinned.

"We've found a small sheltered bay, hidden from roads or signal towers. To load, *Sea Spirit* must have two bow anchors and a stern one to hold her stern close to the shore. That way, we can carry the kegs onto the boat. If the sea is rough, we will use ropes to pull the tender with kegs from the shore to the boat. Then pull the empty tender back for a quick reload."

James liked his choice of helpers.

"We plan to store the kegs below the fish. The crates with bottles will go into double hull. We will take the first load to Yealm, just outside Plymouth. The rest will go to London, and the larger southern towns. In two weeks, there's no moonlight. It will make *Sea Spirit* hard to see from the land. The timing could not be better. We must return to England and confirm the transport in Plymouth."

Philippe took James aside.

"As you requested. I purchased the first batch of the jewelry previously belonging to guillotined aristocrats. They include samples of Marie Antoinette's necklaces and Louis's rings. The price is a fraction of the real value."

Many people wondered why the English did not rescue French royalty from the guillotine. Yes, there were generations of war and contested land between the two countries. The French financed the American War of Independence. But royalty claimed to be linked to God, and so, to each other. The worst royals were better than the revolutionaries 'Le Peuple', and their 'Reign of Terror'. Imagine what it was like for royals in the prisons. Sharing a bucket with no seat, no way to wash, no beds, just hard benches, and little food. Every day, they dragged some of them away, transported by cart through the streets of cheering crowds, to be taken to madam la guillotine. Now they had Bonaparte, both a genius and a tyrant.

"Will buyers think the jewelry is stolen?"

"No, many aristocrats sold it to their guards who got their signatures. It would amaze you to learn what the aristocrats paid the guards to empty the night chamber, or for a pillow and blanket."

James could buy, import and sell jewelry in England legally, and declare his profit. Then he could safely propose to Edith. Percy would not be able to say the profit came from his father's estate.

James unwrapped and looked at the jewels. He had no way of knowing if they were genuine but they looked beautiful.

"They are amazing. There is a contact in London interested and can confirm if they are genuine. If they are we can sell all you can buy at the right price."

While they were talking, Paul and the crew practiced hauling the cannon out of its hiding place from below the bow deck. A revolutionary new Scottish cannonade, it reduced the weight from earlier ones of three tons to under one ton and increased the range and accuracy. It still needed a carriage with wheels and enormous effort to pull it backwards up a slope onto the deck. They replaced the hatch and positioned the cannon on it to fire over the bows. Paul worried about maneuvering one ton of bronze in rough seas.

"We must set up a series of lines with blocks on the four corners of the gun carriage to keep it safe from breaking free."

They practiced until exhausted. It was different from the monotonous gun practice on a big ship. There you had officers marching up and down, the captain timing with a sand glass. They considered *Sea Spirit* their ship, the cannon, their potential lifesaver.

James examined their work.

"The first time a cannon fires is dangerous. If the casting has hidden faults, the cannon will explode, killing anyone nearby. Roger, row a barrel out to the front of the bay as a target. Alan, collect the powder."

They kept the powder in a waterproof box deep in the bilges. James calculated the powder and selected a cannon ball. Paul loaded the gun. James aimed it and lit a long fuse and they retreated to the stern of *Sea Spirit* as the fuse fizzed. With a mighty roar, the cannon recoiled back. It pulled at the retaining ropes, shaking *Sea Spirit*. Her timbers absorbed the shock. The cannon remained intact. The cannon ball hit the water, causing a splash beyond the barrel, and then bounced across the sea.

"That's impressive, and a longer range than I expected. It will out distance any Excise Revenue cutter or French patrol boat. Let's try again."

They reloaded, aimed, fired and the barrel shattered into pieces.

"Clean the gun and hide her. Each gun needs a name. Any suggestions?"

Paul spoke. "Defiance?"

"Good idea, Captain Wilson would approve."

Yvonne watched the gun practice.

"James, I see your naval training may come in useful. The sailing training on my boat has helped you. I hope my other training has proved useful." She gave James a seductive grin.

"The sailing training proved invaluable as did the fishing, and if our trading goes well I will be able to propose to Edith, and after I am sure we will benefit from your other lessons." It was James's turn to grin.

"I hope you never have to use your cannon but I am impressed with its accuracy. It is exciting that we are working together, and I hope it is as profitable as our last adventure. The fish prices are so low it is hard to make a living. But you still owe me for the black eye, and one day I will collect. The price will be my choice."

They hid ten cases each of wine and brandy, that Phillipe had brought, into the double hull, loaded Yvonne's fish into their hold, then sealed the arrangements over a meal of cheese, dried meats and wine from the vineyard.

CHAPTER 32

During the trip back to England, they fine-tuned *Sea Spirit*, adjusting sails, sheets and fairleads. Getting the best sail shape and minimum weather helm. Paul practiced taking the cannon out of its compartment, a process much harder on a rolling deck. They were all aware that losing control could cause broken bones or a damaged ship. A couple of English patrol frigates passed in the distance. James altered course to avoid them. Dawn showed them west of Rame Head. Beyond, they could see the distant cliffs and hills of Plymouth and just outside Plymouth Harbor, the entrance to the River Yealm. There, they intended to offload their first consignment. James wanted to check the river entrance and take bearings.

As they approached the Yealm estuary, an Excise cutter appeared from inside the river, rounding the headland and bearing down on them. James's first instincts were to run, testing *Sea Spirit*'s speed. Then he remembered the hold full of fish, and the bottles well hidden. Better to get inspected and assure the Excise that they were just fishing.

"Alan, get busy repairing the fishing nets. Paul, reduce speed, ease the main sail and make us look clumsy. Tony, get one bottle of unlabeled brandy. Leave it in the galley. Be careful in sealing up the hull. It will take the cutter a good ten minutes to reach us. They will have telescopes watching us. Move slowly and unconcerned. We're just tired fishermen. It is normal for them to be interested in our new boat."

James went below and hid all the charts and navigation equipment. He left out a false log of their theoretical fishing trip.

The cutter stopped them by coming head to wind right in their path. An officer, using a hailing trumpet, called out, "Heave-to and stand by for boarding and inspection."

The voice was strangely familiar. A small whaler left the cutter with six seamen, coxswain and officer. James compared them to when he and Paul had done similar boardings. The crew loading into the boat was clumsy, their oars not synchronized. James thought about what he would do if the French boarded *Sea Spirit*. He needed to develop contingency plans as, once on board, the French would arrest them.

The whaler came alongside. Rumor suggested that failed Navy crews manned the Excise boats. The clumsy officer struggling to climb on board confirmed it. He looked up.

Paul called to James

"Good god, its Midshipman Jeffries."

Jeffries, who had put on weight, struggled out of the whaler.

"Now Lieutenant Jeffries, of His Majesty's Coastguard."

James said, "Congratulations. So you left His Majesty's Royal Navy and *Defiance*, a frigate, for a better job in the Coastguard on a cutter! How can we help you?"

Jeffries squirmed inside. Already James had embarrassed him in front of his crew and made him nervous. It was supposed to be the other way.

"I am your senior and you will call me sir."

"Actually we are civilians, and have no need to call you anything, and etiquette requires you respect us. But why are you boarding our boat?"

"It is our job to know everything that happens along the coast. We have been wondering why a naval officer would resort to fishing and why you need such a big boat?"

"The answers are simple. Being laid off by the Navy left me no income. All I know is the sea. I do not want to be a clerk, a coastguard or end up in debtors' prison. The boat is big so it can trawl the new bigger nets for herring. A normal boat does not have the power to pull them. If the war ever finishes, the owner intends to conduct coastal trading."

Jeffries had hoped for this chance. He would finally repay James for all the times he had been humiliated, and at the same time get promotion for finding a smuggler.

"Open up the hold."

Roger and Alan pulled off the canvas cover and then the heavy boards that covered the opening in the deck to the fish hold. Jeffries expected to find contraband. His face fell with disappointment at seeing the volume of fish sloshing about.

"What are you hiding below the fish? Bring the probes."

The Excise seamen fetched long poles from their whaler and started feeling and tapping the hull below the fish. They worked from one end of the hold to the other.

"There is nothing there."

Jeffries looked disappointed.

"Let me see the cabin."

James let him go down by himself. He searched in the cupboards and lockers, checked the logbook and simple charts. He could find nothing. It infuriated him.

"You're free to sail on, but we will be watching for you."

"It was a pleasure to see you in such an exalted position."

Jeffries seethed inside but planned the revenge he had waited so long for, since the first knife incident.

After Jeffries and the Excise men left, James noticed that the bottle of brandy had vanished. Excise officers and the men were not paid much and expected a small present. So Jeffries had already sunk that low.

It took an hour to sail into the River Yealm and another hour for them to check out the Wembury Wood creek for future rendezvous, then half an hour to anchor off Newton Ferris. At dusk, they rowed ashore to the Swan Inn. Built on the coast, it had to withstand Channel gales, so they had made it of stone with a heavy slate roof, unlike the normal inland thatched farmhouses of Devon. The beams were low, forcing James to bend. The wood fire warmed them. Fishermen and beached Navy seamen filled the bar. Somehow, you could always recognize them. They looked different to the farmers. The Excise men who had inspected *Sea Spirit* with Jeffries occupied the corner.

Paul set up conversation with the seamen and then included the Excise men. His ability to get men talking impressed James. Paul soon discovered that Jeffries was disliked. When the Excise men learnt Paul had sailed with him on *Defiance* where Jeffries was considered an idiot, the Excise men bonded with him. They would become a useful information source. Strangely, Paul could never make conversation with women. He became tongue tied, even with the friendliest barmaid.

James moved to the saloon bar. Standing on the shelf among other bottles with its distinctive shape, was the brandy from *Sea Spirit*.

The innkeeper asked, "What will you have?"

"Do you have a good brandy?"

"It's hard to get brandy these days, but I have one of the best. The price is double."

"I will try one. We have been fishing for a week and have developed a good thirst. Tomorrow we head into Plymouth to unload. Hmm… This brandy is excellent. If we chanced on more bottles, is there a market for them?"

The innkeeper leant forward to talk in a low voice,

"We have to be careful. I am sure we can find customers for many bottles."

The opportunity to make his first sale excited James. It also gave him a chance to pay the crew their first bonus, making real the possibility of them earning good money for the first time in their lives. But the innkeeper had purchased the first bottle from Jeffries. What if the innkeeper reported him and set a trap?

James worked out a plan and said, "I have a friend who might have twenty-four bottles of this brandy. Would this interest you and what would you pay?"

"That's more bottles than I can use, but several inns will take some."

The negotiation ended at a good price.

"A friend will collect you at two a.m. He will have companions hidden. If the Excise come, or you do not have the correct money, there will be consequences."

James briefed Paul, who stayed behind to watch the innkeeper. At midnight, Paul left the inn, pretending to be a little drunk, satisfied that he had made good connections with the Excise crew, and that the innkeeper did not try to betray them.

James returned to *Sea Spirit*, collected the brandy bottles and his pistols, and returned with Roger. They found an old oak tree with massive roots under which they hid the bottles.

Paul joined them and confirmed he had seen no contact between the innkeeper and the Excise.

Roger went early and waited outside the inn to collect the innkeeper at two a.m., watching in case the Excise men set up a trap.

James and Paul also hid to watch for any sign that the innkeeper had informed on them. They heard footsteps and saw the outline of two men, one very tall, Roger, and a shorter, stockier man, the innkeeper. Paul gave the signal, two owl hoots, and Roger took the landlord to the tree. By the sound of the chink of glass, the bottles were being counted. Every noise carried through the night air. James worried that someone would hear and investigate. It seemed to take forever.

"If you ever have any more, please give me a chance to buy them. With excise taxes so high on French wines and spirits, one has to use every trick to survive. Alas, the occasional bottle the normal fishermen smuggles is nowhere near enough for a hard working innkeeper to make a reasonable living."

They waited until the innkeeper paid and left, and then joined Roger. He had informed Roger that to minimize risks, they could offload future shipments into a cave, in a cove just outside the headland. Most coastal villages were organized to aid smugglers. It was rumored that the Cornish miners had dug a tunnel in Penzance from the Benbow Inn to Abbey Slip. Many Cornish still considered themselves as a separate country and resented the English taxes.

CHAPTER 33

The trip back to Lymington with a west following wind was fast but rough. With big waves, no boats were out.

James opened the door to the Ship's Inn. The smell of tobacco, and noise of the packed bar full of fishermen wafted out. He looked for Mr Forest who was sitting at the back in a corner. The customers in the bar, on seeing James and the crew, became quiet. Then someone shouted out, "So you made it back. Did you catch any fish?"

The bar exploded in laughter at the improbability.

Another voice shouted, "They've had as much chance of catching fish in a gale as catching mermaids," causing more laughter.

James beamed and scanned the crowd. Mr Forest watched. Big John, the local bully, pushed his way up to James.

"Lords, or sons of lords, have no business fishing, especially with new bigger boats. Your catch will flood the market, lowering the prices."

"On the contrary, the bigger markets get better prices as more buyers will attend."

Paul tried to intervene. "Back off."

"Thanks Paul, but I'll handle it."

James stood tall, but Big John towered over him.

"You'd best find another inn."

Jenny, the buxom innkeeper's daughter, ran the inn. She flirted with all and sundry, carrying multiple flagons of ale, allowing sensuous views of her generous cleavage as she bent to place the ales on the tables. She kept the boisterous customers in check by threatening to throw them out.

"Come on, Big John. Leave Master James alone, him being local, and a war hero. Behave your yourself."

Her father, from behind the bar, called, "Jenny, let them sort it out."

He was concerned for her safety, knowing the local fishermen were jealous about the size of James's boat.

251

Even James looked small to her, standing toe to toe with Big John.

James said in a calm voice, "I have no quarrel with you. Like you, I'm born local. I have the same rights as you to earn a living."

There were murmurs of agreement.

"But if you want to contest it, come outside. We don't want to destroy the inn. After I've taught you manners, I want to sample the famous Ship's Inn ale and our landlady's cooking."

The inn reverberated with roars of approval.

Big John's eyes flickered. The calmness of James's voice confused him. No one ever faced his challenge. In fact, although he often challenged people, he never fought. They always backed away, frightened by his size. But a lord's son, even though tall, should be easy. He moved his right foot back, squaring off to take a swing with his right arm. John telegraphed his intention and James ducked as John's swing sailed across his head. It left John unbalanced and unguarded. James responded with a quick, hard left jab to the solar plexus. John doubled forward, trying to breathe and holding his stomach, leaving his face unprotected. James finished with a right uppercut to the jaw. John toppled forward and sprawled over a table, knocking over ale mugs and spilling the contents.

James helped him up. Hushed whispers floated around the silent bar.

"Come on, big feller. No hard feelings. We will soon remove your headache with a good pint."

A voice called out, "So what about the fish?"

James, rubbing his sore knuckles, raised his voice. "We were lucky. Despite the storm, we ran into a big shoal. The fish will sell in the market tomorrow."

The silence confirmed the surprise, and for the older fishermen, incredibility.

"We like to share our luck. Landlord, one round for all, on me."

There was a roar of approval and the bar continued with its normal rowdy noise. Jenny looked more closely at James, a man to be liked.

Paul came up to congratulate him. "That was handsomely done."

"Thank you, but I am sorry for Big John. Though I must admit, standing with him over me is intimidating."

James checked for watchers, stationed Paul as surveillance, collected Mr Forest and retired into a small private parlor with a roaring fire.

"That was impressive. I thought you were in trouble."

"I trained with five years of boxing and hand fighting under Captain Smith of the marines, on *Defiance*. Now about our trip. I have the wine and brandy samples. They are better than great. Our first delivery is in two weeks. The economy in France is bad, and gold decides. Since beheading the king and aristocrats, a lot of their valuables, sold by them before they met madame la guillotine, are coming onto the market at a good price. While the rest of England is suffering, our royalty and aristocrats still have money. I am sure they would enjoy the chance to purchase French royal jewelry at a bargain price. I have samples."

He realized their mugs were empty, opened the door and called, "Jenny, how do we get service?"

"Service? Why, Master James, now's that you mention it, a kiss goes part way along, plus the promise of a good tip."

In James's case, she would have accepted just a kiss. He would be an excellent catch. Even though as poor as a church mouse, he was the son of gentry, handsome, always joking, fun, and a gentleman. A war hero and a warrior, and the first person to subdue Big John. The local gentle ladies were no longer available to him. Jenny thought of herself as a splendid wife. Her grandfather, an excellent ale brewer, had purchased the Inn freehold from the church and now her father owned it, and would welcome master James as a son-in-law. She wondered how to get him on her own to start their family and move things forward.

"Jenny, we cannot afford your father's expensive meals! Something modest for my friend and I. A good local stew and to top it off, a ripe blue Stilton cheese and fresh bread. Once we've washed it down with wine, you will have both your kiss and a tip."

"I have no intention of serving such a modest meal. You will owe me that kiss."

James and Mr Forest discussed the jewelry, arrangements for selling off the brandy and wine, and the transport to London, where the prices were better, all while eating a tasty meal of local crab and Hampshire beef.

"Now, Master James, about your plan regarding your brother, it's taken positive turns, and there's room for cautious optimism. But I need you in London. You can stay two or three days and return in time for your first trip to collect the wine from France."

Jenny slipped into the room.

"Excuse me, Master James. There are two strangers, aging thugs, just arrived, sitting at the end of the bar. They've come in the last three nights. They just asked me if I know James Lancaster, and if he comes into the inn, they will tip me if I point him out."

James looked, and sized the men up.

"Say yes, but tell them to double the tip before you identify me."

James watched as Jenny haggled with the men and collected two coins. He summoned Paul into the parlor.

"Paul, what do you think of those two characters at the end of the bar?"

"They've seen better days. Judging by their girth and how much they have drunk, they are not fit enough to cause us problems."

James called Jenny over. "Give them a few free brandies, and add the cost to our bill. Now Paul, this is the plan…"

Mr Forest listened, fascinated and even more impressed with James.

Paul left. James wrapped up his conversation with Mr Forest, who booked a room and the first coach back next morning to London.

Jenny loved helping James. She imagined him staying until they closed the bar, getting her kiss, walking him out, more kissing leading to making love and starting their baby.

James called her to pay the bill, giving a generous tip. Her smile changed, as she realized James was leaving.

"Just a quick kiss today. I will make it up to you next time."

James gave her a gentle hug and kiss. The kiss lasted longer than it should have done. Jenny's father, watching from behind bar, did not appear pleased. Jenny melted and James left. She was in a daze, wondering why gentry kissed so much better than the local boys. She could manage rowdy customers, but not James's kiss. She wanted more.

Then the two men knocked her over, dashing after James. He walked alone and was silhouetted by the moon, heading towards the harbor. They followed, their boots crunching down the gravel. They knew it would be easy for them to take him for a 'forced' conversation.

Jenny was furious at being knocked over, and by thugs who had not paid their bill. She called to Big John and a couple of regular customers to follow her and chase the men down.

The thugs rushed after James, following the dark outline of the path. They tripped over something… a long tree branch, lifted up at either end by Roger and Alan They fell heavily on the gravel, scraping their hands. Paul's strong hands and arms lifted them, banging their heads together. They heard him say, "One needs to be careful sitting in an inn too long. It is harder to see in the dark. Accidents happen."

Paul dropped them on the gravel, leaving them in acute pain, their noses bleeding and broken. The latest of Sweeney's thugs learnt that Lucky Lancaster did not become a victim.

Jenny rushed out to find the thugs on the ground, groaning in pain, holding their shins and heads, blood pouring out of the noses. Her admiration for James tripled. How had he managed it? Where had he vanished to?

"You forgot to pay. It will be an extra shilling or we will call the watch. Make up your mind."

They wanted to get away, so paid.

"And don't come back."

She turned to her helpers.

"These kind gentlemen have just paid for your dinner and ale this evening."

Next time James came she would manage things better.

Mr Forest enjoyed the entire episode. His confidence in James grew. Reading his exploits in the *Gazette* was not as exciting as seeing him in action.

CHAPTER 34

Sea Spirit sailed up the Beaulieu River, helped by the tide and light wind. James piloted using willow wands sticking out of the water, marking hidden mud banks on the sides of the river. Cattle grazed in the fields. Birds and ducks flew and swam around them. Early unripe fruit on the trees in the orchards by the farmhouses forecasted summer. James remembered that as a child, he had loved being with the estate farm workers as they plowed behind the big Shire horses before seeding. The Shire horses were originally bred to carry knights in armor. James used to imagined himself one of King Arthur's Knights of the Round Table, riding the horses into battle. Ploughing season was one of the few times he spent with his father. He too enjoyed watching his shire horses gently, but with enormous strength, work their way up and down the fields, pulling the ploughs that turned the earth for seeding. Flocks of birds plucked the worms that emerged from the turned-up earth.

As they progressed up the river, James saw the grand mansions set on the distant hills. It reminded him of the picnics they had invited him to as a child. Now he was considered poor, working and a fisherman, those invitations would stop.

In the far distance beyond the trees were the chimneys of his father's, now Percy's home. Way off to the right stood Edith's bigger mansion. James had brought her a present from France, a couple of presents. But he could not give her anything expensive until there was no danger of being caught smuggling. He dared not let her know his fortunes were changing as one innocent slip of the tongue could get back to Percy.

The masts of the silent and deserted Navy ships at Buckler's Hard came into view. He expected Nanny Jones would be in her rocking chair, looking out of her window. Before they were ashore, she would have heated water for his hot bath and prepared a meal. He insisted she accept living in a small apartment near his. She insisted on looking after him. Knowing how much pleasure it gave her to feel useful and respected, he allowed it in moderation. One day, he would really look after her.

"Paul, take Roger and Alan and return the fishing boat to Plymouth. I have to leave for London. Tony stays on board *Sea Spirit* to guard. Leave before dawn and they will think I am with you. Get the first coach back. Then buy food for a ten day trip, and have everything ready to leave late next week. I should return in a week."

When James went ashore he found that Nanny Jones had indeed prepared a hot bath, in a large copper tub, 'rescued' from a captain's cabin from one of the laid-up ships. The tub stood in splendid ceremony in the middle of the empty loft. Large pails of boiling water were on the stove top. A bottle of red wine and a cheese platter sat on a small table next to the tub. Nanny Jones, no longer strong enough to carry full buckets of water from the well up to their lofts, hired a local girl, Ann, to help.

For James, the week had been full of long days and nights, firming up the plans for shipping the wine and brandy, enjoying the newness and performance of *Sea Spirit* and firing off the cannon. Also the reconnaissance at Yealm, encountering the Excise and selling brandy. Finally the confrontations in Lymington. He looked forward to relaxing in the hot water, shaving off a week's growth of beard, and thinking about Edith.

In the hot bathtub, ideas often came to him. As he stripped off, Ann giggled in excitement rather than embarrassment. Most working families lived in small cottages and shared bedrooms, with nudity normal. But this was a six-foot man, at least six inches taller than the average man, muscled, with broad shoulders, sandy-red curly hair and well hung. It reminded her of the stories told in church about Samson. She wished he would notice her.

James wanted to think undisturbed about Edith. He called out, "Ann, keep lots of water boiling and topping up the tub. Nanny Jones, what's for dinner?"

"Game pie, and a rich one, thanks to our friends up at the Lancaster estate. Also, the gamekeepers who were grateful for that bottle of wine you sent to them after your last trip. All is not well at the mansion. Bills and staff have not been paid and the tenant farmers have been forced to pay rent before the harvest."

While James was sorry for the staff, vendors and tenants, the news of Percy's problems did not disappoint him. He slipped into the hot water, and once ensconced, into his imagination.

James left on horse during the night, taking a packhorse with the samples of wine and brandy, and in his own pouch, the French royal jewelry. He traveled on the forest paths to Cadnam, north of Lyndhurst, there to pick up the London coach. Once on the outskirts of London, and to avoid Whitehall and Sweeny's spies, he got off the coach and hired a chaise to Swan Inn near Inns of Court. He left the wine and brandy samples to be collected by Albert. Making sure not to be followed, he went to his office. It felt strange to think of it as his office.

"Mister Forest, I have left samples of the wine and brandy at the Swan Inn, and have the first of the French jewelry for you to see."

Forest sent Albert to collect the wine and distribute the samples to the wine merchants. Then took his time to examine the jewels, squinting through his spectacles.

"These are beautiful. I am not knowledgeable but the court jewelers tell me that if we can confirm that they come from the royals, they are collector's items. With the bill of sale, however unorthodox, they are worth more than stolen ones rumored to be on the market. We have a close contact in the court to Her Majesty Queen Charlotte, and to her jewelers. As you know, the royalty do not pay quickly. Her Majesty's jeweler had to seek bridging loans from our bank. He will be pleased to assist us. I am sure there are several ladies who would like to boast they are wearing Marie Antoinette's jewels. If we can sell at least one piece to the palace, many nobles will want them. The price is so good I recommend we buy all you can."

"All?" It surprised James. "That is an enormous investment."

"When you do something, do it right, or not at all. Even if we cannot sell them immediately, the value will go up."

James loved working in his father's office and living in the apartment upstairs with meals provided by the inn.

"Master James, your father hoped you would take an interest in expanding the bank business. So do I, and that you will get involved and discuss the decisions with me until you inherit on your thirtieth birthday."

James spent two days studying the current opportunities the bank had. Forest explained how they weeded out the weak ones.

"We want good people who make the initial investment, and are involved with businesses that have growth potential. We are especially interested in modern technology, such as the new weaving machines, modern printing presses, steam engines able to lift coal up from mines way below the surface, tapping into thick coal seams that before were too deep to mine."

Word came that the wine merchants would buy all the wine and brandy. The merchants faced no legal problems. Excise did not mark imported bottles. Once a bottle reached London, they had no way to prove tax had not been paid.

James hoped that during his visit he could get to see Edith. Albert said that it would be difficult. Edith never left the house without her mother.

Forest interrupted. "I think we could arrange for Edith to receive an invitation to a salon hosted by Missis Bell, Queen Charlotte's dress designer. Invitations are considered an honor and Lady Rowley could not refuse her daughter attending."

"Forest, you are amazing. Is there anyone you cannot get to?"

The invitation surprised Edith's mother. She interpreted it as a signal that Edith had the queen's approval, leading to them receiving more social invitations and better marriage prospects for Edith.

"Of course, you must go."

The guests, friends of the queen, were surprised to see a new younger woman. Missus Bell explained Edith was the daughter of Lord Rowley, related through a friend, and visiting London. Edith ignored the scrutiny and enjoyed chatting and bubbling with her normal enthusiasm. She received invitations to call on some of the ladies.

During the reception, Missus. Bell asked Edith to take a private moment with her. Edith entered the room and recognized the shoulders and back of James's head. Her heart jumped. It was impossible.

"James, what are you doing here?"

He turned and grinned, "I am here to see you. We only have a few minutes. I needed to let you know that my plans are coming together. Christmas is the real target."

She fell into his arms. "James, you are full of optimism, but is it based on reality? Truthfully I am worried."

"It is going to be all right."

"I want to trust you, but it is so difficult."

He kissed her again, and she gave up logic and just accepted.

"Why are you are in London, and here? You said you are a fisherman."

"I am a fisherman, and my major catch will be you."

"I don't understand."

"You will soon enough."

"James, my father has to return to the estate, and thank goodness, insists that we go with him. It is an excuse. He does not like my mother spending so much to find me a husband."

They held each other, kissed with passion, until interrupted by a discreet cough and knock at the door. James pulled back.

"I must go, love you, will see you soon. Keep faith and free until Christmas."

He slipped away though a side door, leaving a very flustered Edith being steered back to the main reception.

Sweeney heard, or partially heard, what had happened in Lymington to his latest watchers. He was furious. "You were told to sit in the inn and wait until he came. Then report on what he did, who he met with. Only then were you to get him on his own, rough him up to get the information about Squire's Bank. How could he have known you were watching him? How could you trip over, letting him disappear into the night?"

The men did not admit that they were drinking, or that they were drunk when James left the inn. Neither did they mention that they had their heads knocked together.

"Get out and don't come back."

In a way, Sweeney admired James. It must have been he who arranged for his watchers to be tripped. His youthful looks hid his cunning. A worthy opponent. Sweeny would raise the level of the game. He had too much to lose to let James continue.

CHAPTER 35

Back at Buckler's Hard, James found the crew and *Sea Spirit* ready. The time had come. Even though the clouds showed signs of winds, they set off on what they described as a fishing trip.

They had a fast but wet journey across the English Channel. Black clouds were building, the sea choppy, and the advanced rain showers forewarned of a storm. Rocks littered the entrance to the cove that Yvonne had chosen, and the route through them, only known by local fishermen, was tricky, especially at dusk. James followed Yvonne's hand drawn chart. The difficulty assured James that they were unlikely to be disturbed by a French Excise boat. Once through the rocks, the sea surge reduced and the small bay proved calm and excellent. They anchored just two boat lengths from the shore and placed a stern anchor up and onto the beach. Then positioned *Sea Spirit*'s transom just feet from sand. They waited until dark. From out of the trees behind the dunes, dark shapes emerged, Yvonne's team silently carrying the kegs and crates on their shoulders, that they had hidden during the previous week. No one said a word, so they used hand signals.

All were fishermen from Yvonne's fleet and related by family or generations living in the same village. Smuggling and wrecking was in their blood, as was their bond of secrecy. With one night's smuggling they would earn the equivalent of one month's fishing money. It was obvious that Yvonne had gained their confidence and was their leader. None of them would have tried to fight the English sailors, as she had apparently done when they stole her boat. They filed down the beach, into the water, and waded out to *Sea Spirit*. Roger took the casks and crates and passed them to Paul, Alan and Tony to load them into the hold.

Yvonne whispered to James, "Brittany has never accepted the control from Paris. We do things our own way. None of our fishermen will inform on us."

Philippe watched long enough to ensure all was well, and to transfer the next consignment of royal jewels, taking payment for them. James wanted Philippe to clear off the beach in case they were discovered. He needed to protect the vineyard from connection to the smuggling. The kegs and crates took four hours to load, and another hour for Tony to replace the false hull. Then they loaded the hold with the fish that Yvonne supplied. Every minute, James expected a rush of French soldiers. Paul stood ready to cast off the anchors and head out to sea.

But Yvonne assured James, "I have Maurice and Leon watching the roads and we will all escape long before anyone arrives."

They finished and James passed the purse with the payment. There were quiet handshakes all around and for James, a hug with Yvonne, which she held onto for longer than Leon liked, and confirmation of their next meeting date. The Bretons slipped over the dunes and vanished into the woods.

The peaceful calm of the cove changed once they had cleared the rocks. Dawn showed a veritable storm developing with mounting waves. It took them sixteen long and cold hours to get to the River Yealm. Channel waves tested the construction of *Sea Spirit* and its crew's stamina. A lantern signal confirmed Trevor was waiting with his men to unload the casks and crates onto packhorses. It had taken a lot of detailed planning and preparation, but it had gone well. They were all exhausted, but it gave James optimism for the future.

After unloading the goods and getting paid by Trevor, they anchored in the Newton Ferris pool just inside the River Yealm's entrance. Paul lit the wood stove so they could get warm and dry. James fell asleep in his bunk thinking of the first time he saw Edith at the party for his sixth birthday.

CHAPTER 36

They woke refreshed. The storm had passed, leaving the sea calm, and a strong west wind pushed them back to Lymington to sell the fish. On shore James avoided the Ship's Inn. After unloading the fish, they returned straight back to Beaulieu, checking the new jetty and barn at Ginn's Farm.

James felt buoyant about how all the plans had come together. If all progressed, they could make four trips between now and Christmas, perhaps six, depending on wind and weather. He would pay for the boat and be financially independent. Most importantly, he would ask Lord Rowley for permission to marry Edith.

Their peace was shattered when, as they approached Buckler's Hard, James saw the unmistakable round figure of Sweeney, his brother's lawyer, waiting on the dock, with, judging by their hats and coats, the two thugs who had followed James to London.

As *Sea Spirit* drifted towards the dock, James sat on the deck, loading his three pistols and strapping on his father's cutlass. Paul, the bulldog, stood bristling for a fight, marlinspike in one hand and cutlass in the other. The rest of the crew held cutlasses.

Sweeney, waving a legal-sized envelope, called out in his squeaky voice, "Master James, here is a warrant to take possession of the boat. It belongs to your brother."

"Mr Sweeney, I am the legal captain of this vessel and am duty bound to protect it from pirates. I will shoot anyone who tries to come aboard before we fetch our local magistrate to check your papers. If you try to board, you will discover real pain. You may remember the last time we met, that things did not go well for you. Nor for any of those hounds you sent. This time will be worse. Paul, Roger, Alan, keep these people off the boat while I write a letter and instruct Tony what to do."

Sweeney turned to his men. "Take possession of the boat."

The thugs took a step forward. James turned back from going below, and drew a pistol from his belt. His crew drew their cutlasses. The thugs hesitated.

Sweeney shouted, "This is a legal warrant from Southampton. If you harm anyone, I will have you put in prison."

"This is not Southampton. Our locals do not accept corrupt magistrate's warrants."

"Your visit to my office is not forgotten. You will pay for it."

Turning again to his thugs, Sweeney shouted, "They dare not hurt you, take the boat."

As they hesitantly took a step forward, James fired at their feet. The wooden deck of the jetty sent out splinters as the lead ball struck it. They leapt into the air.

"Stand back. The next forward step will earn the man a wooden leg."

Sweeney's thugs moved back, to be jabbed in the back by a stick. They spun around to find Nanny Jones, her ebony walking stick pointing at them. She led a hostile crowd of Buckler's Hard boat builders. They blocked the exit to the dock. The thugs might take on boat builders but they were not used to being confronted by an elderly gentle lady with a flowery hat, wielding a black ebony steel pointed walking stick. They did not know what to do.

The crowd parted to let Tony off the dock with James's letter to fetch the local magistrate. James wondered why Sweeney wanted the boat. Were things so bad for his brother? The boat, if sold, would not make a dent in his brother's debts. Had Sweeney penetrated their private world? He doubted it. Mr Forest would know somehow and would have warned him. Maybe Sweeney just wanted vengeance for James pushing him over?

James's confidence and use of the pistol made Sweeney furious. He had expected, with the warrant, to just take procession of the boat with little resistance. He felt sure the envelope James took from him led James to Squire's Bank, where his father had left money for him. Yet the bank clerk Sweeney bribed could not find out anything. Sweeney had thought that threat of losing the boat would force James to confess to him. Percy's gambling debts and wild London parties had drained the estate. The gaming clubs continued to let Lord Percy gamble. They gave him credit, ignoring Sweeney's warning that the estate could not pay.

Sweeney needed the fees from the Lancaster estate and the money he filtered from it on the side. Without it, he could not continue his lavish lifestyle. Over the years, he had lost most of his clients. When Lord Lancaster died, and his useless son had taken over, Sweeney became his lawyer by promising to raise the income. Through his creative bookkeeping, he erased his own debts. Now, standing in the scorching sun, trapped on the dock waiting for the local magistrate, he felt vulnerable.

He looked around for somewhere to sit, but found nothing. He attempted to exit the dock and tried to push through the crowd.

"Let us through."

But that infernal woman with the stick pushed it into his stomach. The crowd moved around to support her.

"Madam, I—"

"You'll stay until the magistrate arrives, even if it takes days."

Sweeney retreated. His men were useless. He should have fired them after the fiasco in London. Though the fiasco had exposed James's secret bank account. What a shame James was not his client. Few young gentlemen could survive in his circumstances. Most were useless without an income. James had shown himself to be frustratingly competent.

Sweeney looked up at the boat and saw James sitting with calm confidence, pistols in his belt and cutlass in hand, alongside his well-armed crew. Sweeney never faced physical combat. He always relied on his words, lies and money. He would try to reason with James, and called out, "It will be much worse for you once a magistrate arrives. Let's discuss this. Perhaps we can make a deal for you to keep the boat?"

James laughed and Sweeny felt impotent. James knew that one of the best ways to defeat an opponent was to make them wait. As time passed the heat made Sweeney sweat. His clothes became damp and smellier. He looked around, seeing water on both sides of the dock. He could not swim. There was no escape. His heart raced. He had a hostile crowd behind him and a pistol in front. He always used others to do his dirty work. Now he was on the front line and scared. Once the magistrate arrived, he would get satisfaction. The gout in his feet hurt. His legs were giving way. He had to let them go. He sat with a thump on the dock, to a roar of laughter from the crowd behind him.

Tony ran to the mansion of Lord Rowley. He had always knocked at the servants' door before, never at the front door where James sent him. He arrived out of breath and uncomfortable. Morgan, the butler, looked down on him disdainfully.

"The servants' door is at the back."

"Your honor, I have a petition."

"His Lordship does not receive petitions at the mansion, especially from laborers."

Tony plucked up the courage to say, "Master James Lancaster asks for Mister Morgan to give the letter to Lord Rowley in his position as chief magistrate, or he should tell me where to find a magistrate."

Morgan seemed reluctant to take the letter. "I am Morgan, are you sure it is Master James Lancaster?"

"Yes, your honor. There are pirates at Buckler's Hard, and Master James captured them. A magistrate is needed."

Morgan was incredulous. "Pirates at Buckler's Hard? Master James captured them!"

"Yes, sir," Tony spluttered.

Morgan wondered what would happen next. Lady Edith arriving in her father's coach at breakneck speed to collect a book for her father's court. Lady Rowley dashing the family back and forth to London. They had just returned. It took days to get the trunks unpacked and all the clothes cleaned. Master James becoming a fisherman. Now pirates?

"Most unusual, but as it comes from Master James, I will give the letter to His Lordship. Wait here."

Calling for a magistrate gave James the right to stop Sweeney for however long it took. It could be a week. He hoped someone would arrive in a few hours. James hated having to ask for help from Edith's father. But he needed a magistrate and Lord Rowley was the local chief, and reputed to be tough but fair.

The wait seemed interminable. The crowd grew quiet. James sensed that for them, it became an event, a bit like going to the fair, and one that would be talked about in the Master Builder inn for months. Nanny Jones had gained a flowered umbrella to keep the sun off. She enjoyed her role as agent provocateur and organizing the boat builders into a small army. Poor

Sweeney seemed to melt away, sitting on the rough-hewn timbers that made the dock. Sweeney's thugs stood to the side, trying to keep out of his sight, away from the crowd and James's pistols. James almost felt sorry for them.

After three hours, James wondered what to do if no magistrate arrived. Behind Sweeney the growing crowd turned, as a grand carriage rolled up. The crowd parted. A constable led the way followed by Lord Rowley, and behind him, Lady Rowley and Edith. So, they were back from London. James was nervous. So much at stake. What if Lord Rowley agreed with Sweeney? Edith looked stunning with her hair around her shoulders and an elegant long light cloak over her summer dress. Her slim look and tight waist contrasted with her mother's formal dress and flowered hat.

He had wanted Edith to see *Sea Spirit* on their own, never imagining this would be the occasion. Edith's mother coming seemed a good sign, or he hoped so. She never mixed with the laboring people, except at the annual village fair. There she walked around smiling, but avoided meeting the villagers, unlike her husband. James had to concentrate on Lord Rowley. Sweeney confronted him, waving his papers in the air as he struggled to stand.

Lord Rowley realized that the situation was dangerous, with a sizeable angry crowd, facing a fat little man sitting on the dock struggling to get to his feet, and two thugs. There was a new boat with young James and crew, armed to the teeth, looking more like pirates than the fishermen. He recognized Sweeney, a nasty little lawyer from Southampton. He represented James's brother and appeared before Lord Rowley to evict tenants. James's father had seldom evicted anyone. He worked with them when they ran into problems, such as bad weather and failed crops. Unfortunately, the law had forced Lord Rowley to find in Sweeney's favor, but he did not like it.

Sweeney had trouble getting his portly body back onto its feet, but was relieved to see Lord Rowley. He had appeared before him a few times, always getting the decision he wanted. So he assumed that Lord Rowley liked him.

"Your honor, I have a warrant to take possession of this boat on behalf of Lord Lancaster."

"Let me see it."

Lord Rowley took the warrant out of Sweeney's hands, tapped him aside with his silver topped stick, and walked towards the boat.

Sweeney disliked being treated with such indifference. "My Lord, I must explain."

His Lordship turned and glared, a glare that stopped Sweeney's protests.

"Constable. Keep Mister Sweeney, and those two unsavory specimens, company."

James had only a moment to recover, standing and passing his weapons to Paul.

"Well, young James, are you going to invite me on board? I've heard so much about this boat. I am pleased to finally see it."

"It is kind of you to come in person, my Lord. I am sorry to trouble you."

"You are lucky that we are just returned from London. But are you going to leave Lady Rowley and Miss Edith on the dock, or had you thought of inviting them to join us? Perhaps we can talk in the cabin, if you have one?"

"My Lord, I apologize. I had not thought they would board such a poor vessel."

"Nonsense, this is the only boat built here for a year. It brought much needed work to our people. Rumors are that it is full of innovations."

James was relieved. Thank goodness they had cleaned the boat on their return trip from Plymouth. Lady Rowley, uncomfortable with the situation, needed help to board. Edith, smiling from ear-to-ear, skipped down the dock and boarded in a flash.

Lord Rowley took his time looking over the deck. Then descended cautiously down the steep companionway ladder into the cabin. He helped the ladies, looked around and sat in James's seat at the mess table. The ladies squeezed into the bench. James sat perched on a stool.

Lord Rowley looked at the writ.

"James, this may be serious. I need to study it. Then we can talk. Perhaps you can show the ladies the boat for a few minutes?"

Lady Rowley interrupted. "After struggling down the steps into this cramped cabin, then squeezing into this bench, I will stay put. But what more can be seen? It is a small fishing boat, and not one I would venture on, even in the river, let alone out to sea. But you may show Edith."

Lord Rowley looked up, surprised but pleased. He had always liked James and enjoyed all the naval dispatches mentioning him. If James had an income, or if his wife was flexible, he would like him as a son-in-law. That his wife suggested Edith be alone with James for a few minutes surprised him. What plan was she developing?

Lady Rowley had her reasons. Edith's interest in James had caused tension between her and her daughter for years. It had to be snubbed out. When they had returned from London, she had agreed to let Edith wait until Christmas Day to see if by some miracle James became financially sound enough to marry her. Lady Rowley knew James would fail. No fisherman, even one born to be a gentleman, could catch enough fish to become rich. Lady Rowley felt sure that once Edith visited the fishing boat, she would realize how low James had sunk. Especially if Sweeney confiscated James's boat in front of her. Lady Rowley had made a deal with the mother of the actual husband she wanted for her daughter. She feared the mother would not wait much longer. If Edith was persuaded about James's inevitable failure, it would speed up her plans. Her daughter deserved a lord, and the social life that came with it, plus, Lady Rowley wanted her grandchildren to inherit titles.

James led the way up to the deck. Edith looked radiant. He explained about the innovations of the boat, but she interrupted him.

"James, the boat looks fantastic, but we must talk. When Daddy said he received an urgent request from you, I thought my mother would say he should send his clerk. Instead, she insisted on us coming with him. She is up to something. She has never even been to Buckler's Hard before. Her coming here is strange. She is sure you cannot make the Christmas deadline. I promised that if by Christmas Day you cannot propose, I will marry her choice. What happens if you lose your boat?"

"I won't lose the *Sea Spirit* as she is not mine to lose. But that is another story. You can depend on Christmas Day."

"James," Lord Rowley's voice boomed up from the cabin.

James helped Edith down the companionway steps.

"If you really are a fisherman, I would expect you to have on board, some French brandy and wine for the ladies."

"Well, on our last trip, we met a French fisherman and purchased exactly what you are asking for."

Lord Rowley passed the warrant to Edith. "Give me your opinion of this."

Her mother rolled her eyes.

Then Lord Rowley sipped the brandy. He took a second sip.

"James, this is not a brandy that a poor French fisherman would sell to his English counterpart. It is excellent. Is there more?"

"I might find some."

"Mark me down for twelve bottles. I will pay top price for them."

So, thought Lord Rowley, *James is supplementing his fishing income. I hope he is not discovered and brought to my court.*

Edith seemed to take forever, reading each word. She looked up, and her father asked, "So, what do you think?"

"I see that a Southampton magistrate issued the warrant for property in our district. It omits there being a prior summons, or a court notice to James to appear to answer the claims. There is no mention of any documents proving ownership."

James noticed Lord Rowley beam with pleasure, but Lady Rowley frowned. She hated when her husband encouraged their daughter to show her learning and legal mind. Women were expected to remain uneducated to please their husbands. Edith had read every book in their library. Her father claimed she knew more law than any of the nincompoop lawyers who wasted his time.

Edith's expertise impressed James, and he felt proud of her.

Lord Rowley looked at James. "This warrant claims you are the owner of the boat. That you are bankrupt, and you purchased it with an undeclared inheritance from your father. Therefore it belongs to your brother."

James took out the ship's papers from a waterproof canvas case.

"My Lord, I am poor but not bankrupt. As you can see, a bank in Scotland financed the boat building, and they own the title. I am embarrassed to show you my small retainer as captain, and share of profits."

Lord Rowley studied the papers. It shocked him to see how little James got paid. He was disappointed that James did not own the boat as it would have shown that he did in fact have money.

"I see that the taxes and stamp duties are paid and certified and the boat belongs to a Scottish bank." Lord Rowley's face spread into a grin. "Could you not find a bank further from Beaulieu? Edinburgh is the furthest town in the kingdom, and many days' travel!"

"It's luck, my Lord."

James thought, *so the lord understands our game, and why the owner is far away, and under Scottish law.*

Lord Rowley hoisted himself up. "Luck is more often created than just happens. But we are happy to believe you. The warrant is invalid. Let me see that worm Sweeney."

He climbed up to the deck, followed by Lady Rowley, Edith and James.

"Mr Sweeney."

Sweeney, who in Southampton received respect, resented being left on the dock. He was sitting under the heat of the sun, sweating, dizzy, in need of water and boxed in by the crowd led by Nanny Jones. Under the watchful eye of the constable, he climbed with difficulty to his feet and hustled over to the boat.

"How did you get this warrant?"

"I applied to the magistrate in Southampton."

"I read that. But what notices did you serve in advance of the hearing? What evidence did you submit to prove that Master James owned this boat?"

Sweeney had been so sure that James owned the boat that he got the warrant without notice of the hearing and without evidence, from the magistrate whom he bribed regularly. One who asked no questions. Now he sensed trouble. Before this, Lord Rowley had been easy to persuade. Damn this James.

"Well, er... we asked, and everyone said James Lancaster owned it."

"You got a warrant without giving the defendant an opportunity to answer your claim?"

"He was away at sea."

"Constable. Lock this man up for two days for false representation and those two fellows for trespass."

"My Lord, I protest, I am a lawyer. You cannot lock me up."

"Constable, make it three days." He turned to Sweeney. "Now Mr Sweeney, is there anything else I cannot do?"

"My Lord, I apologize, but I am entitled to know who owns the boat."

"You are not entitled. If you go about it legally, you will find out. But I do not want you wasting more of my time. It is owned by the Edinburgh

Maritime Bank. They paid all taxes and stamp duty fully. While you're resting in our local jail, I will write to my friend, the chief magistrate, in Southampton to inform him of this serious situation. Also to ask him to investigate the other warrants you obtained from the same magistrate."

The crowd cheered as Sweeney and his men were led away.

Lord Rowley turned back to Edith. "What does the law say about a captain's responsibility to defend his vessel?"

"If pirates attack, and a captain does not use his best efforts to protect it, the owners may hold him responsible for their loss."

"How does the law react to people firing weapons?"

"If the people trying to board have no legal reason, they are pirates. The captain must use all resources available to stop them."

"Excellent. It's a shame women cannot be lawyers. Now, James, it seems your growing legendry good luck has served you again. But for a fisherman, you are causing too much trouble. Try to avoid that Sweeney character. He and your brother do not have your best interests at heart. Come, ladies, we must leave."

"My Lord, I cannot thank you enough."

"Then don't, in case you cause more problems."

James wanted a word with Edith, but her mother marched her away and hustled her into the coach. Edith turned for one last look at James, standing on the deck.

The crowd's expectations of having a good time were not disappointed. James beamed at Nanny Jones, standing as proud as the queen.

"Nanny, you would have been a great general. Would you like to invite your army on board for a tot?"

Nanny's army responded with a cheer. The bottles, removed from the hiding place, were put to good use.

Back in the coach, Edith's mother felt vindicated. "Can you believe such a thing? A gentleman sunk so low, employed, a fisherman, not even owning his own boat. He looked like a pirate when we arrived, standing so tall, suntanned, with long hair blowing in the wind, pistols in his belt and a curved cutlass. Not a gentleman's sword."

She regretted James not being born the first son and inheriting the estate, and title Lord Lancaster. She would never admit it, but James was handsome. Handsome did not always make for a good husband. She had selected a better one. *A mother knows what is best for her daughter*.

Edith tried not to shed a tear and hid it with a handkerchief. Her tummy hurt with anguish. There seemed no hope. James's income was tiny. How could he still promise to be ready by Christmas Eve? She adored the boat and also loved the way James looked with his open shirt, a week's growth of beard, his pistols and sword and wild hair. If that was how pirates looked, she wanted one. Not just anyone, but him.

"Hmm…" Lord Rowley said, which meant he wanted to say something important. "A ship's cutlass is for close quarter fighting and much more practical than a gentleman's rapier. Rapiers are fine for the idiots who want to duel, but not in an intense battle. He knows how to use his pistols, sword and perhaps his fists."

Lady Rowley became impatient. "Husbands do not need to fight but to provide. You have to agree there is no purpose in Edith waiting until Christmas. James is a lost cause."

Edith's heart jumped. So that was why her mother insisted on them going with her father when he told them about James's letter. She wanted to change their agreement to wait for Christmas.

"Hold on there. We agreed to Christmas. Once that is past, one way or the other, we'll lose Edith. I intend to enjoy our daughter's company and legal help every day until then."

Edith felt like a condemned person, with a small reprieve.

Lord Rowley's eyes were no longer sharp. Edith had become his right hand in running the estate, and the legal assistant he hoped a son would have been. Her father continued. "James is the luckiest young man alive, or the cleverest we have ever known. I would not bet on which one it is. He earned the name Lucky Lancaster for good reason. If you had looked at the deck of his boat, you would have seen the nets were folded naval fashion, looking unused. Fishermen and their wives repair the nets the moment they return to harbor. James did not purchase that brandy from an ordinary French fisherman. He has more available. When Sweeney goes to Scotland, the local bankers will not like a slimy English lawyer asking them about their business. If he goes to court to find whom the bank represents, it will take him six months. It is possible James owns the boat and has been clever enough to have it fronted by a bank located as far away as Scotland. I expect there will be half a dozen more owners before they can trace it back to him. The only problem will be if James's father separated some of his wealth from his idle son Percy to give it to James. Then James must hide it for five years and maybe ten. I wonder how far his luck will stretch?"

"Ten years!" Lady Rowley yelled. "Edith will be an old maid by then, and too old to have children, my grandchildren. I won't have it."

Edith felt like a shuttlecock bouncing between two players, but she knew when to keep quiet.

Lord Rowley became firm. "We agreed Christmas Eve and so it shall be, but not a day more. We will announce Edith's betrothal at our annual party."

So, Edith thought, *even Father has determined to marry me off, regardless of my feelings*. She thought about *Sea Spirit*. From the coach it seemed so small, especially when she compared it to the frigate she had visited. But once on-board, she loved it. The wood, mast, deck, cockpit, the cabin. She wanted to sail. Of course, she would have to reorganize the cabin and galley. One day James would take her on a voyage. She had read that owner-captains of merchant ships sometimes took their wives with them. With James being captain of a boat, they could elope easily.

Edith closed her eyes, thinking back to when she had persuaded her father to arrange a visit to *HMS Defender*, a sister ship to *HMS Defiance*, docked in Portsmouth. The captain loved having a lord on board. You never knew when you might need help from one. He had called the senior midshipman when Edith asked to see their mess. The small size of the captain's cabin had surprised her. When she had entered the midshipmen's mess, it had shocked her to see that six to eight midshipmen lived and slept in such a small space. How did James cope? She had gone to the gun deck to see the gun battery where James had responsibility. She could not imagine being there when all the guns fired, recoiling with violence, smoke and noise. Back on deck, they had showed her how the minute glass and log worked. She had looked up the main mast where James often went to identify ships seen by the lookout. How could anyone climb up there? Especially when the ship rolled?

"Edith, stop your daydreaming and wake up to the real world."

Her mother never gave up.

CHAPTER 37

The trip to London had been fast. The roads were dry. James wanted to get away while Sweeney sat in jail, and put into action the plan suggested by Mr Forest, to evade followers. The London streets were busy. Did all these people make a living? How did they cope with the smells and dirt underfoot? Where did they get the amazing assortment of costumes and hats they wore? He saw no one looking for him or whom he recognized at the Whitehall Coach Inn, but went through the front doors of a series of inns and out at the back, and safely made his way to the Inns of Court. Mr Forest, his glasses on his forehead and rubbing his chin in excitement, seemed full of energy.

"Do not worry about our friends in Scotland. They are expecting to hear from Sweeney, and a surprise awaits him if he ventures there himself. With the problems that will be on his desk when he gets out of jail, I doubt he will go. Your plans are admirable. The profits from the first shipment are better than expected. If you can get the rest of the wine and spirits from the vineyard here in the next months, it will make you for life. With the additional revenue the jewels bring, you will manage the other business we started, without having to draw on capital. I always enjoyed your father's business, but while being riskier, this is much more fun. I must caution you. Once the transfer of the vineyard's wine is completed, you must stop free trading. The authorities will know about the sudden influx of spirits. They will become more vigilant. The good news is that our jeweler friends say the palace will buy from the Reine Antoinette's collection. Now let's plan the details and get you back to your boat."

Jails were run as private businesses. The town paid a low daily fee for each prisoner, and the jailers were free to supplement their income. Many jails were converted houses with deep stone cellars. The warden put Sweeney in the general cell packed with prisoners, many of whom were sick. Dirt, vomit and excrement soiled the floor. He slept sitting up on a stone bench. The food, made from rotten boiled vegetables, smelled foul.

"Warden, this place and food are vile."

"What do you expect?"

"Is there any way I could rent a private cell?"

"The one available is a small furnished apartment. It's expensive."

"I will take it."

"For an additional fee, I could allow the local inn to send you food."

His men did not fare so well. He considered they deserved it.

Sweeney never forgot the fear and humiliation he suffered from James's confrontation. He returned from jail as dangerous as a wounded rat trapped in a corner. On his desk were a series of new demand notices for IOUs signed by Lord Percy Lancaster. He did not know Percy had amassed such debts. He had even played hazard again at White's with the Duke of Wellington. However, his first priority was to calm things with Portsmouth's chief magistrate. He called in a few favors and looked after the magistrate's clerk. The chief magistrate's gout restricted his movements and he would soon retire. His clerk needed to save for a pension. Sweeney paid a bigger bribe than usual, and charged it to the Lancaster estate. Then Sweeney wrote to his friends in Scotland to find out about the Maritime Bank. His spy reported that James had taken the coach to London. Sweeney expected information from the boys at the Whitehall Coach Inn he also paid to watch for, and follow James. It was an expensive operation.

CHAPTER 35

After the stress of the first shipment, the next trips were easy, almost an anti-climax. Not that James minded. They transported the kegs and crates to the beach, loading them on to *Sea Spirit* with no problem. They filled the hold with fish provided by Yvonne. Predictable summer southwesterly winds took them across the Channel to the Beaulieu River. Late at night, the kegs were offloaded into the hidden vaults below Ginn's Farm's new barn. Then they sailed to Lymington to sell the fish and returned to France for the next shipment. For the next two months, they didn't stop; they coped with summer storms, dodged French and English Excise boats, delayed transportation of the kegs from the vineyard to the beach because of French troop movements and waited for Yvonne to catch enough fish.

Albert met the boat as they returned to Bucker's Hard.

"Mister Forest thinks it is time to set the trap, and that you should make a quick trip to London."

The summer journey was fast. James followed Albert's training, and after getting off the coach made a point of asking several people the directions to Squire's Bank. He noticed the young runners following him. He led them to the bank, making a poor job of evading them. On entering, he announced his name out loud. The clerks looked up, startled, and James asked to see the senior partner.

"Mister Lancaster, several people have asked us if you or your father have an account with us. On principle, we refuse to discuss our clients' names and business, but now you arrive wanting to open an account. It is strange."

James pretended to be naïve. "Did my father have an account?"

"No, but if he did, we would report it to his heir, the current Lord Lancaster, but we will not discuss clients with third parties."

"And if I open an account, can I depend on your discretion?"

An hour later, having completed his business, James left the bank, confirmed that the young boys were still following him, and entered the nearest inn, leaving them outside the front door, ordered ale and a cheese plate, changed his hat and coat, and slipped out of the back door. Then he weaved through narrow alleyways, and when he knew he was not being followed, headed to the Inn of Courts. Three days later he was back on *Sea Spirit* sailing out to France for the seventh and the last shipment. They had managed much more than he had originally estimated.

On passing Lymington, an Excise boat stopped them. Unusual, normally they checked boats as they returned. There were a few bottles on board for personal use. James left a bottle of wine for the Excise men to take with them. They picked up the bottle and examined it.

"Any brandy?"

The question warned James. The Excise were tracking the source of brandy appearing ashore.

"With the price of fish being so low, we are lucky to buy the odd bottle of wine, let alone brandy."

The inspection took a long time. After, they took the last of the ebb tide through the Hurst Narrows, past the Needles into the English Channel. There were an unusual number of coastguard cutters patrolling the Channel. They put out their nets to show they were fishing, and under the cover of night, pulled them in and continued to France. Yvonne waited for them south of the Channel Islands.

"We will have the last shipment on the beach in two nights."

Yvonne continued fishing. James selected a secluded cove where they anchored. He talked to the crew about his feelings that their luck was changing and asked for their thoughts. The crew relied on James's luck. Their low point was when Sweeney had turned up at Buckler's Hard. James had managed that so well, as he did many of their previous adventures. They voted to continue. James needed to collect the last jewels, for which he had already paid a large deposit. Even if they had voted not to collect the wine, he still had to get the jewels, which would be easy to hide. They took it in turns to keep a watch from the headland and noticed more French Excise boats were patrolling. The French had spies in London. If the English Excise were trying to find a smuggler, the French also knew that wine and spirits were leaving France.

James used the waiting time to write to Edith. He had not seen her since she was on board with her father. James had sent a few notes via Woodsman, reassuring her all was well, but heard nothing back from her.

Edith was depressed. There seemed to be no way of getting out of marrying her mother's choice. To make it worse, her mother refused to name the man and family she had chosen. For aristocrats, marriage focused on strategic relationships, strengthening one's family's economic and political power. The marriage vows made the women agree to love, honor and obey. If they liked their husbands, it was a bonus. Some even grew to love them. If they did not, they learned to manage. Husbands spent most of their time hunting, fishing and shooting, and at their London clubs. Lords went to London for sessions of parliament. Wives produced babies and ran the household.

Edith immersed herself working hard for her father. She hoped to make herself indispensable to him by running the estate and acting as his unofficial legal assistant. Maybe he would agree she did not need to marry. It was normal for top families to arrange marriages. Society expected them to make the best of it. Still, she filled her eloping bag with clothes and her jewelry.

James calculated that by the time they were back from this trip, and after he delivered the jewels to London, there would only be a few weeks left before Christmas. It excited him, being so close to independent wealth, but he still needed to explain how he came by it, so his brother could not claim it.

Back on *Sea Spirit*, hidden in the small bay, Paul worried. He had watched James grow from a boy into a man, never seeing him look so concerned. He sat gazing out to sea with an expression forecasting a gale. Did the forthcoming trip, or the ominous weather signs, concern James that much? He remembered their first storm, and did not want to suffer that again.

Paul did not know that James's concern focused on how to get free from his brother's control and to claim Edith's hand. Perhaps he should make a deal with him? Instinct told James that once he opened the door to a compromise, his brother would want everything.

Paul also worried about how hard they worked *Sea Spirit*. The hemp ropes were stretching and constantly needed tarring and tightening. If they encountered the Excise boats, he knew they would outrun them. But one broken shroud or stay could cost them everything. He upgraded and used bigger cords for more security. He made the crew practice getting the cannon out of the hidden hold, even in rough weather. They seldom fired it for fear of attracting attention. The noise of cannon fire traveled miles.

Paul had responsibility for the victualing, ensuring they had enough food and water to keep them at sea for weeks, in case the French or English Excise chased them, and also, so they could stay at sea during storms, when most boats would be in harbor. In fact, storm weather became their friend, when the Excise boats always stayed in harbor.

After this trip, they would lay-up for the winter. Paul would go back to his Dartmoor cottage, wealthy for a seaman, get help to remove the rocks, to have a barn built, and to see his lass. He had visited her the few times when they sailed into Plymouth Harbor, and hoped she would welcome his advances. Having no relationship with women, he did not know how to proceed. He would ask James, who had an easy way of communicating with women. Paul had seen the barmaids in the inns rush to serve him, how Miss Edith had looked at him when she came on board. Even Lady Rowley, while pretending to be cross, had admired James's physique when he helped her on board *Sea Spirit*.

Paul looked again at the clouds. They worried him. With a barometer on board, it would tell them the decrease in air pressure. But he did not need a barometer. His body told him. The clouds were forming, and the wind dropped. Soon, the southwest wind would lose the battle with the northwest wind, and that would bring the first early winter gale. Already the upper clouds were streaking, indicating strong winds above. He hoped they could enter the cove and load before the waves increased in the cove, making loading kegs and exiting difficult.

James went to the headland. "There are no French in sight, let's get underway."

The surf was already entering the cove. They dropped two bow anchors and reversed towards the beach, easing the anchor lines until they were as close to the shore as they dared. Yvonne's team came out to help their tender through the surf onto the beach and run a stern anchor ashore. They tightened all the anchor lines to keep *Sea Spirit* in position, but she pitched and rolled. The French team were not able to walk the kegs out through the surf. They ferried them in the tender, two at a time. It took much longer than normal. The cold water made the team take turns standing in the surf to control the whaler. Others pulled the whaler to *Sea Spirit* with lines.

With Sea Spirit moving so much, it made it difficult and dangerous to maneuver the heavy kegs into position and to tie them down in the hold.

Ashore, James made the final arrangements. He had become very close with Phillipe Valente, the vineyard manager. James said that the bank wanted to buy more land and expand the vineyard while the war continued and land prices were low.

"We have a history of wars in Europe. Once the war finishes, and they always do, the English and French people will be friends once more, things will stabilize, trade will restart and land will become expensive again."

James paid Phillipe for his share of the sales, then arranged to return in the spring to discuss how to ship this season's wine. He paid Yvonne and her men for assisting, and for the fish they had caught, though, with this weather, it proved impossible to load the fish.

"Yvonne, we do not expect to do any more trips until next spring when we will ship this year's wine. I will contact you."

"James, is that all you have to say to me? I know you are being loyal to Edith, but as you once said, one is able to love more than one person at a time. Most people love their parents, siblings, pets and their wives all a little differently. There is no conflict. Every man always remembers their initiation. So I expect a kiss." Yvonne grabbed him, and in front of everyone kissed him. The kiss was still wonderful and Yvonne held on a lingered a lot longer than she should have done.

"I see you have not forgotten your lessons. Use them well, and remember that you still owe me for the black eye, and one day I will collect."

After that James had to concentrate and deal with the agents for the jewels, and pay them a large amount in gold to take procession of them. He had no experience with jewels. The first group was authenticated by a French court jeweler who had escaped the revolution and was now living in London, working for Her Majesty's jewelers. Even Reine Antoinette had signed away her vast collection. James felt the buyers of the jewels were hypocrites. They demanded signatures of sale but ignored the circumstances that created the signatures. Even so, he felt lucky to have been able to buy them.

The weather deteriorated. With the last kegs on board and secured, they said their goodbyes. If one keg got free in the storm and started rolling, it might break the hull and sink them. The whaler was also on board and strapped down. Now they had to leave through the rolling waves surging into the cove. They would need Roger's strength on the skull oar and the rest of them on side oars to row *Sea Spirit* out through the gaps in the rocks. Once outside the cove they should be able to raise the reefed sails.

CHAPTER 39

James asked Paul to steer. Roger manned the stern oar. Tony took the port oar and James the starboard. They rowed up to the anchors. Once over the anchors, all except Roger rushed forward to assist Alan pulling on the lines and raising them. Then they rushed back to row before being driven onto the shore and shipwrecked. They made little progress against the wind and waves. James feared his luck had run out. He worried they would not have the stamina or strength to row out of the cove over the surging waves. How long could they last? Then he heard Paul's voice, the dominating one he used as coxswain on the *Defiance*, urging his rowers to beat the other long boat.

"Row, you black hearted scoundrels. Row for your lives, row or never again see your sweethearts, row together, in… in…"

His demanding voice penetrated through the howling wind. They forgot the pain. James thought of Edith and found extra energy. Each of them dug deep inside to muster the energy and row, motivated by their own interpretation of Paul's words. Alan started singing the mermaid's shanty, "The mermaid's a singing, calling us to her, row you sailors row, She's calling you to kiss you, row you sailors row,…" and the rhythm of the shanty helped. Slowly, *Sea Spirit* moved forward. Alan secured the anchors then joined James on the oar.

Once clear of the rocks, they raised a storm headsail and a reefed mainsail. The seas were building. They crawled up enormous waves to rush down the other side into a deep valley, wondering if they would keep going down into the sea and sink. From the bottom they looked up thirty feet to seas all around them. Somehow, the bow lifted and the boat started up the next wave. James used the speed gained descending down the waves to help drive them high enough on the other side to catch the wind in the top of sails to drive them up to the top of the waves. Then the boat pushed through the wave crest before starting the down slide again.

It was relentless but they were not in a hurry and were unlikely to meet any hostile boats. James issued rum tots all round, passed out dried meat and cheese and sent Roger, Alan and Tony below to rest. Through the night they worked two hour watches, then four hours off, steadily heading away from the shore and danger, though danger still lay ahead. They had to clear the Channel Islands and the Alderney rocks, tides and currents. With the wind from the northwest, it would push them sideways towards the islands. Later they would tack towards the southwest, into the Bay of Biscay before tacking for a clear trip across and up the Channel to England. James regained his confidence despite Paul's insistence that old sailors said that mermaids had been seen on the Alderney rocks.

After a long night, dawn revealed a landscape of boiling white water, spray and a black sky. In the far distance to starboard were the Channel Islands. The west tracking ebb tide had taken them further west and away from Alderney, a good thing, as they might avoid tacking. A winter northwest storm would take two or three days to blow itself out. There was nothing to do except go as carefully as possible, checking rigging, and the bilges for water.

Sea Spirit remained a very sound and basically dry boat. Water raced down the decks, and the violent motion of the boat as she slid down the waves at an alarming speed caused them all to hang on for their lives. The wind whistling through the rigging made the situation sound even worse. To talk to the crew, James had to wait until the boat arrived at the bottom of the waves, where it was sheltered from the wind and became quiet. There was no attempt at conversation. It was a powerful lesson in the vulnerability of life. Each man knew they were at the extremities of their physical and mental endurance, and made different silent vows as to what to do better, if and when they survived.

Late in the morning, Alan shouted, "Sail ahoy, off the starboard bow."

The first look showed nothing but waves. Then, at the crest of the next wave, a mast appeared about ten miles away. As they mounted the next wave, they saw it was a French Excise boat. James calculated that with big waves, the French were unable to launch a whaler to board them. They were windward, but coming towards them. With a bit of luck, *Sea Spirit* should pass in front of them and out to the main English Channel. To escape, they needed to clear the Channel Islands without tacking. It required more sail, but that also created risk by putting more strain on their mast and rigging. At the top of the next wave, James estimated that they had less than an hour to make their escape.

"Paul, shake out one reef from the main sail. God willing, and assuming your rigging holds, we can head up closer to the wind and pass Alderney to get clear ahead."

Paul had come to the same conclusion. He felt confident. But then he saw another sail dead ahead, coming from around the north end of Alderney.

"Enemy sail dead ahead. Another French heading towards us."

This was no mistake. It would stop them escaping. Now two French boats, with crews of thirty each, out in a storm, were both heading downwind towards them. They were in a trap. To flee south they needed to turn around in theses extreme waves, almost impossible and dangerous. Even if they managed the maneuver the French would follow them to the coast and block them. There seemed no way out.

Paul asked, "What are they up to? They cannot board us in this weather."

The answer came with distant cloud of smoke followed by a bang. A cannon fired from the starboard boat, demanding they heave-to. It confirmed that even with these seas the French could still fire on them. James's tingling came to him. After all this effort, the French would not stop him. He would fight, even if the odds were terrible. Here were two boats to windward, each with six cannons and thirty-five to forty men, compared with their single boat, one cannon, and five men.

James shouted above the wind, "Belay undoing the reef. Roger, Alan, Tony, get our cannon on deck as quickly as you can. Paul, keep us steady to give us time on the top of the waves to make an accurate shot. The good news is that their bow chaser will have half our range. The bad news is that if we miss, and they get close, we will not survive their broadside."

It was difficult and dangerous moving a cannon in these conditions. Roger rigged double tackles to stop it from moving around while the boat bucked and twisted. They dragged it up the ramp out of the hold onto the deck, then replaced the false deck, and positioned the cannon pointing it to the left of the bow and the mast stays. The entire operation took fifteen minutes. James appreciated Roger's size and strength and all the training Paul had given as they crossed the Channel each time.

The gap between *Sea Spirit* and the French cutters got smaller. Both French boats fired another warning shot, demanding *Sea Spirit* heave-to.

James had been calculating. "I am afraid our chances are not good. One lucky cannon shot is unlikely to stop them. We will use double shot. Two cannon balls joined by a chain and aiming for their masts. It will shorten our range but might cause more damage."

The two French boats were closing in on them. As *Sea Spirit* crested the waves, James aimed the cannon. Often the French boats were hidden behind deep waves. Only the tops of their masts were visible until they rose and appeared, just as *Sea Spirit* rushed down her wave into her trough.

They had missed half a dozen chances to fire and now they were getting too close. Soon they would be in range of the French bow chasers. Through his looking glass, James could see the French crews at the bows preparing their cannons.

One French boat fired, but they were still too far away. *Sea Spirit* rushed down into the trough. The cannon ball splashed into the sea half a mile in front of them.

Once again, Paul marveled at James's patience. He appeared calm and secure, even as two powerful war machines were bearing down on them. It would be hard to escape their fire. Paul had no regrets being with James, except he hoped to propose to the lass in Plymouth. If lucky, and they were not drowned, it would be difficult to propose from a French prison.

James called out over the noise of the wind and crashing waves. "Paul, hold her steady on the next crest."

Paul became very focused. He eased off the wind to gain speed to climb the wave. As they crested, they synchronized with the port French boat, now only a half a mile away. *Sea Spirit* was now in their range.

James shouted, "Stand by, wait for it, fire."

The cannon roared and recoiled. At the same time a puff of smoke came from the French bow. The French shot passed over them.

James did not see where their shot went. The French boat slid into the trough and disappeared. As *Sea Spirit* slid down their wave, the second French boat fired. Their cannon ball passed to the side.

"Reload."

It was now a precarious situation. Two French boats, both within range, manned by full crews and both with bow and side cannons. *Sea Spirit* had no way of escaping unless the waves hid them.

It took forever to mount the next wave. The starboard French boat disappeared behind a deep wave, and the one had they fired on had not reappeared. When it did, it showed a broken mast, and the deck covered by a tangled mass of rigging and sail. *Sea Spirit*'s two cannon balls linked by a chain had made contact.

James felt the tension slip out of him. His luck had not left them. Paul and the crew also felt relief and shouted hooray, but James silenced them.

"Belay that. Paul, bear up and put the hulk between us and the other French. They won't fire at us for fear of hitting their own. Those poor devils will need luck and help to survive. They have enough sea room and four or five hours. It might give them time to cut away the mess and set up a temporary spar. Perhaps they can get a tow from the other boat, before they get washed onto the Brittany rocks."

Paul thought it typical that James thought more about the fate of the enemy seamen than of celebrating their escape.

On the crest of the next wave, they saw the second French boat had altered course towards their companions. It was a moment of relief and relaxation. The tension flowed out of them.

"Paul, Roger, Peter, get the cannon stowed. Alan, take the helm."

James went below to check the charts and tides. On returning on deck they were securing the cannon in the hold and replacing the deck. It had been a mammoth task to maneuver it and used all of Roger's strength. He stood up and pumped his fists with the victory sign.

James saw an enormous wave coming for them.

"Hang on."

The bow was covered with water, and it rushed down the deck, filling the cockpit. It stopped *Sea Spirit* and she took her time to emerge from the wave. When she did Roger had gone.

"Roger!"

They looked back at the boiling white water and the enormous wave now behind them. Nothing was said. Roger was not to be seen. Even if he had been seen they could not turn back in these waves. James was in shock. He was responsible. It was Paul who broke the silence.

"He could not swim so at least death would have been quick. I cannot count the number of times I told him to always hang on with one hand."

The journey back through the storm should have been a celebration, but everyone was quiet, remembering moments with Roger, his gentleness contrasted with his size and strength.

CHAPTER 40

Sweeney felt happier than he had for weeks. He'd resolved the problems with his local magistrate. It had cost more than expected, but he'd escaped being censored. At last, he had received confirmation of James's account at Squire's Bank. The runners had followed James to the bank. The clerks had heard James being introduced. He had spent over an hour in the office of the senior partner. But his name still did not appear on the client register. Sweeney deduced that the bank must have a secret register and he intended to get it.

The Scottish situation proved more difficult. His informer confirmed that a substantial London organization was behind the boat. Sweeney had reacted to 'substantial' with excitement. It must be Squire's Bank and James. He had brilliantly deduced James's plans. Lord Percy Lancaster's debts were now out of control and only a miracle, or finding James's hidden wealth, would save both the lord and him. He needed to retain a London lawyer, but all wanted up front retainer fees. None would accept Lord Lancaster's promissory note. Sweeney found it strange that the gambling clubs still accepted Lord Lancaster's signature, but not the London lawyers. All the law houses seemed to know of Lancaster's problems.

London intimidated Sweeney and its fast pace overwhelmed him. His unfashionable clothes made him feel inferior. In Southampton, he was a powerful lawyer. Here they viewed him as a rural bumpkin, not understanding the real world of the Court of the King's Bench. He had visited several top law firms. They wanted payment up front. Luckily, a lawyer's clerk bumped into him.

"Morning, gov. You've been walking around for a while. Are yous looking for a lawyer or barrister?"

"Who are you?"

"I am a clerk, but knows everyone who is anyone."

"I am looking for a hungry barrister who knows inheritance and finance law."

"That would be the Milman offices in the Inns of Court."

"Thank you. What's your name?"

But Albert had vanished.

Willman Milman agreed to represent Lord Lancaster, with fees to be paid afterwards, but only if Sweeney personally guaranteed the payment. He felt he had no choice but to stand as guarantor. The fees could not be that much.

For twenty-five years Forest had worked for James's father and enjoyed every minute. They'd always been careful and the business had built up solid assets. Lord Lancaster had rewarded Forest very well. Few, including his wife, knew what he actually did. None knew of the link to the Lancaster estate. Forest had no children, so he focused himself on his work. His Lordship seldom spoke about personal matters, yet, as his health declined, he had confided in Forest that he now admired James, his second son. He regretted that he had failed to get to know him better. He no longer understood the behavior of his first son, Percy. Forest had promised Lord Lancaster to keep the business hidden from Percy and instead to train James.

When James proposed bringing the wine and brandy they owned from France, his first reaction was to say no. Then he rationalized that if they could get it to England, they would remove assets from Napoleon's reach. This would help the war effort, bring much needed beverage into the country and make a handsome profit on their investment in the vineyard. When the jewelry opportunity happened, giving James declarable income, it impressed Forest. He worried about the danger to James, so approached the whole thing as a war game. He doublechecked James's plan at each step.

Then James proposed his third secret plan. To use a war metaphor, it equaled Agincourt, where six thousand English warriors beat thirty thousand French using the new weapon, the longbow, with a little help from the rain and mud. James's 'weapon' was equally brilliant. In war, one watches the enemy. Sweeney watched James, so Forest watched Sweeney. It was easy to bribe Sweeney's chief clerk as Sweeney did not treat him well, every day threatening to fire him. Even before Sweeney left Southampton for London, Forest knew his plans. He circulated enough information to ensure that none of the major London barrister partnerships would touch him. Albert had followed Sweeney since his arrival at Whitehall. Forest let him suffer a couple of frustrating days. Then he arranged for Albert to bump into Sweeney and to introduce him to a barrister whose firm accepted deferred fees. Mr Forest personally drafted the barrister's contract, which Sweeney signed.

Sea Spirit sailed slowly away into the waves, leaving the French Excise boat struggling to cut away its broken mast and erect a jury rig.

James looked back at them with concern.

"Those sailors are going through hell. It might have been us. They are putting out a sea anchor to reduce the battering by the waves, but it will be difficult for them to erect a jury rig in time to avoid the Brittany coast. Thank goodness they have a companion boat. Otherwise we would have remained to help rescue them."

Paul thought about it. "But they would have sunk us with no thoughts of saving us."

"Paul, we could not let thirty innocent seamen die. Years ago, the French were our friends. They will be again when our leaders stop this war. Alan, steer closer to the wind so we clear the Alderney rocks. They were expecting us. It seems the English and French Excise are actually working together. Under these circumstances, we cannot go back through the west end of the Solent. We will go the long way round and use the flood tide to set us to enter the Solent at the east end, off Portsmouth, late tonight. The ebb current will help us up the Solent to Beaulieu. If this gale holds, it will help us slip home unnoticed. Before we return to France, we will have to alter the paint, rigging and lines of *Sea Spirit* so they cannot recognize her. After today, they will never forget or forgive us."

The crew remained silent as they battled across the Channel. Each thought of Roger, realizing how closely they had avoided disaster. Luck, even James's luck, did not last forever. They still must get past the English Excise, sail at night up the Solent and past the infamous Brambles sand bank, enter into the Beaulieu River in the moonlight, and offload the cargo.

The free trading profits, already made, had set them up for life. They had debated the wisdom of doing this last trip, but voted for it. Now they nursed *Sea Spirit* across the Channel and up and down its storm waves, grateful for the moonlight.

Paul felt especially emotional. He had trained Roger, but obviously not well enough. Once again, James's planning and skills had carried them through a crisis. He did not doubt James would navigate them back to Beaulieu, although few naval officers would attempt to sail up the Solent on a dark night. But then what? He hoped to find the words to persuade his lass to marry. Yet he also wanted to continue going to sea with James. Could this be their last sail together? What were James's future plans for *Sea Spirit*?

The Isle of White showed through the storm spray and the late afternoon light. Just before dark, they confirmed sighting Bembridge Cliffs.

Once under the lee of the island, the waves reduced, and they were not thrown around. James thought about those people who never experience the power and noise of a sea storm. It is impossible to explain the relief that comes when one arrives at a relative shelter, but still the wind howled. They worked their way up the Solent, avoiding its unmarked sand banks and being seen.

In the early hours of the morning, having offloaded the cargo at Ginn's Farm, they moored at Buckler's Hard, exhausted. But James insisted on one more task.

"We must offload the bow chaser and the false hull panels and hide them in the boatyard. The Excise people will soon learn of the French boat's dismasting. They will search for a fishing boat big enough to have a cannon. We must make *Sea Spirit* look like a tired fishing boat caught in a storm."

Sunrise came before they finished. James turned to Paul.

"We will get a message to Roger's family and send his share to them. Rest up for a couple of days, then I want you to accompany me to London. I need you fit and well. Bring the boat's pistols."

Paul had heard about London. He could manage storms, but not crowds and strange people. If James wanted it, he would go. But why? What were the pistols for?

Nanny Jones knew James had returned and she and Ann had prepared his hot bath. Nanny had been surprised at how many girls had offered to help her. She did not know that Ann had told all her girlfriends about James.

It took the full two days to prepare for London. James checked the arrangements at Ginn's Farm for shipping the cargo. He visited Lord Rowley, with the pretext to deliver the brandy he had ordered, but really hoping to see Edith. Lord Rowley appeared friendly, and interested in how they had coped with the storm. But he made it clear that Edith would not be available. James left resolute. He would be patient.

Then he visited his old home. He had not been to the estate since his brother had kicked him out. Percy was in London again, trying to win back his fortune. James wanted an update from the staff. Montague greeted him with enormous affection but explained that Percy had not paid staff wages and local merchant bills. They were having trouble getting credit and obtaining supplies.

On returning to Buckler's Hard, Tony warned him that Jeffries and Excise men were on *Sea Spirit*, asking difficult questions. James knew Paul could handle them. He returned to his loft, put on his fisherman's clothes, looking humble and poor when men came knocking.

"Excise, open up."

James opened the door to see Jeffries with three men. "Jeffries, good to see you again. How can I help you?"

"We are here to search your rooms."

"Do you have a warrant?"

"No, but if you have nothing to hide, does it matter?"

"What are you looking for?"

"French wine and brandy."

"I could make you wait. As strangers to this area the magistrates might delay you days. But I have nothing to hide. Your men may come in, but you will have to remain outside."

Jeffries looked at James and knew he would not be able to enter. Once again James had humiliated him in front of his men. One day he would pay for it. The men entered, embarrassed to look at Jeffries. James closed the door in his face.

His loft contained a small bed, stove, bathtub and a small table and four chairs, a bucket of water and a night pot. Humble, even for a fisherman, and especially for the son of a lord.

It surprised the Excise men how modestly James lived. Finding nothing, they reported to Jeffries waiting outside.

"Are you sure you checked everywhere? Did he try and bribe you?"

"Begging your pardon, sir, but you could not hide a mouse in that room. Why, even me Magi and me live in a bigger space. There is nowhere to hide barrels and bottles. As for a bribe, there wasn't even one bottle for the taking."

Jeffries asked about the trip. Were they in France? Seen any French Excise boats? Noticed a privateer pretending to be a fisherman? Why out in the storm? Why did they build such a big boat? Who was the owner? How come they returned at night when navigation was so difficult, especially entering the Beaulieu River? The questions were endless, but easy to answer. James had expected a coastguard visit and rehearsed the answers with Paul. They both said the same thing. Jeffries did not believe them. There were large quantities of smuggled French brandy and wine turning up in the top clubs and restaurants, some in parliament and even at the palace. Once in a restaurant, there was no way of knowing if taxes were paid. The Excise hated to be made to look foolish. They did not like the French, but cooperated with them to stop smuggling. The French had reported trying to stop a smugglers' boat, equipped with a new generation of a light-weight, long-range bow cannon. It had de-masted one of the French boats. The smugglers were operating like privateers. The French drawing of the boat looked similar to *Sea Spirit*.

"Most fishing boats are alike. Why would a fishing boat have a cannon? We barely make a living wage fishing, especially after losing a week's work with the storm."

"We will find these men. They will rot in prison. You should cooperate and tell us who did it, then we might give you clemency."

"If I see the smugglers, I will report it."

"Lancaster, your luck will not last forever, and I will be waiting."

"I would not depend on it if I were you. It might be better if you used your energy on learning your trade. Even the Coastguard dismisses captains."

Jeffries left infuriated and frustrated. He had promised his bosses that he would find the smuggler, confident it was James. Now he would be sent back on patrol, on the wet and leaking cutter, for days bouncing in the Channel's rough water. At least on *Defiance*, most of the time the ship just passed through the waves and one did not feel them as much.

James knew Jeffries and his colleagues would be watching so he would have to be even more careful.

Soon after, someone else pounded on the door.

"Wait a minute."

James primed his pistols. A fortune in la Reine Antoinette's jewels were hidden in the roof timbers. He opened the door and backed up, aiming the pistols at the bodies outside. A bailiff, in formal attire and official hat, looked at the pistol, and said, with little confidence, "No need for the pistol, sir. I believe you to be James Lancaster and I am serving you with two letters."

Once the bailiff had left, James opened the letters. One was from Squire's Bank. They had been summoned to appear in court to give evidence about James's bank account. They needed his permission. The second was a summons for James to appear in the Court of the King's Bench in London next Tuesday, to answer a writ from Lord Percy Lancaster about James's account at Squire's Bank. Sweeney had taken the bait, and the battle begun.

CHAPTER 41

The cold weather made the trip to London uncomfortable. Because of James's concern for the jewels, Paul rode as bodyguard outside the coach, with his pistols primed. The coachman wondered what they carried that warranted so much security. He did not ask, being grateful for the protection. He told James, "Highwaymen spy on the coaches and passengers at the inns while we change horses. With your companion armed, we are unlikely to be bothered."

Once in London, they walked closely together, giving little chance for their luggage to be snatched. The two made a big target and easy for the Sweeney's boy runners to follow.

James first stopped at Squire's Bank, asking them to make it as difficult as possible for Sweeney to get the information he wanted. James would cover the legal costs.

Then he led the runners into a trap in an alley. Paul pounced on them and held them while James slipped away and delivered La Reine Antoinette's jewels to Her Majesty's jeweler.

Afterwards James rejoined Paul, letting the boys follow them to the White Hart Inn where they booked rooms. Mr Forest, unseen, used the back door to visit James. The boys reported to Sweeney who rushed to report to Percy.

"James has arrived in London. He first visited Squire's Bank, staying for some time. They could not have known we knew about his account. Now it is too late for them to hide it. The London barristers we hired have made special arrangements for an emergency hearing on Tuesday in front of a friendly judge at the Court of the King's Bench. The people in Scotland have reported that the Scottish bank financing James's boat is working for a large London institution. At the court we will expose James's illegal inheritance, the fraud of funding the boat via a Scottish bank, take control of James's Squires bank account, and have James in put in jail."

Mr Forest joined James for lunch in his room at the White Heart.

"Master James. London is full of talk about an English smuggler. During last week's storm, he shot down the mast of a French Excise cutter, and escaped from a certain trap. They say it was a remarkable piece of seamanship. They are crediting the smuggler with bringing French brandy and wine into England. The authorities pretend to be upset that a privateer is operating with such a cavalier attitude. In reality, they are happy that the French received a bloody nose. Rumors abound. The newssheets are full of speculation as to which of the famous beached Navy Captains is responsible. No one has suggested that it might be a midshipman. I am interested to hear how you think a captain achieved such a feat."

James enjoyed telling Mr Forest how he imagined it might have happened.

"If your father were alive, he would be proud if that privateer was you. I hear the jewels were delivered, and the palace has agreed to buy them for Her Majesty the Queen. Now it should be easy to sell the rest, and this gives us the legitimate money source for your other scheme."

James could not have heard better news. If his brother contested the profit from the jewels, he would have to go to court and involve the king. The establishment would not allow that.

"On more unpleasant issues, the court hearing with Sweeney and Squire's Bank is on Tuesday. It is Sweeney's last hope to find money. He is convinced that your father left you an inheritance at Squire's Bank. Sweeney and your brother are increasing their debt by hiring the top barristers and securing a special hearing before a senior judge in the Court of the King's Bench. The court normally deals with major cases and those of aristocrats. Our bank has indirectly guaranteed the barrister's fees. Unfortunately the judge will appear to be friendly to their request. Your brother will be in the court with Sweeney and we will have the two together. We will plan your defense over the weekend.

"Keep your coxswain Paul close to you these days. London is full of mischief and we cannot anticipate how low Sweeney will sink. We have three days left before the hearing, so Albert plans to give you and Paul a tour of London, Westminster Abbey, Westminster Palace, the admiralty, the Academy of Art in Piccadilly. The painters your father liked, Constable and Turner, have paintings in this year's exhibition. The outside of the St James' Palace and the docks are all unique and worth seeing. I have managed to get scarce tickets to Sans Souci Theatre in Leicester Place for Charles Dibdin's evening of heroic and patriotic sea and war songs. He is the most popular artist in England and even bought his own theater."

They had a fun weekend and were impressed with the size and details of the buildings, the number of merchant ships unloading in the docks, the Tower of London with its history of intrigue and executions, Westminster Abbey with the tombs of thirty kings and queens, Westminster Hall which Guy Fawkes had tried to blow up in 1605 along with all the lords, and wonderful meals, but most of all they enjoyed the Dibdin's recital and his famous songs.

Paul said, "If we had those songs on board *Defiance*, the crew would have been inspired to work three times as hard. They would not need the starters and cat o'nine tails. They make me want to be back on *Sea Spirit* as soon as possible."

James read to them the newssheets discussing the de-masting of the French ship and speculating which captain had achieved such an outrageous feat. The young runners followed them everywhere. James made sure they were fed while they waited outside the excellent restaurants that Albert selected.

On Monday afternoon, while James worked with Mr Forest at the inn, a letter arrived post haste from Nanny Jones. It originated from the Navy and was addressed to Midshipman Lancaster with the admiralty stamp on the outside. The contents were simple and to the point.

Midshipman James Lancaster is requested and instructed to report to the Second Secretary of the HM Royal Navy with outmost haste. Come in civilian clothing. It was signed *William Marsden.*

James thought he might get a posting on a ship. Then he remembered midshipmen and junior lieutenants were appointed by captains. Midshipmen never met the second secretary. Even captains, sometimes admirals, waited weeks or months for an appointment. But why civilian clothing? Was he being dismissed?

Mr Forest confessed, "For once, I do not know. The secretary has run the Navy for years. In reality, he appoints all the senior officers to ships. Your father helped him many years ago. He will never forget that. But being instructed to go in civilian clothes is ominous. You cannot go tomorrow so, if all goes well, go on Wednesday. You need a decent suit for the appointment. Albert will take you to a tailor."

CHAPTER 42

The Court of the King's bench was housed in Westminster Hall. Major cases were in the main hall and others in side halls. On the walls hung portraits of judges looking serious and mean. The décor and paintings were intended to intimidate the litigants and build up the judges' dominance.

James could not be connected to Mr Forest, so had a barrister with him. In the courtroom, the imposing judge's bench looked down at everyone. Sweeney and James's brother, Lord Percy, were sitting on the front left side of the court when James entered. They had six wigged barristers alongside them. The senior partners from Squire's Bank sat with one barrister by themselves, to the right. James joined them with his barrister. Mr Forest had chosen a younger barrister, not much older than James. James wondered how they could win against such experienced opposition.

He had entered the building full of confidence. Now, sitting way below the judge's bench, with his brother, Sweeney and their senior barristers to his left, he was full of doubts. Lords received special legal privileges. Captain Wilson had told him many times, "Be sure to give your powerful enemy a way to escape rather than trap him in a corner." James needed a plan to let Percy escape, but empty handed.

His Honor, the judge, entered from a door behind the bench.

"All rise."

He walked with the attitude of self-importance, wearing a heavy red robe and an elaborate wig, a man of senior years with a wrinkled, lined face. He'd spent considerable money on food and beverages to gain his girth. He was a devout man and justified his legendary impatience and reputation for sending men to the gallows by quoting the Bible: Mark 12:17 'And Jesus answering said unto them, Render to Caesar the things that are Caesar's, and to God the things that are God's'. He worked for the king, today's Caesar, so administered his justice. The guilty could confess to a priest for their forgiveness.

He acknowledged Lord Lancaster. "My Lord, it is a pleasure to see you in my court."

Forest had warned James that the judge would be friendly to his brother, but this personal greeting showed a terrible bias, and that the private lords' club was very real, making James even more insecure.

"I understand this is an urgent issue of inheritance. The English law treats inheritance seriously, especially when connected to a grand estate and family, such as Lord Lancaster."

The barrister for Squire's Bank stood up.

"Your honor, if it pleases you. William Headly, representing Squire's Bank.

"Carry on, Mr Headly, but be direct."

"Thank you, my Lord. Banks, like lawyers, are allowed to protect their clients' privacy. This demand for our client to provide information about their clients, and the balances in their accounts, is an unprecedented intrusion into their business."

All morning, the lawyers argued back and forth. Sweeney started to sweat. James's brother Percy became impatient with the barristers representing him. It looked as though Squire's Bank would win their right not to divulge information. Then the judge, wanting his lunch, intervened.

"Is James Lancaster in court?"

James's barrister stood up. "He is, my Lord."

"Who are you?"

"William Roger-Sumner, my Lord."

"First time in my court."

"Yes, my Lord."

"Thought so. Why are you standing? I asked for James Lancaster."

James's confidence dropped another two notches.

"Mr Lancaster."

James rose to his feet. "My Lord."

"We wasted the morning with legal babble-gaggle. No one will be happy if I have to return this afternoon after lunch. If the lawyers and bank cannot tell us, you can. Mister Lancaster, are you the younger half-brother of Lord Lancaster?"

"Yes, my Lord."

"Do you own an account at Squire's Bank?"

300

James's barrister whispered to him.

James paused, looked around the court room. Mr Forest gave him an encouraging smile. His brother Percy held his breath in anxiousness. Sweeney's puffy face expected victory. James looked at the judge, smiled and simply replied, "Yes, my Lord."

Sweeney shouted in delight. "I told you. Now we have him."

The judge banged his gavel. "Silence in court. Mister Sweeney, I do not know how you behave in the courts in Southampton, but here you will keep quiet. Mister Lancaster has confirmed that he has an account in Squire's Bank. Does the bank object to telling the court if the late Lord Lancaster also held an account in the bank?"

The bank partners and their barrister discussed for a while. Mr Headly stood up. "Your Lordship, as the previous Lord Lancaster is deceased, and if you agree that the bank is not creating a precedent to the detriment of their living clients, then Squire's Bank is prepared to answer your question."

Sweeney and Percy were ecstatic.

The judge leaned forward. "The court agrees."

The senior bank partner stood. Sweeney beamed in excitement. His plan had worked and he would save the estate.

"My Lord, Squire's Bank never met the late Lord Lancaster, nor did we receive any money from him."

Sweeney jumped to his feet and shouted, "It's a lie!"

The judge banged his gavel again, even more loudly. "One more word from you, Mister Sweeney, and I will hold you in contempt."

The judge looked hard at the bank's barrister and senior partners.

"Your bank has a first-class reputation. Do you swear on the Bible you never had money from, or an account with the late Lord Lancaster?"

Both men stood. "Yes, my Lord."

One of Sweeney's barristers intervened. "My Lord, we are entitled to know when James Lancaster opened his account, how much he has in it, and the source of the funds."

Sweeney looked relieved. The judge looked at James.

"Mister Lancaster, please answer."

"My Lord, I do not believe that my brother has the right to pry into my affairs. He banished me from my home, and has stolen most of the small inheritance my father left for me."

Both Percy and Sweeney reacted. How, and what, had James discovered?

"But to avoid wasting more of Your Lordship's valuable time, I will answer. The Navy laid up many ships and put me ashore as midshipman with no pay, but a small share of prize money. I live in an old sail loft and found work as a fisherman, receiving a small retainer and share of the catch. A month ago, I opened up an account at Squire's Bank and deposited the princely sum of... five pounds."

Percy shouted at Sweeney, "Five pounds! You promised me at least ten thousand pounds."

Sweeney realized he had been outwitted, and it devastated him. How had James tricked them into thinking that his father had left him money in Squire's Bank? If not there, where? James had been one step ahead of him all the time. *How did he plan so far ahead? He must be protecting something of enormous value.*

"My Lord. I protest. If his inheritance is not at Squire's Bank, where is it?"

The judge slammed his gravel. "Mr Sweeney, your writ specifically referenced 'in Squire's Bank'. Now you want all London? You have already wasted enough of the court's time. Is there any reason I cannot close these proceedings?"

Sweeney sat back in his chair, distraught, a broken man. Percy, always a gambler, did not believe it was over. James felt a weight lifted from his shoulders.

A hushed silence fell over the court. It was similar to the silence at weddings when the clergy asks if anyone knows reasons why the marriage may not go ahead. No one expects an answer, but then a voice from the back spoke.

"My Lord!"

The judge looked up and recognized the speaker as a famous barrister in his wig and gown, flanked by four constables.

"Sir Bingham, what is your involvement here?"

"My Lord, you eloquently outlined the importance of the inheritance laws. As important, is a gentleman's word and signature to promissory notes. I hold notes signed by Lord Percy Lancaster and guaranteed by Mister Sweeney, to the amount of one hundred and forty thousand guineas.

My clients made frequent requests for payment but can get no satisfaction. Unfortunately, a lord cannot be put into debtors' prison. Therefore, we request that Mister Sweeney be held in debtors' prison giving Lord Lancaster a week to pay, or we take title to his estate."

Confusion reigned. Sweeney and Percy shouted at each other. Their barristers said that Sweeney had specifically retained them for the issue with Squire's Bank, and as that matter had been resolved, they were leaving. Squire's Bank asked and got permission to leave. James saw Mr Forest on the visitor's balcony, watching. James remained in the court.

"Silence, silence!"

When the judge regained order, he reviewed the papers passed up by Sir Bingham.

"This is serious. Lord Lancaster, is your estate worth this amount?"

Lord Percy Lancaster went white and speechless. Sweeney stood up.

"Your Honor, we talked to the note holders and Lord Lancaster has been paying them back what he can."

Sir Bingham responded, "My Lord, our client now owns all the promissory notes. There has been no response or intent to pay, and Lord Lancaster has continued to build debt. Mister Sweeney refuses to honor his guarantee. He gave it irresponsibly, and therefore criminally, as we doubt he has one hundred and forty thousand guineas."

"One hundred and forty thousand guineas! My Lord, my only guarantee is to pay the legal bills for today's hearings."

Sir Bingham rolled his eyes. "My Lord. If I may show you. Mister Sweeney's note refers to debts incurred by Lord Lancaster and does not reference any specific debts or creditors."

"Mister Sweeney, is this your signature?"

Sweeney shouted, "They tricked me. This is a conspiracy. I never agreed to pay Lord Percy's debts. For two years, I begged him to stop gambling.

The judge banged his gavel. "Lord Lancaster, is it your signature on these notes?"

Percy now turned grey, and delayed answering.

"Well?"

Reluctantly he said, "Yes, my Lord."

"Can you pay them?"

"In time, my Lord."

Sir Bingham intervened. "My Lord, here are copies of the power of attorney granted to Mister Sweeney by Lord Lancaster. Also, the agreement, signed by Mister Sweeney as attorney, giving the Lancaster estate as security for the debts. We therefore propose to confiscate the estate and hope that it will sell at a price high enough to pay off the debts."

"I never agreed to that!" yelled Percy

"Silence in Court! Lord Lancaster, it appears that your attorney has compounded your mistakes. Luckily for you, I cannot lock up a peer of the realm for debt, but I will hold you in contempt if you keep interrupting. Mister Sweeney, will be committed to debtors' prison until arrangements are made with the debt holder. I would suggest, Lord Lancaster, you negotiate with them, as under the law they can take your estate."

The remaining blood drained from Percy's face. "My Lord, if you let them take my estate, I will become a pauper. What will I do? Where will I go?"

"Lord Lancaster, it is a bit late to be considering that. A lot of Londoners live on the streets. Unless your friends take you in, I expect you will join them. Bailiff, take Sweeney away."

They grabbed Sweeney, dragging him squealing off to the cells and from there to the debtors' prison. Lord Percy stood lost and confused.

The judge turned to James, now friendly. "Mister Lancaster, I knew and liked your father. You remind me of him. Please approach the bench." The judge leaned over his desk and spoke in a low voice. "This is an unfortunate turn of events. Your father was respected. Your brother being made homeless, even though he deserves it, will not go down well with the establishment and will tarnish the family name, and by association, you. If, as I suspect, you have influence with the creditors, I recommend a certain leniency. That way you can keep the mess out of the press."

James remembered Captain Wilson's words, "Let a trapped rat have an escape route."

"Good advice, my Lord, thank you."

"Court adjourned."

The young runners were waiting outside the court to follow James, not knowing that Sweeney, their employer, was in jail. James told them the news, paid them, and sent them home.

Paul asked, "Begging your pardon, Captain. How could anyone get into so much debt? Why would anyone buy all those promissory notes, when the estate is not worth that much?"

"My brother will find that no one will ever lend him more money. His clubs will suspend his membership. His friends will be too busy to see him. Sweeney will discover the horror of debtors' prison. The debt holders will negotiate with my brother. After we shall have the answer to a lot of your questions. Now let's celebrate a minor victory and plan for my meeting at the admiralty tomorrow."

CHAPTER 43

They had built the new admiralty offices next to the Horse Guards and close to prime minister's office at ten Downing Street, in Whitehall. Made of stone and red brick it looked more like a palace than Navy headquarters. The entrance was through a guarded gate, into and across the courtyard and through enormous doors into a large marbled reception area with a black and white marble checkered floor. Dominating the reception was an imposing staircase ascending to the offices. Many an officer had climbed the staircase to learn his fate, watched by those below waiting their turn. Uniformed officers filled the reception area, trying to arrange an appointment to beg for a ship. There were insufficient chairs, so junior officers ceded them to senior ones. Stories were told of officers waiting weeks for an appointment and then, when they entered the inner sanctum, being dismissed in minutes.

The clerk was key to getting an appointment and rumored to be the best paid person in the Navy as everyone gave generous tips for his help. He took names and sent them up with uniformed pages to the offices above. When the important people entered, the waiting crowd stood in respect. Whenever a new person entered seeking an appointment, watchers tried to identify him. When anyone exited a meeting, friends tried to find out the results. If a captain received an appointment to a ship, there were ten lieutenants wanting to sign with him.

James entered the hallowed area, and no one bothered to look at him, a young man, out of uniform, not important. He looked around, intimidated by the number of senior officers waiting. He found the clerk at his raised desk looking down on everyone with an air of respectful indifference. He ignored James, who waited and waited.

"Yes?"

"Here are my instructions to report to the second secretary."

James passed the letter up to the clerk, who looked at it with surprise. The general conversation stopped. Something unusual was happening. Based on his age, he could be a new lieutenant, but not out of uniform. The second secretary did not see anyone below admiral or senior captain. Officers watching James concluded that his father was a senior politician or an admiral, who had requested the meeting.

The clerk became more attentive, knowing how the second secretary worded his summons. The letter started with 'request' but ended with 'utmost haste'. Not an ordinary meeting.

"Mister Lancaster, please find somewhere to wait. You might be here for hours. If you need to go for lunch, please tell me."

He dispatched a page, who ran up the stairs with the letter.

No seats were available. James leant against an unoccupied column. He was thinking of Edith, and the coming deadline of Christmas, when the clerk signaled him to approach.

In a whisper he explained, "Mister Lancaster, the secretary is waiting for you. The page will escort you."

It surprised the clerk that the secretary would see James so quickly and insisted on discretion. A captain complained that a young civilian got to see the secretary before he did.

The clerk responded, "Sir, may I suggest you tell the secretary yourself." But he guessed he would not.

An elderly page, in a blue uniform bearing polished brass buttons with crossed anchors, led James up two flights of stairs and down long corridors with the walls adorned with paintings of famous ships, including Henry the Eighth's *Mary Rose*, and the Battle of the Nile showing Nelson's fleet cutting between the anchored line of French ships and the riverbank. The French ships were all on fire. It made James realize how inconsequential midshipmen were to the management of the Navy.

He entered the wood paneled oversized office of the secretary, with windows looking into the King's Green Park and onto Buckingham House, which King George had purchased for his wife, Queen Charlotte, and their fifteen children. A coal fire made the room warm. James had never been so nervous. The secretary could make or break an officer's career. James had imagined a big man. It surprised him to find a small and thin man, in his late fifties, balding and rather dwarfed by his big desk. Small piles of files and ships' logbooks covered his desk and floor.

"Sit down, Mister Lancaster."

The secretary lived up to his reputation of being direct.

"The Navy has a problem. There has been a flood of smuggling, and as I am sure you know, the dismasting of a French cutter."

James cringed inside. The Navy could not know of his involvement, or could they?

"The Excise and politicians assume it is impossible for a privateer to operate without the Navy knowing. We checked all our ships and their activity. No Navy ship was involved."

James became even more uncomfortable. As the secretary talked, his sharp unblinking eyes stared into James's eyes. James did not want to appear weak by looking away, nor rude by staring him down, so he focused through the secretary's eyes and listened.

"The newssheets think the privateer is an unemployed Navy captain. At the moment, there are many, though most do not own the skills shown by this privateer. The French reported that a large fishing boat dismasted one of their vessels. It was a fishing boat that sails fast, points high and has a very modern bow-chaser cannon. Going against two bigger and heavily manned boats, in a storm, and accurately firing a cannon from a small boat was a masterful piece of seamanship."

James could only assume the worst. After successfully smuggling, buying and selling the French aristocrats' jewels, being a few days away from to proposing to Edith, he was now facing a court martial, or worse. As he had not resigned from the Navy, even though unemployed, he was technically under their rules.

The secretary continued. "Three years ago, the Navy ordered six new experimental light-weight cannons from the Carron Company in Scotland. They are a vast improvement on the traditional cannonades and much easier to aim. We took delivery of four, but because of the cutbacks, canceled the others. The foundry accepted an order from a Scottish bank for one of them. The carter collected it, and headed to London, then received instructions to head further south. The cannon ended up at Buckler's Hard in Beaulieu."

They had caught him. James was tense, but he remembered Nanny Jones' advice. When confronting a disaster, smile and pretend to be confident. He found it difficult to smile.

"Buckler's Hard builds Navy ships. This year they only built a large fishing boat that matches the description and drawing provided by the French."

Should James confess and beg for mercy? He tried to say something.

"Sir, I—"

But the secretary interrupted. "Wait until I finish. The admiralty has three interests. First, we want to assure the Excise department and parliament that the Navy was not involved and." He paused and looked harder at James. "Second, it will not happen again."

James tried to respond, but the secretary did not allow it.

"Our third interest is to find how this boat is so fast, and sails so close to the wind. Then put it to work close to France to keep track of Napoleon's activity, and do the occasional discreet trip ashore. If we could find this boat, we would charter it for the Navy and use its current captain. However, the minimum rank to command a ship is lieutenant. We reviewed your midshipman career, your training, language capabilities and your many mentions in dispatches. You returned from the Caribbean in command of a prize ship as acting lieutenant, but because of the cut backs, missed being confirmed. We will confirm you, as lieutenant, with seniority as of your departure from the Caribbean. The admiralty will charter the boat and crew. Neither the charter nor your active duty will be posted. It will remain a secret. You will report to me, continuing operating out of Beaulieu. By the way, I considered your father a good friend and a fine man. He would be proud of your efforts, though I doubt he would condone you upsetting the Excise so much."

James had trouble absorbing the news. The Navy knew everything, but intended to keep it a secret. They had promoted him to lieutenant, and he would be entitled to back pay. Most important, he would command his own boat and crew, and conduct secret missions. The news overwhelmed him, and his head started spinning with ideas.

"Sir, thank you so much. For this work, I need to make modifications to the boat. If we do not carry heavy cargo, we could carry side cannons. Also, we need to change her appearance. I am sure the French will look out for her."

"There is a lot to be done. You cannot appear in uniform as the French spies will connect you back to your boat, which everyone must believe is a fishing boat. Over the next days, we will formalize an agreement to charter the boat, create a separate identity for you and the boat in case they catch you, so you and the boat can never be connected to the Admiralty, and set up an operating budget to bypass the normal Navy bureaucracy. You will liaise with my aide, and assuming you are available, we will get this sorted out over the next two weeks."

"I am available, sir, but with one firm commitment, to be in Hampshire for Christmas."

"That is only weeks away, and you must be operating by March. Be here tomorrow at nine a.m."

James rushed straight back to the Inns of Court. Mr Forest's face beamed with the news.

"Well, Master James, your various plans are working. Your brother had to beg a bed from a friend as his club kicked him out. Sweeney did not enjoy his first day in jail. The note holder's representative laid out the basic terms and will collect all the Lancaster estate papers from Sweeney's office in Southampton. There will be lots to learn from them. Lord Percy and Sweeney are trying to get legal help. But lawyers are unlikely to get paid, so no one has agreed. Now we have a lot to do. I want to teach you the bank business, and involve you in the decisions.

For the next two weeks, James worked around the clock, mornings at the admiralty and afternoons and late into the evenings with Mr Forest.

James sent Paul back to Buckler's Hard with detailed instructions for the improvements and changes he wanted made for *Sea Spirit*, including changing the name.

"But Captain, it is bad luck to change a boat's name."

"Not if you sacrifice to Neptune and the four winds. She will be named *Edith*."

Paul then took the coach to Plymouth to see his lass. Before he left, James spent some time giving him advice on proposals.

"But Captain, I cannot just tell her I am in love with her, want to marry her, and will look after her the rest of my life."

"Paul, that is exactly what you are going to do. Look her in the eyes, give her the silk scarf and ring you got from France. Keep it simple."

Paul practiced the words in the coach, but did not believe they would work. It needed something much more elaborate.

James reported to the admiralty.

The admiralty clerk coughed, and in a low voice said, "We will not need any names, sir. The secretary wants you anonymous. Matthew will lead you."

The page led him straight upstairs to work with the first secretary's aide.

The Navy's assurance satisfied the Excise. They assumed the Navy handled the rogue captain. Gossip still speculated about which captain had de-masted the French. With good news in short supply, the newssheets exaggerated the story. Several captains, when asked if they did it, did not deny responsibility.

James found he had become part of a well-organised, ultra-secret, military and diplomatic intelligence department whose origins went back to Francis Walsingham in Elizabethan England, the man who had intercepted and deciphered Mary Queen of Scott's letters, leading to her execution by Queen Elizabeth. He discovered they had agents in nearly all the courts of Europe, inside Napoleon's headquarters, and in a number of the bigger foreign army regiments.

James was to provide the missing cross-Channel link and to become an operative agent.

"Normally the Navy would have given you months of training but you have already done successful missions in France and possess the basic skills, so we will have to improve them as we progress."

In between the meetings at the admiralty, Forest taught James about business decisions and controls. Forest would continue his management of James's expanding interests, but with James's active participation and mutual approval.

The reports from the lawyers handling Percy's promissory notes were positive.

James had sent messages to Edith telling her that his plans were on track, but received no reply. Once again, her mother had intercepted the note.

Edith had no news from James. Rumors had him back in London again. Why London? Had he abandoned the Christmas date? She worried sick

311

about who her mother had planned for her to marry. She busied herself giving legal advice to local wives, while planning to elope with James, packing and repacking what she would take with her.

Mr Forest entered James's office. "We collected all the Lancaster estate papers. It turns out Sweeney helped himself to some of the estate income. We found cash in his safe and took it and his property in Portsmouth. The deeds to the estate, farms, etcetera are in order. They belong to the note holder, as Sweeny, using his power of attorney, pledged them. It is unnecessary, but in the long term, it would be best that your brother also signs. He is living in a hotel which, as you requested, he believes his friends are paying for. He has no cash or credit, so is not gambling. I think it is time to meet with him."

This was a meeting James knew had to happen, but not one he wanted.

"Will you be at the meeting?"

"No. We must keep me and the bank secret. The note holder lawyers, and William Roger-Sumner, the barrister who was with you in court, would be best."

"But he is so young."

"And so are you. He is very intelligent. You need a lawyer your age to grow with you, as I did with your father. Give him a chance. You will find him an asset. He is also a fine horseman, fencer and linguist. He may be of help in your new admiralty ventures."

Percy resisted the meeting, then agreed for the morning of December 22nd, making it difficult for James to get to Beaulieu by midnight on the 24th. The meeting was to be held in the offices of the note holder's lawyers, in their big wood-paneled board room with a table for twenty people. Portraits of past and present law partners covered the walls. James and William Roger-Sumner arrived first and waited with the other three lawyers. Percy arrived twenty minutes late. He looked old, thin, walking bent as though carrying the world on his shoulders. His eyes were red from a hangover and from coughing.

Percy shouted, pointing at James, "What in hell's damnation is he doing here?"

William stood. "My Lord, these proceedings will go much better if we remain civil. Mister Lancaster has interests. Please take a seat."

"You think you won. I will take my seat in the House of Lords and see you all in court there."

"My Lord, we expected that. After two or three years of litigation you will lose again. The lords know of the public criticism of their privileges, especially since the French Revolution. They do not like one of their own making a spectacle. You will not be received well. How do you expect to live? Your clubs threw you out. We have repossessed your London house. You have no cash or credit. Friends are paying for your hotel. But they inform us that support stops today, unless we come to an amicable agreement. Your luggage is packed and waits by the door. Bailiffs will stop you from entering the New Forest estate. You are a pauper, and cannot even pay for your scarlet wool, white miniver collared robes you need to enter the House of Lords."

William impressed James. He was respectful, firm, and knowledgeable.

"What do you want? Why is he here?"

"In Sweeney's papers, we found he stole money from you. We recovered some and reduced your debt a little."

Percy relaxed a bit.

"We also found a copy of your father's will."

Percy looked worried.

"We will transfer the Apple Blossom Hill farm to your brother."

"Let the shit take it. He always enjoyed playing on the farms. He goes from a fisherman to a farmer, and can rot there."

"If you start more legal proceedings, we will sue you for theft of the farm and the inheritances for staff at the estate. So let's be civil. Against our advice, the note holder is offering you the use of a substantial manor on Dartmoor, Baskerville Hall, and a modest income for life. If you accept you must agree never to return to London or the New Forest."

Percy thought for a moment and jumped to his feet. "I accept the offer, but not the restrictions."

James stood and confronted him, lifted him by his jacket lapels high off his feet, held him a moment staring into his eyes, then dropped him into his chair. Percy had never felt so powerless and frightened.

"Sit and listen. The restrictions are for your good. You have many enemies who have lost a fortune because of you, and who want to skin you alive. You have no heir to support so they will not feel guilty if you die. They will skin you slowly if they find you out of Dartmoor."

Percy had feared James, now he was terrified.

"Face reality. Thanks to you stealing my inheritance, I had to get work as a maritime trader. Now I am a supplier to His Majesty, amongst others. I own your notes, our estate, and I will let you rot if today you do not sign the agreement. The offer is for today only, out of respect for our father and our family's long history and excellent name. If you leave without signing, you leave as a pauper and in the rain. Your hotel will not let you in. You will have to beg your friends for a bed. Every shadow may hide the people waiting to take revenge."

Percy started crying. "What guarantee if I sign?"

"A contract, and my word, which unlike yours, has always been good. So for Father's sake and to keep our name out of the broadsheets and scandals, I am offering you a comfortable and quiet life in Dartmoor. Take the offer or leave."

Percy hesitated, but realized he was out of options. His shoulders sagged even lower. "I agree."

Percy curled into the chair in the fetal position, sobbing and clearly unhinged. It was a pathetic sight.

James whispered to William, "Well done. Give him the quill and make him sign before he is completely out of control."

William put the quill in Percy's shaking hand, and moved the hand to each place he had to sign in the contract.

"There, that was not so difficult."

James passed the contracts to the lawyers.

"Thank you, gentlemen. I would like all this wrapped up early January. William, I must leave to Beaulieu. Get my brother a coach with a guard to ensure he gets to the estate on Dartmoor. We will send his personnel effects after Christmas. Can you be in Beaulieu straight after Christmas? There is work for you. Happy Christmas to you all."

He left without a word to Percy.

CHAPTER 44

Edith was desperate. Christmas Eve, two nights away, and still no news from James. Her mother was busy preparing their annual Christmas Eve party. There would be food, music, dancing and games for the children. By tradition, all the major families in the area attended. Edith was certain her mother's choice for her future husband would be there and be announced. She had sent a message to Nanny Jones to learn what news she had of James. Nanny responded that James was still in London though Paul had returned ten days ago reporting that the court case went well. James wanted changes made to *Sea Spirit*. Since then, Nanny had heard nothing. Edith was more perplexed. What court case? She should have been there to help. What changes to the boat? Was James continuing as a fisherman?

"Edith. Make yourself useful and supervise the decorations. We are copying Queen Charlotte's new fashion of bringing a yew tree into the house and decorating it with ribbons. At the party you must make a special effort to look fresh and pretty. No talking politics, law, or any un-lady-like subjects. I have laid out the dress you are to wear."

"Mother, you selected my dress!"

"You need to look demure and submissive."

"I insist on knowing who he is."

"You will know at midnight at the party. Now get to work."

James had booked the midday coach out of London. It would take two full days and he would arrive just in time for the Rowley's Christmas Eve party. Not having an invitation would not matter once Lord Rowley knew everything. The rain poured down, making the roads soft, and it was turning cold, making the journey slower than normal. They arrived at the halfway overnight stop late, and in the dark. The men were wet from walking to lighten the coach on hills. A wood fire helped them dry, and a mulled wine warmed the insides.

James talked to the coachman.

"I must be in Lyndhurst tomorrow afternoon. With the roads so bad, would two extra horses help us go faster? I will pay."

The coachman remembered James from the time when he rode up front with him. But he had changed. He seemed bigger, and more confident and still with his pistol and sword. A man to be admired, or for some, feared.

"I will talk to the hostlers. They will want payment up front. It is more work for me."

"You will be well compensated."

Next morning the hostlers added the harnesses and reins and two more horses to pull the coach. It took time, as did getting the passenger loaded after a late night drinking. They left an hour late. James's frustration eased when they made better progress, but it looked as though they would not arrive until early evening. Changing the horses at each stop took longer, as the inn hostlers were not expecting to add the extra horses. Clouds and rain made it darker earlier, then snow started falling.

Lady Rowley was rushing around, supervising the preparations for the party. She was actually quite good at it and hosted three main parties each year. She assigned each of the regular staff temporary help hired from the village, whom they had been training for two days. The villagers fought to be selected as it was their only chance to experience gentry life, to sample the leftover food, and earn extra money.

The kitchen worked at full speed to prepare the buffet for one hundred and fifty guests. Cook made enough food to ensure there were leftovers for the staff. The orchestra was rehearsing. Presents for all the guests were laid out in the banquet hall. Wood fires were heating the reception rooms. Morgan was training village temporary staff in the protocols to receive the guests and take their cloaks. Woodsman was in charge of all the drinks and preparing gallons of mulled wine and punch. The weather was taking a turn for the worse, the rain poured down, and the gardeners who had cultivated the Christmas flowers in the greenhouse were concerned it might snow,

The regular maids would take care of the female guests. Some would arrive with spare clothes in case the rain or snow entered their carriages. Most women would want time with a mirror before entering the main salon, where Morgan would announce them to be greeted by and Lord and Lady Rowley and Edith. While the women preened and powered themselves, the men would wait in the lobby, where they would be served a punch and boys would brush any mud off their boots and shoes, and polish them.

The guest list was set at one hundred and fifty which meant that each year two or three families were dropped and new ones added, causing much gossip and stress, especially for the wives, for those who were uninvited. The main gossip was whether Lord Percy Lancaster would attend. He had not been seen for some time and rumor had it that he had lost a fortune trying to beat the Duke of Wellington at cards and was heavily in debt.

The stables were prepared with ale and cold cuts for the coachmen.

Edith used the confusion to smuggle her eloping bag and a heavy cloak downstairs and into the office by the front doors. She was sure James would arrive.

Lord Rowley had long ago learnt to keep away from the preparation. Sitting in his study, in front of the fire, he wondered how he would cope without Edith, once she was married. It was a shame that James had failed to appear. Lord Rowley was infected with Edith's enthusiasm for him and her certainty he would arrive with a miracle solution. But Rowley suspected there was no hope. His wife's choice of a husband for Edith was all right, but not the best; she deserved much better. His own marriage had been arranged, and they managed well, but without the affection he hoped for, or that James would have received if he had married Edith.

He had heard that Percy and Sweeney had summonsed James to the court and expected that it was to do with the ownership of the boat. He doubted that even the Court of the King's Bench would penetrate James's ownership arrangements. Then there were all the stories of a privateer dismasting a French boat during the same storm that James had been out in, and by a boat whose description was remarkably like *Sea Spirit*. The gossip said it was such an audacious action of seamanship that only a top captain could have achieved it. Could James be that captain at his young age? But James's absence led to the reality that he had not solved his financial situation, and Edith would be betrothed before midnight.

Night came early, the snow was falling heavily reducing visibility, and the coach moved even slower. The coachman could not risk the horses breaking their legs by falling into potholes hidden under the snow. Lyndhurst was only ten miles, but in these conditions it might take two hours. The Rowley Manor was an hour further. The coach lurched to a stop, pulling the horses up.

"Everyone out. The rear wheel is in a hole. Get the luggage down and help lift the axel to get the wheel free."

The women passengers tried to get protection from the snow under one of the coachman's waterproof blankets. The men shivered, getting wetter and muddy as they worked to lift the coach. James urged everyone on. It took half an hour. It was already seven-thirty by the time they moved again.

The guests started arriving, their coaches drawing up under the covered carriage entrance so the guests could alight, protected from the snow. As they entered the main salon, Morgan called out their names. It always impressed Edith how he remembered them. Then, standing side by side, Lord and lady Rowley and Edith welcomed them. Her mother had chosen her dress. She hated it. It made her look like a young timid maiden, rather than a fully formed woman. She still did not know which husband her mother had chosen. There were several men of the right age whose mothers looked at her closely. She would not have considered any of them, but it did not matter, as once she eloped no one would want her.

The coach continued slowly, but once again came to a sudden halt.

"Everyone out. The axel broke. We will have to walk to the next inn and stay there until it is fixed."

The passengers became angry. Most had been trying to get home for Christmas, and were cold and wet.

James intervened. "Calm down everyone. I have a better idea. I will take one of the coach horses and ride to the Lyndhurst inn and ask them to send help and a coach. In the meantime, you can stay in the coach, even if it is tilted a bit, and keep dry and out of the wind."

"Your honor. These are coach horses and may never have been ridden."

"Never mind. I will get to the inn one way or another and inform them of the problem, and have them send out a rescue party and prepare food and hot drinks for when you arrive. I will leave your horse there. Please leave my bags with the innkeeper."

James checked the horses, touching their backs. Most shied but one did not object. Perhaps it had been ridden when it was younger. James unbuckled the harness, cut the reins short, and jumped onto its back. The horse bucked, but James's legs gripped him like a vice. He tapped his neck.

"Hold on, my beauty. We have a long, tough journey together."

Did the horse remember better days when it was younger, before being demoted to the cruel life of a carriage horse? It calmed down and picked its own route through the snow, mud, slush and potholes. They had at least two hours to go and James pushed the horse as fast as he dare while trying to stay warm.

The guests were impressed with the decorated yew tree, searching out their present which by tradition they opened after midnight, comparing the size and shape of the packet to the others, and started to book dances.

Lord Rowley took his wife aside. "When are you going to tell Edith?"

"She will learn when you make the announcement at eleven, an hour early. That way, she cannot make a scene and cause a big upset. Afterwards, they will have music, dance and time to get to know each other.

The dancing started. Edith's card filled up. Several men asked for the last dance, but she kept it open. She kept looking hopefully at the doors but all the guests had arrived and the doors were closed. The announcement was to be at midnight. She would slip out at ten and have time to escape before they realized and tried to find her. She looked for her father and found him taking a quiet moment in his study.

"Daddy, I cannot bear it. James promised to be here. Something must have gone wrong. I trusted him."

"Edith, I am so sorry. I would have been very pleased to have him as my son-in-law. But people do not just get rich quickly. It has taken our family generations to get to where we are. It is impossible for a fisherman to earn enough to provide for you and your children. He is a sailor, and once the war restarts he will be back at sea for years and you would be alone. Your mother and I have managed our arranged marriage, as do most people. I am sure your mother has chosen well and in time you might become fond of your husband and even love him."

"Daddy, remember I love you."

Edith did not want to create suspicion, so rejoined the party, smiling.

James, and a tired horse, arrived at Lyndhurst in at ten p.m.

"Mathew!"

The landlord appeared, frightened by a wild looking man, soaking wet, face and clothes covered in mud, armed with a pistol and saber. For sure an outlaw. He was about to call for help.

"Mathew, it's me, James Lancaster."

"Master James. You scared me. I thought you were a highway man. In god's name, what has happened to you?"

"The coach has a broken axel and is full of cold wet people about nine miles up the road. Send help and blankets, and prepare rooms, food and hot wine for them. I need a horse, the fastest, not the tired nag you rented to me last time, and I need it now. Also a generous tot of rum to get me warm."

"The rum is on me and you will have my hunter, look after her."

CHAPTER 45

Edith announced she had to go to her room to freshen up. She slipped out of her dress and put on riding clothes. She would take her horse, ride to James's boat and wait for him. They would never look for her there. The servants' stairs lead to a discreet door in the front hall. She slipped into the office, retrieved her bag and cloak and headed to the front door. As she opened it, Woodsman appeared from behind a tapestry.

"I am sorry, Miss Edith, but your mother positioned me here, with the promise of being sacked if I let you leave the house."

"But please, Woodsman, look the other way. I will make it worth your while."

"I am sorry, Miss Edith. If you go back upstairs the way you came, I will say nothing. No one will need to know."

Edith returned to her room and cried. She would not let her mother see her like this. *While there is life, there is hope.* She went to her wardrobe and removed the dress she had wanted to wear. It showed off her figure. She let her hair down, adjusted her make up and put on the diamond necklace and dangling earrings bequeathed to her by her grandmother.

The main staircase led down to the lobby and the party. As she descended, she could feel all the eyes of the guests looking at her, men fascinated, perhaps some intimidated by her beauty, style and confidence. Many women were jealous. Her mother was furious. Her father beamed with pride, reflecting how well she had blossomed from the tomboy she used to be.

Lady Rowley turned angrily to her husband. "Make the announcement now."

"My love, let the orchestra finish this dance while I collect my notes from the study."

As Edith descended her mother blocked the path.

"Edith, what do you think you are doing?"

"Letting my future husband know how lucky he is."

The snow continued in heavy squalls, but gaps opened in the clouds and the moon helped James as he urged the horse forward. Up on the hill, he could just see the silhouette and lights of the mansion. Only another ten, at worst, fifteen minutes and he would arrive.

Morgan instructed the orchestra to stop playing once the dance finished and do a drum roll to introduce His Lordship. The staff prepared glasses for the toast, with English sparkling wine. Champagne was better, but not available because of the war.

Lord Rowley did not want to make the announcement. He reached for a glass of brandy, realizing it came from one of the twelve bottles James had delivered. He was embarrassed, remembering that he still had not paid him. He and Lady Rowley had visited his future son-in-law and his parents. He was all right, but not impressive. His parents were wealthy and promised he would have a generous allowance until he inherited the estate. The young man said he spent his time hunting, fishing, shooting. "I waste little time reading. I go to London for the social season, and to play cards." Edith could have a comfortable life, but dull until she created her own social life. Now he wished he had been stronger and supported Edith with her romance with James. Would she ever forgive him?

The gates of the Rowley estate were open and the gate keeper watching for late guests who had been delayed by the weather. Then he saw a mad highwayman galloping up the lane. He tried to close the gates, but the horse knocked him over. He rang the bell to warn the grooms outside the house of an intruder.

As the drums rolled, Lord Rowley slowly mounted the stairs to be seen by everyone. His wife told him to keep his speech short. She stood close by him on the floor two steps below, holding Edith's hand, pretending that she need support, but really to hold onto Edith to stop her running away. Lord Rowley would not be rushed. He was about to lose his daughter, a moment too important for a brief speech.

"Friends, Lady Rowley and I are happy you could be with us tonight. It is not only Christmas, for which we give thanks, but we have some exciting family news."

Lord Rowley paused and scanned the guests, slowly smiling and building up the suspense.

"We are overjoyed to announce the betrothal of our daughter, Edith. Before I name her lucky fiancé, first let me tell you a little about her."

Edith felt despair run though her, a condemned person facing the gallows with no escape.

Edith's mother whispered, "Announce the name and then talk."

Suddenly the door burst open, and a groom rushed in.

"My Lord, there is an outlaw with sword and pistol galloping up the drive. The gate keeper sounded the alarm."

Lord Rowley looked at Morgan with a shocked expression. "Outside with a cudgel and release the mastiffs. Everyone, please remain calm. Now, what was I saying?"

Edith, for a moment was excited that it might be James, but then resigned herself to reality. It was a highwayman, who must be desperate if he was trying to rob a mansion.

They heard the dogs barking wildly, shouts, and Lord Rowley raised his voice.

"It was when Edith had her sixth birthday party…"

It horrified Morgan to see the outlaw approaching at a full gallop, riding past the flame torches that lit that last section of the long drive. Morgan could see a mud face, mud and snow covered clothes, and a lethal looking saber and pistol in his waist belt. Thank goodness for the mastiffs. The best guard dogs ever. Even Morgan never went near them, unless they were muzzled and leashed. The outlaw drew to a halt jumped off his horse and shouted a greeting to the dogs… who rushed up to him… and licked him. James and Edith had played with them when they were puppies.

Morgan turned to the amazed servants, watching from the safety of the door.

"Get weapons and be quick."

"Hold up, Morgan. It is me James, James Lancaster."

Morgan thought he'd recognized the voice. As James approached, he raised the cudgel and stared frozen in indecision. It was indeed Master James, looking half like a wild scarecrow and half a mud animal.

"Make way. I must see Lord Rowley."

"That is impossible. They did not invite you. Anyway, you can't go in looking like that. Lord Rowley is announcing miss Edith's betrothal."

"Morgan, even though you have delivered to me some unpleasant messages, I always liked you. However, if you do not step aside, I will knock you aside."

James moved to his left. Morgan moved to block his path and James dodged around to the right and charged through the doors, knocking the staff aside.

Lord Rowley continued to address the guests, whose attention was split between him and the activity just outside the main doors.

"When Edith was fourteen…"

James burst in, women screamed and men shouted, but none advanced.

"What in damnation! Fetch me my sword and hurry."

"Lord Rowley, you do not need a sword."

Edith, Lady and Lord Rowley each recognized the voice coming from the outlaw standing before them.

Edith turned from fear, to joy, to anguish. Was James drunk. Was he a vagabond? She had trusted him. Perhaps her mother was right.

James's outlandish appearance delighted Lady Rowley. Now Edith could see how bad her choice of James had been.

James determination impressed Lord Rowley. James must have gone through hell to get here. However, such a dramatic entrance and interruption was inexcusable.

"James, I admire the effort you have made to be here, but you must go."

"My Lord, we agreed I have until midnight Christmas Eve to report my good fortune. There is nearly an hour left. I am here to ask your permission to ask for Edith's hand in marriage."

There were exclamations from the guests but others called for quiet. The drama was too good not to be able hear. Some even wondered if this was a staged event to make the party more fun.

James turned to Edith. "You said you would marry me as a poor fisherman. Will you marry me as the owner of the Lancaster estate?"

"I would even marry you as you are now."

As James knelt and took out a small box, Lady Rowley interrupted.

"You're the owner of the Lancaster estate?"

"Yes, and by appointment, supplier to His Majesty and others."

Lord Rowley looked down from the stairs. "His Majesty!" Lord Rowley imagined James was selling the king wine and brandy. "If this is true, and only if it is true, you may propose."

A tall, thin, regal looking woman called to her son. "Arthur, we are leaving."

The young man meekly followed his mother out.

Edith was shocked. Her mother had chosen Arthur Westbury!

James slipped Marie Antoinette's diamond ring onto Edith's finger.

Edith's mother had never seen a diamond so big and clear. She would manage Lady Westbury later.

"Yes, yes, yes!" Edith said loudly, pulling James up into her arms, ignoring the mud.

The guests applauded and broke into conversation.

Lord Rowley waved to the orchestra to start playing. The music competed with the noise of the gossip.

"James, the staff will help you clean and find dry clothes. Your fiancée will want to dance and after we will talk."

"Thank you, my Lord. May I ask for some additional favors? Please send a coach to Buckler's Hard with a message for Nanny Jones asking her to pack a bag and go with them to our home. Also, send a message to our butler, Montague, that Nanny and I will be there tonight and get the house warm. I will need transport later. The horse I arrived on has to return to the Coach Inn at Lyndhurst tomorrow."

"But you can stay here tonight."

"Thank you, but I must let our staff know the news, so they can enjoy their Christmas."

Edith rushed to change into a clean dress, but also not to cry in front of James or her parents. She was a mess with emotions. How was it she had been made to suffer so long thinking James was poor when all the time he was dealing with the Palace? How had he acquired his estate? Was his brother dead? Why had James waited to the very last moment to propose while she feared her parents were going to force her to marry? She looked at the ring as it reflected the light from the candles and dazzled her. Was she really engaged? She would deal with the questions later. Now she wanted to show James the wife he had acquired. She rang for Mary.

Percy's journey to Dartmoor was not much better than James's to Lyndhurst. The road was muddy and the journey slow. His excessive lifestyle caught up with him. Unable to get warm, he shivered and coughed in the coach's corner, watched by the bailiff sent to ensure he arrived.

He did not understand how a penniless fisherman, a commoner, had taken control of his promissory notes and was also a supplier to the king. He should never have trusted Sweeney. The house, in the middle of Dartmoor, was rumored to be haunted. How did James obtain it? It did not matter now. He signed the papers rather than become a pauper and shamed in front of his ex-friends. All this happened because he'd stolen James's farm and small inheritance.

The moor had weeks of fog when one could not leave the house. There were marshes and unless you were a local, and knew the secret paths, you could not cross the moor except via the few tracks for carts, which were terrible. Dartmoor, in Princetown, had a new prison for the French war prisoners and also for some from the American War of Independence. It was a few miles from his future home. The few prisoners who escaped were recaptured or died on the moor. He, too, was now effectively in prison. Unless his health improved, he would not live long, and James would inherit the title.

Sweeney sat chained and dejected in his crowded cell in Newgate Prison, no longer able to pay for privileged accommodation and meals. They put him in one of the 'yards' with the common prisoners and he was forced to eat slop. Many would receive the death penalty, to be hung outside the prison in front of a crowd of spectators. If Sweeney was convicted of stealing, and not hung, he would remain in prison for years. They moved the long-term prisoners onto the hulks of old warships, which were stuck in the mud at Woolwich, on the Thames shore, downstream from London. If the damp and pneumonia did not kill them, scurvy would.

James returned to the party in borrowed clothes to find Edith wearing a beautiful red flowing dress and looking even more stunning.

"Did I tell you how beautiful you are and how much I love you?"

"No. But from now on you must tell me every day. You gave me the ring but did you actually ask me to marry you?"

"Will you marry me?"

"I will consider it, if you dance with me."

"But at sea I never learnt to dance, except the hornpipe, which the sailors performed on Sunday afternoons."

"Then you will dance the hornpipe."

"In front of everyone."

"Yes. That is not a lot to ask, for the right to marry me."

"For the right to marry you, I will do whatever you ask."

James spoke with the orchestra, and to everyone's delight and laughter, he danced the hornpipe.

Edith smiled to herself. Not all her mother's advice had been bad. "Start out by establishing that he is to look after you."

"Now, will you marry me?"

"I expect part of our honeymoon to be on *Sea Spirit*."

"It can't?"

"Why not? You said you would do whatever I ask."

"*Sea Spirit* is now called *Edith*. So on *Edith* will be the start of our honeymoon."

"James Lancaster, I will be your wife, but you must learn to dance."

CHAPTER 46

After the guests left, the staff started to tidy and clean up. Edith, her parents and James retired to the study. James made a point of sitting on the sofa next to Edith, and much to her mother's annoyance, held her hand.

"James, we took you at your word, but now we need to know the truth."

"My Lord, I came across the opportunity to buy, at a very low cost, a lot of the previous French royalty's jewelry. Through palace contacts, Queen Charlotte and her friends now own most of them. Edith is wearing Marie Antoinette's ring."

"I am? It's fantastic. The most beautiful diamond ever."

Lady Rowley looked at it closely. "It's much better than anything Lord Rowley ever gave me."

"My love, there is time to buy you more jewels. But James, the jewelry could not have paid for the Lancaster estate."

"I am embarrassed to admit that my brother was deep in gambling debt, guaranteed by the estate. The holders of the promissory notes know how difficult the law makes it to sue a lord. I guaranteed to buy the notes signed by Percy up to a value of one hundred and forty thousand guineas at twenty percent of the face value, so twenty-eight thousand guineas. The jewels paid for it. As it is a gambling debt, they risked little. Edith and I now own the estate.

"Incredible. How did you learn to do this?"

"That is a story for another day, and it is late. May I visit the day after tomorrow, and talk about our wedding?"

Edith's mother stood. "No. That is two days away."

Edith was shocked. Was her mother still trying to stop them?

"We have a simple family meal Christmas late afternoon, as the staff spend most of the day clearing up the party. You're now family, so we expect you here at six this evening. As you are not yet married, do not spend long kissing Edith good night."

"James, I am sure there is more to tell, and I look forward to tonight. There is a covered trap and driver waiting for you outside."

Edith went outside for the kiss and took her time. James held her gently but firmly, exploring her lips. Shivers went through them both. It became known as 'their kiss' and Edith would ask for it every day.

When she returned, her father was sitting on one side of the fire, her mother on the other. Her mother looked at them with a satisfied grin. Lord Rowley knew the look. She spoke with an air of pride.

"I told you James would come through. He just needed the motivation. If we had given into him earlier, he would not have worked so hard to find the solution."

"What?" exclaimed Edith. "Mother, how can you say that?"

"Your father and I planned all this, didn't we, dear?"

Lord Rowley, at a loss for words, just shook his head and mumbled, "Yes, my dear."

Edith did not believe her mother, but learnt from her.

"Mother, you're a genius. I am looking forward to hearing all your plans for the wedding, but it needs to be soon."

"The earliest will be straight after Easter. The church does not do weddings leading up to Easter. But that is not a lot of time to organize the major wedding I have been thinking about for years. One small favor."

"Yes, Mother."

"You have to help me explain to Lady Westbury why you are not marrying her son."

"Westbury! Mother, how could you? They are rich, but so dull."

Montague and Nanny Jones were standing at the door as James arived.

"I am sorry it is so late, but I thought you and the staff deserved to enjoy Christmas. There is much to tell but to keep it simple tonight, Lord Percy has taken early retirement and is on his way to live in Dartmoor. Next week please pack his personal items and ship them to him. I now own the estate."

Nanny Jones nearly fainted with surprise. "James, you never cease to amaze me. But how?"

"Master James, that is wonderful. But we can no longer call you Master James so would Squire be all right?"

"Master James is fine with me, but if you prefer Squire, then feel free to use that. Next week, we will pay all the salaries and merchant bills. I will meet the tenants and our farm managers and get things in order. Also, my father left you and the staff inheritances which I will distribute."

Montague gave a sob and turned away.

"Montague, what is wrong."

"Master James, I apologize. We worked hard for your father most of our lives and thought there was a mutual respect, perhaps even affection. When, after his death, there was not even a mention in the will we were devastated, thinking that we had wasted our lives. So it is not the money he may have left, but knowing he did care for us that is so important."

"Montague, he thought of you as family."

"But James, we are dying to know how you managed this."

"Nanny, all in good time. Montague, later today I would like to have lunch in the main dining room, and with all the staff. Now, a hot bath, a glass of excellent wine, if you have hidden any, and a warm bed. Nanny, think about which apartment in the mansion you want. By the way, I am getting married to Edith."

"Getting married. Wonderful. Then I will have another baby to look after. Perhaps I can bring Ann to help? My apartment downstairs is fine and while the baby is small I will sleep in his room."

"Nanny, is it not time for a girl in the family?"

CHAPTER 47

On Christmas morning Paul visited his lass, Jennifer, trying to pluck up the courage to propose to her. It was Jennifer who prompted it.

"Paul, this is your seventh visit. Today is Christmas day and special. Is there something you want to ask?"

"You know I am a stranger with women and not good with words."

Jennifer sat patiently, willing him to find the words.

Paul tried to remember the long proposal he had worked on in the coach.

"Jennifer, I have been at sea since…"

Jennifer wondered if he would ever get to the point.

No, thought Paul, this is not the way. *Do as James said.*

"Jennifer, you are beautiful, I love you, I want to look after you and I have good savings. I want to marry you. I have this ring and scarf for you."

Jennifer had never expected such a wonderful proposal. Paul, when talking about the sea and James, was a poet. On a ship he was full of confidence and a leader, the rest of the time, tongue tied, and with women a disaster.

"Yes, Paul Bulldog, I will marry you."

"You will?"

Paul could not believe it was so easy. "Wonderful. After a simple wedding we can move to my cottage."

"Paul, I waited thirty years for the right man. I always thought I would find a real man, and you are perfect. Well nearly perfect, but you will be. I need to teach you a lot about women. For the wedding I need a new dress, you a suit, and we will marry in a church with our friends and have a party. Your house needs some improvements before I move there. Now I need a kiss."

Paul hesitated not knowing the proper way to kiss. Jennifer recognized his problem and was thrilled she was his first. She gently pulled him forward and touched his lips with hers and then Paul pulled her close. He was learning and experienced his first kiss at thirty-eight years old. After, he cried.

CHAPTER 48

Christmas evening dinner with Edith's parents was very enjoyable. The meal was anything but modest. Surprisingly, Lady Rowley was humorous and fun to be with. Edith's father asked probing questions.

"Were you at sea in the storm the same day a big English fishing boat shot down the mast of a French excise boat? Do you know what happened?"

"Of course I cannot be sure, but one can imagine that it happened a little differently than reported by the French, or by the English newssheets and gossips. Perhaps the so called privateer was on an innocent voyage, free trading, when confronted by hostile…"

"James, the detail you imagine makes it seem as though you were there. By the way, I owe you for the excellent brandy. Will we see any more of it?"

"Not regularly. But once a year I expect enough might appear, and at the same time some very good wine which His Majesty is now enjoying."

"What will happen to your boat now you can give up fishing?"

"First, I have promised Edith a trip. We have to make alterations for it to be suitable for her. Then the owners have asked me to test new fishing equipment."

Lord Rowley smiled. James still pretended not to own the boat and it was unlikely he would test fishing equipment. What was James up to now?

"I will miss Edith's help with the estate and Tuesday's magistrate's court."

"It is up to Edith, and I have not discussed this yet with her, but I do not see why she cannot continue assisting you in court and running the estate. I have been thinking about all our farms and tenants currently selling the produce to Giles, the middleman who sends it to London, taking most of the profit. We could combine our crops, transport and sell direct to Covent Garden. Transport is profitable and easy. Also, we can combine buying, and with group negotiation, save money. Edith could manage the whole thing, with the two estate managers and an assistant, who she will need when she gives birth to your first grandchild."

"James!"

"Are you suggesting my daughter actually manages both estates?"

"Lady Rowley, she already helps manage your estate, and according to everyone she is very good at it, and she is a better lawyer than most men. Edith, what do you think?"

"I love the idea. Once it is organized with a good manager, one normally only needs a day a week except at ploughing and harvest time. And I love helping Father in the courts."

"Edith, a woman's place is in the home, making babies and running the staff and social life."

"Mother, you have trained me well and I will have no problem running the staff or organizing our social life. If we are lucky to have a lot of babies we can adjust."

"James, that sounds very much like doing business."

"My Lord, it is. The industrialists are taking over England. It is controversial for gentry to be seen to participate in business, but already the big landowners in the north are opening coal mines. We cannot ignore what they are calling an industrial revolution. We must be part of it or be left behind. They say that the farm workers will go to the factories who pay better and soon a steam engine will replace shire horses for ploughing."

"God forbid."

"And that a steam carriage will travel as fast as twenty miles per hour."

Lady Rowley was incredulous.

"James, you're living in fantasy land. That speed is impossible, and it would blow my hat off. If God wanted us to go faster he would have made stronger horses. I would never travel in such a dangerous machine. Next, you will suggest men will fly!"

Edith was excited. She loved James the hero sailor, but she was thrilled with all his modern thoughts and that he wanted her to have a real role.

"James, I love your ideas, and also want time to write some suggestions to improve the law for our tenants and workers."

Morgan entered.

"Excuse me, my Lord. Montague, Master James's butler, has sent over an urgent letter."

James recognized the seal and tried to cover it as he opened the letter.

It came from the second secretary of the admiralty. *We need you to be ready by February. Report to me in two weeks. Marsden.*

"The owners of the boat want me to test the new fishing systems in February. They expect me in London in two weeks to discuss it."

Hmm, thought Lord Rowley. *An urgent letter on Christmas Day, with the Admiralty seal which James tried to hide, about fishing equipment! Industrial revolutions! Wives managing business and estates! This is no ordinary son-in-law.*

Edith went to bed thinking of running two estates, her kiss, their wedding and James kneeling and confirming he loved her. She planned for him to do it every day, starting on their honeymoon, partly on *Edith*. Of course, the boat would need changes to make it more comfortable, perhaps converting the fish hold so they had their state room with a proper sized bed, separate from the salon, and a separate kitchen for the cook. She slipped into her dream of James laying with her, kissing, cuddling... and more. But then she worried. Why did James have to rush to London in two weeks and test new fishing equipment in February, when the winter storms were at their worst? He had pretended to be poor while actually being a jewel merchant and selling to the king. Daddy said James was probably also smuggling brandy and wine from France. What else was he hiding? She would find out.